P9-ELT-376

Book of Judas

Forge Books by Linda Stasi

The Sixth Station

Book of Judas

Book of Judas

Linda Stasi

A TOM DOHERTY ASSOCIATES BOOK

NEW YORK

This is a work of fiction. All of the characters, organizations, and events portrayed in this novel are either products of the author's imagination or are used fictitiously.

BOOK OF JUDAS

Copyright © 2017 by Linda Stasi

A Forge Book
Published by Tom Doherty Associates
175 Fifth Avenue
New York, NY 10010

www.tor-forge.com

Forge® is a registered trademark of Macmillan Publishing Group, LLC.

The Library of Congress Cataloging-in-Publication Data is available upon request.

ISBN 978-0-7653-7875-0 (hardcover)
ISBN 978-1-4668-6336-1 (ebook)

Our books may be purchased in bulk for promotional, educational, or business use. Please contact your local bookseller or the Macmillan Corporate and Premium Sales Department at 1-800-221-7945, extension 5442, or by email at MacmillanSpecialMarkets@macmillan.com.

First Edition: September 2017

Printed in the United States of America

0 9 8 7 6 5 4 3 2 1

With Great Love To:

My husband, Sid Davidoff, a relentless cheerleader who kept me on it—even when I wanted off it.

My best man and best critic, Damien Miano, who never refused to read it one more time, always—amazingly—coming up with startling new ideas and fresh perspectives.

My dear friend, Antonia Katrandjieva, who read, reread, and reread again, inspiring me anew each time with her brilliant knowledge of all things spiritual and esoteric.

Acknowledgments

Thank You

Liza Fleissig, my agent, defender, promoter, protector who, as we New Yorkers like to say, don't take no crap from nobody! You are the best, the brightest, the bravest in a world of cowards who *do* take "no" for an answer.

Bob Gleason, my smart-as-hell editor, who believed in me then and believes in me now, and who made my career as a novelist possible.

My family, Jessica Rovello, Kenny Rosenblatt, Marco, Dean, and Reed Rosenblatt, whose everyday successes from nursery school to grown-up work and from "Lil' Wins," to big, astounding achievements are a source of wonder and joy to me every day.

Dana Isaacson, an amazing and brilliant freelance editor who helped me rethink, reshape, and then (ugh!) rewrite this book.

Thank you forever, Connie Simmons, my dear friend and Emmy-winning producer/director who has been my motivating/

meditating partner who created the wonderful *Book of Judas* trailer. Check it out at: www.lindastasi.com.

Dr. Michael Horodniceanu, president of MTA Capital Construction of the Second Avenue Subway, NYC, who took me deep underground to walk into the construction of the unfinished (and very scary) subway tunnels, as well as through its hidden byways, which helped change and shape the book.

Tal S. Perelman, a brilliant *nephew*-by-marriage, who took me to places in Israel tourists never see—but places that they really, really should see. His knowledge of ancient history and the Torah as well as unlimited patience with his American "aunt" will never be forgotten.

Thanks, too, to all the other American and distant Israeli artist-relatives who brought me into their desert home and down into the three-thousand-year-old tomb/burial chamber in their "basement." Still wondering, though, what did it mean when the lights went out completely the second I walked in and went back on the second I stepped back outside?

Eran Frenkel of Jerusalem Experience, (jerusalemexperience .com), who helped me re-create everything I'd seen in the old city in Jerusalem after I'd come back, with his video tour of every place I needed once again to see—and some that were completely new to me as well.

Introduction

A few years ago, right after I finished writing *The Sixth Station,* the first novel featuring New York City reporter Alessandra Russo, I flopped down on a couch in a house my husband and I had owned for twelve years.

I spotted a book in plain sight on the bookshelf, which for reasons I can't explain, I'd never seen before. It must have been left by the previous owners, or even the ones before that, I thought, because the book, *I, Judas* by Taylor Caldwell, had been published in 1977!

I picked it up and read it, fascinated. It was a novel based on the idea that Judas had been more a misguided believer than a traitor.

Three days later, my daughter and I were browsing a bookshop in Princeton, New Jersey, on our getaway girls' weekend and there on the front table of the shop was another Judas book, *Reading Judas: The Gospel of Judas and the Shaping of Christianity* by Elaine Pagels and Karen L. King, which I immediately bought. This non-fiction book interpreted and explained—as much as possible—the esoteric teachings that Jesus had—according to what was left of the rotted manuscript—imparted to his most trusted disciple, Judas (he had been Jesus' "treasurer," after all).

I had now gotten two messages about or maybe *from* Judas in one week!

But it wasn't until I began digging into the history of the Gospel and the journey that Judas' nearly two-thousand-year-old codex had taken from the time of its discovery by peasants in an Egyptian cave in the 1970s to its final rediscovery in New York in the year 2000—that I really freaked out.

The long-lost, once-pristine papyri—after three decades of having being roughly passed around, lost and found again on the black market—had ended up in a safety-deposit box in a Citibank branch in Hicksville, Long Island.

Why did that set my hair on end? Because that was the *very same* bank branch where I'd had my first bank account; the same one in which my parents had banked!

To quote Rick in *Casablanca,* "Of all the gin joints in all the towns in all the world, she walks into mine."

There are literally uncountable numbers of bank branches in the world, and for the pages of Judas—written by the man whose name had been haunting me for days—to have ended up in my own teenage-era bank? Insane. And it was believed that some of the pages had gone missing during those decades.

So, the universe had spoken, and damn! I had no choice but to send my protagonist, Alessandra Russo, on her second great quest—this time to discover what those lost pages of Judas contained.

It was a journey I took with her to Israel and into places not seen by Americans before. Such as a three-thousand-year-old burial chamber underneath a private home in the desert and a tunnel cut deep underground into the bedrock of NYC, which was closed to the public.

Those places, which were opened to me, were just a tiny part of the adventure, which I took with Alessandra, and with Judas. It's one that I hope you will take with me as well.

The story is fiction, but the truth that's been hidden for two thousand years isn't.

Book of Judas

Preface

المنيا

AL-MINYA, EGYPT, MID-1970S

Everyone in the Jebel Qarara hills in middle Egypt knew the story.

A great and glorious book, one that may have held the secrets of life itself, lay hidden within one of the ancient burial caves that dot the countryside.

Many of the hidden holy relics and scrolls had long ago been covered by the shifting sands, while others that had been found had fetched kingly sums for the lucky *fellahin* who had discovered them. But some were still there, hidden, just waiting . . .

The village of Qarara is dry and arid, even though it is just a few minutes' walk from the Nile. The grave robbers who were searching that day weren't criminals by local standards—they were farmers who hadn't been able to raise enough crops to keep their families fed. Finding something of real value could mean food enough for their children, wives, and parents for weeks or even months.

The area around the village, like much of Egypt, Israel, and Palestine, was at that time so strewn with artifacts like shards of ancient pottery, coins, even religious statuettes—some authentic, most not—that they didn't fetch much from the scouts.

These scouts were the middlemen who brokered deals between the peasant farmers who found the objects and the black market antiquities dealers who wanted to buy them throughout the Middle East and beyond. It could be a profitable but very deadly way to earn money. The rarer the find, the more likely it was that it could get a man killed.

Besides the danger from the criminal element, anyone caught tomb raiding and stealing the artifacts within them would be subject to a punishment so severe, it was not spoken of aloud.

That morning, as one man stood guard outside, grave robbers made their way into a burial cave they'd found. Strangely, unlike most of the graves in the area, it had remained untouched by human hands.

Inside they found the skeleton of a man wrapped in a shroud, with the bones of his family or perhaps his servants around him.

Next to the skeleton lay a limestone box, and within it, a codex—a manuscript bound in leather. Had they found the book to which the local legends had referred? They couldn't read the ancient Coptic script inside the bound papyri, which was still in excellent condition, but the local scout to whom they'd handed it told them that it was a very important find indeed.

What they had unknowingly given to the scout was the legendary, ancient, lost Gospel of Judas.

It was a transcript in the words of Judas (יְהוּדָה), the disciple who was the most trusted by Jesus, but also the one forever known universally as the man who had betrayed Him.

This codex, it had been rumored, contained the most important secret in the world—something so great, so terrifying, and so dangerous that only one earthly being had been entrusted with it: Judas.

The betrayal of Jesus, the codex maintained, was necessary for the process of crucifixion and resurrection—which would change the world—to begin. So even though Judas would remain the most hated man throughout eternity, he had no choice but to obey his Lord Jesus by betraying Him.

The discovery of the lost Gospel of Judas was a find so revolutionary, so controversial, so dangerous, so unique, that the tomb raiders believed they would become very, *very* rich men when it was sold.

That codex, however, never did make those *fellahin* rich, but conversely brought misfortune to almost everyone associated with the sale. Was it cursed, wondered the black marketeer who had unsuccessfully tried for years to sell it, first for $10 million, then $3 million, and finally for $1 million?

Yes, it *was* cursed. The Gospel of Judas—the greatest discovery since the Dead Sea Scrolls—was brought to New York in 1984 for a possible sale, which never occurred, and then it was unbelievably left behind, unattended, to rot into nearly one thousand minuscule pieces inside a Citibank safety-deposit box (number 395) in Hicksville, Long Island, until April 3, 2000.

Worse still, it was later determined, as experts attempted to put together the bits of rotted papyrus, that of the pages that remained, eighteen leaves of the original codex were missing.

Most of those eighteen pages were eventually recovered, but some believe that two or three remaining pages still exist out there somewhere.

It is those lost pages which may contain that which no human should ever know. Is it the secret to life itself—or the power to unleash Armageddon?

1

"The son of a bitch is dead. Wanna get drunk?" It was my pal Roy on the other end.

"What?"

"You know, hammered?"

"Roy? You sound like you've gone nuts."

"Yup, nuts," he answered, barely suppressing a laugh. Roy had been my best friend since high school. Death wasn't something he usually took lightly—especially not since 9/11 when he'd lost so many of his firefighter buddies.

"Who's dead?"

"Seriously, Russo?"

"Wait! Let me take this off speaker. I'm in the newsroom," I said, wondering who and what he was talking about.

"I don't care! I want the world to know. Ding dong, the ole son of a bitch is dead!"

"Oh my God! Your father? He died?" I asked, trying to keep my voice controlled.

"Finally!"

"I'm sorry. I mean, I know he was horrible to you, but your attitude is . . ."

"You sound like a girl," he said, which he knew would rile me up because I liked to think of myself as a woman who's tough as any guy. The soldiers I was embedded with in Iraq used to say I could take it like a man. And I can.

I answered his poke with one of my own. "You should show some respect for the dead, Roy Boy."

"You mean the same kind of respect dead Morris always showed me?"

Roy's dad, Morris Golden, had always been an abusive brute—to his wife and to his son. His abuse got even worse, if possible, after he found out that his hero firefighter son was gay. He could no longer beat him—Roy'd become a big, strapping man—but verbal abuse from a parent can be a punch to the gut at any age.

"Jesus, you didn't kill him or anything?" I asked, a little panicked now. Silence. "Roy? Did you kill him?"

What he said was: "Have you ever heard such great news on such a winter's day?"

"It's spring."

"It is?"

"Shut up and stop being an ass. I'm sorry about your dad, Roy. I mean that, but I'm seriously concerned that you—"

He cut me off. Roy was trying to string me along, which had been our pattern since we were kids. But this was no time for games.

I was late for the news meeting but I was equally concerned that Roy had finally snapped and killed the old bastard.

"That is not the attitude I expect from my oldest friend," he mock-sighed. "Elation. Unmitigated joy. Piss-in-your-pants happy. All good. Feeling sorry that he's dead? Not so good," he said instead.

"Roy, cut the shit and answer me! How did he die? Tell me you didn't kill him."

"That's two questions. And you yourself, Ali, didn't answer my first one. Do you want to go get drunk?"

Getting more concerned by the second, and losing my patience with his games—and it took a lot for me to lose my patience with Roy; he was the one person besides my oldest girlfriend, Dona, to whom I allowed this kind of slack—I sucked it up and said, "I'll ask you one more time. Buddy, did you kill your father?"

"Nope. I wanted to, but I didn't. He called, I went over. Dead!"

Just then, a copy kid started hovering around my desk.

"Ali, the meeting's starting in five," he said. Then, "The editor said to get your ass in there. And he means it."

I gave him a look—learned at my mother's knee—that could scare a Taliban leader out of his sunglasses. It seemed to scare whatever courage he had left, right out of him, too.

"*I* didn't say that—Mr. Brandt did," the kid choked out. "He said to quote him exactly!"

"OK, OK," I snapped, "but as you can see, I'm very busy on the phone, here. With a source. Tell that to Mr. Brandt."

Now the kid looked like he might projectile vomit. I brushed him away, warning, "Go ahead, tell him. You can't be timid in this game, kiddo. Get moving!"

Apparently twenty-two-year-old males have no understanding of the dangers of continually poking sleep-deprived, water-retaining new mothers who also happen to be dealing with friends who sound like they're on the edge.

Back on the phone, Roy was still talking, saying, "I been called a lotta things in my time, but a source? Soused yes, source no."

"But how did he die?" I repeated.

"Here, ask him," he said. "He's right here! In his house. We're—*I'm*—waiting for the coroner."

"Jesus, Roy. You're in your old house in Hicksville just sitting there with your dead father?"

"It's like a pre-shivah. But with the dead guy present, and without the snacks or the crowds. Not that this old bastard will have anybody to mourn him, or that I'll even sit shivah. But I'm always up for some nice *hamentashen* and dry pound cake."

The copy kid came back from the conference room, hovering again like a fly on bad meat.

"I said I'll be right in dammit!" The kid turned on his heels and scooted away just as the HR lady walked by. She gave me the look that said, "We don't speak to other employees like that."

I wanted to tell her to drop dead, but we don't speak to other employees like that. We used to all the time—it's a newsroom, for God's sake, not a yoga retreat—but even we reporters are now supposed to be civil. *What is this world coming to?*

"Roy, I gotta go. And please, go wait outside or something. Don't just sit there . . ."

"Outside? And give up the comfort of the living room? Or maybe I should call it the dead room now?"

"You're in the living room? With the corpse? For Christ's sake, Roy!"

"Hey, this was a long time coming. Let me enjoy the moment, will ya?"

"Ugh, that's rough, even from you. And by the way, how did he die again?"

Once more he ignored my question and chirped, "Yup—me and dead Pops—we're in the living room and I'm staying right here. I want to make sure he's really dead."

"You're a sick bastard."

"See you tonight and we'll celebrate?" he asked, as though I hadn't just called him a sick bastard.

"All right," I said. "I'll meet you tonight, *if* I can get a sitter." As I sort of mentioned, I was then the proud (read: harried) single mother of a six-month-old bouncing baby boy named Pantera Russo. Or Terry for short, because, as my mother reminded me daily, "Pantera is no name for a child."

"I'll drive into the city," Roy said. "Got the old man's car. I should say the old man's old car."

"Not the '85 Buick?"

"None other. Whaddaya say we meet at El Quijote—seven-ish?"

"*Ish,* and *if* I can get the sitter to stay. I'll text you. Gotta run or I'll get fired," I said, while running to the conference room, cell phone to my ear.

"You're a Pulitzer winner, they can't fire you."

"I never actually won. Bye!"

"Oh, Russo?"

"What? Please, honey, I'm late for the morning news meeting!"

"I forgot to tell you something."

"I know you're in a bad way, but I will be, too, in about thirty seconds if I don't get in there . . ."

I remember that I was standing in *The Standard*'s newsroom just under the big screen that digitally flashed the headlines right next to the ancient clock that didn't do anything much. You tend to remember things like where you were when your life changes forever.

He couldn't be stopped. "Just listen to this one last thing," he said, now sounding—what? Desperate? Excited?

"On his deathbed—yup, the deathbed confession really does happen—even though that was last night and I didn't know he was dying." Roy continued, somewhat out of breath, "Old Morris, he grabbed my hand, my good beer mug hand at that, in his boney mitt, and said, 'Son'—like the old bastard ever called me anything but 'Useless'—'Son, I need to tell you that I stole something.'

" 'Yeah, like what—my childhood?' I told him, so he squeezed my hand like he wanted to break it, which he probably did, and wheezed out, 'Stop whining, Useless.' I swear he said that. Then he said, 'What I stole were some pages. A codex. When I was bank manager.' He called it a 'Judas bible' that had been left in a safety-deposit box in his bank branch in Hicksville. He claims he only stole some pages because he wanted to save them from rotting."

"Wait a damned minute!" I said, stopping short and putting my rush to the morning meeting on a brief hold. "I've heard about that. It was called the Gospel of Judas. I know it because we covered it when *National Geographic* negotiated for it. But—I swear—even though it was mentioned that it had been left in a Citibank in Hicksville, I never made the connection that it was our branch— our Hicksville branch. But, Roy, it was supposed to be rotted into a bazillion pieces."

"Well, not all of it was found then, my father told me. He said he stole it way back in the 1980s or something. Then he sealed it up in a brass tube in the house."

"Jesus! No pun intended. How many pages did he steal?"

"He didn't say."

"But why those particular pages? Did he tell you that at least?"

"Yeah, but get this: he said he stole only the pages that revealed Jesus' secret to resurrection. Like Jesus' resurrection was nothing but a magic trick." He spat with such disgust, I felt like I'd have to clean my phone receiver. Roy's Jewish faith was solid—but he'd always had a real soft spot for Jesus. Thought He was a cool dude. His words, not mine.

I wasn't swayed and like the good reporter that I am, stuck to the storyline. "Did Morris expect you to use this resurrection magic trick on him or something?"

"I sincerely doubt that. If that were the case for sure he woulda chosen somebody else," he answered, knowing that I knew their brutal father-son history. "But my father also said that the stolen pages were like two thousand years old and because of what was in them, they were worth—are you ready?"

I was more than ready. A great story like this would take me off the "she's-just-back-from-maternity-leave-so-stick-her-on-the-easy-boring-city-council-since-she'll-have-to-rush-home-beat," and put me back where I had been before I took maternity leave. I knew that even thinking about the story opportunities as my oldest friend was sitting next to his father's stiffening body was probably so awful it would condemn me in my next life to manning a toilet-bowl brush in a public toilet in China, but still, I am a reporter at heart.

"He said these resurrection pages or whatever the hell they are, are worth," pause, pause, "ten million bucks!"

I nearly dropped my phone and just stood there stock-still with Bob glaring daggers at me from inside the glass-walled conference room.

"How much did you say?"

"Ten million."

"You inherited something worth ten million from that tightwad? Oh, I'm sorry, your father, that tightwad." How could it be that dour, dull Morris the bank manager was actually an international man of mystery? Impossible. The guy rode a bike to work to save fifteen cents on gas—way before it was hip to ride a bike to work. He had three suits, all dark blue, and one good pair of shoes that he resoled over and over again for thirty-five years. "Bastard!"

I wasn't going to be cleaning the toilets in Hebei province in my next life for saying *that* at least. Roy's father was an abusive terror. I remember he made Roy work like Cinderella around the house for an allowance, which he was made to use to pay for his own piano lessons, which Roy despised in the first place. Roy would be left with zero money for regular kid stuff like the ice cream truck, and when his mother got caught slipping him a couple of bucks out of her tightly controlled grocery money, Morris knocked her around so bad that she ended up in the hospital. She told the doctors she'd fallen down the stairs. How many times a day do doctors hear that one?

"There's a hitch though," Roy continued.

"A hitch?"

"He said that if these pages are unlocked in the wrong way without the proper keys, it'll release Armageddon."

"Armageddon? That could be a hitch, yes," I sort of joked back.

Then, "See, though, even if all the spells or whatever the hell is needed to open it properly are followed, he said that if terrorists got hold of it, it would give them the power to raise the dead and control who lives and who dies."

"You're talking all the power in the world! Jesus H., Roy."

"I realize that," he said, perhaps finally taking in, or maybe believing what his old man had said.

"Hey, kiddo? Forget El Quijote, I'll come out to Hicksville."

2

I walked into the morning news meeting with a look of shock on my face. I mean, how do you absorb something like, "I inherited ten million dollars but it's in a tube that could unleash Armageddon?"

I tried to walk in unnoticed because I was so late. Good luck with that, sister.

"Good afternoon, Ms. Russo," Bob Brandt, the editor, snarled at me as I opened the glass door. I mumbled an apology that I didn't mean.

The twenty-two-year-old hipster geniuses were already reading off their story ideas for the day—all gleaned courtesy of BuzzFeed or one of the other 24/7 news/pop culture sites.

One dope in a wool cap with dirty hair peeking out said, "A woman in Peoria, in Illinois—right? She exploded her Chihuahua in the microwave by putting him in to dry after his bath." Talk about a laugh riot! Or so you'd think by the reaction in the room.

"Get it up right away," Bob barked, I mean, growled—dammit—I mean, *said*. At sixty-two, Bob had survived the paper wars and was still up and taking nourishment—the guy was a phenomenal editor—and had steered *The Standard* from print to almost all digital without dropping dead or losing old-time readers.

The old tabloid maxim, "If it bleeds, it leads," is, in this digital age, being replaced by a new one: "If it clicks, it sticks." If a story doesn't get the clicks, it doesn't stay on the homepage for long. Everything is tracked instantly and constantly.

"Exploding pet? That will explode with clicks and shares," he joked, (sort of), taking a slug of his mocha latte.

What happened to newsroom bosses who came in drunk and drank their coffee black with a shot of Scotch?

"Who doesn't love a good exploding dog story," a seasoned reported moaned. *That's what news media has turned into,* I thought to myself for the ten thousandth time: clicks, hits, shares, and lifting from other sources lifted from other sources. And by sources I didn't mean actual people like cops and politicians and insiders looking to drop a dime or some keystrokes or whatever on somebody they disliked to a reporter they trusted. No, no, no.

We reporters were no longer encouraged to cultivate human sources; now we were encouraged to scour other sources for stories in this 24/7 news-cycle world. Quicker, easier, and a whole lot cheaper than sending someone to Peoria to interview the dog exploder. Leave it to TV news, with their big budgets, to chase those stories.

As soon as a story went live (online), anyone/everyone could crib, sorry "advance," that story, which means that by adding a factoid or two, anyone could claim a new version of the same story as their own, with even, yes, a new byline. (As the exploding-dog lady would surely be any minute now.)

Reporters are now required to have the hacking skills of Julian Assange, the writing chops of Hemingway, and the ability to churn it all out in thirty minutes or less. Failing that, you work for one of the millions of pop-up Web sites, or are a self-professed expert/YouTube sensation without credibility but millions of followers, all of which helps legit news to become less and less important every day.

The one or two old-time columnists/drunks still around weren't around that day since they rarely made it in before noon unless they had slept on their desks in a drunken heap the night before. None of them, however, had this story. I had it and it was all mine!

Man! A possible ten million dollar find in *my* best friend's house! The lost pages of the Gospel of Judas, completely intact. Maybe.

I was deep into my own head when I realized that Adam, the digital editor, was asking the assembled group for a roundup of the best overnight stories. Some new and unknown boy, also in a wool cap—it was spring for God's sake!—talked about a new scientific breakthrough in which there were ten ways to lose weight while eating pizza and tacos. Ten—count 'em—ten!

This new form of news—ten this, twenty that—is called lift and list. Lift someone else's story and highlight it with a list of bullet points. We used to call those bits cover lines—the things you see on the covers of magazines—now they're called news stories.

"Great!" someone else chimed in. "Let's order in some pizza!" *Ha-ha. What a card.* "Tacos!" someone else added in a near explosion of hilarity. "Let's chow down!"

I reflexively looked down at the slight bulge where a concave area once called my flat stomach had been. Six dreaded baby-fat pounds to go! "Only the Kardashians can eat pizza and tacos and then have babies in order to shrink their waistlines," I chimed in.

At nearly forty-three, I was in good shape and was at least chic enough to avoid wool watch caps except in blizzards. I dressed like a reporter should—black jeans, black silk shirt, boots, hoop earrings. Work casual without being work slob.

I have three good natural assets. Good, thick, black, Italian hair; a good haircut, which I usually keep chin length; and red lipstick. Some may not consider a good haircut or red lipstick natural assets, but I believe they are. Height is not, tragically, one of my natural assets. I lie and say I'm five three, but five two is more like it. On a good day.

At the time of Roy's announcement, being a new mom with six months of maternity leave under my belt, it wasn't that I exactly felt out of it—it was more like I didn't quite feel back in it, either. Look, I'd been to the mountaintop—literally—and in my current circumstances, I didn't imagine ever getting there again— facing life, death, or even getting the shot at that kind of story. But back then, I had no clue that the whole mountain—not just the top—was about to explode.

Too bad that the newbies in this conference room wouldn't have as much chance to exhaust themselves doing a surveil and experience the horrible scut work that turns a cocky know-it-all into a real reporter the way I had, I mused to myself. OK, yeah, they might get to the mountaintop, but for sure it wouldn't be with a man like Pantera.

Bob looked at me. "Russo—hello?"

I looked up.

"Not to disturb you, but what are *you* working on?"

Besides my swollen boobs from weaning Terry off the teat? I

wanted to say, but instead I said, "Just something *yuuge,* as Donald Trump would say. This, while *you* thought I was on the phone with my sitter."

Everyone laughed. I got along with all the reporters and editors, and my desk tended to be hangout central, and everyone as far as I knew thought I was terribly clever. Even the hipsters in wool caps. Hanging out with a Pulitzer finalist was almost as great as hanging out with Justin Bieber and his naked girlfriends. Or failing that, being the first to lift and list a Trump tweet.

They all looked at me, waiting for pearls of wisdom or a wisecrack. Ah, shit. *May as well spill,* I thought, hoping none of these jerks were interviewing at Newser or Google and would lift and list *my* story.

"Well, I was on the phone with an old friend," I started to say, wondering how much I'd give away—and how much was even real. "He's broke as Bernie Madoff, but unlike Bernie, never had more than three dollars to his name."

"You always hung with the best people," Bob joked.

"Wrong!" I answered. "He *is* the best. Roy, that's my friend's name, was a firefighter at Ground Zero. Maybe the only gay Jewish fireman I ever knew. Got PTSD, took early retirement."

Bob looked bored. "And?"

"And he just inherited something worth ten million bucks from his father who was an abusive tightwad still living in his old Levitt house in Hicksville. The guy was so tight he needed 3-in-One Oil to move. Anyway, the old man—on his deathbed—told Roy that what he left was something he'd stolen, that was worth a lot, but that if Roy sold it he'd unleash Armageddon." By the skeptical look on Bob's face, I thought it wise to skip the part about Jesus' secret personal resurrection formula.

"Sounds like the ravings of a crazy man," Bob said, with Adam eagerly agreeing. *Horses' asses!*

"Yeah, well, what if it were true—that this thing he left him, which he said was two thousand years old—*was really* worth ten million? Or maybe even a lot more . . ."

They all shut up and stared. I couldn't help myself, and went for it—sort of—risking the smirks of the assembled. "And better, what if it *is* cursed?"

"Holy shit," said one wool cap.

"Fuck me," said a rewrite guy.

"Sounds like the plot to *The Amityville Horror,*" said a pretty twenty-one-year-old intern in a crop top, leaning her chair back onto two legs for no reason.

"That was about a haunted house," I corrected her.

"Yeah, that's what I mean," she said. *Anybody home?*

More to the point was what Bob now said, which was, "Do it! Go out there and talk to this Roy guy, Russo. Now."

"I will, but I can't now," I answered.

"And why the hell not?"

"This Roy guy, as you call him, is now sitting with the stiff—that would be his recently deceased father—in the father's house, in— get this—the living room, ironically enough. They're—well, I mean *he's*—waiting for the coroner, who has to sign off on a cause of death since no one was present when he passed."

"Well, shit, can you get him to take a selfie?" Adam asked, so excited he jumped up from his chair, picturing the lead online story complete with selfie of Roy and the corpse. I imagined the photo composite of a giant cartoon bag of money next to them.

"A selfie with a stiff? Isn't that even below *The Standard*'s standards?"

After a second or two of quiet, a chorus of "hell no" and "abso-
lutely not" broke out.

Question: How many stiff drinks does it take to get a gay Jewish
ex-firefighter/oldest friend to pose with a stiff?

Answer: None. If you didn't know him, you'd have thought by
the sound of his voice when I called Roy back that he was already
through half a bottle, but I knew it was just from pure joy. In fact,
I'd never heard him sound anything but morose when he tied one
on, so I surmised that he hadn't, in fact, been hitting Morris's
Manischewitz. Roy Golden was truly a happy man for the first time
in his forty-three years on this Earth. And he deserved it.

It took him about two minutes to send a pic of himself standing
next to his dead dad in the hospital bed in the middle of his living
room. Mr. Golden, or the corpse of Mr. Golden at any rate, died
with a snarl on his puss, while his son was grinning like he'd just
won the lottery, which in a way he had. But Roy would look like a
greedy, heartless man yukking it up with his dead father's corpse
on the front page, so for his own good, I asked him to take another
selfie where he looked somber.

I couldn't help but search his two sent JPEGs for what might be
bullet holes or stab wounds on Mr. G. But the corpse was clean. It
looked like ole Morris Golden had just dropped of natural causes
at ninety. (Roy was the sad product of Morris's second marriage,
and his only child, thank the Lord!) But these were grim pics nonetheless, and a helluva nasty way to start the day.

I wrote the preliminary story to accompany the photos, leaving
out some of the details like what exactly he'd found. I reported only
that it was an ancient relic from the time of Jesus that was report-
edly worth millions and that the dead man's last words indicated

that the relic carried a deadly curse. Armageddon seemed a stretch—even for a tabloid.

Details would come when I had investigated everything thoroughly. My story went up on *The Standard*'s Web site immediately.

In my hurry to get the story up and out, we never thought about how revealing even that much info could be dangerous. Dumb. Especially in this day and age of instant news, instant access, and instant crazies armed with a bit of info.

Even Lotto winners get themselves all lawyered up before coming forward.

But who would have the nerve to steal a stolen relic?

Who would even think they could get away with it? Oh, right, Morris got away with it for decades.

3

Within thirty minutes both the pic of Roy with his dead father and the story of the possible $10 mil find with a curse attached were up online as the lead story. *My* lead story.

Five minutes after that, the story had seventy-eight thousand clicks and ten thousand shares (and two million Facebook and Twitter shares by 2 P.M.). Within minutes of the story going viral, news vans were lined up outside Mr. Golden's old Levitt house in Hicksville. They captured the undertakers loading the body bag into a hearse with Roy standing by, looking handsome as can be with his crazy red hair, two days' growth of beard, a shit-eating grin on his face, wearing a NYFD T-shirt barely containing his shit-kicker shoulders.

Too bad there's not an off-the-job-firefighters calendar because my boy Roy would be Mr. February—everybody's fantasy valentine, I thought.

Before I left, I asked the librarians—yes, newsrooms still have librarians who can help you with research—to collect whatever they could find on the Judas Gospel. And there was a ton. What I was interested in—and what turned out to be confirmed in the digital clips—was that yes, the Gospel had been found in the same Citibank branch where I knew Morris had in fact been the manager. And yes, it had moldered into thousands of pieces—some totally unrecoverable.

I told Bob I was leaving to get Roy before he spilled to someone else—which was true in a way—but I actually headed home first on the subway. I needed to spend an hour with Terry if I was going to be out that night, and I needed to see if the sitter could stay late.

As I was climbing down the slippery subway stairs—it had started to rain—I called Roy. "Don't say a frigging word to anyone. If you talk to any other reporter, you drunken sot, I will make sure you end up with Morris!" I was joking, but not really.

"Like I would." He laughed. "Anyway, I'm heading back to my own place. My fifteen minutes appear to be over already. The news vans thought it was more interesting to follow the corpse than to follow me."

"Fickle bastards. Thank you, Jesus! And I say that with all due respect to Orthodox Morris. I'm going home to spend an hour with Terry and get my car. I'll be out to you in two hours max."

I knew this was a bigger, hotter story than the other news fiends realized because I knew Roy and I knew Morris Golden and they didn't. I needed a good look around that bad house.

It would be weird to see the place—we'd lived next door to each other when we were growing up—but Roy spent most of his time at our house, since his dad didn't want kids around.

Like I said, Morris was as mean as he was tight. He had been the bank manager of that Broadway branch of Citibank in Hicksville,

Long Island, for as long as I could remember. There was nothing fancy or even interesting about the branch—just a regular dumb suburban kind of place, where my parents had their account and where I even had my first savings account. It might have moved and changed since, but it was definitely the same branch back then.

Mr. Golden was one of those men who were tyrants at home and to his employees at work but managed to be so obsequious to his bosses and anyone with money (of which there were very few in Hicksville) that he rose from teller to branch manager. He had the job for at least twenty-five or thirty years until he retired. I knew him to be dull and gray. What I never ever figured him to be, however, was a bazillionaire international black market antiquities dealer. That was as likely as my having had a secret life as a Brazilian butt model.

It was all as unlikely as Roy surviving at all, and managing to even become a legendary surfer out of Atlantic and Gilgo Beaches on Long Island's South Shore, while being gay among all those Irish Catholic macho surfer boys. . . . But that had happened, so who knew what else those Golden men were capable of?

I was the first—and only one—Roy came out to when we were fourteen. I came out to him at the same time and admitted I would now have to stay a virgin forever since I'd planned our lives up to and including four kids. Well, between my stints as a war reporter and his as an astronaut, I mean. I did become a war reporter anyway.

Roy taught me to surf; I taught him to shop. We taught each other how to kiss. I (we) fantasized about killing his father when I wasn't planning out the rest of our lives. I grew out of that fantasy. I sincerely hoped Roy had.

I hopped off the subway and walked the six blocks home to my bundle of a baby boy, Pantera "Terry" Russo. Big name for such a little guy.

Terry had my last name, Russo, which left everyone wondering who his father actually was. My ex-husband, Donald Zaluckyj, swore it was his, because we'd had one, just one, relapse, after crying in our margaritas over missed stories. And that had happened just before I was handed the biggest story of my life, ironically. But Donald was wrong about Terry's parenthood. So wrong.

I didn't need (and didn't take) a DNA test to know that Terry was the son of my one true love, Yusef Pantera. OK, yes, I had only known Pantera for less than one week before he was killed by a sixty-eight-year-old crazy-ass female former assassin for the CIA (don't ask), but the love we shared didn't die when he did. I still loved him. Dead or not, I pined for the man. *Always will,* I thought. Who was I kidding? Life with Pantera would never have been normal. He would never have been a good father, not really. Always running off to do whatever the hell he did.

Seeing Pantera gunned down was the worst moment of my life, but during that earth-shattering week we'd shared—uncovering such a gigantic story—we managed not only to fall in love, but to produce our miracle baby. I grieved that Terry would never know his father, but I rejoiced that he did have such a man *as* his father.

Back when I was married to Donald I had been told that I could never conceive and I guess that was what eventually drove us apart. Without the glue of a child to hold us together, we—Donald is a wild man photojournalist, and I, a risk-taking reporter who'd had my share of ups and downs—were each too driven, too hungry for the great "get" (exclusive story) to stay in one place with each other long enough to make it work. We were always off to cover some war or other tragedy, usually separately.

How in hell did we ever think it would last? We met during the invasion of Iraq, got married with bombs in the background, a few of our drunken reporter friends as witnesses in what was left of the only decent bar in Baghdad. It was a wild, passionate, and dangerous marriage. Of course it was destined not to last. But it was fun while it did. Sort of.

Now I found myself with the infant I was never supposed to have, with acclaim I never expected to get for a story that I could never have imagined would have happened, and yet still fighting to stay on top of the game.

In the olden days—like ten years ago—a reporter had time to research a story, get to the truth. Now we're all so worried that someone else will grab it and get it up online before we do that, too often, we rush to write and upload before all the facts are in. It's just the way it is.

As soon as I got home, I grabbed up my Terry as he laughed his wondrous baby laugh, and swirled him around the room. My glee was short-lived though as my sitter/nanny, Anna, had some news of her own. All bad. Her mother in Guiana had suffered a stroke and was in critical condition. Anna had to fly home ASAP.

Great. My sitter had to leave for who knew how long, my parents were off on some do-gooder mission in Africa (my mom's a pediatrician and my father, a social worker), and I was sitting on the biggest story to come my way this year and had no one to watch Terry.

Let me backtrack a sec. Sure I'd been a Pulitzer finalist, and sure I was a hard-nosed reporter, but the truth was that newswomen just can't take maternity leave and expect to come back to the same position. The news doesn't wait for a mother to bond with her baby. Period. Men usually don't take maternity leave but if they do, people think they're sensitive and special. When women do, we need to fight to get back to where we were before we left.

But the cold hard facts right that second were that I had a baby to support and I had to get back on top—and stop being viewed as the "older" reporter in the room. I was forty-freaking-three, not ninety-freaking-three!

And now I was a forty-freaking-three-year-old reporter without a sitter. "Of course, Anna," I said, hugging her so that the three of us were in a circle embrace. "Do what you have to do." I wasn't going to put her in the position I'd been put in—for taking time with her family. At the same time, I was freaking out. I mean, Terry was six months old, and I was sitting on a hot story, which I might not be able to pursue, and I could actually lose my job for taking another leave.

As I was walking down the hall to throw out a bag of garbage in the compactor room, I ran into my neighbors, a retired couple, Raylene and Dane Judson. They'd been my neighbors for nearly a year, and I liked them a lot, within reason. Raylene was kooky and dressed like an old hippie, which she was. Ditto Dane, who had a long, gray ponytail. They could often be seen meditating out by the East River path next to our apartment building. They'd even gotten me into the practice. Sort of.

They knew all kinds of interesting, esoteric stuff, and seemed to be loaded—they had made their money in an herbal alternative-medicine company—and were always jetting off to some exotic locale here or there. I'd water their plants and collect their mail. In a way they were similar to my parents—also aging hippies. Imagine being in your late seventies and still spry and curious and healthy and fun. And yes, in love.

Why they didn't live in some high-end condo I didn't know, but I was glad they had decided to move here and was even happier that they'd ended up just down the hall from me, modest as our building was compared to what they could have afforded.

They were approaching the elevator when I came trudging down the hall with the garbage bag. "Alessandra! We just saw the story you broke online! Wow. Good for you," Dane said. He was dressed in one of those short-sleeved Caribbean suits that never look good outside of the Caribbean.

"You go girl!" chimed in Raylene, apparently channeling Janis Joplin today, her curly hair loose and crazy. "We're so proud of you! Where do you go with this story now? I always find that reporter process so interesting!" She tended to talk as though every sentence ended in an exclamation point.

I shrugged. "It's a problem, unfortunately, but one I'll figure out I'm sure."

"Whatever do you mean, dear girl?" Dane asked. "This is huge. Even I know that and I'm just a guy who spent half my life looking for herbs in the jungle!"

I pursed my lips. "Anna's mother had a stroke and my parents are in Africa. I don't want a stranger babysitting."

"What about your ex-husband? He seems like a nice enough fellow," Raylene said.

"Yes, he is. Sometimes. But he has as hectic a job as I do," I answered, "but hopefully he can pitch in once in a while."

Just then the elevator came, and as she was getting in Raylene added, almost pleaded actually, "Let us know if we can help you out. We're usually free as birds!"

Could I? Nah.

I thanked them and heard her saying to Dane as the door closed, "I think she figures we're a couple of old potheads."

The elevator went down before I could hear his answer.

4

I called Roy to tell him about the Anna situation.

"Hicksville no, Quijote *sí*," I said, not knowing really if I'd "*sí*" or not see him later. He could always just come over to my apartment for some takeout.

Next I called Donald the ex, of the too-sexy long hair and new ridiculous handlebar mustache. I was hoping he'd help me out by watching Terry later.

"Hey, babe," he said. "You knocked it outta the park today with the ten mil story! Great get."

"Who could imagine Roy of all people could be part of such a story," I said, still shocked myself.

"Ah, your pal Roy," he said, and I smiled to think how Donald would be shaking his shaggy head. "I swear that guy just pretends he's gay so he can grab your ass without getting in trouble. I should try that. But damn! Now the guy's rich, so he can come out of the closet, admit he's straight, and sweep you off your feet. Come to think of it, I'd even go gay myself for ten mil."

"You are such a jerk! He's my best friend—or my best guy friend, anyway—as you know."

My best girlfriend was Dona Grimm, who was seven years my junior in age and almost a foot my senior in height. She was a cocoa-skinned beauty who was a helluva reporter, even though at over six feet (not counting her spikes and towering retro Afro) she could have been walking the catwalks of Europe. I would have asked her to babysit, but I knew that I'd be leaning on her heavily to help me with Terry in the coming days.

"So Donald—"

"Let me guess," he cut me off, "you must want something or you wouldn't be calling me. The answer is no."

I could hear music and glasses clinking in the background.

"Are you in Afghanistan or just some dingy bar somewhere unspeakable?"

"Dingy bar yes, Afghanistan no, unspeakable probably."

"Dear God. A strip joint in the daylight? Are you insane, or more importantly are you in New York?"

"Yes, I am, and I'll have you know it's not just any strip joint. Clippers. I've got a credit here. Joey the owner owes me three K. I'm having their breakfast special, steak and eggs."

"Breakfast is over," I reminded him. Then, "They cook breakfast there?"

"No."

"Never mind, I'm terrified to go further with this conversation. I need a favor."

"I hate to repeat myself, but no."

"It involves Terry."

"Oh, my son! Well, that's different."

"No, I mean, the one who isn't your son. *That* Terry. Are you by any chance free tonight to help me out by watching not-your-son?" I knew I was pushing my luck here. Adding, "Anna has to fly back to Guiana and I need to meet Roy about the story."

"This is the kind of person you leave my son with—someone who just up and leaves?"

"Her mother had a stroke, for God's sake, and I'm leaving him with *you,* am I not?"

"What time?"

"Six thirty? But have you been drinking?"

"No. I'm sober as a judge."

"That's what I'm afraid of."

"Of course I'll be sober. You're trusting me to babysit our son, aren't you?"

"Oh, Jesus. You're like a child yourself—always have to get the last word. Not your son . . ."

"He is," he said and hung up, getting the last word, of course. The guy does have a certain charm, which is how we ended up together in the first place. Bad boys have always been bad news for me.

Take Yusef Pantera. I knew Donald had always been my excuse for not ever getting involved with anyone of any substance. Then Pantera happened to me.

Astrophysicist by training, assassin by birthright (hey, nobody's perfect). He had also been the appointed guardian/father of the baby who became the man who became the accused terrorist/savior Demiel ben Yusef. Pantera became my lover because, well, because it happened. Fate. Oy. I *had* turned into my mother, after all, with all that silly fate stuff.

But the thing is, I had no intention of ever falling in love with Yusef Pantera. I mean, at first I mistook the guy for a German, or a Seventh Avenue garmento with his bespoke suit and slick haircut. Worse, I thought he was trying to kill me. When a man blows up your car, you can't help but assume he's trying to kill you, right?

But then Montségur happened. And Carcassonne happened. And the relic with the DNA of Jesus happened.

I never really accepted Pantera's death. Not in my heart. Of course I saw the pillar fall on top of him, followed by a collapsing, burning wall. I saw him get shot. But the thing is, I never saw him *die,* and I never found his name on the Red Cross's rolls of dead-and-missing in the unit set up in the mountains of Manoppello after the earthquake.

Yes, I *knew* he was dead, he had to be, but I didn't accept the fact that he *was* dead. One thing I did absolutely know though? If he were still alive, he would have come when his son was born no matter what shape he was in.

Stop! This isn't helping anyone. You can't whine over what can't be when you have to deal with what is right this second. And right this second you don't have baby backup.

After my daily self-slap for pining for what couldn't be, I did what I could: I reserved Anna a seat on the next flight to Guiana (check), convinced Roy—again—not to talk to any other news outlet (check), called Bob several times to assure him I was on the story like black on pavement (check), and did my mommy chores (check, check).

After Anna left in tears despite my assurances that strokes weren't fatal like in the old days, as though I really knew anything about it, I got Terry ready for a walk in the beautiful late spring air. Why not? I'd earned my keep for the day and was going to be working that night.

"Who wants to go for a walk with Mommy?" I tickled Terry's tummy, just so I could hear him laugh again.

I kissed his face, fed him his bottle, then changed his diaper and sang, "Don'tcha pee on me, little Terry, don't pee on me!" at which point he of course sent a giant stream right into my face.

Laughing, I cleaned us both up, bundled him up, put him in the stroller—which was about the size of a 1970 Buick—and walked out, babbling to him the whole way.

"So Terry, here's the place where you will probably get your first ice cream cone," I said, pointing out the Mister Softee truck. Terry looked over, intrigued by the jingle, which the driver wasn't allowed by NYC proclamation to continuously play anymore. Terry was apparently the only person in New York who loved it. We walked from Twenty-Third Street to Forty-Second Street, crisscrossing from First Avenue to Second Avenue. Then, "Here's where Mommy used to work," I said, pointing out the old *Daily News* building with the giant globe built into the floor. As we walked on, and approached Dag Hammarskjöld Plaza, abutting the United Nations, memories, good and bad, came flooding back. It was, after all, the park where I first laid eyes on Yusef Pantera.

Dona met me and we bought a couple of hot dogs and split a knish. As we were catching up on the bench, our food on napkins between us, I looked up and saw the Judsons walking arm in arm, apparently coming from the U.N.

"Oh geez, just what I don't need—my neighbors. I only saw them an hour ago. Don't encourage them," I warned Dona.

They saw us and waved and of course came right over and hovered. I wasn't going to ask them to join us. Dona and I only had just so much time together and I didn't want to share it.

I could see Dona the fashionista was intrigued, however, with their getups—they'd apparently had a post-lunch change of clothing—and she was encouraging them to sit down rather than making them go away. Raylene was now done up in a pair of wide-legged orchid bell-bottoms, a deep purple crushed velvet jacket, a sequined black cloche on her head, and a four-thousand-pound cross with what looked like genuine—huge—diamonds, rubies, and emeralds.

Dane had somehow turned his long gray ponytail into braids and was wearing a Crayola-blue corduroy suit with an open-neck, wide collared blue shirt with giant patterns of star systems embroidered into it. He even had a walking stick with a silver dog's head. When I looked closer I saw the dog was baring its teeth. Jesus.

The Judsons, as I feared they would be, were equally intrigued with the gorgeous Dona. After sticking their heads into the stroller and coo-cooing Terry, they informed Dona about the dangers of preservatives in hot dogs and asked her why such a gorgeous woman would think of drinking Diet Coke (apparently rotting from the inside out wouldn't matter to someone who looked like me).

They finally left, after eating up ten minutes of my time with Dona.

"How cute are they?" she gushed to my great annoyance.

"Cute? They look like folk singers from the land that time forgot," I sniped back, uncharitably.

"Adorable," she scolded, "but I will give you that they are kinda buttinskies." After another ten minutes, Dona split and headed back to her desk at Fox News, and I strolled Terry home in the brisk air. It was enough to put him out cold for the rest of the afternoon, and time for me to work my sources on the phone. Yes, after a stint with monks and nuns on last year's story I actually had relic sources! Even so, I came up empty.

At six thirty-five Donald, bless his rotten heart, showed up to babysit. I handed him step-by-step baby care instructions, as well as the Judsons' numbers in case of an emergency—as though they could do anything that he couldn't.

"Don't drop him, don't feed him a sandwich, or give him a beer," I said on my way out as Terry giggled as though he knew what I had said. "He had a long nap, so he might not go down for the night until like eight thirty."

"Got it."

As I waited for the elevator—the hallway outside my apartment is not as brightly lit as it could be—the Judsons were *again* just coming home. Their insane-people outfits did however add enough brightness and festivity to light up the hallway like a Christmas tree in a dark window.

Geez, it's getting harder to avoid these two than Starbucks.

"A date or chasing that story, Brenda Starr, Girl Reporter?" Dane quipped.

"Same story."

"The cursed papyrus?" Raylene asked. "We read about it, after we saw you in the park."

"How did you know it was papyrus? I didn't mention it on purpose in the story."

"Oh, you didn't? I could have sworn you did!" she said, exclamation point.

Dane jumped in, tapping his ridiculous dog-head walking stick for emphasis. "Well, some other reporter must have mentioned it! I'm afraid your friend the fireman could be leaking like one of his fire hoses. You'd better stop that leak or you'll lose out on another much-deserved Pulitzer."

I should never have told them about my near loss. Nosy bodies!

She changed the subject. "Dane and I were at the U.N. lecturing on alternative food sources in third world countries. Cockroaches are full of protein, ya know."

He added, patting his stomach, "Too many *hors d'oeuvres* with the ambassador, I'm afraid," Dane added tugging on Raylene's arm. *Ambassador?*

They hurried away as casually as though they'd said, "A big day of bingo down at the senior center."

Concerned that Roy had leaked, I cabbed it to El Quijote, home of the twenty-six-dollar lobster.

El Quijote has been on Twenty-Third Street in Manhattan since Jesus was in swaddling Pampers. Its old booths and brown-and-white murals of Don Quijote, and paella are strictly a secret for locals.

Roy, in jeans, an NYFD T-shirt, and sneakers was already sucking down sangria at the bar when I got there. He looked shaken. Roy is a big guy—six three or four, red flattop, tats with the names of all his brothers who died on 9/11. He's also a real looker except for the fact that hard drinking since his "retirement" was beginning to show. That plus years of abuse as a kid had all added up to make Roy look like a lumberjack with a cross to bear—which is why women were hitting on him all the time. I always told him that taking himself out of our side of the game was a blow against womankind. He himself had had just one semi-long-term relationship—with another firefighter who'd died at Ground Zero. The death of his guy, and his other friends and colleagues, kind of did him in. He was never the same after that.

We grabbed a booth and I took his hands in mine. I could tell just by looking at him that he hadn't leaked to anybody, so I didn't even need to ask. The waiter brought over a bowl of chips and salsa and we ordered another pitcher of sangria, which means, appropriately enough, "bleeding."

"Hey lovey, what's wrong—I mean besides your father dying and finding out that you're sitting on a cursed gold mine? You looked kinda banged up."

"Ah, dealing with a lot. I didn't think about him dying, ever. It's a lot to swallow. Freedom and fury at the same time."

I cocked my head questioningly. He took a piece of paper out of his jacket pocket. "And crazy shit. This is nuts but my old man had this clutched in his hand when he died. The funeral director gave it to me, along with his socks. Jesus. Rigor mortis had set in so they found it when they were doing whatever they do to bodies."

It was a crumpled-up Post-it Note with an inscription:

ان المنتصر يملكه العالم

I recognized it as Arabic from my tours for *The Standard* in Iraq.

"And then there's this thing called the Voynich Manuscript," he added.

"What the hell is the Voynich Manuscript?"

"Beats the shit outta me; some kinda old book. When I went back to the house to look for his papers that the undertaker needed, I saw that he'd left another Post-it Note on the book's binding—in his office on the shelf. It's real old and it's full of writing and weirdo drawings of plants, astronomical charts, and bathtubs with tiny naked people. Who knew he ever looked at anything but a ledger?"

"And the mysterious tube he spoke of—the one holding the bazillion-dollar relic?" I asked, the reporter in me worried that Morris had lied. One last mean-spirited jab at his hated son.

"Yeah, a brass tube. But I couldn't find it," Roy answered glumly before lighting up. "Until"—he raised his eyebrow and leaned forward—"I pushed on the back of the bookshelf there—where the Voynich Manuscript was—and saw that the wood was buckled behind it, and sure enough. It was a fake back. I popped it out with a screwdriver and found it back there. Has the same writing on it."

He reached into his old canvas messenger bag and pulled the tube halfway out. It was an ancient-looking brass tube about two inches in diameter. It looked sort of like the pneumatic tubes department stores and giant libraries used to use to send money and requests from floor to floor. On the top was the matching inscription: ان المنتصر يملكه العالم

He passed it to me under the table. Turning toward the wall so it couldn't be seen, I turned it over in my hands and tried to unscrew the caps on both ends. No go. "It's sealed solid. How can you even get into it without breaking it?"

"Don't know, but I'm thinking that if it's got those old papers in it, they could crumble if it's not opened in the right environment."

"Ya think?" I said sarcastically.

"I don't know, but right now," Roy whispered, turning to see if anyone was watching us, "that's not my main concern. Right now my main concern is hiding it."

"Hiding it. Of course, but we also need to get it opened by an expert and get it appraised."

"I don't want to keep it in the old man's house and I don't want to hold onto it in my place."

"Why not your own apartment, for heaven's sake? Who's going to try to break in? You're seventy feet tall and built like a brick shithouse."

"I swear from the time I left to the time I went back to my old man's house, someone *had* been in there. Things were moved, some stuff knocked over. So I don't trust my place or his."

"You're getting crazy. You locked up your father's house when you left—right?"

"I'm a firefighter for God's sake. I know how to secure a place."

"Right. Sorry. So couldn't the mortician's guys have knocked stuff over?"

"Possible yeah, probable no, since I was there. I didn't see them move anything. Keep it for me, will you?" he said.

"Oh, and this was back there, too." It was an ancient, really ancient-looking key. Like something you'd see in the Mesopotamian exhibit at the Metropolitan Museum of Art. It was corroded over in green crust—so it must have been brass—a few inches long, with a round circle on top that had points inside the opening, on top of a long shaft that had designs along it. The bottom part, the part that fit into a lock, had three intricate half-inch-long protrusions—two with teeth facing up and one with teeth facing forward. The key was pretty heavy considering its size.

"What's it go into—some kind of door or something?"

"Beats the shit outta me, but he hid it for some reason. That's why I don't want to leave it there. So you'll keep this stuff for a day or two?"

"I don't know . . ."

"Please, Ali," he said, taking my hand again.

"Well, all right. If you really need me to. But I don't have a safety-deposit box in my apartment, you know."

At that we both cracked up. "That's exactly why I want you to keep it! Who knew bank managers could steal from them?"

"I don't think they can. Morris was in cahoots with someone . . ."

"Clearly. But whoever it was, it ain't good."

"Agreed," I said, putting it into my oversized shoulder bag. "I'm sure I can find someone to have a look at the tube thing. *The Standard*'s librarians have research on everything. They'll find me someone. If we can open it. An expert."

"If there is such a thing . . ."

Then I remembered that of course I knew someone, and I smacked the side of my head. "Duh. I might know a guy."

"You're kidding," he said, grinning and shaking his head.

"Remember that priest, Father Paulo, that I traveled with last year—the guy from the cloning story?"

"The old guy?"

"Yeah. The old guy. He's a horrible snob, but a brilliant scholar of ancient religious artifacts. He'd for sure be able to help. He's our backup—in case."

"OK," Roy said. "I knew you'd know a guy. Or for sure you'd know a guy who knows a guy," he said, holding my hand, then dropping it and picking up the giant menu. "Let's order. Everything. I'm starving."

We got lobsters and another pitcher of sangria. "Here's to being a wealthy man!" He toasted to himself and we clinked glasses, although I was seriously uncomfortable toasting to the fact that we were celebrating a death.

As we chowed down, Roy reached into his jeans pocket. "Oh and there's this . . . I forgot. It was taped to the side of the tube."

"Anything else you forgot?" I said, shaking my head. "You'd never make it as a reporter. You're like a clown with magic pockets. You keep bringing stuff out of 'em."

He handed me a tiny manila envelope, the kind that stamps would fit into. "May I?" I asked before opening it.

"Sure. It's an earring."

I shook it out onto the table and sure enough a small, antique-looking, post-back, ruby stud earring—just one—fell out. I picked it up and turned it around.

"Too bad there aren't two. Probably worth something as a pair. But what do I know? Was it your mother's?"

"Not if he gave it to her it wasn't. As far as I know he never gave her anything of value."

"Your grandmother's?"

"Possibly. But there's only one, so I guess it kind of doesn't matter."

"I guess . . . but who knows? Everything matters sometimes. You want me to hold on to this, too?"

"Sure. I'll just lose it."

"Maybe you want to get your ear pierced?"

"Nah. I'd feel like the Village People."

"Was there a gay Village People fireman?"

"Weren't they all gay firemen?"

Switching subjects, I asked, "So what are you doing about funeral arrangements?"

"Tomorrow at nine. You'll be there with me, right?"

"Of course. Where?"

"Here's where it gets even weirder. My father, the good Jew? Get this: he wanted to be buried in a Catholic cemetery."

"What the eff?"

"It's in his papers. He converted to Catholicism, which is news to me, and had his lawyer certify that he wanted to be buried in that cemetery in Queens. Bought a plot there—a single plot, mind you—my mother's in the Jewish cemetery. He didn't want to be cremated or put into the plot at the Jewish cemetery next to her, which is probably a blessing. He wanted to be buried at St. John's."

"You can't be serious! I know that place. In fact I did stories about it when John Gotti died. You know who else is buried there?"

I asked, still shocked that old man Morris, who wore a yarmulke half the time, had gone Catholic.

"Besides a bunch of my buddies from my ladder company who died on nine eleven?" he said, fighting back tears.

"Yes," I said, putting my hand over his. I could feel him shaking. Roy really did still suffer from post-traumatic stress syndrome. He was afraid he'd even go postal one day, so he was on meds and seeing a shrink. "Well, Morris will be in interesting company. They're all there: Lucky Luciano; Governor Mario Cuomo; John Gotti; Geraldine Ferraro, the first female VP candidate; and even Robert Mapplethorpe, everybody's favorite homoerotic photographer."

"He'd hate knowing he's in the same hallowed ground as both a Democrat and a 'faggot,' as he liked to call me."

I, too, was glad the S.O.B. was dead. Terrible to even think of all the sadness he had caused.

"Waiter," Roy called. "Please, another pitcher!"

The waiter brought another pitcher of sangria. "I'm letting you drink another pitcher, but I'm not letting you drive home. I'll get you an Uber. Drink up, buddy."

We were both dying to know what the hell was in the tube—was it the missing pages from the Gospel of Judas? Would they still be intact? And what about the Armageddon curse and the business about the resurrection code? Were they just some superstitious stories Morris had cooked up in his aged mind or were we talking about real danger here? But whatever it was it would make a helluva story, maybe even a book. Oh man. I was so back in the game. Too bad I was so dumb in so easily dismissing the danger.

We talked until eleven, when I knew I'd be wearing out my

Donald favor so I put Roy into an Uber, gave the driver his address in Astoria, and kissed him good night.

Roy's father's old Buick was parked in front of the restaurant, so I offered to drive it to my apartment building and put it in the garage there overnight. Instead of meeting him at the cemetery, I'd pick him up in the morning and we'd drive there together.

"Here's to dying young and leaving a beautiful corpse," Roy said.

"Here's to dying old and looking as good as possible," I answered, kissing him again through the window.

"I'll be out in front at eight o'clock tomorrow morning. Don't be late." I realized I'd have to take Terry to the cemetery, which wasn't my favorite idea, but that was the only option. I watched the car drive off, Roy sticking his hand out and waving good-bye through the window as the car traveled farther away from me down Twenty-Third Street.

5

"Honey, I'm home!" I jokingly called out to Donald as I opened my front door.

Oh shit. The friend from hell was there with him.

"Hello to you, too, Larry," I dripped sarcastically, throwing Donald a look. His friend dopey Larry had shown up, apparently to keep the boys company—emphasis on "boys."

I surveyed the mess that the two man-boys and one baby had made.

"Hey, Ali," Larry said. "I didn't smoke anything."

"Good for you!" I said, not knowing how the hell one was supposed to respond to such an announcement.

Donald picked up his camera equipment—he'd come straight from work—and tapped his chest to make sure he hadn't lost his Marlboros while caring for the baby.

"I got some good genes," he said. "The kid is fearless."

"I'm afraid to know what any of that means. Was everything all right? Baby didn't give you any trouble?"

"Aside from stinking up the joint, no."

"You sure that was the baby?" I asked, eyeing Larry, who had the same satisfied look on his face as dogs do when they fart and wonder why everyone is running for cover.

"Babe, I really appreciate you pitching in at the last minute like this . . ." I said, kissing Donald on the cheek as he tried to turn my mouth to his. "Jesus, Donald. Not in front of the child," I joked, meaning dopey Larry.

"How's Roy?" He showed me a photo he had of Roy on his camera. "The freakin' guy was all over the news today."

"Really?" I snarked. "It's my story—remember?"

Larry chimed in, "That guy, he's the fairy fireman, right?"

"What the hell is wrong with you, Larry? It's not 1950. People don't talk like that anymore. Fairy, my ass. He could take you out with one punch."

"Eh, I'm only kidding. So he's really rich now?"

"Not yet, he's not."

"What's this about a cursed stone tablet?" Donald asked.

"It's not a stone tablet. I never wrote that. Hello? It's some ancient papers in a sealed brass tube." I reached into my bag to show him.

Then I stopped, thinking, *Maybe Roy is paranoid about someone messing around in his dad's house, but then again, as they say, just because you're paranoid doesn't mean somebody's not after you. Don't play free and loose with something someone has entrusted to you.*

I quickly shoved the tube back into my purse before they got their grubby mitts on it. But Larry had seen it. "Geez, it's only us. It's a brass vase?"

"No." I left it at that, and gave Donald the *look* that meant, "Not in front of dopey Larry." He nodded slightly so Larry didn't see.

Donald put on his coat to leave. Larry, of course, didn't follow suit. "Well, thanks for stopping by, Larry," I said, hoping he'd get the hint and vamoose. He didn't, so Donald grabbed him and shoved him out.

"You wanna hit Clippers?" I heard Larry ask him as I was closing the door. When I heard the elevator ding and voices in the hall, I peeked through the security peephole and saw that Mr. Buttinsky had corralled Donald and Larry. He'd gone to the compactor room to throw out some garbage *just* as Larry and Donald were about to get in the elevator.

Jesus, what a bunch. Who's worse, the Buttinskys, or Larry and Donald, the gossips? I wondered and double-locked the door. I walked back to Terry's room to check on him. He was sleeping with his little butt up in the air, happy as a clam.

I pulled down the Costco-sized box of diapers from the top shelf in his room, figuring I'd hide the tube in that giant box. But when I reached for the tube, I got a shock from touching the metal.

I picked it back up, holding it by a paper napkin, figuring it was the same as when you get a shock from touching a metal object indoors when it's too dry and hot, and stuck it inside the diaper box, knowing that nobody goes into a diaper box unless absolutely necessary. The earring went into my locked jewelry box. *Oh, the key. Right.* I wrapped it in a sock and put it in my top dresser drawer.

That night I fell into a restless sleep, waking up over and over with my heart pounding, then falling back to sleep only to wake again in a panic. *Bad sangria dreams.*

I woke for the final time at six fifteen—not because I had to get Terry and myself ready to drive out to Queens, but because it was now freezing in the apartment. I jumped out of bed, threw on a robe and fuzzy slippers, and checked the windows in my room, the living room, and the kitchen. All locked. I walked into Terry's room.

It was really freezing in there—what the hell? But stranger still? The baby was sitting up in his crib babbling and giggling to himself. He'd never sat up by himself before!

"Oh my little star!" I gasped. "Sitting up!" It was odd since he normally woke up crying to be picked up, fed, and changed immediately—but then I realized why it was so cold. The window in his room was open and a fierce breeze was blowing right on him.

But the window simply couldn't be open, I knew. I had these steering wheel club-looking locks on every window in the apartment. But it *was* open. Not much. Maybe half an inch, but still. I made a note to call the super as soon as we got back from the funeral. Did that idiot Larry break the lock? *Moron!*

When I checked, I could see it hadn't been broken at all. I relocked the window and reached for Terry, but he wasn't even interested in being picked up. Instead he was babbling away to himself in baby talk in the freezing cold room. I picked him up and put a blanket around him.

Rubbing him up and down, I cooed, "That's Mama's good boy. Ooo, so cold. Mommy is a bad girl. I didn't know your window was open!" But I knew it hadn't been open when I had checked on him the night before. I *knew* it wasn't.

I looked at the clock: 6:25. Instead of being overjoyed that finally Terry had slept through the night, I was a little weirded out. Even if he slept through the night, why hadn't he cried to be picked up when he did wake up?

My mom the pediatrician would have told me that Terry had hit a milestone and that was a good thing. I knew that she would have been right and I was probably just having new mom anxieties—it wasn't easy raising a baby alone since my bleeding-heart parents had gone to Africa to help other women with their babies. So why, then, was I feeling anything but good about this new milestone in baby Terry's progress?

Then, as I was putting Terry onto the changing table, he spoke. "Mama!" I stood there immobilized for a second. Terry had also just said his first word! Make that two giant milestones in one day, or three, counting the fact that I was about to take him to a funeral of a Jewish man in a Catholic cemetery.

I felt momentarily excited and bereft at the same time because no one was there to share the moment with me. More to the point: his father wasn't there to share the moment with me.

Then Terry put his hands up, and I heard what I knew I couldn't have heard. "Mama! Up!" *What?* I nearly dropped my baby off his changing table.

6

It was too much to take in—alone—so instead I managed to chalk the weird incidents of the morning up to, well, weird incidences. And that was my second mistake. My first was taking the tube into my home.

I fed Terry, dressed us both for the funeral, went down to my building's garage, took the car seat out of my own car and put it into Morris's Buick, and strapped Terry into it in the backseat. It was a tough go. Buicks from 1987 were not designed for modern-day car seats, which require the skill of the *Top Gear* guys to attach even to a modern car, let alone an old clunker. I finally figured it out and stuck a Binky in Terry's mouth—knowing he'd drop it in five seconds, at which point, he'd immediately scream for it again.

Instead, Terry fell asleep before we even got into the Midtown Tunnel. He was still fast asleep when I pulled up to Roy's apartment building in Astoria. I waited and waited. No Roy. I called his cell. He picked up after three rings.

"Where are you? I'm waiting outside. Funeral? Hello?"

"Oh shit. I overslept—what time is it?"

I waited another ten minutes and *my* cell rang this time: Roy. "I'm outside. I don't see you."

"In front of your building, and I'm double-parked!"

"My apartment building? I went back to the old man's house. I slept in Hicksville. And I slept like the dead."

"Oh for Christ's sake! What now?"

"I'll call a cab and meet you at the cemetery. You head over. I'm really sorry, Ali, but I thought you knew I was staying here. If somebody had messed around here, I didn't want to leave it unguarded."

"You could have told me last night."

"I was drunk. Your fault."

"My fault. I accept full responsibility. Now please get to Saint John's. I don't want to bury your father alone while carrying my baby!"

I turned the car around and headed for the cemetery.

I got there just before nine, asked directions to the gravesite from the guard who gave me a map, and drove around the vastness of the grounds.

It had started to rain again—it was one of those nasty, cold mornings. Perfect day to bury a nasty, cold man. Finding the site was easier said than done. It's not like I could type it into the GPS or anything.

Even on a gorgeous day the St. John Cemetery is creepy as hell with giant mausoleums and horrible gravesite statues of giant, scary, looming angels; weeping angels; Jesuses who are posed like Rodin's *The Thinker*; and God knows what else, no pun intended. "Catholics sure know how to do up the afterlife," I mumbled aloud. Coming from a long line of agnostics, I never understood how I ended up with as many priests as friends as I have. Maybe because we all liked arguing about God. Yes, I've got some set.

Speaking of priests, when I finally found gravesite # 42.7121-73.8662, a lone priest was standing next to a giant hole that had been covered with a grave blanket, the casket resting on a bier.

Since Terry was sleeping and I was able to drive right up, I left him in the car with the window cracked open a tad, and began to make my way, under my umbrella, attempting to keep my heels from sinking into the wet grass as I trudged the thirty feet or so.

"Good morning, Father," I said. "Is this the funeral site for Mr. Morris Golden?" I asked, feeling rather foolish asking a Catholic priest if he was there to bury this Jewish man.

The priest, a sallow-faced man in his fifties, with a clear plastic raincoat over his priest blacks and collar, was holding an umbrella and looking upset. He grabbed my free hand and said, "Are you one of Mr. Golden's, ah, er, friends?"

"In a manner of speaking . . ." I said, not sure where this was going.

The priest started to cry. Cry! "I am Father Elias," he said, unclasping my hand to take out a handkerchief to wipe his eyes. "Morris—Mr. Golden—he converted just last year, you know, after years of devotion to Jesus."

I pretended that I did and nodded my head. "Yes. Devout. Tragic that he came to it so late in life. Catholicism, I mean," I lied.

"He came to me for conversion. The man was a saint!"

A saint with a strap for his son, and a stolen artifact, I thought but didn't say.

"I can't believe there is no one else here," Father Elias moaned, looking for any approaching cars. "A life like his and nary a mourner, except for you, Miss, Miss . . ."

"Russo, Alessandra Russo."

A look of recognition crossed his face. "Ah. The reporter. You wrote about the missing holy pages that his son now possesses?"

"Well, yes . . ." *How did he know they were pages?* I decided to play it cool.

"And where is this son, may I ask? Is he not coming to say a final farewell to his beloved father?"

"He's on his way. We had a mix-up."

"I see," he said, not seeing at all, obviously, by the look of disdain on his face.

Then, "Have you seen it? The relic, I mean?"

As inappropriate as it clearly was for him to bring this up, what with dead Morris in the casket right next to us and all, I still managed to bite my tongue. But seriously, what had been appropriate about any of this from the first call I had received yesterday anyway?

I simply said, "No, no, I haven't."

"Well, has the son found it yet—the papyrus?"

He knows it's papyrus? I thought.

"Roy, his name is Roy Golden. But no, he hasn't located it. No, not that I know of. Why, may I ask, do you think it's papyrus that Mr. Golden left?"

"Well, Morris told me! It's what brought him to the conversion in the first place—these pages are simply among the most important Christian relics of all time. The world needs them. Mr. Golden promised to will them to me"—he made a quick course correction— "I mean to our church, not to me personally."

"I see. And which church are you affiliated with, Father?"

He slightly pulled on his collar, as though it was too starched, and answered, "Why, Our Lady of Vilnius. Mr. Golden told me about the pages in confession one day."

"Confession?" *What priest tells what he learned in confession?*

He got out of it by quickly saying, "I can only tell you that because we had many, many conversations about it after that."

Right.

So Morris had told him what he had! *I'm not going to get into it with a weeping priest while standing in the rain at a cemetery, over the body of a Jew who left a ten-million-dollar Christian relic.*

But I did. "That's what he told you?"

"Of course. I was his father confessor."

"So you mentioned. Do you know then how the relic came into his possession, Father?"

"Again, yes. He was given the pages by the owner."

"Yes, of course," I said. "But did you know, unfortunately for St. Vilnius parish," I began as tactfully as I could, until I was stopped.

"Our Lady of Vilnius." Elias sniffed.

"Sorry. Our Lady of Vilnius. You see, Mr. Golden's will says something different," I said, watching the priest's eyes narrow. I continued, not knowing what the hell Morris's will said one way or the other, "He left everything to Roy." I wasn't about to let this unknown priest or his church steal Roy's inherited relic any more than I was about to let another reporter steal my story. Wasn't happening.

Just then I saw a cab pulling up with said-heir Roy in the backseat. *Oy,* I thought. *How do you answer something like that?*

"Speaking of which . . ." I said, waving to Roy. I tried to signal to him not to slam the door, but he did, which woke Terry.

I slogged back in the soggy ground to unhook Terry's car seat and kiss Roy at the same time. Terry woke screaming his head off, so I picked him up and pulled a bottle out of the diaper bag and began trying to feed him as we walked. He was having none of it, kicking and wailing. He screamed even louder when he saw Roy.

"I have a way with kids," Roy joked as we walked back to the gravesite and the morose Father Elias.

Mourners at the next funeral over shot us nasty looks. "Who takes an infant to a funeral?" I knew they were saying.

This graveyard was like the Leonard's of Great Neck of cemeteries. "Golden funeral! Party of three."

Terry continued carrying on like he was possessed—until we got right to the grave, that is. Father Elias made the sign of the cross on my baby's forehead, and he immediately calmed down, looked up at Father Elias, and smiled.

"Mama. Up," Terry babbled to Elias, while trying to scramble out of my arms.

"Mama's here, baby. Right here . . ." I baby-cooed to him.

Roy whispered, shocked, "The kid talks?"

"It just started. Clearly he's a genius!"

Too bad the genius wouldn't stop trying to squirm out of my arms. Finally Father Elias reached for him, took him from my arms gently, and Terry again immediately quieted down and smiled up at him. "Mama!"

What the . . . ?

The last damned thing I wanted right then was my newly fluent infant to be held by a priest over a grave, so squirming or crying or not, I held out my arms and the priest gave him back after making the sign of the cross again on Terry's forehead, this time with the holy water he was carrying to sprinkle on the casket. This seemed to quiet him down enough to at least be given back to me, his own mother. Roy and I shot each other looks.

"If no one else will be attending . . ." Father Elias sighed, disappointed, searching for any approaching mourners. He finally began.

"Would you like to say anything?" he asked Roy, who shook his head, looking down at the grave.

That really seemed to offend Elias. "Well, if you don't choose to—I'm sure you're too upset to speak," he snarked, "then I shall." Roy nodded.

Father Elias described in detail Roy's father's conversion to Catholicism. "After Morris miraculously was given a relic of enormous importance to the Catholic Church," Elias intoned.

"Given? After he stole this relic of enormous buckaroos, you mean," Roy whispered to me as I was standing there trying to rock the fussing Terry into some kind of quiet.

Elias must have heard him because he repeated, annoyed, "Right after Morris miraculously came into possession of this relic, he found *Jesus!*" The rest was a bunch of purple prose about the sainted Morris Golden, who'd spent the last years of his life in total devotion to his personal savior, Jesus Christ. Finally, the funeral ended, and even though it wasn't the Catholic way, we threw handfuls of dirt on the grave in the Jewish tradition. Terry started screaming again.

And so good-bye, Morris Golden, and hello to what we both thought would be the beginning of a life without shame and shackles for my boy Roy. Who knew how wrong two people could be?

"What a pile of horse shit," Roy said as we headed back to the car after thanking Father Elias for taking the time to come out to Queens all the way from—well, he never actually said from which borough or town, although we assumed it was Hicksville—and for throwing such a swell funeral.

Elias, however, followed us. He handed Roy his card with just a phone number and his name. "Please call me. I must discuss the find that your late father left."

"Yeah, sure," Roy said, as in, *Screw off. It ain't happening.*

The priest kissed Terry on his forehead and he momentarily—again—stopped bawling. Roy shot me a look, which I pretended not to notice.

"Father, you have the magic touch," I said, wanting to get back into the car and out of the rain.

Father Elias brought me up short, however. "I only possess that which comes from my Lord Jesus Christ. Not magic. Belief!"

Oy. How do you answer something like that?

Roy took Terry from my arms and tried to hook him back into the car seat, but he screamed loud enough to wake the dead, no pun intended. I nervous-giggled, hoping this guy would just leave us alone.

Father Elias grabbed my sleeve as I was turning to help Roy deal with Terry, and sneered at me. "This is no laughing matter. I know who you are. I know what you did last year with that terrorist. I know you helped him. Do not let yourself get caught up again with the Antichrist. The thirteenth daimon has you in his sights!"

"Who?"

"The Satan. 'And I saw a beast rising up out of the sea, having seven heads and ten horns, and on his horns ten crowns, and on his heads a blasphemous name.'"

What a freak! I thought, but in reality the freak was freaking us both out.

I jerked my arm free and snapped back as calmly as only a reporter can when faced with a nut job. "A news story is a news story, Father! And that so-called terrorist was an innocent . . ." *Why in the hell are you getting into this?* I thought to myself before Elias cut me off, now shaking his finger at me.

"Well, Ms. Russo, what is now in Roy Golden's possession," he said, looking at him but speaking as if he weren't there, "is as dangerous now as your so-called innocent man was back then. The only place for the papyri is in my church where we can consecrate them in the name of our Lord." He turned and walked away without another word.

"Well, that's one priest I won't be calling 'friend' anytime soon," I said to Roy.

Over Terry's screams, Roy answered, "What the hell was *that*?"

"Morris must have had some crazy friends. But actually, I have no idea what the hell that was. I'll look up this Vilnius parish and maybe I'll go pay Father Elias—not that I trust him—a visit. He might be able to shed some light on the locked tube."

"Or he'll knock you over the head with it and run off with some underage boy."

"Shut up. Like I'd take it with me. Geez. This is who you trusted with the tube? Someone you consider an idiot?" I joked. Then, "You're also a huge weirdo, by the way."

"I'm the weirdo. Right," Roy said as we got into the car and I turned back onto the highway. "Astoria or Hicksville?"

"I think we should go to your dad's house and look around."

"Breakfast first? Here, look, the best diner in the world," he said as we drove past a typical Queens diner that looked like Versailles. "It was even voted 'best diner' by, well, I don't know who, but it must be true, it says it on the banner," Roy implored, pointing his finger.

"That banner was new in the Carter administration," I cracked and then I pointed—to the backseat and the wailing child.

"Oh, right. Scream Boy," he said. "Never mind."

"I don't know what's wrong with him," I moaned, turning around and trying to see if he was OK. "Roy, can you try sticking his Binky back in his mouth? It's hanging on the ribbon on his onesie there."

"What language are you speaking—Binky, onesie? That priest must have possessed you with the thirteen daimons—because you're speaking in freaking tongues."

"The thing on the ribbon pinned to his onesie—p.j.'s. It's called a Binky. A pacifier." Finally, Roy did as he was told and I turned the car toward Hicksville.

When we pulled up, I unbuckled Terry's car seat and used the handle to carry him, and walked inside the old Levitt house. Terry was still fussing. "Maybe he's teething," I said, not really knowing what I was talking about. Mommyland was still a strange and unusual territory for me.

The house had had a makeover since the old days. The former shingled facade had been changed to resemble a Tudor castle plopped over a row Cape Cod house, sitting smack in the middle of Long Island suburbia.

The inside had remained relatively unchanged, however—1970s kitschy kitchen with avocado-green appliances, as it had been back then. The living room walls were covered in what looked like very good, very old paneling. Somebody had added deep purple velvet drapes. I peeked out of them to see kids riding their bikes and nor-mal life going on, while inside there was this ugliness. For a split second I thought when I had looked out that the scene looked old—or fake. The bikes the kids were riding looked like 1950s Schwinns, and the girls were wearing dresses. I peeked through the velvet drapes again, but the kids weren't there—must have ridden away.

Looking around the room, attempting to lighten the mood from the feeling of dread inside that house, I said, "Well, now I know where the rest of the drapes from Tara went." I thought I was feel-ing all the bad vibes from the years of abuse in that chamber of hor-rors, and of course from the fact that the chief horror master had died in that house the day before. I later learned it was much more than that.

We walked back to the second bedroom on the first floor, which had been converted into a library/office with floor-to-ceiling bookshelves filled with every manner of old book imaginable. It was musty and dusty and even creepier than the living room. The good thing, however, was that the minute we walked into that library room, Terry quieted down.

"There's Mommy's good boy," I said, putting the pacifier in his mouth and a blanket around him. It was especially cold in that room. Freezing, in fact.

"There's probably a few thousand in books here," I said to Roy, easing down an old leather volume and feeling the beautiful binding.

Every book seemed to be about spiritualism: *The Divine Pymander,* translated by John Everard; *The Chaldæan Oracles of Zoroaster,* by W. Wynn Westcott; and *The Secret Doctrine,* the masterwork of Helena Petrovna Blavatsky, in what looked like a first-edition binding. Books on sacred geometry, code breaking, magic, and even necromancy (communicating with the dead).

"Where did you ever find that book, the . . . the . . ."

"Right."

He walked over to the shelf where he returned the book he'd been holding very carefully. Old habits die hard. He jumped a foot high when I put my hand on his shoulder from the back. "Your father isn't coming back to yell at you for messing up his books," I said gently.

"I hope . . ."

"He's not. He's dead. You can torch them if you want—although you'd be out some hard cash—and he can't say anything about it,"

I said, throwing one random book on the floor, which made him jump. Roy fake-laughed and handed me the ancient leather-bound Voynich Manuscript.

Just then Terry began wailing again. "The bang must have scared him." I picked him up and soothed him, the tears running down his little cheeks.

"Mama up! Mama up!"

"I think I better head back to the city. It's been too much excitement for one day for this little guy. Can I borrow this one and some of the other books?" I asked. "I want to see what the hell they're all about and begin calling around to see who knows how to unlock that tube."

"I'll drive you back," Roy said.

"No, it's OK. I'll call a car service. At least we still have that perk at *The Standard*. I *am* on a story, after all. Oh, let me copy down the info from that priest's card."

Instead he dug it out of his pocket and handed it to me. "Here, I don't want it."

The card was made of fine-grade vellum—not your standard-issue parish priest kind of card. It read in a fancy typeface: Father Arturo Elias, with a +40-008 before the phone number.

"Curious," I said, looking at it. "I'll give this guy a call. I'll go over to the church, see what he's all about."

"Sure, whatever." Roy shrugged.

The car arrived and Terry and I got packed up to leave, Terry squawking the second we got outside that House of Creepiness. "He's the only kid that ever wanted to stay inside this dump," Roy said.

"That's because he's the only kid ever allowed inside that dump besides you. Remember?"

He nodded. "I can't forget, unfortunately."

"So, you leaving or what?" I asked, taking his hand.

"No, I need to clean up some stuff."

"Clean up? Like what? Don't want to leave evidence of the crime," I joked.

"Exactly," he joked back.

7

I got home, fed Terry, and put him down for his nap. He had finally calmed down as soon as he was back in his cozy crib.

I called Bob Brandt to say I'd attended the funeral and was working on the follow-up from home. "There's a bunch of research I gotta do. And Bob, I went back to Roy's father's house, and it was weird with a capital 'weird.' I mean, the guy, this shadow of a man, had a library full of black-magic books."

"Watch the quiet ones," he said.

"Oh, and Roy gave me the relic to hold on to until I can find the right experts. It's safe though."

"I hope 'safe' doesn't mean your apartment, Russo," Bob said, somewhat incredulously. "You're holding a possible ten-million-dollar relic—for *safekeeping*? Where? In your refrigerator?"

"Not to worry."

He didn't trust it. "Jesus Christ! Put it in a safety-deposit box!"

"You didn't seriously just suggest that, did you? The thing was stolen out of a safety-deposit box—remember?"

"Oh, right. My bad. Bring it in. I'll put it in the safe in the office."

"No can do," I said. I wasn't about to tell him my sitter had gone home to Guiana and I had no clue when she'd be back. "I'm having it analyzed by an antiquities expert," I lied. "I can't open it."

"Just don't lose the damned thing. This could be big. Very big."

"As big as the exploding Chihuahua?"

"You are such a pain in my ass," he said.

"You mean that in the nicest possible way, right?"

"Right."

Whew! I'd dodged another bullet. The longer I could work at home, the shorter the time until Anna returned. If she ever did!

I rang up the old number I'd had for Father Paulo. Damn! *"Questo numero non è più in servizio."* This number is no longer in service.

Ten minutes later my cell rang. Unknown number. I picked up anyway.

"Ciao, bella!"

"Father Paulo?" I was stunned. But then I shouldn't have been. Either his number was still in service and he had that outgoing message for whatever reason or he had read my story, which had gone viral. Paulo was nothing if not a news junkie.

"Sí," he said pretentiously, as though he hadn't been born in the U.S.

"I tried you but the message said your number was no longer in service."

"That's correct," he said, simply. "That old number is no longer in service. I'm in Israel now, and I've been waiting for your call."

Father Paulo, at eighty-four, was still attached to the Vatican—sort of like their CIA—and had been part of the whole story of the cloning that I broke last year. But I wouldn't trust him as far as I could throw a battleship. That being said, there was no denying his scholarship, his brilliance, and his knowledge of things esoteric. He understood the spirituality that had been lost in the pomp and circumstance and big-deal money matters that the Church had devolved into over the millennia. The fact that the Vatican had rented out space to McDonald's within spitting distance of St. Peter's was a particular source of annoyance to him.

"What is it that you have exactly? This relic?"

"Are you sitting down?" I asked, meaning it sincerely.

"I am."

"Good, because this is a doozy. My friend Roy's father, well, he was a real S.O.B. He was a bank manager during our growing-up years, and believe it or not, he was manager of a Citibank branch in Hicksville, Long Island."

Clever and devious as old Father Paulo was, I heard a sharp intake of breath on his part.

"Do you know where I'm going with this?" I asked, to see if he'd give anything up.

"Possibly. It's well known that the so-called Gospel of Judas had been stashed by some fool Egyptian black-market thief in a Citibank branch, yes."

"One and the same as the branch where Mr. Morris Golden, father of my friend Roy, worked."

"I do know that the so-called Gospel took a very circuitous route, and ended up in that not-safe safety-deposit box—and moldered into thousands of pieces. Case closed," he said, somewhat smugly. Well, very smugly.

"But it is my understanding," he continued, "that after it was found by peasants in Middle Egypt, the codex, which became known as the Codex Tchacos, had been moved all over the Middle East and Europe among dealers who tried selling it for years at what was then an extraordinary price. Finally the fool—I believe his name was Hanna, who'd kept it, lost it, found it again, all very disreputable—took it to New York. He thought he had a buyer there, but didn't. Somehow it ended up in the safety-deposit box to rot. Tell me what I don't know so far." I could practically see him puffing up his chest. "Case closed?"

"Case just reopened," I answered. Paulo and I had been through hell and back together last year. He wasn't an easy man to like, but a very easy man to respect.

"This is the sound of me being intrigued."

"Well, I hope you took my advice and are sitting down, Father. I think I've got lost pages from the Gospel of Judas. Roy's dad must have stolen them right out of the bank vault."

"Dear Jesus! How can that be? It's only been a vague rumor that such pages exist." He was a scoundrel, but I knew he would be the only one who could open the tube, and once he knew what I potentially had, he'd be desperate to get his hands on such an ancient text. His call had been a fishing expedition, and it had paid off. Rumors travel fast among his crowd.

"And so, Father, I'd like your help."

"Of course."

"I don't know for sure what I have, though."

"Excuse me?"

"Whatever it is, it's sealed in a tube, and it can't be opened. Or it can be, by someone who'd know how, but I also know that if it is what I think it is, opening it could make it rot immediately."

"Well, not immediately. It lasted for nearly two thousand years without rotting—until it hit that bank vault."

"True. But I don't want to take that responsibility on my own."

"If I open it for you, I must be the one who interprets it."

"Of course. But there's also a practical side to this, Father. I need to sell it on behalf of my friend. I don't want to go into the specifics over the phone, but you know me well enough to know I wouldn't do anything illegal." Dead silence on the other end.

"Geez. You think . . ." I added, trying to spur him along.

"I don't think anything," he said, cutting me off. "But if it's what you say it is, I know of a buyer who'd pay handsomely."

"My friend is looking for ten million dollars, nonnegotiable."

"Let me get back to you on that. But are you sure your friend is willing to part with the relic?"

"He already has."

"Meaning—what? That you have it?"

I didn't answer.

He knew the answer by my silence. "Is it in a safe place?" he asked, somewhat panicked.

"Of course. Safer than a safety-deposit box, that's for sure. That's exactly where it sat rotting away for decades. All rotted, except for . . . well, what was stolen."

"Or so you assume. You told me it's sealed in a tube of some kind. That would be the proper storage, I believe, but in fact, you don't even know if the tube is empty."

I hadn't even given that possibility any thought. What if?

He went on as though he hadn't given me new food for thought: "Where did you store it, may I ask?" he said calmly. "This is too valuable a find to be sitting around in your home or somewhere foolish like that."

He could tell by my silence that yes, it was in my home.

"You need to get it to me. In Israel."

"In Israel? I can't just drop everything and take off for Israel. I have a baby, you know."

"So I've heard."

"You did?"

"I did."

"You heard I'd had a baby—while you were in Israel?" I asked incredulously.

"I assure you I *am* well informed."

"So *I've* heard," I said, parroting his smugness.

"I merely want to keep the relic safe forever, if it is what you say it is."

"We both know you're talking about the Vatican, so why not cut right to the chase, Father? But can't you come here?"

"My health is not what it should be," he answered. "My heart condition has worsened and I'm under a doctor's care here. I'm not supposed to travel for another month. At least."

I figured he was lying to get me to come to him, but how do you say that to an octogenarian priest? "Oh, I'm sorry to hear that," I said instead. We knew each other well enough to know how to play the game. Then, "Can you hold on a second, Father? It's getting very cold in here and I have to put on the heat." My teeth were actually chattering. When I went to turn up the thermostat in Terry's room, once again, I found the window was opened. *What the hell?* I'd shut it tight and relocked the club window guard thing. Terry slept through it all.

Who the hell had opened Terry's window?

I picked the cell back up. "I have to get back to you on all that. See, my sitter has taken off for Guiana and I'm here alone with the baby."

"Bring him."

"I don't think so." When did he turn into Father Mary Poppins?

"I'd like to see the boy. Even though he's the son of . . ." he started.

"I'll get back to you, OK?" I ventured, reaching for a sweat-shirt.

Damn it's cold!

He didn't respond so I continued, "Lemme see what I can do."

"You do that," he finally said.

What could I do, *really*? My parents were due back in a couple of weeks. But could a find like this wait that long?

Answer: Absolutely not. Nor was taking Terry a possibility. He didn't even have a baby passport. There were just so many things to think about that you never think about before you become a parent. A single parent.

My next call was to the super in my building.

Question: How could they have installed such an important item as a child safety lock that didn't lock properly?

He ran right up, panicked, waking Terry in the process.

Answer: These locks are foolproof and break-proof and most definitely childproof. There was nothing wrong with the lock.

If it couldn't open on its own, then how in hell did it keep open-ing on its own?

The super decided the best way to prove it was the way men have been proving things since caveman days: gaffer's tape. He secured the lock with the fix-everything tape, then sealed the window sides, bottom, and top with more of it.

"If that comes off, missus, you either got one helluva strong baby or you got a ghost." He laughed. Funny guy. I gave him a ten for his efforts and made a mental note to call the housing authority if it happened again. It was the law, after all, that child safety locks must lock, for Christ's sake!

As I was changing Terry, the doorbell rang again. I ignored it. The super would just have to come back. It rang again.

"Geez, Terry," I said, picking him up off the table to get to the door. It wasn't the super. It was the Judsons. "We saw Gerald, the super. Everything OK?"

"Oh sure, thanks, the lock in the baby's room keeps opening."

"You want me to have a look?" Dane asked.

"Sure, thanks."

"Dane can fix anything!" Raylene exclaimed, holding out her arms in the universal "Can I hold the baby?" gesture.

"Mama up!" he exclaimed happily to Raylene.

"May I?"

"Sure," I said. She proceeded to sit down and feed Terry his bottle while I heated up a jar of mashed peas.

"I'll be damned," I said. Raylene looked proud as punch that Terry was eager to eat the peas she proffered.

"I can't get him to eat anything. I'm afraid I'm not so good at this mother thing," I moaned.

Raylene smiled and pshawed. "You're a fine mother. I was a good mother back in the day, too . . ."

"Why, Raylene! I had no idea you had children. I mean, you never mentioned . . ."

"'Had,' my dear. I had a son, Makenson, but well, he died. Tropical disease. I don't want to talk about it."

"Of course. I'm so sorry," I said, rubbing her shoulder.

Terry was done, but she wasn't budging, so I picked up one of the books from the stack I'd taken from Morris's house. "I have about five hundred hours of research to do," I said, hoping that she'd take the hint and leave because I really did have five hundred hours of research to do.

"Let me bring Terry to our place, give you some time to work," she said as Dane came out of the nursery. "Looks like the super did a super job." He laughed. "Gaffer's tape! The tape of the gods."

"Dane," Raylene said. "We're gonna take Terry to our place for a couple of hours. Give Alessandra some time to work." *Did I say that was OK?*

"Excellent!" Dane said.

"Well, excellent then it is," I said, throwing up my hands. I packed up a diaper bag with bottles, diapers, and Cheerios. "You're like twenty feet from my door, but still . . ."

As they were about to leave, Dane turned back. "Alessandra, I know you're very busy, but we're having a few friends in for a small dinner party tonight. Even a local politician. We'd love it if you could join us . . ."

That was the last thing I felt like doing. "Gee, I'd love to but I haven't got a sitter."

"Don't be silly," he said. "Bring the baby."

"A screaming baby is not exactly great dinner company."

"He'll be fine. Why, look. He's quiet as a lamb of God," he said.

"Yeah, that's funny because he's been the devil spawn all day so far," I joked.

"Dinner at eight," Raylene said, whisking away Terry, who was happy as could be to be whisked away. They were quirky, but nice people, and frankly I was glad for the solitude. "I'll pick him up around five . . . ," I tried telling them as they rushed away.

I sat down at my desk in the living room and cracked opened the Voynich Manuscript. As soon as I opened it, I heard a loud bang, like a crack of electricity. It seemed to emanate from right near where I sitting, but there was nothing there. Scared it was an electrical problem, I smelled all the wires near me. Nothing.

Between the cold and the crack, my apartment was turning into one of those self-contained climate laboratories. *What next, indoor rain?*

Again, it just seemed coincidental and so I blindly went back to studying the book.

As Roy had said, the Voynich Manuscript was an ancient, illustrated codex of weird plants and other oddities, which were hand illustrated and written in a language I'd never seen before. But this volume wasn't just any old book. This copy of the Voynich Manuscript looked to be ancient and hand created. The pages looked to be real calfskin parchment. *Jesus.* What I didn't know then was that only one of them was supposed to have existed and if another one existed, it sure wasn't supposed to have been in Morris's Levitt house.

I was carefully—very, very carefully—turning the pages when I came upon a note tucked into the book somewhere between the middle and the back.

It wasn't that there had been a note tucked inside that made me sit up and take notice, it was what was written on that note that did it.

8

To my son,
Once the tube is in your possession, contact Mr. Myles Engles,
Engles Rare Books, Lexington Ave., New York City.

Respectfully
your father,
Morris Golden

PS: the chains of our Lord did not bind him. The secret is
above where he hung below. 31.780231° N, 35.233991° E

My God, what a creep, I thought. And what a lunatic.

On the back he'd scrawled a phone number with 011+44 before
it; it was the country code for England. Odd because the note said
that Engles' shop was in the U.S.

The vellum reminded me of the card that Father Elias had given
to Roy—also with a different country code on it. I took it from my

bag, and looked up the church online. The Wikipedia entry startled me: *Our Lady of Vilnius,* it read, *was the national parish church of the Lithuanian Catholic community. Despite a landmarks preservation debate, the church was demolished in May 2015.* Demolished? What the hell? New York City? *Why would a ninety-year-old guy travel to New York City for a priest, anyway?*

I dialed his number, but it just rang. No answer, no voice mail, no nothing.

I next Googled *Arturo Elias, priest.* But came up blank. Then I e-mailed *The Standard*'s librarian, Scott, to see what he could dig up on the church and this Father Elias guy. He e-mailed me back a few seconds later repeating what I'd already learned about the church and that there had been a huge protest when the diocese closed it, and worse, when they sold it to developers. The last parish priest there was not named Elias, but Frank Lowry, who had retired. I e-mailed Scott back to see if there was any info on where this Lowry had chosen to retire. That was a lot easier to find, so I dialed up the seminary in Maryland where he was now semiretired and teaching.

He got on the phone immediately. "This is Father Lowry, how may I help you?"

I explained who I was, but only said that Father Arturo Elias had presided at my friend's father's funeral and that my friend wanted to contact him to thank him but that we couldn't find him since the church where he'd told us he worked, Our Lady of Vilnius, apparently was no longer there.

Father Lowry took a moment and said, "That's correct. It was demolished. But Ms. Russo, and I'm loath to say this, someone was pulling your leg."

"At a funeral?"

"Yes. There are some very weird people out there, as you know. I was there for twenty-two years and we never had a priest named Father Elias. Well, let me be clearer on that: there wasn't a priest by that name during *my* time there."

"Oh?"

"That's why it's so curious that this man would use that particular name."

"What do you mean, Father?"

"Because Father Arturo Elias was the name of the very first pastor Our Lady of Vilnius ever had."

"When was that, Father? I need to find him."

"Find him? You'll find him in St. John Cemetery in Queens! The church was built in 1910, so dear Father Elias died back in the 1940s."

"But . . . this man couldn't be more than, say, midfifties."

"I'm afraid the man you encountered was a faker, Ms. Russo. Father Arturo Elias is long dead."

"But why would someone fake it?"

"I have no idea. I mean, it's possible that this priest is a distant relative of the first Father Elias, but to say he was associated with Our Lady of Vilnius? Preposterous."

"I'm more curious than ever now," I said. "Are there any archival photos of the parish priests back when the church was first opened?"

"I doubt it. Before I got there, there had been a fire in the rectory and adjoining office. All the old records, photos, paintings—all gone." We hung up, and I was more confused than before I'd called. Who the hell was the man pretending to be Father Elias, anyway?

I phoned Roy next and told him about my conversation with

Father Lowry, but Roy, unfazed, let it roll off his back. "What a shock," he said drolly. "My old man had friends who are as crooked as he was? Wow. That guy's probably some petty thief who got a priest's costume at Abracadabra on West Twenty-First Street. I got my *Chorus Line* Halloween outfit there last year."

"Oh, shut up. Aren't you even concerned that your father's funeral was presided over by a fake Catholic priest?"

"Ali, are you seriously asking me if I care that my abusive Jewish-father-turned-last-minute-Catholic had a fake Christian burial? The guy was probably just some shyster who read about the relic and thought he'd take a stab at stealing it. Jesus H."

"But how did he know where the burial was?"

"Funeral directors post those things online now. Sometimes when there was a bad fire, we'd have to work with the funeral directors to make sure they'd inform the cops so that they could block traffic after they posted it. Disasters bring out more mourners than a Mafia funeral."

"But he knew the relic was papyrus."

"Stab in the dark, Ali. Just a nut. Trust me."

"I'll let you know if I find anything," I promised.

Next I tried the phone number for Myles Engles, who picked up after one ring. He was in fact boarding a flight from England back to the U.S. at that very moment.

He hadn't read my story, but said he'd be more than interested in seeing the relic. He'd have to know something more about it because it might not even be within his area of expertise.

"Well, I hate to discuss this over the phone, but did you ever hear of the Gospel of Judas?" I heard him gasp on the other end.

"Who hasn't?"

"Well, did you know that some pages were missing?"

"Rumor, speculation, but frankly that has never been verified because the manuscript—when it was found back in 2000 in a bank vault—was literally in thousands of pieces, much too rotted to know what if anything was actually missing. It breaks my heart to even talk of it. One of the greatest finds of the ages, left to molder and rot . . ."

"What if some of it was, ah, rescued?"

"Rescued?"

"Stolen. Out of that safety-deposit box where it had been stored way before the rest of it was found."

He gasped again, visibly shocked. "Oh. You're there now? At that bank?"

"No, but I am in possession of the pages. I *think*."

"We're about to take off," Engles said. "Can you bring what you have to my shop on Lexington Avenue first thing tomorrow morning?"

"Nine?"

"Nine. And Miss Russo? *Te-he-zah-ree.*"

"I'm sorry, I didn't understand you."

"Yiddish for 'be safe.' "

"Oh. You, too."

I thought he was just looking for me to wish him a safe flight. Some Jewish thing I didn't understand. I was wrong.

The rest of the day flew by as I tried to make sense of the Voynich Manuscript, which I had neglected to mention to Mr. Engles. I've learned in my years of reporting that it's one thing at a time. Don't give it all up at once.

Since the Voynich Manuscript made zero sense to me, I stored the book safely—well, as much as a two-bedroom NYC apartment allows. No, not in the Pampers box this time, but in the hutch in the dining area in the top drawer. Wow. No one could find it there! But I live in such a secure building, no one ever worries about robberies. For those of you who don't live in NYC, I know, it sounds odd, but I've always felt safer in a doorman building in the city than in a house in the suburbs. We had a doorman on duty 24/7, security cameras all over the place, and if I ever thought—ever— that someone was breaking into my apartment in the middle of the night, I'd just pick up the intercom and call the doorman and security would be up in a New York minute, which is approximately thirty seconds.

I then Googled *Gospel of Judas.* I discovered that it had been found by peasants in Middle Egypt probably in the mid-1970s. The codex was then named for Frieda Nussberger-Tchacos, the woman behind its rescue (i.e., the Codex Tchacos). Decades later. It was then transferred to the Maecenas Foundation for Ancient Art in Basel, Switzerland. The Gospel of Judas had taken a very circuitous route for several decades before Tchacos got ahold of it. It had been carelessly huckstered around the Middle East and Europe among dealers who had tried selling it for a small fortune.

Finally an Egyptian small-time seller of antiques by the name of Hanna got it, kept it, lost it, found it again, and took it to New York, where he thought he had a buyer, but didn't. So—and here's where it gets really weird—Hanna got disheartened and rented the safety-deposit box in a Citibank in Hicksville, Long Island, of all places and flew back to Egypt.

The codex was left to rot for sixteen years and somehow along the way it even spent time in another disreputable dealer's freezer, where it suffered further damage.

It was almost impossible to believe that such a priceless relic was tossed around like a cheap library paperback that somebody had forgotten to return.

I next called Roy to tell him about the note and the phone call with Engles. He sounded good. "Well, that's better news than the last call. Here's even better news," he said. "I have a date. We hooked up on Zoosk."

"Be careful. You're semifamous now—and maybe rich soon, too."

"You sound like an old lady. I'm a giant guy. I know how to take care of myself, Gramma."

"You're right. Have fun. I'll let you know what happens at the bookstore tomorrow."

I hung up and started digging into what the Gospel of Judas itself was about—what was left had been pieced together by experts working with *National Geographic,* although most of it was beyond repair—but when I glanced up at the clock again, it was already five! Holy crap, where had the day gone? I ran down the hall to pick up Terry at the Judsons' apartment. As I approached I could smell something delicious cooking. I walked in and found Terry happily playing on the rug. When he saw me he said, "Up Mama!" Then, "Cookie!"

"Did he just say 'cookie'?" I asked the Judsons, astounded.

"No, dear," Dane said. "Our little Terry is a smart boy, but I don't think he's into making culinary suggestions just yet."

"Cookie Mama!" Terry repeated himself. Maybe he was!

Raylene, who'd managed to set a beautiful table for eight with china and silver, chimed in, "He's such a delight! A real pleasure!"

"Thanks so much for taking him. I really appreciate it," I said, marveling at all she'd accomplished that afternoon. "How in the world did you cook and get the table set with this little monster around?"

"Oh, it's easy, honey. Like I said, a pleasure!"

Gee, she really must have been a wonderful mother. I can barely order out when Terry's going baby-berserkers.

"Smells great, Raylene. What's cooking?"

"Turkey a la Dominicana, stuffed with rice and pigeon peas," she answered, opening the oven to baste the turkey. "And *pastelón de arroz,* plus my own favorite, *bollitos de yuca.*"

"You made Spanish food?"

"Dominican. When I was a little girl I lived in the area that they now call Punta Cana in the Dominican Republic. But it was still mostly jungle then. My parents had a big place in Santo Domingo, but they let me stay with my *abuela*—my grandmother—during the summers. She was a *mambo,* a voodoo priestess."

"Really," I said, astounded. These two never stopped surprising me.

"The mambos—the women—were looked down on by Christian priests and nuns and were horribly harassed by them. My grandmother was Haitian, but she moved across the island to the Dominican side—after the Christians drove her out of Haiti."

"You grew up in the Dominican Republic," I said, more as a statement than a question. It seemed impossible. She nodded her head.

"Well, I'll be." I let that fact sink in before changing the topic, grabbing a dish towel for no reason other than to look busy. "So what can I do to help? You must have your hands full."

"I'm fine, dear, just get yourself prettied up. The politician we told you about is single."

"Who is it? I must know him from my job."

"Don't you worry about that," she said, grabbing the dish towel and scooting me out the door with the baby.

"Can I bring anything—wine, dessert?"

"Just yourself, and Terry, of course."

She managed to watch the baby, make dinner, and set the table while all I did was try unsuccessfully to figure out an old book. The woman's amazing.

Terry was not happy to leave, but I got him home, gave him a nice bath, and put on his best jammies. After all, he was going to his first dinner party.

I took a quick shower (very quick), while he was in his jumpy seat then riffled through my closet looking for something that fit.

Little black dress and big, fat stomach? Too little, too fat. Black sweater and skinny pants? Too drab. Navy sweater and pencil skirt, big loop earrings and killer spikes? Perfect.

Who are you trying to impress? The world's kookiest dressers or the mystery dinner politician? Wait a minute here—you are trying to look good for their unattached male guest! You've come a long way, baby. You who said you'd never look at another man again.

I was surprised and even a little pleased that yes, maybe I was getting ready to get ready to start dating again. Someday. Not that day. But someday. Maybe.

Right. Wait until Terry starts fussing or stinking up the place during dinner. That should clinch it with said unattached male politician.

Ready! I opened the door, took a deep breath. This was going to be a boring evening at worst or somewhat interesting at best—if the guests were. I walked across the hall to the Judsons' apartment. I was barefoot and I carried Terry in his baby seat in one hand, my spikes in the other, diaper bag on my shoulder.

I rang the bell. The door opened and on the other side stood all six feet two inches of gorgeous: Councilman Alonzo Curry.

"Well, I'll be darned! Alessandra Russo as I live and breathe," he said, shocked.

Alonzo Curry! I can hardly *breathe.* "Well, hi!" I smiled, shaking his hand, managing not to spout out his secret newsroom moniker: "Hot Curry."

Alonzo took the baby—seat and all—from me as I put my spikes back on and walked inside. He watched me and then smiled his killer smile when I was three inches taller. "I liked you just the way you were!"

"Charm is not going to get you favorable press, Councilman," I joked. *Man, what a babe!*

"No? Damn," he joked back.

Councilman Curry was a New York City up-and-comer in the political world. He was forty-five, divorced, African-American. He was a lawyer and now a politician with his eye, everyone knew, on the mayoralty one day in the not-too-distant future. We knew each other slightly from my having covered city politics.

He was everything pervy, serial-exposer, former council member Anthony Weiner was supposed to have been and turned out not to be. Curry had taken his old seat after Weiner resigned during the first of his many, many sex scandals. I figured Curry, though, was the real deal. But who can ever say that about any politician?

On the other hand, what in hell was *he* doing here with my hippie dippy neighbors? I had to find out—reporters can't help themselves. "Alonzo, you're the last guy I ever expected to see here. How do you know the Judsons?"

"Everyone knows the Judsons." He laughed. "Can we actually go three more feet inside before you ask the next question? A born reporter!"

"And you're a born politician! Can you actually answer that first question?" I joked back.

"OK! The Judsons were early supporters," he said, inching his way with the baby into the foyer, where Dane had set up the bar. "They came to all my meet-and-greets back when there was no one to meet and greet! But they believed. They kept showing up. Threw fund-raisers. They're like second parents." *Like the son they lost,* I thought. *I'll bet their son would be about Curry's age now.*

"Who knew they were political animals," I said, thanking him for holding Terry and taking him back in his little seat. "So, meet and greet my little guy, Terry."

He play-shook the baby's hand. "Aren't politicians supposed to kiss babies?"

"Not anymore. Parents these days are afraid of Zika . . ."

"And all germs, chocolate, nuts, bikes, skateboards, and . . ." And so we entered laughing. Nice.

"Let me ask you, how did we ever grow up without wearing helmets and knee pads to ride a Big Wheel back in the day?" he asked.

I like this guy. No, I really like this guy. A normal man. I must be getting wise in my old age! Or maybe my bad-boy radar is on super high alert and Hot Curry's really trouble-in-disguise.

The hostess was rushing toward us, arms out. "Raylene, can I just stick Terry in the extra bedroom back there?" She was wearing a low-cut cocktail dress circa 1975 with that enormous bejeweled cross dangling between her breasts, which still looked surprisingly perky—especially to a woman like me who'd just stopped breast-feeding and whose breasts were now not even close to Raylene-perky.

"Oh, no. That's Dane's private study. I don't know what the hell he does in there, but it's locked." She laughed. Come to think of it, I'd never seen the third bedroom door even opened.

"Just put him in our bedroom," she said. "We can hear him

better from there anyway in case he cries. But he's such a good boy," she said, snuggling him, the giant cross close enough to his mouth for him to bite it.

The rest of the guests began showing up as Dane, dressed in an embroidered coat and satin pants, served up every manner of exotic cocktails and Raylene fussed with hors d'oeuvres—from fancy pâtés to—yes—everybody's favorite, pigs in a blanket.

I tried not to stuff myself like one, and drank a glass or maybe two of champagne.

Best, Terry fell fast asleep in his baby seat and I was able to put him in the master bedroom where I could hear him if he woke. Perfect so far.

The conversation turned to my big story, which I was glad to talk about—show off about, really—in front of the councilman. It just so happened that one of the guests, a middle-aged woman named Aaminah Safar, was a professor of antiquities at New York University. How coincidental could you get? But, like the man said, there are no coincidences.

Safar was quite beautiful, fiftyish, and dressed in black with a vaguely Middle Eastern head wrap that hinted at but was not a full-out hijab. It suggested religious belief while remaining true to the belief in fashion first.

I was telling them about how my source's relative had stolen a relic from a safety-deposit box in Hicksville, Long Island, where I'd coincidentally grown up. *Shut up!*

Safar knew exactly what I was talking about. I assumed it was because the pages and their discovery had been big news. She then, unbidden, said that stolen pages from that Gospel had been rumored for years but that it seemed impossible that they'd actually been found. *What the hell?*

"Pages?" I said. "We don't know what the relic actually is yet," I answered stiffly.

She then asked if she could see it—the relic—apparently not believing me, so I explained that it was locked away, and that I was picking it up in the morning to take it to a Mr. Engles, an antiquities dealer. She raised an eyebrow in the most condescending way and glanced sideways at her dinner companion, Dr. Heliopolis Amarande, a pretentious, bookish man in a broad-striped suit, with eyebrows so gigantic they looked like a new life form. Alonzo and I also exchanged "what a bunch of weirdoes" looks like a couple of fifth graders.

I thought to myself: *A couple of glasses of wine and they expect me to spill the beans like a blind chef in a vegan restaurant. Don't take the bait.*

I realized, however, that they were familiar with Engles, and that he was a dealer in rare manuscripts—not just any old antiquities.

"Ah, so they are the missing pages!" Safar exclaimed. "But surely," she added condescendingly, "you can't mean you'd consider taking such a relic to a *commercial* book seller?"

I smiled and nodded, just as patronizingly. "You bet."

"Well, I can't imagine!" Realizing I'd turned into Trump's seventy-five-foot-high impenetrable dream wall, she softened. "But I certainly would myself like to see . . . it."

I smiled, nodded, and thought: *Not going to happen in this lifetime, lady. I should never have opened my mouth in the first place.*

Eyebrows, feigning casual disinterest, asked oh so nonchalantly, "Where did you say you'd stashed the . . . the . . . what is it you said it was?"

"I didn't." I smiled just as condescendingly.

This was like the Nuremberg trials with costumes.

"But I thought you said it was in a safety-deposit box." Eyebrows nudged me, trying to get me to give up more information.

His suggestion, however, brought gales of laughter from the assorted oddballs. "No, but it is safely locked in the guarded safe at my newspaper office," I lied, adding, "The rightful owner is meeting me at six tomorrow morning. Engles is leaving for Europe and will open up early for us." I don't even know why I kept lying, but for one thing I just wanted them to shut up and give me a reason to get out of there, and for another, the whole thing was beginning to not sit right with me. Yes, people are always curious about a big story, but something was creeping me out about their particular curiosity.

Curry, sensing my discomfort, tried rescuing the evening by changing the subject, and talking about the mayor's stance on racial inequality in the NYPD. The group of liberals was all over it like goop on tar, and I thought all done with quizzing me, too. Wrong.

By the time dessert came, they started in again, so I made my excuses—baby needs to get back into his crib, very early morning appointment, blah, blah, and pushed my chair back to leave.

Eyebrows leaned on his elbows and looked around the table to make sure he had everyone's attention, clearly getting ready to say something profound. Instead he shockingly said, "Engles, you say, is meeting you at six A.M.? That one wouldn't get up early for his own bris."

What an anti-Semite! I thought but let it go because the last thing I wanted to do was stay there and argue some more, but I *was* curious about one thing. "You know him personally then?"

Councilman Curry cut in before Eyebrows could answer, which annoyed me, but he also must have had enough of these awful people himself. Eyebrows mumbled something about how he'd run into him or something, waving his hand dismissively.

Curry had made his excuses right after I did, and following some air kissing and thank-yous the councilman and I escaped together. He even picked Terry up in his seat to walk me to my door down the hall.

"I wanted to hear how Dr. Eyebrows *really* knew Engles," I said as the door closed behind us.

"Oh, sorry," he said, his long legs slowing down to keep pace with me. "I got so pissed at that anti-Semitic remark," he fumed, "that I had to leave or really get into an argument with that pretentious pain in the ass."

I laughed out loud. "You got that right. Horrible guests. I'm very fond of the Judsons," I said as we walked, "but they can be exhausting, too . . ."

"They have tremendous energy, yes," he answered, back to being the politician.

"That's not what I mean."

"I know," he said, giving me a look and a giant smile. We both laughed again.

When we got to my door, he handed me back my baby and said, "Can I call you?"

"Sure. You have a story to slip me?"

"Politicians *always* have a story. But I don't want to call you for business. I'd like to get together socially." He paused as I just looked at him blankly, forcing him to play-smack his head. *"Duh, Ms. Russo!"* Damn, the guy was sexy.

"Oh! You mean like a date?"

"No."

"Ahh," I said, somewhat embarrassed.

He laughed out loud. "No, not *like* a date, an actual date."

"Got me!" I found myself ginning back. "I'd like that. But I warn you, I'm not allowed to let a source buy me dinner. We have to go dutch. So I'm a cheap date to boot."

"I want to take you out, for God's sake," he said. "I pay." Then he did a double take. "Wait! You're sure you're a cheap date, though, right? Otherwise it's off."

We laughed and said our good nights. This guy was funny as well as smart. Oh boy. So why then was I feeling guilty? Pantera was dead and nothing I could do would bring him back. Still, no one would ever replace him.

Hey, idiot! You have to start at least putting your toe back in the water.

Nice self pep talk but the truth was that nothing I could do would make me stop pining for Pantera, loving him, wanting him.

I carried Terry into his room, deciding not to wake him but to put him right into his crib without changing his probably wet overnight diaper since he was fast asleep.

I wish I could get Terry boy to conk out like that when he wasn't at the neighbors' apartment, I thought, gently placing him down and putting his blanket over him.

As I was removing my makeup I saw something remarkable—shocking even—in the bathroom mirror: Me. I looked relaxed, pleased even.

Huh. A date.

I got cozy in bed and picked up my cell and called Roy. I wanted to see how *his* date had gone. I knew he'd be thrilled to know I sort of had one planned, too. Roy'd been almost as bad as Donald about the mysterious Pantera. "He sounds like a jerk for letting himself get killed," he'd say, especially when he'd knocked back a few.

"And you don't know your ass from your elbow," I'd answer back. Very mature, Roy and me.

Roy didn't pick up. It was still fairly early: 10:15. Damn though, I wanted to dish with him about the weirdoes, the hunk, and, well, all of it. I was also desperate to find out how his Mr. Zoosk had turned out.

But I just couldn't keep my eyes open for some reason. I conked out, but the last thought I had was: *He must be a hottie or Roy would be home by now. Or maybe he is home—with Mr. Zoosk. We both deserve a little joy about now* . . .

9

The phone rang at six o'clock, waking me out of a near-coma of bad dreams. Again it was freezing and I pulled the covers up and reached for my cell, vaguely aware that the baby was not crying to be fed, but the ringing phone immediately set my brain into panic mode. *Dad, Mom, Africa, accident, sick, stroke, coma, dead.*

It was nearly as bad. "Ali," Roy's panicked voice screeched out. "Fuck."

Zoosk. *Rape. Beaten. Sex tape. Robbed.* "Oh my God, Roy. Zoosk?"

"No. They say they now think the old man was killed."

"What? Who?"

"They say they got a tip that he was smothered."

"What?"

"Homicide!"

"Who, the cops?"

"Yeah. They didn't say they think it's me, but I think they think it's me. They said *somebody* offed the old bastard with a pillow while he was in his bed in the living room. Jesus, I sound like Clue."

"I asked you a hundred times if you'd killed him and you swore to me you didn't. You didn't, right?"

"I didn't. I swear. I wanted to. But I didn't."

"Oh shit."

"They want me in for questioning. That can't be good. I just got in and there was this voice message. Some Nassau County detective saying they want me in for questioning."

"You just got in? Did you spend the night with Mr. Zoosk?"

"No. He was a creep. He had read that I was the firefighter that inherited a bundle. Suddenly I was his dream man. I'm too old for this shit. I'm too old, too tired, and now I'm in trouble for no God-damned reason."

"Calm down, OK? But well, where were you all night, then?"

"Gee, Ma," he said sarcastically, "I was depressed, so I grabbed my board and went out to Gilgo to catch some waves."

"Like you said, you're too old for that shit. Jesus, do you have no regard for your own safety? So you went out alone. In the middle of the night on the most deserted stretch of beach on the eastern seaboard to surf all night."

"Yeah. Surfline was reporting moderate to high so I went. That's what I do when I can't sleep. I was upset about, well . . ."

"I know, but now you've got bigger problems than some online gold digger, surfer boy. The cops. I'm sure they're just fishing. Some stupid neighbor with a grudge or something."

"They want me to go in to answer a few questions."

"You don't have to go in, you know."

"But I figure I should, ya know—so they know I've got nothing to hide."

"Bullshit. And that's exactly why you shouldn't go in, because you do have nothing to hide. Don't go."

"I'm going."

"Oy vey, what a pain in the ass. OK, Roy, I can't talk you out of this?"

"No. I want to get it over with."

"All right, but play up your firefighter status and nine eleven. Got it? Don't say much to the cops, but don't seem uncooperative, either. I'll call Mad Dog Rosenberg and I'll call you right back."

"I need to lawyer up?"

"You need to lawyer up. You know Mad Dog?"

"Fred Rosenberg, the Mafia, gangsta lawyer? Jesus, Ali. Didn't he defend Sunny 'Hams' and Way-Ren Hawkins?"

"You bet your ass he did. Got them off, too. Dog owes me. I did him a couple favors and recommended some clients that upped his media profile if that is even possible."

"Well, I appreciate that, but shit. I'm just some schmuck head-case ex-firefighter. I can't afford Mad Dog Rosenberg."

"You can afford anything now. Remember?"

"Not yet. Who knows if *ever*. That tube is stolen property, remember?"

"Whose stolen property? Some probably-dead-by-now Egyptian black marketeer from the 1970s who didn't give a shit enough about the pages that he left them to rot in a bank vault in Hicksville, Long Island, for God's sake!"

"Still. A Mob lawyer? That wouldn't look very good."

"Shut up. Somebody got to the cops good enough. You don't want them digging up your old man, do you?"

"Hell no," he said, sucking in enough air to fill a Macy's balloon on Thanksgiving.

"Just hold tight. I'll call you back," I said, hanging up.

Enter the columnist's conundrum: What do you do when a friend becomes the story? Do you use your access to him/her to further your career with exclusives that favor your pal because you want to help? Do you recuse yourself because it is clearly a conflict of interest? Do you stay neutral and if you feel the friend is guilty, do you write that? Do you encourage your friend to spill only to you because you have his back? Or do you hide what you know, hoping the story will go away and your friend won't suffer needless humiliation?

If O.J. had had a best friend columnist, would she have defended him in print or on TV? Immediately these and other crazy thoughts flew into my mind. Could I be as objective as the great Ann Rule had been when she discovered that she had unknowingly been sitting next to and had befriended serial killer Ted Bundy when they were colleagues at a suicide hotline in Seattle?

Screw it. I'd kill for Roy, no pun intended.

So I called Mad Dog. Dog's personal trainer answered his cell and said the man himself was deep into squats with hundreds of pounds and he'd call me back. Dog became a power lifter the day after he recovered from getting beaten up in seventh grade in Jackson Heights for being "the skinny Jew kid."

All this had happened, I realized, before I'd even gotten out of bed. *Jesus. I took my nightgown off during the night.* I remembered being very hot, although now it was very cold. What the hell kind of champagne *was* that anyway? I put on some sweats and socks and tiptoed past the baby's room, listening at the door. All quiet on the East Side front. In the kitchen I warmed up a bottle and walked into his room. It was really freezing in there again, but the gaffer's tape had held tight.

What the hell is causing this cold?

I found Terry sitting up, playing with his fingers—not crying—in his crib. "Mama up!"

"Yes, baby. Yes, up!"

Then, "Baba, Mama. Baba."

"What did you say, baby?"

He immediately repeated, "Baba, Mama, baba."

I picked him up, and embarrassed as I am to admit it, I was getting a little freaked out by my own son. Did he mean he wanted his bottle? I tried to change him, but he insisted, "Baba, Mama," quite clearly while grabbing for the bottle. I lay him down and handed him the bottle as he was being changed.

Every time he'd go to sleep, he'd wake up with a new word on his lips. Was it the cold that was making him wake up smart or was he Mozart or something? I mean, yes, his father was a genius, but seriously, this required my mom.

When we finished, I tried Skyping my parents in Africa. No luck, so I e-mailed. After the usual niceties, I asked: *Is it normal for a six-month-old to say words? Yesterday Terry woke up saying, "up," "Mama," then "cookie." Well, I think he said that, and today he woke up and asked for his "baba."*

Damn them that they had to go help helpless, single mothers in Africa when here I was, their own hapless, single-mother daughter alone in the city!

I then checked the thermostat in the nursery. Sixty degrees even though the weather app on my phone said it was an unseasonable seventy-two outside. I turned on the heat. Terry and I were both shivering.

As I was feeding Terry his cereal—now both of us with blankets—my cell rang: Mad Dog. "Russo. Wazzup?" Rosenberg thinks he's one of the boys. He's not. Well, he was but not any-more.

He was a Queens College wrestler, NYU Law top of his class, street kid made good. He keeps his accent not because he sounds like a tough guy but because the white-shoe lawyers still think of him as a low-rent Queens boy whom they can get the better of, which they never can.

The bigger the case, the fancier their Harvard accents, the worse his Queens accent becomes, and the more he humiliates them in court.

I explained Roy's story to him. He had read my news story about the stolen relic and the curse with the ten-million-dollar price tag. He asked a few questions and I answered a few, as best as I could. He said the case would be with Nassau County Police Commissioner Randy O'Neil. That was good. They'd gone to college together. Murder suspect? That was bad. Calling Roy in for questioning? That was questionable.

"I'll call Randy then I'll call Roy then call you back." He tended not to take any pauses between words when he was on a mission. The turn-around took ten minutes.

"They got shit," he said before I had a chance to say hello. "Well, they got shit on your boy anyway. Everybody knows he hated his ole man. Ole man hated him. Tol' somebody—or many somebodies—every time he went to Smit's on Old Country Road that he'd like to smutha the bastid. Then after the fact, the morgue assistant de-cides to say the stiff had classic bloodshot eyes. I said, 'Jesus Christ, Randy, the father was six hundred years old. Whaddaya expect his eyes to look like? Brad fuckin' Pitt?' Randy says the assistant M.E. swears there was fibers in his throat, too, a pretty good sign of a pillow fight."

In English that means: Morris Golden was very old so naturally he had bloodshot eyes. In addition to the bloodshot eyes, which are a classic sign of smothering, the assistant swore to the Nassau Police commissioner that Morris had fibers in his throat, which would indicate suffocation by pillow.

"So besides Roy telling other drunken sots that he wanted to kill his father," I asked, almost losing my breath since this didn't sound good, "how does it lean toward Roy actually going through with it?"

"Like I said, they got shit. Other than the fact that Roy found 'im dead and stands to inherit ten million big ones? Not much. Although, may I add," he continued at his usual breakneck speed, "nabiz saw Roy's car there five hours before he called nine-one-one."

"Oh."

"Yeah. Oh. What they were doin' lookin' out the window at that hour I dunno. If I need to, I'll send one a' my associates out dere. Prolly not, though. I may go myself if he needs me."

"Thanks, Dog."

"It's fine."

"Should I come out, too?"

"Do me a favor. Stay the fuck away. Last thing I want is to attract attention. They got nuthin'."

"You have such a way with words."

"Whatevah." He hung up.

I called Roy. "Mad Dog says they got nuthin'," which he already knew.

Roy told me, "Dog said if it got hairy, to shut up and call him and he'd come down or send somebody." Mad Dog was headed to court for a client—a hip-hop record producer accused of drugging a female rapper and raping her. It was big news. Just another day in the life of Mad Dog Rosenberg.

In the meantime, Terry was itching to go, go, go. I called Bob's voicemail, knowing it was too early for him to be in the office, and left a message that I was taking the magic tube to an antiquities dealer and would be in later, failing to disclose the latest info about the murder accusation, Roy's being questioned, well, all of it. Such a bad move on my part.

Like I said, revealing a friend's trouble was the columnist's conundrum and I'd broken rule one: Never let friendship get between you and the story. It's bound to bite you in the ass. Rule two: if you don't put friendship first, it will bite you in the ass anyway.

This Roy breach wouldn't just come back to bite me in the ass. It would come back and bite my head off.

10

Meanwhile, back in reality, I packed up Terry in his stroller, stuck the ten-million-dollar tube and the ruby earring deep into my purse (I'm a New Yorker—what mugger would think a woman with a baby carriage would be carrying the multibazillion-dollar Gospel of Judas with a curse on it around in her purse?), and headed out the door to walk over to Engles Rare Books. The second we stepped onto the sidewalk, however, the skies opened up like Noah was in town for the boat show.

"Shoot! Just what I need!" In New York City, the minute even one drop of rain falls, all taxis disappear and Ubers are as rare as the white buffalo.

As if sent from God, who was rushing toward me, large umbrella over their heads, but Raylene and Dane.

"Oh, honey!" Raylene exclaimed, of course, taking the stroller from me and pushing it under the building's awning. "It's pouring out!" *No, you're kidding.*

"I have an appointment," I said, scooting under the awning to join them. "Wouldn't you know it? It just started to pour. I even left my umbrella upstairs. My app said no chance of rain."

Dane, ever the gentleman, handed me his oversized brolly, as he called it. "Please, take mine."

"Gee, thanks. You guys are always in the right place at the right time. And that was a great dinner party you threw last night. Wow!" I lied.

Raylene, who was decked out in some sort of bizarre sequined pants number like she'd knocked over Liza Minnelli's closet, exclaimed, "Easy peasy!" Of course. Then, "Why not let us watch the baby? He's such a joy!"

At that, as though he understood her, Terry put his arms up to her. "Up, Mama! Up!"

"Oh, you sweet baby!"

"Oh, no, really, I couldn't impose."

"No imposition. I promise! It gives me such happiness. I'd for-gotten what . . ." She dropped the rest of the sentence, and Dane gave her an extra squeeze.

"Up, Mama."

How could I refuse? And besides, how could I get anything se-rious accomplished with Mr. Engles if Terry started squawking to be picked up? (Although he seemed to be squawking for Raylene, not me, lately.)

"Really? You're sure you don't mind?"

Dane's look said it all: Terry is the grandson Raylene could have had if our son hadn't passed. *Wait, she never did say it was Dane's son, did she? She had said, "I had a son," not "we had a son." Hmm.*

"So where are you headed this morning? How long will you be?" Raylene asked. "Not that we're in a hurry to give him back!"

"Oh, I'm going over to that bookshop I was telling you about last night." Oops.

"But didn't you say you had to be there bright and early? We just thought you'd already come and gone," Dane said.

Shit! I forgot about that lie.

"Ah, Mr. Engles' trip was canceled. He said to meet him later."

"Well, how about if I accompany you?" Mr. Buttinsky said. Raylene had the look that said: "I'm doing you a favor here, the least you can do is indulge the old guy and get him off my hands for a bit."

"Ah, um, sure, let's go."

"For heaven's sake, where is the tube you spoke about?" Dane asked, peering into the stroller as though I'd given it to the baby as a rattle.

I tapped my giant shoulder bag. "I can fit a washing machine in here if I had to." I gave Raylene all the instructions as though I were going off to war, and she happily marched Terry inside as Dane and I sloshed through the rain to Engles Rare Books.

Mr. Engles, a man in his eighties, was waiting inside his shop, which had to be one of the only rare book shops left in New York that looked like a rare book shop should look. Like something out of Dickens on Lexington and Thirty-First, while all around him, the city had turned into an ugly, soulless, sun-blocking glass-and-metal mess of Gaps, H&Ms, Banana Republics, Sephoras, Starbucks, and cell phone stores. It was only a three-story building, occupied by Engles on two floors and a tax accountant/lawyer/notary on the third.

When we entered the beautiful old shop lined with rare treasures, the leathery smell of polished bindings hit me. There was even a bell over the door.

"This is what people think New York is still like," I said, reaching out to shake Engles' hand. He even looked exactly as you'd expect a rare bookseller to look. Small, gray, trimmed beard, slight English accent, and elderly, but spry.

"This is what New York should still be like," he said. "Ms. Russo, I take it?"

"Yes. Thank you for meeting me this morning." I was praying he wouldn't say anything that would give me away about the fake reverse trip I made up. "This is my friend Mr. Judson. Dane Judson."

As they shook hands, Engles cocked his head inquisitively. "Mr. Judson, you look so familiar. Do you deal in rare books? Antiquities? I know our paths have crossed at some point—no?"

"No." Dane smiled benignly. "I doubt it, Mr. Engles. I'm just an old Commie. Alternative natural medicines was my field."

Engles still looked doubtful. "I could swear . . . You never came to me looking for a copy of the Voynich Manuscript?"

How many times is this damned book going to come up this week? I thought to myself.

"Many years back," Engles continued, "maybe even twenty-five, thirty years ago?"

"How can you remember anything from so far back?" Dane laughed. "I wish I had your memory, sir!"

"I remember it because in my fifty-five years in this business only two people have ever asked me for the Voynich Manuscript."

"No, I'm afraid not," Dane replied. "Unless it had magical medicinal remedies of the peyote kind," he said by way of a joke that fell flatter than Gwen Stefani's abs.

"Well, yes, it's said to have great medical secrets," Engles said, still eyeing Dane, desperately trying to place him. "It's said to even hold the secret to life and death."

"Well, that's a showstopper," I said, grimacing.

"Ah, not to worry, Ms. Russo. The thing is, no one has yet been able to interpret it." I deliberately didn't mention the fact that I was holding on to that book in my apartment. Besides, something told me to hold off and see for myself where this was going.

"No one's figured it out even with a computer?" Dane asked, as though he already knew the answer.

"Yes, perhaps. A professor at the University of Bedfordshire claims to have cracked the code. But there was only one or possibly two in existence. One is cataloged in the Beinecke Rare Book and Manuscript Library, and a Spanish publisher is making a limited edition as well. But it's impossible to know if another is hidden in a private collection somewhere."

"Sounds positively fascinating," Dane said, somewhat dismissively, I thought.

Engles ignored him or didn't catch it, and answered, "Thank the dear Lord, I was always led to believe, anyway, that the incantations in the Voynich Manuscript alone weren't sufficient to create life or raise the dead." Then, realizing that he sounded a bit loony, he added, "I guess that's true, because I personally haven't heard about any resurrections since Jesus!"

"As far as you know, Mr. Engles," Dane said, again trying for humor and landing on his ass, totally unaware that he had no sense of humor. We both looked at him. Instead of humorous, Dane's remark had come off as oddly and unnecessarily aggressive. Especially for Dane, the love, peace, and granola man.

"But as I said, only two people in fifty years ever asked me for it," Engles continued, attempting now to bring the temperature down a bit. I figured here was a businessman who wasn't about to let an uncomfortable moment ruin what could turn into a perfectly good multimillion-dollar deal. "In fact," he continued, moving behind his beautiful antique desk to turn on his state-of-the-art Mac Pro, "I managed to acquire—after years of trying—maybe the only remaining copy—for my client," Engles said, trying not to stare uncomfortably at Dane.

"And who was that?" I asked as Dane suddenly started busying himself perusing the bookshelves.

"It was a man named Morris Golden," Engles said, spreading his hands out on his ancient desk and motioning for us to have a seat. Good thing, because I almost fell down. Dane hovered without actually taking a seat, and instead moved to study the framed, signed letters lining the wall in back of Engles' desk.

Engles said, as he logged into his Mac and scrolled down, clearly uncomfortable with Dane over his shoulder, "If you go back to the left, back there, I have a signed letter from Alexander Hamilton."

Dane nodded behind Engles' back, but clearly was more interested in snooping over his shoulder to see what Engles had been searching for. I was beginning to feel like I was in the middle of an old man pissing match.

Good thing old guys can't piss far.

Just then, Engles cried out, "Bingo! I knew it!" as he pointed to his screen. "I made the sale to Golden on March 10, 1985. It was a Sunday. I remember because normally I'm closed, but for a big sale like that, I would have opened more than just my shop. I would have opened Fort Knox!"

"How much is 'big' if I may ask?"

"You may not," he said, all business now. "Client privilege. So what have you brought me, Ms. Russo?"

I hit him with the big one. "Mr. Engles," I said, pulling out the tube, "Morris Golden is the very reason I'm here. He had the missing pages from the Gospel of Judas! That's how I came to have them in my possession."

He was visibly taken aback, and actually stopped breathing for a few seconds. "Morris Golden? From Hicksville, Long Island?" He gasped.

"Yes, one and the same. But you look like you've seen a ghost."

Engles raised his eyebrows in an "as if" gesture.

"Mr. Engles, I assure you," I said, to try to calm him down, "if it's Morris Golden you're worried about—that you gave away his secret or anything—don't worry. Mr. Golden passed away."

I wish Dane would stop trying to peek at Engles' screen, dammit! I shouldn't have let him come with me!

"Look—in this business you come across all kinds," Engles said, leaning forward in a conspiratorial kind of way. "It's rife with international black marketeers. You have no idea. But that one? Golden? He was a meek bank manager, but when he came back to pick up the book, he came in like a real thug."

"A thug?" I asked, surprised.

"A thug," he continued. "The man had a pistol in his bag! He had insisted the transaction be in cash, which is not really a legitimate way to do business. Not for that kind of money certainly. Then—and here's what's even more disturbing: that night my shop was broken into and my safe cracked! I couldn't make the accusation that it was him, but . . ."

"Did they get the money?"

"I'm smarter than that, Ms. Russo. I had an armed escort bring it to the bank immediately after Golden's car pulled away. My personal banker opened up just for me that day."

I was desperate to know how much we were talking about, but I'm a reporter. I know when somebody's done spilling for the day.

"Back to your tube," he said, rolling it around in his ancient hands like he was holding a ten-million-dollar piece of delicate crystal, not a heavy brass tube. "This inscription here on the end? It's Arabic. It means something like, 'The world is owned by Victor.'"

"Victor? Who is Victor?"

"I can't imagine," he answered. "Maybe a friend. Maybe someone who has a claim to it?" Then, "Speaking of which, to whom does this Morris Golden treasure belong now?"

I explained the circumstances, how Roy had inherited the pages, eliminating the part about him not being able to come, seeing as how he was even as we sat there probably in some precinct telling cops how he didn't kill pistol-packing Morris the Miserable. "He's with his lawyer," I said, fudging the truth that he wasn't with a lawyer of the estate kind, but of the criminal kind. "He couldn't be here," I continued as Engles examined the tube.

"Oh, and this was taped to it," I said, handing him the little envelope. "It's just an antique earring," I told him, pulling it from my bag.

Engles emptied the envelope and took out the earring. "Hmm. Very interesting," he said, picking up a magnifying glass and looking at the earring and then looking at the tube.

"Taped to it, you say?"

"Yes, my friend said it was taped to the side."

"Ah. You see this?" he said, holding up the earring as Dane leaned over his shoulder to get a better look. I shot Dane a look in turn that said, "Back off." Embarrassed, he did.

"The earring has a screw back," Engles said, pointing out the minuscule threads on the earring's gold post that spirled unusually from end to end.

"And?" I said. "Unfortunately it doesn't have the earring back that must have screwed onto it."

"Not necessary. I have a feeling . . ." He held up the tube and showed me two tiny holes that I hadn't seen before. "May I?"

"I'm not sure what you mean . . . but whatever it is, you know best."

Engles inserted the earring post into one hole and began turning. I heard a tiny click. But when he inserted it into the second hole, not only didn't it fit, but it seemed to give Engles a shock—like the one I'd gotten. He jumped and dropped the tube on the desk.

As soon as the tube hit the desk, Dane clutched his chest, desperately trying to breathe. Panicked, we jumped up to help as Dane reached into his pants pocket and managed to pull out a vial and shake a pill under his tongue.

I grabbed Engles' phone and began to dial 911, but Dane's big hand slammed down on mine to stop me. "No, no. No ambulance. I'm fine. Fine," he gasped, tapping his pocket. "Angina unfortunately can't be cured with natural alternative medicine. Do you have any brandy, Mr. Engles?"

He sat in Engles' chair while I ran to get him water and Engles ran to get a bottle of port that he must have had sitting around since the Eisenhower administration.

In the thirty seconds it took to get back across the shop, I saw Dane recovered, alert, and yes, looking at Engles' computer screen.

"There's another earring out there somewhere," he said, as calmly as though he hadn't just nearly had a heart attack and given us one, too.

When Engles came back with the bottle, he poured Dane a small glass, and said, "I will call you a car. I think we'd better finish our discussion at another time. Frankly," he said, locking the tube up again with the earring post and handing it back to me in the tiny envelope, "even if I had the other earring or whatever, I could not open this without the owner's permission, and in sight of that owner."

"Oh, but . . ."

"I'm afraid that's not ethical, Ms. Russo. But would you like me to keep the tube in my safe for you—until your friend can come back with you, and I can do my research on how such an antique tube may be opened and how to best secure the contents within?"

Dane, miraculously robust once more, said, "Well, you said you had a break-in once. I don't think that's very wise!"

"That was more than thirty years ago, Mr. Judson. Of course, I now have twenty-four-hour security and monitoring." He shot me a look.

Going with my gut, I told Engles to lock it up for me, and he said, "All right then," and took out an official-looking form—a hold receipt—filled it out, and called the notary upstairs to witness it. She was about nine hundred years old and probably had been using this same seal to make a living since she worked for the Mayans.

Dane was visibly pissed when we ran out to the car that Engles had called for us. It was still pouring. "I don't trust that man," Dane said as I climbed in. "He deals in the black market, and my friends, who are scholars, said last night that he wasn't trustworthy."

"Geez, calm down or you'll have another coronary," I said as Dane plopped down in the backseat next to me. "It's not like he's going to steal it. And your friends didn't say he wasn't trustworthy or in the black market. What they said about him, if I remember correctly, consisted mainly of anti-Semitic remarks."

He ignored me and simply looked straight ahead like he was punishing me. "There's another earring out there. What if Engles has it?" He huffed. "And that business about that book, the Voltaire

Manuscript! Such nerve." I knew he'd deliberately used "Voltaire" instead of "Voynich" to make Engles sound even more off-base for accusing him of wanting to buy it.

Now I was getting pissed. "Voynich, it's Voynich, not Voltaire, and you're getting yourself upset again for no reason." He glared at me as we sat in an uncomfortable silence the whole way home. I felt like I'd been on a date that started well and went downhill from "Hi, I'm . . ."

Why did I ever let Mr. Buttinsky come with me in the first place? Big know-it-all.

Only thing is? Dane Judson did know it all, but I just didn't know at the time that he knew it all.

11

_____

By the time we'd black car'd it home in the pouring rain, Dane had calmed down and as soon as we walked into the apartment, he was back to being all yoga Zen. It occurred to me that I'd never been in his presence without Raylene before. Either she was his guru and calming influence or she scared the hell out of him when they were together, which seemed like all the time.

I walked in and smelled cookies baking. "I know he can't eat them yet, but I'm practicing for when we can bake cookies together," Raylene said, wiping her hands on her frilly long apron with WORLD'S BEST COOK spelled out in rhinestones.

"Isn't that right, my sweet, little itty bitty, teeny boy?" Terry was so entranced you'd think he was sixteen and had just been kissed by Rihanna.

Raylene spun around to show off her rhinestone apron. "I love my BeDazzler! There's nothing you can't glam up with rhinestones."

No kidding.

I picked Terry up off the play mat she'd obviously bought for him—thank God it didn't have sequins for him to swallow—where he was happily trying to crawl, and attempted to drag him out of there and back home. He did *not* want to leave and started crying, "Mama! Mama!" at Raylene.

"Hey, kid, your mother's over here!" I said, a little jealous of how dazzled he was by the BeDazzler lady.

I took his hysterical self back to our apartment, and got Dona to come over so I could head to the office for a few hours. Enough with Raylene. Dona was working the *Fox and Friends* morning show that week and luckily had the afternoon free.

Terry wasn't any happier to see Dona than he was to see me. "I don't know what's gotten into him the last few days. He must be teething or something," I said by way of excuse.

"Your neighbor Raylene must have the magic teething formula because you marveled that he never cries when she's around," Dona said, picking Terry up and bouncing him around, trying the Binky, a bottle, anything. I was feeling very guilty about leaving her with the fussy (OK, miserable) baby.

"I know. Weird, right? She told me she had a son who died."

"Really . . . how old was he?"

"Don't know. She wouldn't really talk about it. But the woman's a helluva babysitter. She must have been the best mother on earth. She sees Terry and she just lights up."

"From what you've told me, he lights up even more when he sees her."

"He does! I'm very lucky to have them around, what with my parents off saving the world and all."

"Aren't they due back?"

"Yes, thank God. Two weeks. Then I won't have to rely on the

Judsons so much. Not that my parents don't work, but they swear they'll cut back when they're back in the States."

"Good . . ." Dona said. "I kinda get a weird vibe off those two. The neighbors, I mean, not your folks."

I told her how Dane had acted out at the shop and she gave me the mouth sneer *plus* head nod. That's the big duo. "Oh no, not the *look*! You were so charmed by them in the park."

"I don't know." She sighed. "Maybe I changed my mind."

Time was a'wasting, so I gave her complete instructions, left Terry screaming his head off, and said, "If it gets really bad, I e-mailed you Raylene's contact info, or you can just drag him down the hall to get her to calm him down if you need to."

Roy called as I was rushing to the subway. "Like you said, the cops were on a fishing expedition," he said. "I did like Mad Dog said and kept it simple. I told them that after I left my father's house he was alive and I went to Oak Beach and Gilgo looking for the best surf."

"Wasn't it storming that night?"

"Jesus, Russo, I surf the Atlantic. 'Get me outta here, it's raining, and the waves are too high. I might get wet!'" he mocked. "Anyway, the cops were more interested in surfing than in the old man. They're not digging him up so fast. Some of these guys surf. I recognized one or two back from the Long Beach competition."

"Can I ask you a question?" I didn't wait for an answer. "Why did it take you so long to call nine-one-one after you got to your dad's house and he was already dead?"

"Why? I don't know. First I freaked out, then I drank some of his nine-hundred-year-old Scotch, then I just, well, I sat there with him. I told him all the shit he did to me over the years that left me broken. I told him that I loved men, lusted for them, in fact. I told him how I wanted to kill him for hitting my mom." Roy's big, burly voice cracked.

"Oh, honey. I'm so sorry."

He actually started to cry, great, heaping sobs. "I think I'm gonna go out to Gilgo tonight. I have to . . . whatever."

I asked him to just listen a minute as I was heading down the subway stairs and we'd be cut off. I explained about Myles Engles, the book shop, and all the rest of it. He said that he'd meet me there tomorrow if that was cool, and we'd see what the next step was.

Bob was all over me when he got back from lunch. In fact he found me kicking the never-working copy machine. PAPER JAM TRAY 3 kept flashing.

"They can send a probe to Saturn but no one can get a frigging copy machine to work!" I screamed, banging the top as though that would kick it into gear. "I called Boris." I pointed to Boris the tech guy's office, fuming. "But he said now we have to call India first to get a ticket number so that he, who sits twenty steps away, is allowed to fix the goddamned copier!"

Bob totally ignored me. "The ten-million-dollar-firefighter story is up to four hundred and fifty thousand—that's *thousand*—Facebook shares and I don't know how many retweets. Number one story online and it's trending everywhere! What do you have for me? We gotta advance that baby!"

"Do you work for BuzzFeed or do you work for a newspaper called *The Standard*?" I said, stalling for time.

"Can it, Russo, whaddaya have?"

Luck was with me. At least for that minute. Before I could make anything up, Jerry "O'Drunken" O'Donnell, Pulitzer Prize–winning putz and the last of the old-time columnists, came wobbling out of his hole. He was one of the only writers with an actual office. I guess they were afraid if they let him out among the females, he'd say something like he was about to say to me.

Just as I bent down to pull out the paper clog from the bottom of the paper tray, he came up close behind *my* behind. "Russo!" he slurred. I stood right up and spun around like I'd been smacked, hands instinctively over my butt.

"Hi there, Jerry. How ya doing?"

"Great stuff you did, kid," he said, but before I could thank him he slobbered onto my shoulder with Bob looking on, ready to explode. "Lemme ask you a serious question."

"OK."

"Why will a woman give you a blow job and then not use your toothbrush the next morning?"

"Jesus, Jerry," I said, pushing him away. "If you smelled your breath you'd rather give yourself a blow job, too."

That was enough to satisfy him, and he chuckled and sauntered back into his cave.

"That stupid son of a bitch," Bob fumed. "If he wasn't so brilliant I'd fire him."

"You'd be a mere shell of a man without those old characters to keep you on the straight and narrow. I'm a big girl, I can take care of myself."

"Yeah, yeah, anyway, you still haven't told me what you've got."

"I'm working on it. Remember investigative reporting? It was this thing that reporters used to do instead of putting up rumor and innuendo as fact."

He ignored me as though I were speaking Olde English. "Whaddaya got? The *News* and the *Post* are all over this, and the *News* even found pictures of your guy when he tried out for the New York City Firemen's calendar. Why didn't you have that?"

"Because I don't live with the guy and he never told me. Probably because he knew I'd laugh at him for being a schmuck." *Son of a bitch never told me—and I was ashamed to even tell him I always thought he should be a calendar boy. Remind me to kill him next time I see him.* Just then my cell rang: Donald.

"They want me to take some pictures of Roy. He was in the firemen's calendar."

"No, he wasn't. He never actually made it."

"Yeah, he was. I need new cheesecake photos."

"Ain't gonna happen," I said.

"Your boss Bob wants 'em." Donald was freelancing for all the papers and news sites these days, which gave him the freedom to carouse—not to mention a lot more money to carouse with than he'd never gotten on staff. I shot Bob a look and hung up, telling Donald, "Let me get back to you on that, sir." I turned on Bob. "Seriously? Cheesecake? The man has just suffered the loss of his father."

"Oh, give me a fucking break, Russo. You told me the old man was a shit head."

"That's beside the point."

"No, it's not. We own this story, Russo. Own *it*! We can't let anybody else find stuff like the calendar photos. You blew that one, big time."

I pulled Bob into his office—which wasn't very private because it had a glass front. I told him that I didn't give a shit about some dopey, old pictures and that we'd have to keep it all under wraps or we'd lose the whole story. I alone had to find out what was in that tube, and keep it to ourselves until we could break it—the story, I mean. "Let them all scratch their asses while the story dies down. Then—*bam!*—I reveal the pages, the curse, all of it. Pulitzer, baby, Pul-it-*zer*!"

I got up and did the happy dance and Bob attempted to do something like it but he ended up swiveling his hips in the most upsetting manner. "Please, boss, sit down. The children can see you," I said, nodding my head toward the wool hats who were staring open-mouthed.

My joy was short-lived, however. Very short-lived.

The world's most disturbing sound broke my revelry: text alert by way of old car horn sound, to which Bob said, "Could you have found a more annoying sound?" It *was* annoying, but with the baby, I needed something loud that I could hear anytime, anywhere.

Text from Mad Dog: U know Roy surfs Gilgo @ midnight?

Me: So?

Mad Dog: U know the old story about the serial hooker murderer out
    there?

Me: And?

Mad Dog: 2 more tranny hookers found. Fresh kill. There's a prossy
    serial killer on the loose for 10 years out there.

Me: I know. So?

Mad Dog: ur surfer boy told cops he left old man to surf Gilgo in
    storm. Same nite another hooker offed. Some kid found remains
    today.

Me: Shit.

Mad Dog: Worse: per randy—the 2 Gilgo hookers dug up last year
    were Morris Golden clients! No follow b/c old bastard had em-
    physema and half a lung, & couldnt have killed & dragged em
    across LI.

Me: How bad does this look?

Mad Dog: Glad Roy boy's got $10 mil. Gonna need it.

Me: Shit.

Mad Dog: Shit on a board, baby.

Me: Where is he?

Mad Dog: Unfolding fast. He's being interrogated Nassau/Suffolk
task force. Going now. good side? morris left no will. tube's roy's.

Me: Where r they holding him? U didn't say

That was it. Mad Dog was off the grid—to me, a reporter, anyway—even though Roy was my best friend—but Dog apparently thought he was straight. Maybe he was thinking we had a thing, Roy and me.

12

"What?" Bob was yelling and standing practically on top of me in his office. "What is it, Russo? What?" Not just the wool caps but even O'Drunken came out to stare at us.

Was I giving up my best friend for a front page? Would I instead compromise my journalistic ethics—a term some now call an oxymoron—if I didn't spill?

I immediately called Roy. It went directly to voice mail. "Call me. Now!" I texted the same thing. Nothing.

I started to sweat. I knew what I had to do and it made my stomach turn.

EXCLUSIVE

Relic's Curse Hits Millionaire Fireman

By Alessandra Russo

Two days ago he was the most famous fireman in the world. Today he's being questioned by the police for the serial murders of at least seventeen prostitutes on Long Island.

World Trade Center hero, Roy Golden, 42, who'd inherited a mysterious cursed relic worth $10 million, has been taken in for questioning by a joint Nassau-Suffolk County homicide task force.

Cops want to question Golden in the unsolved, possibly decades-long case involving murders on Gilgo and Oak Beaches in Long Island.

Golden was originally called in to discuss the death of his father, ninety-year-old Morris Golden, a retired banker from Hicksville, Long Island, who had come into possession of the relic. Under questioning, the retired firefighter, an avid Long Island surfer, happened to mention in conversation with police, whom he'd recognized from various surfing tournaments, that he liked to surf Gilgo, one of the beaches where the remains of four victims were found in December 2010, and six more remains were discovered in March and April 2011.

Yesterday, the bodies of two recently murdered prostitutes were discovered by a teen on his way to the beach. They had been killed within twenty-four hours of the time that Golden had been surfing Gilgo alone.

In addition, two of the previously murdered prostitutes—one a transsexual—had been clients of the recently deceased Morris Golden. The cops had never followed up on the connection because according to a source, the aged Golden was too feeble to have strangled and dragged the bodies of these women from the middle of Long Island to the South Shore.

In the interest of full disclosure, Roy Golden has been a close friend of this reporter for over thirty years. The younger Golden is, in fact, an out gay man and has never frequented female prostitutes. It is well known among Mr. Golden's closest friends, that he had a limited relationship with his father, Morris, the two only seeing one another once or twice a year.

I filed the story, and then went into the bathroom and threw my guts up.

No sooner was the story posted online than Mad Dog was on the phone. My cell practically spontaneously combusted in my hand on my way back to my desk.

"What the fuck you doin'? You're supposed to be his best friggin' friend or whatever you are!" he screamed as I rounded the corner and plopped down in my desk chair, gulping water that I'd left there the day before.

"I am! His best friend, I mean. But I can't not tell the story or someone else will—and they won't be as easy. You know that! Roy knows that!" Or so I prayed he did.

"Fuck you!" he screamed, rushing all his words together. Then, "OK, OK, I know . . . So, for Christ's sake, Russo, do the right thing."

The next call was a collect one from the Nassau County Correctional Center: Roy.

"Ali. How the hell did I end up here? I need help."

"I'll do whatever you need."

"Mad Dog says the prosecutor's gonna ask for a ten-million bond."

"How convenient! Just what the relic's worth."

"Screw the relic. Sell the thing. Get me outta here."

"But I can't, because we can't open the tube."

"My time's up. Open it. I'll give Mad Dog permission to make you the seller. Sell it all. I know you can do it. What about that old priest—your friend? You said he was a genius with this stuff? Sell it to him."

I didn't want to tell him that he was in Israel and besides, the reality was I couldn't open the goddamned thing (literally) without the other ruby earring.

I scrolled through the cell phone numbers. I hit "unknown caller" to see if by some miracle I could call Father Paulo back. What planet did I think I was on? I e-mailed him, but I got an "undeliverable" message back. How was this all happening? Three days ago I was navigating the choppy waters of single mother-hood and scrambling to get back on top at *The Standard*. Today I had a great story, but a terrible situation. The world was caving in on my friend and I was knee-deep into the quagmire and felt like I was sinking fast.

It can't get worse, I thought. Then it did. My office phone rang. "Russo here."

Dona. I could hear the hysterical baby in the background. "Honey, I've tried feeding him, playing with him, rocking him, roll-ing him. He's inconsolable. He just threw up. More like projectile vomited all over from being so hysterical."

"Oh God. I'm so sorry. I'll be right home. Dona, let me ask you something. Is it cold in the apartment?"

"No, in fact, I thought it was too warm so I turned on the AC. Should I take him down the hall to the neighbors?"

"Yes, if you have to, but I'm heading home."

"Hurry!" she said, sounding frantic.

If I was new to this mothering thing, Dona wasn't even out of the box, although who in hell knows how to calm a screaming baby? Well, besides Raylene, I thought. "Yeah, Dona, call her. I left the number."

"Let me run, it's the doorbell," she cried.

Without hanging up, I could hear her opening the door. "I heard the baby from down the hall. Can I help?" Raylene, bless her heart, I thought. Terry seemed to immediately stop wailing. The phone disconnected.

Thank you, Jesus, or whoever, for bringing those kooks into my life and right down the hall.

Immediately after that mini-crisis seemed to calm down, another old car horn blare, another text. I could hardly keep up. The address bar on top read: "Fr. Paulo."

Fr. Paulo: Are you free to speak?
Me: Can I call you back?

I really need his number.

Fr. Paulo: No.
Me: Then can you call me? Yes, I'm free to speak.

My cell immediately rang. Unknown number. "I need to keep this brief," Paulo said in his ridiculously affected way. I could just see him sitting in some café in Israel, even now making some deal for the relic. What was the choice? Roy—*we*—needed to make bail, or bond anyway, and put up a retainer for Mad Dog in order to make his case. Dog was a friend, but this friend didn't come cheap.

"I see that Mr. Golden, the relic's owner, is in quite deep shit, as we say in the clergy." He chuckled at his own cleverness. Nothing like a little priest humor when you're in the middle of, well, deep shit.

"Bring me the relic in Israel. I can open it. I am the only one who can interpret it, and I am the only one with a network to sell it for at least ten million, if it is what you say it is."

Interpretation: I am the foremost scholar of ancient Christianity, I am a priest who does unknowable things for the Vatican, I am the world's biggest schemer. Don't play games. We both know, too, that I am the only one who can fence this thing but only in exchange for the secrets contained within, even if it does unleash Armageddon. Whatever it is, it'll be mine to control.

"What do you mean you can open it?" was all I said.

"I know who is in possession of the other key—and the incantation that is needed to go with it. Or at least where it is located."

Maybe he really didn't have anything. "Well, it's not a key, it's an—"

He cut me off. "Yes, yes, you have a ruby earring." Never mind. He knows. He was referring to it as a key because it, well, was a key—and was likely in the possession of the Vatican who were probably all over this like incense at mass. I also knew that asking would get me exactly nowhere.

But would I just be handing the pages over under duress once— *if*—I got there? Would I be able to negotiate a fair price for this priceless relic with the Vatican, if that's what Paulo insisted upon in exchange for safely opening it up? If so, would they keep secret the secrets Jesus had imparted to Judas? What if the words really were—as had been rumored—deadly and powerfully so? Was my friend's life worth such an ungodly exchange?

He read my mind long distance. "Alessandra, do you realize what is in your possession? I went directly to—well, to someone who knows about such things—and the pages that you may or may not hold in your possession are the most dangerous writings the world has ever known. They were meant for good, but now, in our age, they are '*Più pericoloso di quanto si pensi*,'" he said, slipping into Italian. That meant he was nervous. If he were a poker player, sneaking in Italian words would be his tell. "Go to the Harmony Hotel in Jerusalem. When you get there, I'll meet you," he said. "Tell no one what you have. Is that clear? I will bring with me the other key as proof."

"You really have it then?"

"Trust me on this."

He's negotiating for the Vatican, I now felt for sure. *After all, who but the current pope could be trusted with such a thing? But unfortunately, none of the rest of those snakes at the Vatican could be trusted with it.*

Pope Francis was a living saint, but he was a saint presiding over a den of devils.

"Does that mean you spoke directly to the pope about this?" I asked. Nothing. "Well, then, how do you know I'll come and if I do, how would you know if you won't give me your contact information?"

He cryptically replied, "I will be where you are. Engles is not the man for this job."

Jesus Christ. How did he know about Engles? Nobody with anything to gain in this game seemed to want Engles in on it. That alone should have commended Mr. Engles to me. Against my better judgment, I asked, "Let me ask you a question, Father. Have you ever heard of something called the Voynich Manuscript?"

"Of course."

"I have it." I heard an intake of air, too steep to hide on his part.

"You have what? A modern-day copy?"

"I have what appears to be a very, very ancient copy of the book."

"Bring that with you as well." Out of curiosity, I took out Golden's note, and asked, "Do these numbers mean anything to you: 31.780231° N, 35.233991° E?"

I could tell he was surprised and tried not to let on. Maddeningly, he just said, "Yes, they do. But not something I can discuss over the phone."

"Ooookay, then, what about someone attached to the Gospel named Victor? Have you any idea who that might be?"

"Victor? No, not that I've heard of but I'll make some inquiries. But please, we can't keep discussing such things over the phone. "

"OK, Father, but I just need to know if . . ."

Too late. I realized he was no longer on the line. Cell phones have taken two great things from our lives: First is the ability to know if you'd simply lost a connection or if someone had hung up on you. The second is your own ability to slam down the phone on someone else, thus turning the act of slamming down the phone into a long-distance act of placebo fury.

In the meantime, I had a screaming baby and a relic to pick up. I just was sort of thinking—it hadn't formed into a full-on actual thought yet—that I would have to go to Israel and meet Father Paulo.

I tried my parents in Africa again. Mom actually picked up. I couldn't fill them in on everything, just the briefest info, including

Terry's sudden ability to talk, which Mom the pediatrician seemed to chalk up to my new mom pride. His talking so early was not reality-based as she would say, but thankfully didn't. Six-month-old babies don't form half sentences. Yes, they do. Well this one did, at any rate.

Anyway, turns out my folks were coming home—*hallelujah!*—maybe even in a day or two. Dad's African *tourista* had gotten the best of him, and once Mom could get his diarrhea under control they'd be on the next flight. Of course they'd stay with Terry.

First I looked up flights to Israel, and then I called Engles, who picked up after one ring. He hadn't been able to find anyone to unlock the tube, and wanted to know if I was sure I wanted to keep a potentially important object in my apartment. I didn't say: "Who'd look in a Pampers box?"

I hopped the subway, and Engles clearly was not thrilled to be handing over what could be a big sale, but I also got the strange impression that he was in some ways happy to get rid of the thing. "I'll keep investigating," he said.

Christ almighty but it was freezing in his shop. I didn't mention it because I figured he had to keep his books at a certain temperature. As I was leaving with the relic-in-a-tube like it was a twenty-five-dollar bed-in-a-bag, Engles grabbed my arm. "I know I've met your friend, Mr. Judson, before—I feel sure he was the one who wanted the Voynich Manuscript. That's why I insisted on keeping the relic in my safe. I just don't trust him . . ."

I didn't want to contradict him—the Judsons had been nothing short of lifesavers for me—but I did say, "Well, between us—please—I've actually got Morris Golden's Voynich Manuscript in my possession now, too. It was with the tube at my friend's father's house. Morris Golden's house."

Engles looked panic-stricken. "Do you have it in your own house, then?"

"Well, yes. At my apartment in Waterside Plaza."

"It shouldn't be there!"

"I know, I know. It's very rare. Would you be interested in possibly brokering a sale for it?"

Engles literally backed up and braced himself against the desk and spat disgustedly. "*Ji-fa!* Filth! Excuse me, I don't mean to upset you. But it's the most unholy book. You need to burn it."

"I can't believe you would say that. Books are your life." He immediately looked stricken, as he turned toward the back room's safe to retrieve the tube, saying quietly, "I know how it sounds, but believe me, some books should never have seen the light of day." If he'd been Catholic, I swear he would have crossed himself.

Now it was my turn to be confounded. Who would have figured *him* of all people to be a book burner?

Then, bringing the tube from the back of the shop he said, "I'm begging you to burn that book. Burn it. Get a holy person to bless it. A priest, a rabbi, a Buddhist monk, an imam, I don't care. Have them all pray over it. Then burn it. *Elohim a-di-rim!*"

"But, it's—"

He cut me off. "Ms. Russo, you seem like a lovely woman and I can't imagine why you got involved with a man like Morris Golden or how you came to actually be in possession of that book, but it should not be in your home. Destroy it."

"You know I can't do that, Mr. Engles. It's not mine to destroy. Nor frankly would I. Too bad Mr. Judson was not the man you thought wanted to buy it. That would be one way for Morris's son to sell it."

Then he grabbed my hands in his. "Never him. Not that man. Please. Promise me that much. He can't know you have it."

"Well . . . OK?" It was more of a question than a statement.

"Please. Does he know you have it?"

"Not exactly. I mean, no, I didn't mention it. Just in whatever conversation we had here in the shop. Reporters keep things close to the vest," I said, remembering how not-close to the vest I was the previous evening, spouting all that stuff in front of those weirdo dinner guests.

These old gents clearly have some kind of dislike of each other, and it has nothing to do with some old book, that's for damned sure.

Engles wrapped the tube in tissue paper, put it inside a velvet-lined wooden box, and handed it to me, saying, *"Teesh-mi-ree Al Atz-Mech,"* Ms. Russo. Be careful."

"And the same to you, Mr. Engles," I replied. I put the box inside my purse and hefted it onto my shoulder. I shook his hand and rushed out to get back home to rescue Dona from the wrath of Terry—and to escape from the freezing cold in the shop.

The last thing I thought when I closed the shop door behind me was that it would be the last time I'd ever see Myles Engles, rare bookseller, alive.

———————

13

I got off the elevator on my floor and was relieved to not hear Terry crying.

Joy at last! At least there was *that* on this very bad day. When I opened the door, I found Dona, Terry, and Raylene happily playing on the floor.

Dona looked up. "This lady is am-*aaa*-zing!" she chirped. "Never seen anything like it. The instant Mrs. Judson walked in—"

Raylene cut her off with a cooing hug. "I told you, please call me Raylene!"

I took off my trench coat—it was cozy and warm in the apartment—and knelt down and kissed Terry's little face a hundred times. "How's my big boy? How's Mommy's baby boy?" He giggled and turned toward Raylene.

"Mama!"

Dona gushed, "Raylene has that magical baby touch. I don't think, even if I ever have six kids of my own, I'd ever have it."

Oh man. Where had my friend gone? She had become a Raylene pod person.

The equally smitten Raylene hugged Dona again. "You modern girls! Mothering is as natural as sex—the first time might stink, but with time, you come to get the hang of it and then never want the good times to end!" Dona and I burst out laughing at the same time.

"What? You think I don't like a nice screwing?" This time our hands inadvertently shot to our mouths. Crime, war, and "if it bleeds it leads" stories we are always prepared for, yes. Naughty sex talk from a senior sitter in sequins? Not on the journalism course roster.

Raylene squatted like a twenty-five-year-old yoga instructor and scooped Terry up from the floor and stood. "You girls finish your convo and I'll finish mine with Terry!"

"It's a love match!" Dona declared of Raylene and Terry or maybe herself and Raylene, I didn't know anymore. She stood up, milk stains splattered all over her shirt and jeans. "I need to go home and hose down. Look at me!" She laughed. Then, turning serious as I put my bag on the table, she asked, "What the *hell's* going on with Roy? I mean, one minute he's the hottie bazillionaire fireman and the next he's a murder suspect? I know we're news rivals, but who came to your rescue today? Who?" She didn't exactly mean quid pro quo, but *almost* exactly quid pro quo. As in: How about a tip, a lead, a minute with Roy to interview him?

"When I can, I promise." I meant it. "I don't really have access to him now. But you know this whole thing is not true, right? Roy would no more strangle hookers than he'd strangle me. You *know* that. Right, Dona?"

Silence.

"Hello?" I insisted.

"Honey, I'm not sure *you* know that. Your story indicated that the cops have some pretty damned strong evidence."

"A million guys surf Gilgo and Oak Beaches at night. Big deal. That effing father of his—the guy was a misery all of Roy's life, well, starting in the eighties anyway, and now we find out he was screwing around with hookers well into his old age—even tranny hookers. And who does it all come back to bite on the ass? Roy, of course. Morris's grip was supposed to end when he did!"

Something was flicking around in the back of my brain. But what was it? I couldn't quite pick it out.

"I'm not saying Roy's guilty of murder. But could he have disposed of the bodies for the old man? Remember the Shulman brothers back in the late nineties—in your old hometown—and Roy and Morris's hometown, too—Hicksville, Long Island. One brother was a mailman who killed hookers and the other, the younger brother, chopped them up and disposed of them in garbage bags along the parkway. What do they put in the water supply out there in Hicksville?"

"Don't even go there," I warned her. "That's not my Roy. He wouldn't cover for that bastard, and he sure as hell wouldn't go dumping bodies for him if his life depended on it!"

"Maybe it does . . ." Dona said. Raylene was so busy listening she almost—*almost*—stopped fussing with Terry for a microsecond.

I gave Dona the eye that Mrs. Buttinsky was listening—not that she called her that anymore, now that they were new BFFs—so we cut it short. Kisses, hugs, thanks, and promises that I wouldn't put Terry the Terror upon her again if I could help it, and Dona laughed. "It wasn't so bad. Oops. I just lied, it was. Roy. Interview. You owe me."

Dane air-knocked on the door just as Dona opened it to leave.

He came in with his recyclable green grocery bag, all cheery, taking out some fruit. "Cherries were on sale. Thought you'd like some . . . Raylene, my sweet, why don't you go home and put up some lemon balm and skullcap tea? Looks like Alessandra's had herself a bad day."

"The baby was a little gassy," Raylene responded as though Terry was theirs and they were discussing the day's baby events. "I made him a nice infusion of fennel seed. Did the job lickety split."

Dane kissed her on the top of her head. She giggled.

They were too sweet, but seriously, I'd had enough for one day. "No, thanks on the skullcap tea, Dane. I'm bushed. Just need to spend some alone time with Terry."

They cocked their heads inquisitively. "I may have to go to Israel for a very short trip. My parents will be home in a few days so they can take Terry while I'm gone."

"You know we'd be happy to keep him. I mean, not *forever*," Raylene said, smiling quickly so I'd know it was a joke, "but so your folks don't have to rush home or anything."

"You've been way too kind already," I answered, knowing that the sooner I could unlock this thing and sell it, the sooner we'd get Roy's defense going. But no, I couldn't . . .

Dane, who apparently disliked Engles as much as Engles disliked him, put his arm around me as they were back at the door. "That Engles person? I called Professor Safar after I got home this morning. She and Dr. Amarande both agree that he's not the man for the job. Bad reputation. Minah and Heli," he said softly, now using the diminutive of their names affectionately, "said he's one step above—well their words, not mine—selling Mickey Mantle baseball cards!"

Apparently this was the worst best example of low class they could come up with. But in my sphere, especially among the sports desk guys, owning an original, signed Mantle? That was as high up the art food chain as we got. Clearly they didn't know that a near-mint 1952 Topps Mantle had sold recently for nearly half a mil!

I decided not to tell him I'd picked up the tube—or even bring up the Voynich business again—because, well, I liked Engles and I thought they were dead wrong. I was right about that at least.

When they finally left, I flipped on the TV. Fox News popped up. (Their number one reporter who had just been here getting baby spit all over herself must have had it on in the background.) And I couldn't believe my eyes.

Roy, my Roy, was in shackles and an orange jumpsuit being perp-walked in front of a crowd of crazed reporters. As he passed them, reporters were yelling, "Did you kill those prostitutes? Were you into transgender hookers?" and all manner of disgusting questions they knew he wouldn't answer. The camera cut to some babe in leather pants and a second-skin tight sweater in front of the court-house reporting: "The former firefighter who just yesterday was on the front page for inheriting ten *million* dollars will spend the night in jail. He's wanted in the long-unsolved murders of nearly two *dozen* prostitutes in the Gilgo Beach Murders, also known as the Craigslist Ripper. The question is this: Is Roy Golden the Craigslist Ripper?"

The screen cut back to the anchor babe with gigantic Miss America hair and a low-cut rubber dress—like a wet suit for underwater cocktail waitresses. "So, Candace, tell us," Wet Suit Babe said. "Isn't that ten *million* dollars tied up in some cursed relic, though?"

Candace: "Yes, Lacey, it *is,* and now we wonder if the curse has already rubbed off on this Long Island surfer dude. Or should we call it the ten-*million*-dollar curse? Back to you in the newsroom,

Lacey!" she said, wiggling. I couldn't tell if she was attempting a sexy gyration or if just she had a bad vaginal itch from all that leather.

Why do these morons always have to exaggerate the dollar amount? Ten million dollars. They'd say the same if the relic was worth one hundred dollars . . .

"Great reporting, Candace!" Wet Suit said.

Jesus, that rubber dress must be hot under those lights. Good thing her boobs are free to catch some air.

I flipped to NY1, where I'd get honest news without the stripper clothes. The news however was the same—bad news for Roy. I called Mad Dog, who was on his way to the arraignment. He said, "They're saying ten million, maybe twenty. You're looking at one hundred to two hundred K just for the bail bondsman, if the judge even goes there. Roy's a risk."

"A risk for what?" I asked, alarmed. "He's a freaking hero firefighter!"

"A freaking hero firefighter who took early retirement because he was mental."

"That's a horrible thing to say. He had PTSD as did *thousands* of first responders." I sounded like Candace Tight Pants.

"Yeah? What about how they'll say he's a nut job who surfed alone at night in giant waves while tranny and straight hookers were being offed in the weeds?"

"OK, I admit, it doesn't sound good."

"That's because it's not good. Can you sell that thing he inherited right away? And failing that, you got an extra few hundred grand layin' around? Like right this second?"

"Shit."

"Shit is right."

I did what I swore I wasn't going to do and called the Judsons. I wanted to know—if possible—whether they could take Terry for one overnight until my parents arrived. Raylene let out such a cry of pure joy it sounded like she'd just realized that it was all a terrible dream and her son was alive and well and cuddled up next to her.

Dane, more practical, wanted to know why I needed to rush to Israel. I made the mistake of telling him the truth.

14

I Skyped my parents, who spent ten minutes baby talking to Terry, who in turn stared at the screen like they were a video game, touching it and trying to move them around.

"He thinks you're a toy," I said.

"He can't possibly have that kind of motor coordination skills at this stage," Mom said.

"I told you. He's a genius." Terry grabbed for my parents' faces and said, "Gagi! Papa!"

"Maybe he's trying to say 'Gramma,'" I suggested, sticking my face into the screen while kissing the baby.

Dr. Mom said, "Yes, perhaps," and rolled her eyes.

"You'll see for yourselves when you get here. A genius!"

They would be arriving in two days and told me if I could get the next plane out, that they'd be there before Raylene and Dane could claim him as their own grandchild.

The next few hours flew by as I booked an El Al flight for the next day, packed a small bag, made sure my passport and everything else was in order, and booked a room at the Harmony Hotel.

As I was stuffing a ratty T-shirt that I loved to wear to bed into my carry-on, the phone rang. Alonzo. Oh my.

"Hi, Alessandra, did I get you at a bad time?"

"Well, sort of," I said honestly, but quickly added, "but I'm so happy it's you. I've had one helluva day."

"So I heard."

"From?"

"Well, Raylene called me all upset about you. She apparently thinks a lowly New York city councilman can spring a man from a Long Island jail . . ."

"She's such a sweet lady. In fact, they've even agreed to take Terry for an overnight until my parents get back from Africa in a day or two."

"Going somewhere?"

"Yes. I need to take a trip to Israel. It's about the story . . ."

"So I guess that means you can't go to the Yankee game with me?"

Gee, what's better, I thought: *a night out with the handsomest, single pol in town, or rushing to Israel with a cursed relic to meet a creepy swindler/priest/CIA Vatican operative with a black market business on the side? And that's when he wasn't swindling rich people into giving their kids secret Vatican-approved exorcisms.*

"Can I get a rain check?" I asked.

"You bet," he answered. "I look forward to it."

"Me, too." How crazy was this? Flirting with a guy while my best friend was rotting in prison.

Next call was to Donald. I told him the story, he offered to go with me to Israel—if he had exclusives on the photos—but I told him Father Paulo would probably freak out. Failing that, would he come over whenever he could in the next day or so to make sure everything was good until my parents arrived?

I could hear dopey Larry in the background, even above the music from whatever bar they were in. "Without dopey Larry," I added.

Apparently the music wasn't that loud because Larry butted in: "I'm not so dopey."

"He's not. He just likes people to think he's a moron," Donald said, and I could practically see the male arm punch.

"He's doing a great job of it," I snarked. *Larry really is such a fool,* I thought.

"Ali, one question," Donald continued. "How do you propose to take a sealed brass tube onto a plane?"

I hadn't thought of that. And then I also remembered that it was very illegal to transport antiquities—especially stolen antiquities—into another country. That was called transporting goods for the black market. *Hello?*

How the hell was I going to pull that one off? Stick a priceless relic—the only intact pages left on Earth that had the actual words that Jesus had spoken privately to Judas, which might be the secret to life itself, or had the power to unleash Armageddon—into checked baggage? Have it travel around the world in the cargo hold? Send it via Fed Ex to a hotel I've never even been to?

What if I was followed and someone snatched the bag? What if I was caught transporting a stolen relic? What if I got arrested and there was no one to take care of Terry? What if my bag went missing and it was never recovered?

And what if I didn't go and Roy couldn't make bail or defense money and he was assigned a public defender, convicted of seventeen counts of murder, and got the death sentence? What if I ignored the most important story I was likely to ever get again? What if . . .

I gave Terry his bath. My anxiety level was out of control and my cozy, warm apartment was starting to freeze up again.

What in hell is going on?

At least Terry seemed to be back to his jolly self and I fed him a nice warm bottle, which he actually asked for, *I think*; read him a story, which he didn't understand, I think; and placed him in his cozy crib. Checked that both the club baby lock was in place as well as the gaffer's tape. All good. Still cold. I put a heavy, wool, baby blanket on him.

Then I remembered the key. Maybe it really was ancient and also worth a fortune. Roy could use the dough for sure.

His diaper pail needed to be emptied, so I left the front door ajar and planned to walk the whole ten feet to the compacter room to throw it out. But as soon as I opened the door, I saw someone leaving the Judsons' apartment. Dear God. It was Arturo Elias! I slipped back inside and closed the door very gently, waited to hear the elevator ding, and picked up the phone and dialed the Judsons.

Raylene picked up. "Raylene, was that Arturo Elias leaving your apartment?"

"Well, I don't know," she said mysteriously. "I was just going to call the doorman. I don't know how he got in, but he said he was looking for the apartment right upstairs from us and got off at the wrong floor!"

"And so you let him in?"

"Well, he's a priest, dear. The doorman said a priest was coming up. When the dear man realized his mistake, he took the lift up one flight. Or so I presume he did."

"Raylene, please listen to me very, very carefully. His name is Arturo Elias, and I don't know if he's a priest but I do think he's a bad guy. He's after the relic! You must never let him in again!"

"Oh my. That's so disturbing. A fake priest? Oh Lord! What next? Fake shamans?" She is the only person in the world, I thought, who could say that and mean it.

"Yes, like a fake shaman," I answered, shaking my head. But she sounded like she was really shaken up, so I told her that I'd call the doorman immediately and straighten it out.

So much for my super-secure building.

When I called downstairs the doorman was all apologies, but said the Judsons had said it was OK to let him in! Then he added, "Maybe they thought it was someone else. I'm so sorry if he bothered you, too, Ms. Russo."

"No, no problem, Anthony," I said, "but please make sure he doesn't enter the building again. Is he still inside by the way?"

"No, he left a few minutes ago."

"He's not who he says he is. I don't even think he's a priest. Please don't let him in again."

"Geez, Ms. Russo, I'm sorry. But we will for sure have him on surveillance video, so we'll post his photo so he never gets in again."

I double locked the front door—not just because that creep had entered my building and my floor and bothered my friends, but considering I also had the book and the Gospel pages inside my apartment, well, Elias had been way too close for comfort.

I opened my laptop and looked up *transporting antiquities*. I didn't even bother to get into the transporting stolen antiquities law, because even dopey Larry would know that was so insanely wrong that I'd probably end up in a Middle Eastern prison camp. But maybe the pages weren't illegal because nobody had claimed them when Morris nicked them. Right.

I found out what I already knew. It was illegal. Taking the relic into Israel meant I was turning into Morris Golden, international black marketeer. Or maybe just a schmuck.

I took the box containing the brass tube out of my bag anyway. I opened it and removed the tube and—*bam!*—dropped it right back into the box in a flash. The damned thing gave me another big shock. *Must be static electricity.* Right.

Yes, it did look like a pipe bomb. No, there was no getting around it. Either I kept it in my bag and got nailed at JFK and arrested on the spot, or I put it in a suitcase and checked it, hoping it didn't get stolen, or removed—along with its passenger—by the NTSB (National Transportation Safety Board).

El Al is so security-driven that they probably even have antique-sniffing dogs that'll tear you limb from limb for trying to sneak even fake antiques in or out, I thought. Not wanting to be ripped apart on either side of my journey, I emptied out a giant Johnson's Baby Powder container into a bowl, stuck the ten-million-dollar tube inside the ten-dollar baby powder container, then poured back as much powder as I could fit, put the top back on, and stuck the container into the velvet-lined wooden box and surrounded it with tissue paper.

I then wrapped the whole mess in bubble wrap—as though X-ray machines couldn't see through bubble wrap. This move, I knew, was the equivalent in dumbness of putting your flashers on when you illegally park.

I finished packing up clothes enough for two days, put three separate luggage tags on my suitcase, each with my cell number and the name, number, and address of the Harmony Hotel in Jerusalem, placed the box in the middle with clothes and sneakers around it, and got ready for bed.

Screw Father Paulo's request for the Voynich Manuscript. One ancient relic at a time was all I was willing to smuggle. If he wanted it for his own perusal, he could get his backside here. This time I had no choice but to bring what I had to him. If he wanted this old book, he could come and get it.

Then I remembered the skeleton key. I hadn't given it a second thought and in fact had completely forgotten about it.

I opened my dresser drawer and took the key from its totally safe hiding place: a lone tube sock I had meant to throw away.

I turned it around in my hand. What the hell could I do with this thing? Nothing.

Then I hit on how to get the key, at least, through security. *Stupid idea, but better than nothing.*

I took the cans of silver and gold spray paint, glitter, and even spray snow that I had in the Christmas decorations box in that same closet. I laid out some newspaper—yes, it was another story about the Gilgo Beach monster—laid the key down, and sprayed the key silver and dusted it with glitter. Perfectly hideous. Perfectly wonderful!

I placed the old, now-garish key on the metal drain chain around my neck—on which also hung my most treasured possession, my *New York Standard* press pass—and checked it out in the mirror. I'd fake it as a cheap, bad-taste piece of junk.

You've just covered a Sumerian or Roman or some other ancient key with glitter and glue. What a classy dame you are, Russo.

I went to check into my flight online and saw that El Al had added an extra flight because of the upcoming high holy days.

Great. I was able to rebook onto the earlier flight instead of the usual late-night JFK–Tel Aviv flight.

Then I made one more call to Mad Dog before I turned in.

No hello, no nothing. He picked up: "He's remanded. No getting out," the Dog said, matter-of-factly. "The judge set the highest bail ever set out there. Ya ready?" He didn't wait to see if I was or not. "Seventy-five million. I cudden believe it."

I couldn't believe it, either. "But Roy's not a flight risk . . ." I attempted to say.

"Not a risk for flight, just a risk to life and limb," Mad Dog screamed in my ear. "And no local bondsman is gonna come up with that scratch. I can get it in the city, but it's gonna be a seven five down."

Seven million five hundred thousand upfront, in other words.

"Can you get that much?" he asked.

"I'm working on it. I'm working on it," I offered despondently. I could only hope Roy would call me collect the next day before I got on that plane. If he was allowed to call me, that is. I needed to tell him he wasn't alone.

"Did he give you permission for me to sell the papers his father left him?"

"Yeah. Do it." He hung up. Sure, Mad Dog was mad but he was also garnering so much publicity for himself as the guy repping the Gilgo Beach killer/hero firefighter/ancient relic owner that he himself was getting seventy-five million in free publicity.

I plopped down on my bed, and as I was lying there trying to sleep the thought that had hit me earlier, the nagging thought that I'd missed something, started running through my head again. But what the hell was it? What had I missed? Something about Morris Golden . . . what the hell was it?

I finally fell asleep, but woke up because my room this time had gone from seventy to zero in sixty seconds. And the window next to *my* bed this time was wide open. I jumped up, nearly breaking my neck on my suitcase, and closed the window, relocking the club thing. In doing so, I noticed that oddly, again, the night air outside was warm—much warmer than the frigid air in my room. In fact, it was, all in all, a perfect spring night.

I got up and checked the thermostat. Fifty-two degrees inside! But how could that be? The AC was turned to "off."

I checked on Terry. He was fast asleep with his little butt in the air, and for once, it was warmer in his room than in mine. In fact, because he was in a toasty onesie, his face was red. It was even a bit too warm in his room.

To prevent myself from breaking my neck next time I got up, I moved my suitcase from my bedroom to the living room and then crawled back into bed. It was 1:30 A.M. *Jesus.*

I finally fell back to sleep, but I wished I hadn't.

I found myself in a dark place, holding Terry in my arms. I was wearing a sort of burqa. Together we descended dank, cold, stone stairs into a dark cave or maybe it was a dungeon. Holding Terry in one arm and feeling my way down the stairs with my free hand, we descended, each step bringing us closer to the hell below. When I reached the bottom step, I hugged Terry closer to me as he started to cry.

Go back! Go back! my brain was screaming, but my dream wouldn't listen.

A single bulb illuminated our surroundings: just a low-ceilinged, cave-like hole hewn out of the rock. Terry and I were completely alone, but I could hear men screaming in agony. But the screams were coming out of the walls!

I could feel "handles" carved out of the stone every few feet along the walls, but they seemed to be handles that held nothing. Hieroglyphs scrawled like ancient graffiti splashed across the screen of my dreams. Just then the light in the cave dungeon blew out, thrusting us into the pitch black. Terry was no longer in my arms. He was gone! I could hear his little screams melding into the screams of the unseen men, but with each wail, I knew he, too, was disappearing further into the walls themselves and I couldn't find him.

Why did you bring him down here—to his certain death? Why?

I shot up straight in bed, soaked in sweat, shaking, freezing, and burning up all at once, and mumbled, "The chains of our Lord did not bind Him!"

What the hell? Or more to the point, what hell was that?

Was this some sign that I shouldn't go? I sounded as superstitious as Raylene! No, it made no sense. I wasn't taking Terry with me. My baby was going to be safe and sound at home with the Judsons. Safe-and-sound.

I turned toward the door of my room and in the dim light coming through the blinds I saw him. Baby Terry was standing at my door!

15

I picked him up, shocked. And shaken. It's kind of terrifying to see your infant standing alone at your door, after all. He was still fast asleep. *How in the world could a six-month-old, who didn't yet walk, climb out of bed and sleepwalk to my room?*

Carrying the sleeping baby with me, I walked from room to room checking to see that no one had broken in. No one had. The child was just progressing by leaps and bounds. *Right.* I took him into bed with me to keep him from doing such a thing again, and he slept through the night. Me? Not so much.

The next day was a flurry of crazy—Terry couldn't even figure out how to crawl that morning, let alone walk, and was doing the baby-rock-back-and-forth-on-all-fours thing.

The hours flew by as I attempted to get all my ducks in a row before setting out for what I knew would be a very short trip and a very long flight. All attempts to reach Father Paulo were unsuccessful, and I hoped that tradition would hold true, and although as unreachable as always, he'd be exactly where he said he'd be, exactly when I got to where he wanted me to be. And that is what I was banking on. What was the choice—really?

Bob was even willing to pay for the trip, on the condition that I'd bring back as big a story as I had with the Veil of Veronica and the cloning of Jesus.

This tube in my possession contained—I hoped—the only words left on Earth said by Jesus directly to his once most trusted disciple, his treasurer, Judas Iscariot. So yes, could be as big. Were they words of magic? Power? Armageddon? Resurrection? And why to Judas? Could actually be bigger—much bigger. Whatever these remaining words were, they were invaluable in terms of what it would mean to the world and nearly as much on a personal level in getting Roy out of prison. I had to trust that the Vatican would do right by them. And pay me enough to do right by Roy. If it had been any other pope but Pope Francis, I would never have considered it, but he is the most decent man to occupy the office in my lifetime. So decent, in fact, I often wondered how the bad guys inside hadn't poisoned him yet.

I pulled on a pair of black jeans; a white, cotton shirt; and then hung the hideous glitter key around my neck and tucked it inside. I didn't feel like explaining myself to the Buttinskys when I had so much other explaining to do—about exactly what to do with Terry every second—that the last thing I wanted was to explain why I was wearing a glitter key. I told them about how he'd climbed out of bed and they assured me that they'd sleep on the floor of his room so he couldn't do such a thing again.

Mollified, and knowing it would only be for one night, I finished up by sticking my iPad, keyboard, an overnight kit, a reporter's notebook, a bunch of pens, and a few essentials in my big hobo purse.

The Judsons arrived at my apartment on time—loaded up with their Omega mega super juicer, a thermal bag, and two giant brown bags of greens, even though we had hours and hours to go.

Of course I was apprehensive about leaving Terry for the first time, especially with his escalating advances, but even though I thought they were nosy and could be annoying, I was thankful that I had friends like the Judsons. I mean, they were thrilled to stay with him until my parents arrived, or none of this would have even been possible. Dona-the-capable was flat-out incapable when it came to Terry when he was on a tear. Donald would have taken Terry to a bar and then claimed it was good for him because he was his son or something equally ridiculous.

"I know you guys are desperate to get some kale juice down this little boy," I said, picking Terry up and kissing his little face while eying their juicer, "but I'm afraid he's strictly a peaches kinda kid."

Raylene pulled out a frozen thing from the thermal bag. "Look! Delicious frozen kale, spinach, and celery root pops! He can suck on them like an ice cream bar! Delicious!"

"I'm sure. But just in case . . ." I opened the pantry and showed them the rows of Earth's Best baby food in every variety known, well, on Earth. Raylene looked like she might faint. "It's organic baby food," I protested.

"Organic, schmaganic!" she proclaimed. "I was in the business. I know from organic!" She kissed her Omega juicer. "Don't we, buddy?"

"I'm surprised you haven't BeDazzled it with sequins," I joked, hugging her.

"Might look nice," she joked back. I think.

I knew Terry would never eat any of that stuff, even as Raylene handed him one of her pureed frozen spinach pops. He turned it over a few times, and stuck it in his mouth, and instead of spitting it out he started sucking on it like she'd just given him a chocolate pacifier. Worse, he kept it there—even though it must have tasted like frozen nasty.

"Yum!" said Raylene as she gently took it from his mouth and he giggled and tried to grab it back. *Go figure. It was green slime!*

"Anyway, here are the numbers of everyone I know," I said, handing them Mad Dog's number as well as everyone else's contact info within the continental United States, including the press secretary to the White House just in case. In case of what I didn't know. Too bad I didn't. Know, I mean.

I was horribly concerned that I hadn't heard from Roy yet and the time was getting near to my leaving, so I called Mad Dog's office, but they said he was tied up and would get back to me—not. One last Skype to my folks, who I was thrilled to find out were actually leaving early. They were about to board the first of two legs of their flight home and said they'd be back in New York probably even before I touched down in Tel Aviv, barring a flare-up of my dad's *tourista*.

So far, so good.

I reluctantly picked up my bag, kissed Terry (feeling serious separation anxiety), and made sure they had the giant list of instructions, which I knew they didn't need. As I headed to the door, I said, "My folks will be here tomorrow, so you've only got to put up with the little monster for one night and you'll be back in your own bed tomorrow. Please, I swear he crawled out of his crib, so . . ."

Raylene shushed me with, "Dear, he's fine. Just a little genius," she said, giving him a sloppy kiss.

"Well, I can't begin to tell you how much I love you for doing this, you guys," I said, starting to tear up.

Raylene, with Terry in her arms, reached out and put Terry up to me and said, "Kiss Mommy good-bye like a good boy. There you go."

Dane walked me to the door and handed me a package tied up in string like something out of the 1940s.

"Open it, please," he implored me. I unwrapped the brown paper. It was a small book, *The Gospel of Judas,* second edition, edited by Rodolphe Kasser, Marvin Meyer, and Gregor Wurst.

"The book, *this* book, is, I think, an interpretation of what was found back in the 1970s. I've made some notations inside."

"Gosh, Dane. I've begun researching, so this will be very helpful. It's incredibly thoughtful of you," I said, hugging him and trying not to tear up again.

"Oh, it's nothing. I'm just an old guy living vicariously through my glamorous, dashing reporter friend down the hall!"

"Hardly," I said, pointing to Terry and all his stuff. "I'll read every word on the plane. See what this demon Judas had to say— or what was left of the words that weren't rotted away, at any rate."

"Apparently, it was mostly rejected by the mainstream scholars and of course the Vatican."

I realized that our little talk had cost me precious time and El Al didn't let you board a minute late.

I had to hurry but still I left with a heavy heart, even knowing Terry was in good hands. As I stepped outside with my big hobo purse on my shoulder and my rolling suitcase in hand, to wait for the Carmel car I'd called, a black-coated, scruffy figure appeared out of nowhere and approached me quickly and spun me around.

"Father Elias! What?" He looked like he hadn't shaved or bathed since last I'd seen him sneaking around the hall. He was positively frantic now.

"Don't do this thing!" he yelled, lunging for my purse. "Give me the papyrus!" I fought him off, dropping my suitcase to the ground but holding on to my purse, which was probably stupid. It would have been worse for him to run off with the suitcase.

"Give it to me—give me the words of Jesus. I must put it in a consecrated place. Morris Golden left it to me and to Our Lady of Vilnius. Give those pages to me!" he screamed. I struggled to break free as he struggled to grab my big red purse.

My doorman came rushing out and grabbed Father Elias by the arms, holding him tight as a small crowd gathered. "What's going on, Ms. Russo? Call nine-one-one somebody!"

"No, no! Just call security. I need to catch a plane and I can't stay to file a complaint!" I said, completely agitated. The last thing I needed was to miss my plane. Shaking Elias off, Anthony held him at bay, trying to get me to change my mind as a Carmel car pulled up. The driver came around, picked up my suitcase, and opened the door, confused, as I rushed in, shaken. I slammed the door and locked it, just as Elias broke free of Anthony and rushed the car door, shoving the driver. He grabbed at my window and screamed, "Give me the codex!" and as Anthony tried to pull him off he screamed, "Thief! That woman is running away with a stolen relic!"

The driver hurried back into the driver's seat and I could hear sirens approaching. Somebody had reported the incident. "Please. Just leave!" The driver didn't want to, but I was the paying customer, after all. "He's just a crazy neighbor."

As we pulled out, Elias followed us. He fell on his knees in the traffic and made the sign of the cross, crying, "The chains of our Lord did not bind Him, Miss Russo! The chains of our Lord did not bind Him! You are a sinner!"

I was shaken to the core. The driver turned around. "You all right, miss? You sure we shouldn't wait for the cops?" His Middle

Eastern accent was thick, and his New York Yankees cap was firmly and proudly in place.

"Yes, yes, I'm fine," I lied. "A crazy man—that's all."

"Lots of crazy people," he said. "A regular nut job."

As I settled back into the seat, I checked my purse, knowing that Father Elias had grabbed onto my bag during that bizarre encounter. Everything looked OK. *Tickets, check. Passport, check.*

"Yes," I answered the cabbie, "just your run-of-the-mill New York nut job." *Not.*

He liked that a lot. I didn't.

My mind was racing: *Is the creep looking for a payday or does he believe the Gospel pages really hold the secret to whatever he and Morris were up to?*

Although the Midtown Tunnel—which miraculously hasn't yet been renamed for a dead politician—was crowded, we made it to JFK just under the wire.

When I got to the El Al check-in line, I reached into my bag to pull out my passport and ticket and felt something I hadn't noticed when I checked my bag earlier. A folded piece of paper.

What the hell? More creepiness from that freak. Father Elias must have stuck this in here!

I opened it. The wobbly script was the same as Morris Golden's and so was the obscure code he'd written before to his son: *31.780231° N, 35.233991° E*

As a great philosopher once asked, WTF?

16

After I got past the initial shock of being assaulted by the now-disheveled and disoriented priest, I get hit with the same code that had been written by the dead and disoriented father of my best friend who was rotting in jail. And to think, just a few days ago, all I was, was merely feeling sorry for myself for losing Pantera.

The check-in line was very long, but since I was cutting it so close, an El Al agent, who I swear are all ex-or-maybe-current Mossad, brought me to the front of the line when I told him I was late.

I began sweating bullets. The last thing one should do—especially when one is smuggling stolen relics in the presence of an El Al ticket/Mossad agent—is to start sweating even small bullets, look guilty, or behave in any way like you are hiding something.

I now had all three going on at once. *Yes! Way to go, Russo.*

The agent looked at the ticket, looked at my passport.

"I have TSA," I said, as though that would change everything. This is the prescreening method that I had applied for and gotten, which allows you to skip regular lines. Unless you're flying to Israel and they don't want you to skip lines. "Oy," as they say in New York.

I rubbed my wet palms on my jeans.

I imagined a locked room and never getting my boy Roy out. Or me, either, come to think of it.

Instead he pulled me aside, checking with his handheld device to see if I was a known smuggler or something. "Why are you going to Israel for just two days, Ms. Russo?"

Never mind smuggler, he's about to arrest me as an international terrorist.

I decided to use the same excuse that I'd used last time I was on the run, at an airport, trying to escape the country.

"I, um, am a publicist for a band. A rock band, so I am, ah, just doing the pre-publicity."

"A rock band," he repeated.

"It's a, well, a retro rock band. We like the 1960s."

"And this band is called—what?"

What the hell did I call it last time? What was it? Shit!

I hoped I remembered correctly, since now everything you ever said or did is recorded somewhere and if any airline would have it, it would definitely be El Al, the world's most secure airline.

"The, uh, the Pan Band," I said, feeling as insane as when I'd said it the first time it came out of my mouth last year.

"The what?"

"The Pan Band. You know, um, they do Jimi Hendrix covers, that kind of thing."

What did you just say? Jimi Hendrix cover band? You sound insane. Shut up before you sink yourself but good.

The Mossad ticket agent looked at my passport and then at my ticket and looked back at me. "Remove your sunglasses, please." I removed my sunglasses but then for reasons I will never understand, I pointed to my blouse and said, "I'm so sorry, but I'm Orthodox."

What? He didn't ask you to strip. You sound insane. Worse, an Orthodox woman in jeans is as stupid as one checking in naked on El Al. Jesus! What is wrong with you?

"Come with me," he ordered.

Shit! Shit! Shit! You went too far.

He checked the computer. "Why did your previous passport say 'Zaluckyj' and the current one lists you as 'Russo'?"

I had just told the guy for no reason that I was Orthodox and now I couldn't say I was divorced and that my maiden name was Russo. "Ah, it's my married name."

"I see. You converted?"

"No, I was born Jewish." *Dear God. Why are you saying all this? You sound like you're about to explode with grenades sewn into your underwear. Shut up!*

He did a bit more checking, and then he brought me right up to the front of the check-in line—and I watched as my suitcase with the precious relic went zipping right onto the conveyor belt to be tossed and beaten up in the cargo hold.

Whew. So far so good.

Security line. *Beeeeep.* "Please remove your jewelry," the security guard said, pointing to the glitter disaster that was now poking out of the button that had come undone on my blouse. *Orthodox slut!*

I put it on the little plastic tray. He called someone else over and they both looked at it.

"My son made it for me in school," I said of the ancient key, as though my son had gone to school with Moses. "It's an old key to our, um, barn." *Your barn, where? In Thebes?*

I was now hot-flashing like a woman in full menopause, the sweat pouring off me. *Oh shit. The glitter is coming off in his hands!*

"She is late for flight four," the Mossad/ticket agent said matter-of-factly, and instead of what I expected, which was: "Arrest her, she put a bomb in her luggage and there's a rare artifact around her neck with glitter on it!" I just walked through the body scanner.

As I picked up the key from the tray, one of the agents, eyeing me suspiciously, said, "Your son should use better glue next time."

Should I wish him a happy Passover? Or is it Rosh Hashanah now? Or maybe Yom Kippur? I am such a freaking shiksa!

Somehow I was through security, so I retrieved the truly terrible key, put it around my neck, and hoped like hell that my bag was being loaded onto the same aircraft.

The gate was, of course, the last one in the entire airport, and I ran like my ass was on fire, and saw—thank God!—that they were still boarding. I handed the woman my ticket, hoping against hope that I'd just get on without anything else going wrong. I'd worry about getting through customs at the other end.

But then something happened. When the agent looked at my boarding pass and passport she said, "Oh. I see. Would you step aside, please?"

Not again!

"Is there a problem?"

"No, no, not at all. It seems you got a last-minute upgrade."

"Upgrade?"

"Yes. You weren't told?"

"No . . ."

Maybe they really think I'm attached to a big rock band? Nah.

"Well, it must be your lucky day," she continued. "Just go back up to the desk and the agent will issue you another boarding pass."

I reluctantly did as I was told and got a boarding pass for a second-row aisle seat.

I didn't understand any of it but nonetheless sent up a prayer to the God I didn't necessarily believe in in the first place.

As I boarded, I looked at the passengers scrambling to put their bags in the overhead compartments and those already seated. Ninety-nine percent of the people on the plane were in some kind of religious garb. Most were Orthodox or Hasidic Jews, as well as a smattering of priests and nuns and a few couples in Muslim burqas and *djellabas*. There are more atheists in foxholes than there are on El Al flights.

I took my seat and then took out my iPad and overnight kit. Immediately a man who looked even more Mossad than the ticket agent took the seat next to me at the window. He was thin but fit, with a well-trimmed beard. He wore a baseball cap, casual but good khakis, a polo shirt, and suede jacket. He took off his baseball cap and was wearing a yarmulke. I also caught a small pin on his polo. Recording device? Possibly.

Stop it. Most Israelis look like Mossad. What? Now you're stereo-typing Israelis?

The guy reminded me of Yusef Pantera—if Yusef had been Israeli, and not whatever he actually was. I realized then that despite my wild and—no pun intended—unorthodox love for the man, I had no clue what he really believed other than the concept of the perfect order of the universe and the belief that he had participated in the "great experiment" to clone Jesus.

I took out my phone to call the Judsons and realized I should have left them an extra iPad so I could FaceTime or Skype with them so Terry could see me. Raylene picked up after one ring. "Hi, Raylene, it's Alessandra! How's Terry?"

"Oh, hello, dear. He's just fine. Just had a bottle of soy milk and a big bowl of mashed turnips."

"And he ate it?"

"You best believe he did. Loved it!"

"Can you put him on the phone so I can talk to him?"

"Well, I just put him down for a nap," she said. "He's sleeping, but if you want me to wake him . . ."

I could have sworn I heard him when she first picked up in the background. "Wasn't that him a minute ago?"

"No, it wasn't. I told you. He's sleeping. And if you wouldn't mind, dear, I'm kind of tired myself and I sure would love to catch some shut-eye while Terry's napping."

"Oh. Sure," I said. "And thanks. I'll call you as soon as I land."

"You do that, dear. Good-bye now."

"Bye, Raylene." Why did I feel suddenly uncomfortable?

I tried Skyping my parents but they were obviously somewhere over the ocean flying home. Good. By the time I landed, they might already be in New York, or at least the continental United States.

One more call: it occurred to me that perhaps Mr. Engles had run into this Father Elias in his travels. After all, Elias was obsessed with the pages so perhaps he was some kind of black marketeer.

I rang up his shop and a woman answered. "I'm so sorry to have to tell you this," she said when I asked to speak to him. "Mr. Engles, we . . ." She paused, clearly sniffling.

My heart started racing. "What happened?" I jumped in, explaining who I was. "Has Mr. Engles been injured?"

"I'm afraid, well, Mr. Engles has passed. This is his niece," said the distraught woman on the other end of the phone. "He . . . he . . . oh God! He was found dead in his shop this morning. There appears to have been an attempted break-in and his assistant found him on the floor clutching his chest." She sobbed. "He had apparently been dead for hours."

Before I had a chance to get any details, the flight attendant came by and let me know in no uncertain terms that my phone had to be shut down. "As the announcement ordered," she added.

I offered my apologies to Engles' niece and hung up in shock and dismay, upset and confused. Sure, he was an elderly man. But a heart attack? Did someone know he'd been holding the relic for me? Was it really a break-in? She had sounded unsure about that.

There is nothing you can do about this now. Maybe it's a horrible coincidence. Right. Teesh-mi-ree Al Atz-Mech, Mr. Engles, Teesh-mi-ree Al Atz-Mech.

More upset with this news than I even comprehended, I looked over at Mr. Mossad. Clearly he was less than pleased with me for talking after being told to shut down all phones. "Mind your own business," I wanted to say and didn't. *Very strict, these Israelis. Like you even know that he's Israeli.*

Then I remembered why I was taking this trip: "Oh my God, *The Gospel!*" I said aloud, realizing immediately that people were craning their necks to get a look at me.

I stood to retrieve it from my bag in the overhead compartment, and at the same time managed to drop the open bottle of water in the console, which in turn splashed the woman seated across the aisle.

"Oh God, I'm so sorry," I said, leaning over and attempting to sop up the water. Forget it. This was first-class, and the flight attendant was there in a microsecond. I was quickly becoming the least popular woman on El Al.

The passenger, a Gisele Bündchen–lookalike, was more gracious than I would have been had someone splashed water on my four-thousand-dollar, perfect, light wool slacks.

The price of her tailored slacks alone could have fed a small third world country for a week. Only old-money young people wear "slacks." The rest of us wear pants. She smiled. "It's fine, don't worry," she said with a slight, unidentifiable accent.

After we were airborne, I washed up, brushed my teeth, shamelessly put on the pajamas the flight attendants had passed out, and walked back to my seat to peruse as much as I could of *The Gospel of Judas* before getting some shut-eye.

Once I cracked the book open, sleep became very much a foreign concept, no pun intended, on my flight to Israel. Forget the stolen relic—how'd they'd let me on the plane with this explosive little book?

17

Since I hadn't had time to read enough about the Gospel itself, what with all the other research I had to do before I left, I had assumed that it would be yet another telling of the story of Jesus, but in Judas' version he would be forgiven or something. I was wrong. Judas claimed in this text that he had been in league with Jesus, and had done His bidding. In short, Jesus asked him to betray Him so that He could be executed. Without an execution, there could be no resurrection or return to His life in another realm.

The original find also contained, in addition to the Gospel, a text titled James (or the First Apocalypse of James), a Letter of Peter to Philip, and something called the Book of Allogenes, whatever the heck that was.

But those weren't my concern—my only concern was the Judas Gospel—the pages that allegedly contained the words of Judas, written down by an unknown scribe and hidden perhaps around 220–340 C.E.

There was barely a full sentence left, however, it having mold-ered for over sixteen years in that safety-deposit box in Morris's bank branch in Hicksville, and then, believe it or not, stored in a freezer where it rotted even more. The codex had originally contained thirty-one pages with writing on both sides, but only thirteen pages remained. Had the lost pages been lost, just rotted away, or stolen? Well, I knew some had been stolen from firsthand knowledge.

As I read what was left of the actual words that Jesus had alleg-edly spoken to Judas, I knew that even those were explosive as an atomic bomb.

It began: "The secret word of declaration by which Jesus spoke in conversation with Judas Iscariot, during eight days, three days before he celebrated Passover."

These pages were *not* about the crucifixion of Jesus, or any of the things about which the other Gospels concerned themselves. This Gospel contained the secret esoteric teachings of Jesus, it was postulated, to his most beloved and trusted disciple, Judas! In fact, according to Judas, he did not betray Jesus willingly but was instructed *by* Jesus to do what he did. Jesus even tells Judas, "You will exceed all of them. For you will sacrifice the man who bears me."

In context, it seemed to me that Jesus was saying that his earthly incarnation as a mortal was nothing more than a suit of clothes that He wore during His time on Earth, and that it had been Judas' job to make sure that his Lord Jesus returned to—where?—Heaven?

Judas hated the other disciples and by the sound of it they hated him as well, but according to this account, Jesus wasn't a big fan of the other disciples, either, often laughing at them and putting them down.

In the intro, the authors also talk of another Gospel, the Gnostic Gospel of Thomas (also disregarded and banned by the early Church). I found it particularly disturbing because in that one Jesus fought with other disciples, Peter in particular, a man who thought women unworthy. Jesus rebuked him after saying that Mary Magdalene should leave them "for women are not worthy of spiritual life."

Jesus slapped him down, saying, "I will make Mary a living spirit!"

You go, Jesus! No wonder we never heard of it.

As I got to thinking about it, the other disciples actually were the big winners in the end—or at least as far as history is concerned—because Jesus' beloved companion, Mary, became known as a whore and/or a crazy woman possessed by the Devil. And it was those disciples who led the Church after Jesus' crucifixion. The winners, after all, write history. To the victors go the spoils. Could the same thing be said of Judas? He lost, but did he? Not if this little book survived. But it hadn't really survived, not *really,* since most of it was so rotted.

But if Morris's stolen pages—the ones that presumably were still intact—really contained the secret to eternal life, or resurrection, or— if used incorrectly—Armageddon, then Judas will still have won because he had written the words that had the power to destroy all of Christianity if not the world—or save it. Would it all be nonsense? Just the ravings of a madman? But why then was the Vatican so eager to get their hands on what we had?

My head was spinning. For example, in Judas' version of his time with Jesus, or what was left of it in *those* pages, Jesus shares with Judas things he never shared with the others. For starters, He tells him that He (Jesus) does not come from Earth, but He's not talking about Heaven, either. It's some other realm.

What realm?

Was it possible that Jesus didn't speak so much in parables as in riddles? The fragments that were left and interpreted in this little book were like reading sci-fi circa 220 C.E. But it was sci-fi at its weirdest. Hopefully, I thought, *When I get to Israel, Paulo will be waiting to interpret what I've got here. And hopefully, he'll keep his word.*

Of course he would. He's the one who called me. Yes, I was glad he'd solve this mystery and put the pages safely in the hands of Pope Francis where they'd be locked away.

And try finding someone else willing to give you ten million dollars to bail your friend out of jail!

Try as I might, the words before me just weren't making a whole lot of sense. I couldn't decide if this was the divine knowledge spoken during His lifetime by the anointed one, the Christ, to His most trusted disciple, Judas, the man we know as the great traitor, or just the rantings of a third-century lunatic who merely put to papyrus what was then 200-year-old oral lore.

Whatever these words were, they seemed to be as weird as if they'd come from another galaxy.

According to the little bits of un-rotted manuscript left, it was only Judas who could comprehend the riddles Jesus was imparting. That's when it hit me—perhaps these words hadn't been parables *or* riddles, but some kind of code! The team of scholars who had been assembled to put the pieces back together and then the others who had interpreted the ancient script had spent their lives studying these languages. They would surely have figured that out—no? Maybe not. *What if this* was *some kind of code?*

Great. Then all I'd need would be to find a clone of Alan Turing walking around Israel with time on his hands to decipher ancient code for me. Or maybe Father Paulo already knew it and was waiting for the rest of the pages to come his way.

I was getting as crazy as Judas, or maybe as crazy as the mysterious writer of this Gospel—whoever that was.

And I do mean crazy. At one point, Jesus tells his disciples in the Gospel, "Do you [really think you] know me—how? Truly I say to you, no race from the people among you will ever know me." As in the human race, the Semitic race, the lunatic race? No. It seemed to me that Jesus was talking about a race from another realm or galaxy!

Then Jesus said the first thing that made complete sense to me—the thing I always seemed to know in my heart and mind even as a little girl without ever being told: "Your God is within you."

Of course no organized religion would go for that kind of talk. When the disciples bristle at such talk in the Gospel of Judas, even from Jesus, He rebukes them, telling them that even the God that is within them is displeased with them. No wonder the Church founders buried this Gospel. Jesus is saying they don't need any priests or church leaders. God doesn't live in churches or temples, and the divine is within and we should self-regulate the good from the bad, the right from the wrong.

The disciples then get all prickly that God isn't happy with them so Jesus challenges them to step forward and face Him if they think they are perfect. However, each shrinks away except for, yes, superhero Judas, who says, "I know who you are and which place you came from—you came from the realm of the immortal Barbelo—but I am not worthy to proclaim the name of the one who sent you."

Barbelo? *Wasn't that a movie with Jane Fonda?*

I was confused: I would ask Paulo if he knew of a town in Israel called Barbelo. Maybe it once existed and now it didn't? Was "Barbelo" an acronym for "Bethlehem"?

It is Judas whom history views as the most reviled betrayer to ever have lived, yet in this book, Jesus takes Judas in a vision into a house so big he can't even comprehend where he is. It is in this "house" where Judas himself becomes enlightened and begins to understand the secrets of the "kingdom"—by which he (Judas) means—what?—the universe? Yes.

Jesus says—the interpreters filled in the missing text here or tried to—that, "Truly I say to you that no offspring of this realm will see that race, nor will any angelic army of the stars rule over that race, nor will any mortal human offspring be able to belong to it, for that race does not come from this realm which came into being . . ." This is followed by a lot of missing text and then, "The race of humans who are among you is from the race of humanity," then more missing text, then, "power which . . . some other forces . . . since you rule in their midst."

Why won't anyone say that Jesus was talking extraterrestrial here and not Heaven?

It seemed, at least according to this Gospel, that Judas was the only one who knew what it all meant. Jesus even tells him how much he will suffer because of his understanding of this extraterrestrial world, and that he is going to be tasked with doing the thing that will make him suffer immeasurably.

"Step away from the others and I shall tell you the mysteries of the kingdom, not so that you will go there, but you will grieve a great deal. For someone else will replace you, in order that the twelve [disciples] may again come to completion with their God."

OK, wait a second here, I thought. *Every accepted Gospel already said Jesus had to die to fulfill our destiny; to become our savior, correct? So wasn't Judas doing what he was fated to do all along?*

It occurred to me also, which it hadn't before, that if Jesus was all-knowing, as they said He was, why then didn't He know that Judas was a bad guy from the start if indeed he actually was a bad guy? Instead Jesus had trusted Judas above all the others, which is clear in all literature, and even assigned Judas the job of being the group's treasurer! That's like the Amazing Kreskin hiring Bernie Madoff to invest his money. I mean, He of all the beings on Earth should have known if Judas was crooked—no?

Perhaps, I began thinking, it was because Judas was the strongest disciple that Jesus had tasked him with the hardest job in the universe: to betray Him in order for the prophecy to be fulfilled. When you look at it with a whole different perspective—like looking at da Vinci's *The Last Supper* and seeing that one of the disciples is a woman—you realize, I thought, that Jesus even signaled Judas to commit the treachery at the Last Supper (or Last Seder, technically) in view of all the disciples! Not in secret, but in public.

Jesus said he'd give a piece of bread to the betrayer and then famously gave it to Judas. I was raised in an agnostic, irreverent family, and so never bought whole hog into the liturgy of the Catholic mass because I always felt that something was wrong—not real—about what they were telling us.

Whose prophecy had been fulfilled?

I turned on my iPad (free Wi-Fi in the expensive seats, not that I knew what the hell I was doing there anyway), and found in the Old Testament attributed to King David: "Prophesied: Even a man, my close friend in whom I trusted, who ate of my bread, has lifted up his heel against me" (Ps. 41:9). Bingo.

But King David wasn't talking about Jesus, he was talking about *himself* and a rebellion by his son and his best friend. It was almost the same narrative as the Last Supper!

Was the whole Jesus/Judas accepted Christian narrative just made up to fit in neatly with King David's prophecy?

When you thought about it logically, it all seemed too well coordinated. In fact, the whole Judas scenario couldn't have happened the way the Bible says it happened, I realized. Jesus was the most famous man in Jerusalem at that time, so Judas would not have needed to betray Jesus by selling His whereabouts to the authorities. Jesus was never in hiding, nor was He unrecognizable. He made His whereabouts known at every moment, as was recorded—and by the way, it would have been like the cops not knowing Elvis was in town. Jesus was the main attraction—and had made Himself very visible on that trip.

Why haven't Christians ever questioned that? I wondered. Wasn't it a huge glitch in the most famous betrayal story in history? Jesus was praying with his men in the Garden of Gethsemane. Jesus. (No pun intended.) That wasn't just a glitch, it was an anomaly of the first order of the first century that had been bought whole for two millennia!

This was getting more intriguing by the minute. I Googled Jesus' activities in the last weeks of His life. Jesus was a total publicity machine whose activities couldn't have been better organized and orchestrated if Madonna (the second one, not the original) had dreamed it up.

And it was all in the New Testament for everyone to see: On His way to Jerusalem, Jesus stopped for dinner at the home of Simon the Leper, where He dined with Lazarus—the very man He'd raised from the dead after he'd been in a tomb for four days! Talk about a media event. And talk about the resurrection formula. Was He trying it out to make sure it worked for Him when His *own* day came?

At dinner, He met Mary of Bethany, who was either Lazarus' sister or a "sinner," aka whore (depending on which sexist apostle you believe). Mary proceeded to massage Jesus' feet with a full pound—yes, a pound!—of immensely expensive perfumed ointment. Then she cleaned the ointment off with her hair!

Not only would dining with a previously dead man be a major event anytime, anywhere, but back then? Any famous stranger coming to town would be big news, but the most famous rabbi who'd brought the dead man back to life would have been a mammoth event. Furthermore, there was what would be today, the reality-TV aspect of it. The town's alleged bad girl gave the resurrection rabbi a foot massage with a king's ransom's worth of perfumed ointment. Seriously?

Imagine, say, the pope getting his feet massaged with precious oil by one of the Kardashians, who then cleans his feet off with her hair. *No wonder Kanye calls himself Yeezus!*

To make it even more of a public spectacle, it was only Judas who complained about the whole tawdry spectacle. In fact I found in John 12:2-9 that Judas complained out loud because it was such a waste of money: "Why was this perfume not sold for three hundred denari and the money given to the poor?"

Man! This had to have been the best show in the known world. It still would be!

It got better: On Sunday, Jesus left the town of Bethany, and rode into Jerusalem in a triumphant procession astride not just one, but perhaps two donkeys! I mean, who rides two donkeys at once besides, say, a rodeo trick rider or someone who wants to attract a huge crowd? That's not exactly the way to stay incognito. Was it to fulfill Zechariah 9 and the prediction of the coming of the lowly messianic king, which reads, ". . . your king is coming to you; righteous and having salvation is he, humble and mounted on a donkey, on a colt, the foal of a donkey." Many interpreted that to mean two donkeys.

If that wasn't a public enough scene, the following day, Monday, Jesus made sure everybody saw Him when He went to the temple and caused a scene by rebuking the money changers and arguing with the chief priests.

On Tuesday—like Joe Namath predicting that impossible Super Bowl win, which Namath also did three days before the big event—Jesus announced the date of His execution three days before it happened. To further make His presence known, He got into it with temple leaders, predicting doom and gloom and the destruction of Jerusalem itself if they didn't start believing in Him.

That's one way to make sure no one recognizes you. What a showman!

On Wednesday, more arguing when Jesus called all religious leaders hypocrites and snakes. Then from the Mount of Olives, He mourned Jerusalem's pending destruction. Now if that didn't catch the eye of the authorities, what would? That could be perceived— or would be today—as a terrorist threat.

Still not enough? On Thursday, the ancient publicity machine was at full crank, and Jesus actually announced where He and his disciples were going to celebrate the Passover meal. Afterward they went to pray (well the disciples fell asleep), publicly in the Garden of Gethsemane at the bottom of the Mount of Olives. It's not like they were hiding in a cave somewhere.

Not only were the Romans and the Pharisees watching Jesus'

every step at that point, and would have already *known* where He was, He would have been as familiar to them as any superstar is to us nowadays. Judas would never have had to kiss Jesus to identify Him. It would be like having to plant a kiss on the pope in order for the authorities to pick him out from the cardinals. Dear God (no pun intended again!), the story, accepted for two thousand years, actually made zero sense if you gave it much-needed, if discouraged, thought.

More troubling still—when *I* thought about it—was the question of *why* Judas would have had to be a traitor when every Gospel proclaims that it was Jesus' destiny to die for our sins in the first place.

If you indeed were a true believer, then logically you would have to believe that Judas helped Jesus fulfill that destiny. *Too bad humanity didn't actually get redeemed by His crucifixion. The world is as much of a cesspool now as it was back then—except on a much bigger scale.*

But what about the whole Judas money issue? If Judas got into it with Jesus for allowing Mary of Bethany to waste the precious ointment on Him when the money should have been distributed to the poor, why would he have sold Jesus out for thirty pieces of silver for his own personal gain (which turns out to be exactly the price of a slave in those days—just in case you didn't find the betrayal unseemly enough already)? And since Judas supposedly threw the money back, according to Matthew, before hanging himself, what *was* the point in the whole exercise that has fascinated Christians for two millennia? The fascination lay in the resurrection. Life *from* death! Life *after* death.

The disciples whose words made it into the mainstream Gospels couldn't have it both ways. That stands to reason. But unreasonably they did have it both ways and then some. Judas was a traitor but he was the one who fulfilled Jesus' destiny. Judas wanted to give money to the poor, but was so greedy that he sold Jesus out for money. And the believers in the apostle stories have bought the scenario for all this time. This despite the fact that they even shut out Jesus' family from their narratives, and apparently from the early Church, as well.

Questions aside, I had to get back to the history of the Gospel of Judas itself. I had to know its background if I was to make this deal. From what I could tell, any pages stolen had seemingly been recovered. A man named Bruce Ferrini, who had somehow come into possession of the pages after they'd been found in the vault, had turned them over—even the pages he'd been withholding (or so it was reported)—so what in hell were the alleged pages flying under my seat in the cargo hold?

I read and reread the few existing pages over and over, looking for what was missing so I'd have some idea of what I was dealing with when I had boots on the ground in Israel. *Good luck with that.*

Just then, the flight attendant came by with a choice of meals. I looked at the menu. It was like flying Air Jean-Georges, well, kosher Jean-Georges. No sense getting on the wrong side of the resident God of this airline when you're thirty-six thousand feet in the air. I ate a little of the lox appetizer and the next thing I knew, that same flight attendant was gently waking me for breakfast. *What the hell?*

Mr. Mossad beside me seemed like he'd just had a shave, shower, steam, and haircut, and was fully recharged for a day ahead. Gisele Bündchen, on the other hand, had changed from the nine-million-dollar beige slacks outfit into a nine-million-dollar white slacks outfit that looked exactly the same.

Instead of dwelling on it, I made my way to the bathroom in my airline pajamas and changed into my jeans, T-shirt, and sturdy sandals.

Mossad and Gisele seemed to be deliberately not looking at me as I made my way back to my seat and the flight attendant announced preparations for landing.

You truly are reaching new depths of paranoia. They're only trying to avoid looking at you because you look like a typical American slob, while they're probably on the international best-dressed list.

I was excited to land and get through customs—for the obvious reason—but also so I could call the Judsons and "talk" to Terry.

I looked out the window as we were descending and could see the Holy Land below, sacred site to three of the world's major religions, the sea, the vast desert. It was big and my making a deal for a huge amount of money seemed as filled with mystery as that desert.

What in hell are you doing, Russo? Have you lost your mind? Yes, probably. Oh well, downward and upward.

18

We landed around twelve thirty. By the time I got to the hotel,
I knew a good part of the day would be eaten up, so I started
sweating bullets. The tickets had me returning in two days. My
God. How could I accomplish anything in that time?

What if Father Paulo didn't show? What if the tube wasn't in my
luggage? What if . . . ?

I made it through immigration without a fuss—thank God I wasn't
stopped or my luggage searched—and turned on my phone and
quickly scrolled through. Nothing from the Judsons or my parents.
Nothing from Paulo. Nothing from Mad Dog. So far, so bad. I was
desperate to open the suitcase but I couldn't do it in the middle of
the terminal, so I tried as casually as possible to walk into the
women's bathroom.

I went into a stall, my heart beating, and opened my bag. Oh
God. The box was there. But was the tube? I unwrapped the fifty-
four-thousand feet of bubble wrap and there it was, still in its vir-

ginal and untapped state. *Whew.* I put it back inside my luggage and rushed out.

Before I got outside though, I tried my apartment where the Judsons were staying but only got my voice mail recording, so I left a message: "Hi. It's Alessandra. Please call me on my cell from my house phone as soon as you get this message. Just checking in and want to say hi to my sweet baby boy. Love you both, too, and as always, thank you, thank you."

I tried calling Dane's flip phone but it just kept ringing. *He probably never put a message on it. But it's nearing six thirty* A.M. *so they should be up and about now, what with Terry waking up with the sun.*

I exchanged five hundred dollars at the Citibank ATM inside the terminal. The best rate of exchange is always at the airport ATMs and not at the currency exchange booths, aka the money changers. Funny that I'd just read about Jesus railing against those guys in this same country, and here I was doing the same thing two thousand years later—just not outside the temple.

The Harmony Hotel is located in Jerusalem, while Ben Gurion Airport is in Tel Aviv. The choice was to grab a *sherut* (shared taxi), which were readily available at about fourteen dollars, or a regular cab for which there was a long line, at seventy-five.

The ride, I was told, was about forty-five minutes, and that was long enough, so I took my shot at a personal cab, hoping the time on the line would make up for the time spent dropping other passengers off along the route with a *sherut*.

I handed the driver a piece of paper with *Harmony Hotel, Yoel Moshe Salomon 6,* written on it, not that I had to. The drivers here speak English and unlike NYC cabbies aren't newcomers who don't know their way around. The driver immediately told me he was Muslim, as though I would have some kind of prejudice against him.

I asked the driver if the Harmony Hotel was located inside the Old City, but he said that it wasn't and was about a twenty-minute walk. My phone dinged five minutes into the ride and I jumped for joy. Home! But it was just a message from AT&T telling me: "Message rates will apply." *Shit.* Angrily, I slammed the phone back into my purse.

A second later it was followed by another text alert.

"Goddammit!" I spat out, causing the driver to look up. "Goddammit" probably wasn't a great phrase in a land of religious people. "Gosh-darned AT&T. I *know* message rates apply," I said aloud.

But this time it was a text from "unknown" so I assumed it was Paulo until I read it.

> We tried to call you, but we couldn't connect overseas somehow. The doorman, Anthony, is sending you this text message from us—Raylene & Dane. Everything is fine. That window in Terry's room wouldn't close again, so we're at our apt. until the super fixes it. Terry asleep/our bed. All good. R & D.

Whew. At least I could rest knowing that one man, the little man in my life—was in good hands.

I texted back:

> Thank you, Anthony, for being the messenger. Please tell Mr. & Mrs. Judson that I'll phone first thing in the morning. Also my parents will be arriving. I left the keys for them with security. Thank you, Ali Russo.

Unknown:

> You got it, Mrs. Russo.

Mrs.? Anthony never called me Mrs. We were very informal in my building and I had insisted early on that he just call me Ali, and besides, I wasn't anybody's missus.

It was a long, forty-five-minute ride from Ben Gurion Airport to the Harmony Hotel; mostly a stop-and-go highway route, and then a crawl-and-stop through the beautiful streets of Jerusalem. At any other time I would have reveled in the ride, but now my brain was racing faster than the slow-moving traffic. Time was wasting and damned Paulo had not tried to reach me. Was he going to internationally stand me up? *Nah.*

The cabbie broke into my thoughts. "Sorry, miss, but there is a situation ahead."

I saw a dozen police cars, lights blazing, and a cordoned-off street. My immediate thought was a Palestinian-Israeli street conflict.

"We have to go around the block," he said. "The police closed the street."

"How far are we from the hotel?"

"Just one block, right there," he said, pointing to the street. "The Harmony Hotel is right there."

"Well, I may as well walk. I don't have a heavy suitcase or anything," I said, paying for the ride with a credit card.

"Be careful, miss. It looks like trouble!"

Not that trouble ever bothered me, although it has always had a way of finding me. I got out, and curiosity led me to where the police situation was unfolding. I stood with the crowd and could see that a body bag was being loaded into an emergency vehicle. There was blood all over the street and on the building.

"What happened?" I asked a person standing next to me.

"Murder!" she exclaimed. "A Christian priest was killed!"

The man next to her immediately took up the argument. "No, I'm sure it was a Jew. Murdered by a Palestinian!"

"Did you see the body?" I asked the man.

"No, but you don't have to see a body to know what goes on in this city."

"Oh. How was the person killed?" I asked, the fear bubbling up. *No, it couldn't be. It just couldn't be.*

"I don't know," the woman answered, annoyed that the man had discounted her belief that the victim had been a priest. "I was right near here! There was no gunfire. Maybe he was stabbed," she said, pointing to the incredible amount of blood splatter.

As the vehicles began pulling away and the CSI teams moved in, the police broke up the crowd up and forced us to move.

Shaken, I walked around the corner to the ancient stone building that housed the Harmony Hotel.

I was amazed at how ultramodern it was inside in stark contrast to the outside and the whole surrounding area—all slick white leather and chrome.

The front desk clerk pulled my reservation right up. "Welcome, madam, here is your room key card. Have a pleasant stay—"

Before she could give me the whole spiel about the mini fridge and breakfast room, I cut in. "Sorry, but did you hear that a murder took place around the block?"

The clerk shook her head and went back to smiling as if I'd just wished her a pleasant day as well. Hospitality 101—always keep the guests happy and—what?—in the dark?

"OK then, can you tell me, has a priest come by or called for me?"

"Well, a Christian priest did come by about an hour ago, but he didn't ask for you. Had some breakfast in the restaurant."

"Would you say the priest was in his eighties?"

"Why, yes. But this city is filled with clerics of the three main faiths. Nothing unusual about a priest . . ." That was it. Nothing more was forthcoming from her about him.

I did, however, appreciate that there wasn't any of the usual chatter that keeps you from getting to your room in a speedy manner. It was a little off, but it was also a relief. I just needed to get started. Doing what? Waiting for Paulo.

My room was on the second floor, but I stopped for a coffee in the deserted lounge off the lobby and tried to call home again.

The Israeli coffee jolted me and I ordered a light bite as I dialed the Judsons' apartment. I knew Terry would be sleeping but I wanted to just check in. Again, no answer. *Must have gone back to my apartment.* No answer there, either. What was going on?

I tried my parents.

"Honey!" Mom's happy voice warmed me. "We just landed. We'll get our bags and head right over to your place."

"Mom! Oh, Mommy!" I said, reverting back to the little girl I always felt like when I knew my parents were around to make everything OK.

"I've been trying to reach the Judsons, that couple who watched Terry overnight down the hall from me?"

"Yes . . ."

"But they aren't answering. It's what? Nine o'clock there?"

"They must have the ringers turned off," she said. "People who aren't used to babies think every little noise will wake them up!"

"I'm sure you're right," I said. "But I'll feel better when Terry's back with Grandma Doc."

"Oops," she said. "The JFK gestapo are coming my way. Not allowed to use cell phones until we're through customs. I'll call you as soon as we're home. Love you."

"Love you back, Mom. My love to Daddy, too."

I took the elevator instead of the stairs because my legs were wobbly from the trip and I needed to stretch out. *I wish the freaking Judsons would answer their damned phone. Any damned phone.*

I walked down the hall, slipped the key card into the slot, threw the card back into my purse, and opened the door to my room. First thing I saw before the door shut automatically behind me was a wall that partially closed off the rest of the room, with a shelf and a mirror. Resting on it was a little nosegay of lily of the valley with a card. I thought they were fake and a decoration. No sense in reading the card. It would just tell me the room service number or something like that. I should have read it. I should also have noticed the coincidence. But I didn't so I didn't.

I managed to also grab a tiny glimpse of myself before the door closed. I always have dark circles under my eyes—I liked to rationalize them away as just part of my Italian charm. But now they'd gotten so bad that I looked like the walking dead.

When the door shut behind me, I hadn't remembered to put the card into the slot to turn on the lights, so when I flipped on the switch the room stayed dark. Because of the glaring sun, the blackout curtains had been drawn. I fished around for a second for the key card in my purse, and dropped the damned thing on the floor. I gingerly made my way into the dark room holding onto the wall. I felt the bed and threw my bag down onto it. I had to open the drapes to find the card wherever it had fallen.

Something was wrong. My bag didn't seem to land on the bed. It made a weird sound like it had landed on something else.

Then I heard a faint, almost imperceptible breath that took my own breath away. Someone was there!

Then a whisper. One word, *that* voice: "Russo." I fell to my knees.

19

In the dark, he gripped me in both of his arms and lifted me—
forced me—back onto the bed as I struggled to break free.

He sat down next to me in the darkened room, still holding me
tightly by one wrist. I didn't need any light to see, to know, it was
him. Not Father Paulo.

With what little strength I had left, I turned toward him and with
my free hand, smacked his face as hard as I could. He released me
but did nothing to resist.

I attacked, punching his chest over and over until I was nearly
spent. I flew off the bed, trying to scratch his eyes out. I felt a patch
over one of them.

"Bastard!" I screamed, clawing at him for all I was worth. "Get
out! You have no place here. Get out!" I was screaming like what I
was, a wounded animal whose fury had been kept in check until
this moment. I felt for the table lamp and picked it up to hit him
with it, even though he still wasn't resisting.

What he did do, though, was to grab onto the lamp and we struggled with it, tumbling to the floor. I heard the bulb break. He rolled away from me and stood up.

I threw the lamp toward where I thought his head would be. Take his other freaking eye out if I could.

Instead it crashed against the wall. In seconds, security was pounding on the door. I rolled off the floor and ran to the door in the dark, throwing it open, the light from the hall pouring in. The hotel guards had their rifles at the ready. This *was* Israel, after all.

"He's right there, officers!" I said, spinning around and seeing him for the first time in the half-light. My heart leapt. Still.

He calmly walked over to them as I stood in the doorway, but he easily pushed ahead, blocking my way. He spoke softly, showed them some kind of identification. I knew they could see me—see how he was holding me against my will—but their faces changed from stern to panicky as they quickly backed out of the door, acting like they'd just had an encounter with God. And God was *pissed*.

What the hell? The door shut behind them, once again throwing us into the pitch black. They had left me alone with him!

He reached around and picked the room's key card off the floor and stuck the card in the slot, which turned on the overhead light. The ceiling had an energy-efficient bulb so it took a minute to brighten as though it were a slow opening shot of a movie. I assumed an offensive position, again ready to do battle, since no one was coming to my aid.

Then I got my first *good* look at him as the light brightened. His face was scarred, not like the last time I'd seen him when it was worn but clear, and yes, he definitely had an eye patch. He had grown a scruffy beard and wore a nondescript broadcloth shirt, khakis, and hiking boots. He was also packing heat.

We sized each other up, neither of us moving in closer for the kill.

Run? Fight? What?

I expected his expression to be furious. Instead, he grinned at me. Grinned. "You look like hell," he said, the gap showing between his teeth.

I was stunned. "What did you say?" was all I could come up with.

"I said, you look like hell."

"*I* look like hell?" I taunted, my voice rising. "Me? That's what you have to say? After all this time? Son of a bitch!"

"True," he answered, nodding his head. He was mocking me.

"And you," I said, "standing there with one eye, all scarred up. You look like Freddy Krueger and yet you have the fucking nerve to tell me I look like hell?"

He rubbed his face and hand. "Yes. You're right. And I think you just gave me a few more. Scars, I mean."

"Scars? Too bad you're not dead," I answered.

He looked at me very seriously. Was he going to go all sentimental on me or did I finally get to him? Instead, he laughed. Out loud. "I sort of thought the patch and scars gave me a manly, rugged look."

I lunged at him. "You think this is funny?" I growled. He grabbed both of my hands with just one of his while I tried to kick the life out of him again. And he just kept laughing. I went to knee him where it would hurt the most, and missed. I would have fallen on my ass if he hadn't been holding me against my will. Without meaning to, a guffaw escaped from me. *What?* My guffaw turned into a cackle, which turned into hysterical laughter; tears were pouring down my face. I simply couldn't stop laughing-crying.

I thought at first that the laughing might have taken him by surprise, because he let go of me. But then in the same motion, somehow, he grabbed me up in his arms and forced me in close and tight as I kept trying to break free. He stroked my hair, which was stuck to my head, wet with sweat. The laughing had stopped at least.

I tore my face from where it had been crushed against his chest, and shot a quick look at him, my grimy face streaked with sweat and tears. I tried to catch my breath.

He took my face in his hands and forced me to look at him as I struggled not to.

"I love you, Russo," he said.

"I hate you, Pantera," I answered.

20

How could this be? How could Yusef Pantera be alive? I had *seen* him die. Or thought I had anyway. Neither his name, nor any of the aliases (that I had learned about in our brief time together anyway) had been on the lists of survivors of the Manoppello earthquake. It was chaos, sure, and the whole Abruzzo region had been hit hard, but still.

I had managed to make it out of that cave and back down the mountain after the earthquake and finally to the Red Cross hospital tent, and had searched row after row of cots with survivors. Pantera was not there.

I went back to the rubble of the Volto Santo church and tried to crawl through the burnt-out wing where we'd been when he'd been "killed." It was hopeless and the authorities soon forced me off. It was in ruins. What the earthquake hadn't destroyed, the fire had. It was nothing but a charred mess of stone, wood, and stained glass.

It had been an exercise in futility in any case, because I had seen him get shot and I saw the flaming wall crumple on top of him.

Yes, I had seen it all, yet here he was and I didn't now know whether to be relieved or remain furious.

I just couldn't ever forgive him. What had sent me into a rage and was still infuriating me was why, if he had been alive all this time, had he not come to me when our baby was born?

It was his life's work to know everything connected with the Demiel ben Yusef incident. I was certainly a huge part of that. No, he hadn't been able to keep them from executing Demiel but he *could* have been with me when his own son was born.

I realized then that he had known not just about Terry, but about everything else as well. Being able to have the information that no one else had is what had kept him alive while living both way outside and deep inside the law.

I couldn't comprehend how Yusef, who had raised Demiel, a cloned baby, *as* his own child hadn't come to me when Terry was born. Terry *was* his own. Not a child made in a laboratory. Terry was Yusef Pantera's flesh-and-blood son made the old-fashioned way. But when the baby was born, Pantera was nowhere to be found.

Then it hit me: Did he think Terry wasn't *his*? Dear God. But in truth, whether he believed Terry was or was not his, like a fool, I had really believed that what we'd had together, however brief, transcended everything.

Shut your brain off, you sound weak, I told myself.

But I couldn't. I *knew* there was no way that one stupid slip-up of a night with Donald my ex could have resulted in a baby when all our years together as Mr. & Mrs. hadn't. That's why Terry *had* to be Pantera's son.

Stop doubting what you know instinctively. At least now you can stop romanticizing the days that led up to that night you had together.

Did he know Terry was his? Or did he show up now because millions were involved? Was this why he was here now and didn't reach out when Terry was born?

As if reading my thoughts, Yusef "the Panther" Pantera, still holding me close, said, "I'm here now."

"But why are you here? Why?" I yelled. "Did you smell the cash from halfway around the world?"

He didn't look surprised, so clearly he knew what I was talking about. He knew I had something worth big bucks. "I don't care about the money. I have what I need."

"Well, how convenient for you then to show up just now, when you haven't been in touch all this time. Even when my son was born." I wouldn't give him the satisfaction of saying, "when *our* son was born."

"I couldn't come then," he said. "It was for your sake. *Your* safety. And the boy's."

"Please. You sound like a two-dollar self-published fanzine. '*I couldn't come to you, my dear beloved!*'" I said, waving my hands theatrically. "But you could come when money's involved even though you don't need any. Am I doing good so far?"

"Quite horribly, actually. Totally off the mark." *Snob. Asshole.*

Then it hit me: Paulo. Pantera was here and it seemed like a reasonably good guess that it had been Paulo's body in the street.

"Did you murder Father Paulo to get a piece of the action?"

"No."

"You know—and more importantly *I* know—that he would never have shared anything with you. Is he dead?" I asked.

"Yes, Paulo was murdered in the street but it wasn't me."

This made two elderly men dead who had been involved with this Gospel—Judas' Gospel—within hours of each other. And the only human connection had been me. Back to reporter mode: Pantera had killed before in his so-called line of work for this mysterious "Headquarters" outfit, so killing an old enemy would be no big deal.

"Bullshit," I said. "You killed an old man in cold blood. Or was that two?"

"Absolutely not. I don't know about any other man, but Paulo was not murdered by me, nor did it have anything to do with me or anyone I am associated with. I was supposed to meet Paulo here," he continued. "I should have tailed him but I didn't. He was killed by someone who wants to get their hands on what you've got."

"I don't believe you."

"I know you don't. But that's why I gained access to your room. I had to make sure it was safe."

"It? I'm an 'it' to you?"

He looked heavenward, as though he had the nerve to be exasperated. "Has there ever been any other human being who is such a pain in my ass as you?" he said. He didn't wait for an answer and continued, "I meant the *room*—'it'—as in 'the room,'" he finished, throwing his hands up in frustration.

"You're spreading around such horseshit you're stinking *it* up—the room I mean," I answered, going into the bathroom to wash my face and hands—anything to get him out of my sight.

He knew better than to try to follow me. "Paulo called me—despite our differences," he said over the running water. "He knew I'd only come out of hiding for you. Old snake that he was. He also said he knew I'd have the contacts to find anything—and any*body*. Of course he went no further."

"Are you saying he was afraid of being killed for what I have access to?" I called, sticking my head out of the bathroom.

"I am saying that he was concerned about that possibility, yes," he answered. "So despite our deep disgust for one another—Paulo's and mine—he put your friend's relic, or the possibility of getting his hands on it, above his own safety. He also knew I'd put *your* safety above anything. That's what was supposed to have brought us together, made the peace between us after all these years."

I let it sink in that Paulo was really dead, that he'd been brutally murdered on the street like a sewer rat. I ignored his telling me how my safety was his main concern. No time for that bullshit. Main question: Was Pantera lying? Did his so-called "Headquarters" bosses order the hit on the old man?

In short, I wasn't buying what Pantera was selling.

"Sorry but no go, bro," I said. "I don't believe you."

"No? Well, what about this?" he answered. "The pressing problem right now is that Paulo's assassin must have taken what Paulo was delivering to you."

"What was he taking to me, Vatican cash? A down payment? What?"

"No, he said he had, and I quote, 'the other key.'"

I came out of the bathroom wiping my face and hands on a towel. *Damn! Father Paulo did have the other key after all!*

What now? The old priest, who had been very connected to the pope, was my link to selling Roy's relic, I thought.

"But I believe he didn't have it—not in hand, at any rate."

I wanted to gauge Pantera's reaction, and said, "In any case, the relic isn't mine. It belongs to a friend. I was just . . ."

Pantera broke in, watching *me* now for a reaction. "Your friend Roy, you mean. The one who's been indicted for the Gilgo Beach prostitute serial murders."

I turned around, pretending I needed to put the towel away, refusing to let him see the surprise on my face. *This one continually confounds and surprises me, even though I should be used to it by now.*

"How am *I* doing so far?" Pantera said when I came back out of the bathroom again. He was rubbing one of the scars on his face and stopped the second I caught him.

"Yes, that Roy," I answered, "but that proves nothing. You could easily have found my column on the subject online."

"Father Paulo told me he was dealing for you."

"That's correct," I said stiffly. "And now he's dead."

"But," Pantera answered, "first he had to get the brass tube opened—the one that has the missing pages of the Gospel of Judas, no?"

I was taken aback. "He told you that?"

"No, he didn't tell me. Suffice it to say I knew."

"Fuck that story. You're dealing with a reporter here, not some schmuck who found a Picasso in her attic and is taking it to *Antiques Road Show,* for Christ's sake. How do you know?"

"Paulo told me just so much, and I figured out the rest on my own. It wasn't hard. Once I knew about the Citibank branch."

"Jesus, no pun intended. I'm dealing with two scammers here. Or only one now."

"Despite it all . . . Paulo and I were teammates *once,* on the—"

I cut him off. "Yes, the so-called 'great experiment.' And you ended up as enemies. Did you two bring me here under false pretenses?" I demanded. "I promised I'd get the money. I smuggled an artifact into Israel with the express intention of negotiating a deal and that the pope himself would keep it safe!" I made that part up, but it's what I would have demanded. With proof.

"And worse, I left my baby son back home with some neighbors," I seethed, picking up the TV remote control to throw at him. "Bastard!"

"Whoa. Calm down," he said, remaining perfectly calm. "I—we—didn't bring you here under false pretenses, I swear," he said, grabbing my hand in what seemed like a microsecond to keep me from throwing it.

"Let me go!" I said, struggling to get out of his grip.

"I will . . . *if* you let me explain." So I nodded reluctantly, rubbing my hand as though he'd injured me, even though he hadn't. Somehow he knew how to do that without actually causing any marks.

"Alessandra," he said, as though he had the right to address me like a friend. "Those pages in your possession are very, *very* dangerous. That's why they are locked up in a tube. They cannot be released to just anybody."

"I know *that*. Do you still take me for an innocent? And you? *You're* not just anybody, I take it?"

He looked at me, or at least his eye without the patch looked at me, mocking. I couldn't help but to think, *Well, yes, now that you mention it, you aren't just anybody, you are the father of my child.*

"Keeping it in your apartment was so . . ."

Son of a bitch! Had I told Father Paulo? I couldn't remember. Either Pantera was telling the truth and he'd been in touch with Paulo as he said, or he'd tortured the story out of him before he killed him.

"As soon as I knew—although I couldn't believe—where you'd kept the pages, I knew I had to get them out of there."

"*You* had to get them out of there? Then why didn't you come and get them instead of making me travel halfway around the freaking world?"

"Would you have just handed them over to me of all people?" he said.

"No. Never," I answered.

Almost pleading, he then said, "Please understand that every second that you had them in your apartment, the baby was being harmed."

"What? What the *hell* are you talking about?"

"Had you not noticed anything different about Terry?" Pantera obviously knew enough not to use Terry's full name—after all, my baby had been named after him—although now that was something I regretted. Deeply.

I continued, "No, certainly not. There is and was nothing different about my son."

"No?"

Then I remembered. "Well, he did start speaking early . . ."

"At six months."

"Yes, he's very smart."

"And? Was it after the tube came into your apartment?"

I thought about it and in fact he hadn't started speaking *until* I put the tube in the box in his room for safekeeping! And then there was the freakish episode when he stood in my bedroom doorway.

What I said, though, was, "Well, he did put a few words together, too."

"And you didn't think this was odd?"

"I did. In fact, I phoned my mother in Africa and she kind of poo-pooed it as though I were a crazy, overly proud mom. Said it wasn't possible. And why am I telling any of this to *you*, anyway?" I shoved him away—he was entirely too close—and I plopped down hard on the bed.

"Let me ask you something," he said, sitting down next to me as though he'd been invited, so I stood again. "Can you rationally explain the temperature changes in your apartment?"

I steadied myself on the night table. "Yes. It did get very cold." I said almost to myself and then, aloud, "And you know that—how?" He, of course, said nothing, and even so I continued, intrigued. "The window kept opening even though they all have baby safety locks on them."

"That's why I had to get the tube as far away from the baby as expediently as possible. He's still an innocent, unformed child. He was totally vulnerable. Even through the metal."

"But was Terry harmed in any way?" I was sickened by the thought.

Yusef stood up next to me and I shrugged him off roughly. "No, he wasn't harmed, I don't believe," he said, "but then again, I wasn't there."

"No kidding! But I was."

"Anyway," he continued, "he would have been harmed had he been exposed much longer." Then, "Who did you say is staying with Terry while you're away?"

"Like you don't know?"

"Actually no."

"Well, my parents are. They've already landed."

"That's good. But you left yesterday . . ."

I started rubbing my face hard. "My neighbors. The Judsons. Nice, kind people. Lost a son and Terry is sort of like the grandson they never had." He stared at me.

"Don't you dare stare at me. You have nothing to do with me or my baby and how I raise him. Got it?"

I had almost said, "You haven't been there since he was born," but caught myself. I didn't want to go there—admit he was the father.

"I want to call them now anyway," I said and picked up my cell and dialed my apartment. It wasn't to appease *him,* really, it was to appease myself. Pantera's dead calm and subliminal distrust had made me nervous. I hated him, but he was the smartest human I'd ever met—and the best informed.

My own landline apartment voice mail picked up, so they hadn't gone back there. I dialed their apartment and after a few rings and then a click, Raylene picked up. "Hello?"

"Oh, hi, Raylene. It's Alessandra." I put it on speaker so he could hear the conversation.

"Yes. I know," she said somberly.

"You're home in your apartment. Is everything all right? Is Terry all right?"

"He's fine, dear, but we're getting ready for a stroll and Dane is already downstairs."

"Oh. Can I say hi to my little man?"

"Like I said, he's downstairs with Dane." No, she hadn't said that exactly. Then, "We're walking over to the Norwegian consulate."

"What? Why?"

"The Norwegian consulate? Why, they're having a breakfast for VIPs."

"And you're bringing a screaming baby?"

She seemed to get angry. "He doesn't scream. Not with me." *Jesus.*

"Well, Raylene, I'm calling to say my parents are on their way. Should be in my apartment within the hour."

"That's nice, dear. I'm sure Terry will be very happy to see them."

"Yes, of course."

Then as she was rushing to get off the phone, she added, "Has Terry ever seen them before? Oh, I'm sure he has and he'll be just fine."

"Yes, of course," I said defensively. *I leave my baby for one over-night with people I trust until my parents come rushing back from another continent to stay with him and suddenly I'm answering questions from an absentee dad and the granola crunchers like I'm the worst mother in the world?*

Raylene was clearly trying to hang up and sniped—yes, sniped!— "But really, like I said, Dane is waiting and so is the Norwegian ambassador. We'll speak later. Ta-ta!" I stared at the phone, very, very glad that my parents would be arriving very shortly to take Terry back into the family fold. Raylene was acting like he was not just her grandchild, but her child!

My mommy radar was pinging, but I wasn't panicking because my parents were on the way. Nothing terrible could happen in less than an hour. Could it?

We hung up and I smiled broadly but insincerely. "Like I said, he's doing great!" Pantera looked blank. "I hate when you have that idiotic blank face."

"What do you know of these people? Did you do a background check?"

"Excuse me? They're my neighbors. And very nice people." Then, in an attempt to wound him, I exaggerated, and said, "The man I'm dating, a councilman from Manhattan, has more than vouched for them. He's known them for years."

"Well, that's reassuring. Who wouldn't trust the word of an elected official," he swiped back.

"This from the mouth of a professional assassin."

"Yes, you're right. A mass-murdering killer for God, and whoever else gets in my way," he mocked.

"Probably, yes. You're here, and so you must have some idea of what the hell happens next. I've got the relic. Somebody else has the means to open it. And we don't know who because it died with Father Paulo."

"I have a pretty good idea who he may have been dealing with," he answered.

"The Vatican," I said.

"But as the buyers, not as the ones holding the key. That's another story. Holding the pages is dangerous, finding and taking the key is dangerous. Terrible things started happening to your friend when he became the relic's owner, and now it's in your possession."

I didn't want to say what I thought: that my harm would come through Terry. Instead I asked: "Do you know—since you were assigned to the so-called 'great experiment' by Headquarters, whatever the hell that is—what powers these pages have, exactly?"

He didn't say anything.

"Talk to me, Pantera!"

"I will, but now is not the time. I swear it's not the time. We really need to move quickly."

"Well, first I'm locking it up," I said, taking the tube out of my bag and heading toward the wall safe. "I really need a shower to wake up and, well, I'm locking it up . . ."

"Oh for God's sake, Russo. You think I'm going to steal it?"

"You are capable of everything," I said and slammed the bathroom door, as though he couldn't pick a hotel room wall safe.

Once inside, I let the water run as hard and as hot as it would get and stripped down. *How could Pantera be alive? I saw him die! Sort of. And why did he abandon his baby and me?* Was he a monster? Was the man in my hotel room whose face bore the scars of— maybe Manoppello, maybe something else—really the man I'd been pining for for so long? Now Paulo and Engles were dead, too. Who was this person? I knelt down next to the tub and sobbed. Who could I trust? *Trust no one.*

Just then the door opened and Pantera walked into the bathroom. He picked up a washcloth and took my hands from my face and gently washed my face where I'd already abraded it.

I was completely confused. I shook my head to clear it, tried to push him away as tears ran down my face. No luck. Yusef held onto my arms, and said, neither harshly nor softly, "Russo, listen to me. You have five minutes to be hysterical, and then you have to pull yourself together. Yes, you need to take a shower, but first lukewarm," he said, adjusting the controls, "and then run it ice cold to get your circulation working. We have work to do . . ."

"You're telling me what to do? You?" It was like another resurrection of the dead. "I don't need *you* to tell me what to do, mister. I managed to bring the whole Demiel business—after you supposedly were killed—to a conclusion. Gave the cloth with Jesus' image to Demiel's mother. I managed to climb out of the rubble and escape the carnage and the earthquake. I looked for you for weeks, and when I couldn't find your body in the wreckage, I walked and hitched rides in army and relief trucks for hundreds miles back to Rome—while I was *pregnant*! I gave birth without a father to help and I've been raising my child on my own for six months. So, really? I don't need you to tell me what the hell to do. It's not about *you*. I'm not crying about you. OK? It's just that my best friend might end up in jail forever, and my other friend Paulo is laying in a giant puddle of blood on the street. I need a minute, OK? And I miss my baby, too."

Then he said what he shouldn't have said: "Our baby."

I glared at him. "Don't you dare go there. Terry is *my* boy. Not yours. Got it? Good."

So he knew for sure. He had never doubted it, I could feel it. *But then why . . .*

He cut off me off mid-thought. "You've used up three of your five minutes."

Right. I had to get moving. But what was I moving toward? In reality, I needed to get rid of this unholy thing—if it was as terrible as Pantera said it was—and never look upon it again. But how could we find the other key? Clearly baby Terry had started acting strangely immediately after I brought the pages into the apartment . . .

"Two minutes . . ."

"Do you know about what the pages—"

He cut me off. "One minute."

The man wasn't going to get deeper into it right then no matter how much I needed facts. He wasn't leaving me alone in the bathroom, either. Maybe he thought I'd try to overmoisturize or something.

"Get out," I said. "Maybe in France or wherever the hell you came from, strangers hang out in the shower together, but not here!" Then I remembered I was in Israel.

Who was he and what was I doing here with this dead man? In reality we were in many ways strangers, despite the days we had had together on the lam. Despite the fact that I thought we had this bond—sexual, spiritual, physical, impossibly magical—it wasn't as though I could have Googled him to find out the who, what, and where of him. He was more elusive than the steam that had fogged up the mirror and twice as hard to make out.

"Just want to make sure you don't climb out the window," he said as he exited the bathroom.

"I won't. And oh, Pantera? You can busy yourself while I'm showering by fucking off!"

"Just make sure you rinse off with cold water," was what he answered. "It'll break the jet lag."

"Get out."

He'd been right about the cold shower. Yes. I did feel better. But that didn't make him right about anything else. My resolve was returning. As I had learned the hard way, "trust no one" meant exactly that.

I slipped into my jeans, pulled on a fresh T-shirt, and walked back out. He was sitting at the desk, holding some kind of smart phone, a kind I'd never seen before (of course).

Who was this man whom I'd mythologized into a superhero? How does he even earn a living, where does he live—now that I know he lives, that is?

21

Yusuf Pantera is the kind of man who can make himself invisible, which is why, as I'd seen, he can be very deadly. You wouldn't notice him in a crowd unless he wanted you to notice him for whatever reason. He was several years older than me—in fact he was in his fifties—but in Olympic-athlete shape. Average height, thin but with a rock-hard body, close-cropped sandy hair with a bit of gray, green eyes, (or eye, now it seemed), and a slightly off-kilter international accent. *Asshole.*

I walked over and saw that he had a map up on the screen. Not a regular map, but an ancient-looking map.

Without looking up he said, "Those numbers: 31.780231° N, 35.233991° E? It's code, I think."

"You went through my bag and found the note?" I asked, exasperated at his sheer nerve.

"You told me to get busy . . ."

"No, what I told you to do was to go fuck yourself."

"I thought that meant go into your bag and look for things."

"You are such a pain in my ass," I said, grabbing back the paper Father Elias had shoved into my bag and looking at it as though I understood the code.

"I think I can find out what it means. Trust me."

I walked away. "Trust no one, Pantera. You're the one who drilled that into my head once—or am I mistaken?"

"Did I say that?"

"You did and yet somehow I still I trusted you. I trusted that you were dead, for starters!"

"Not to be redundant," he answered calmly. I noticed that his slight, vaguely European accent was resurfacing. "But just this once, forget what you thought and trust what I'm telling you."

"I can't. I can't trust anyone with my friend's life hanging in the balance. With Paulo murdered. Not them, not you, not anyone." Why was I feeling now like I also shouldn't have trusted the Judsons? *Shut up,* I told myself. *Your parents are probably in front of your building right now, getting their luggage out of the cab. God knows what they brought the baby from Africa. Probably a book on obscure African dialects if I know them.*

"So tell me the truth, Pantera. Or get the hell out. Those are the options."

Ignoring me, he simply said without any affectation, "I saw you had some decent sports sandals in your bag. That's good. We've got a walk ahead."

"A walk? Where?"

"Here," he said, pointing to the map. "Right here."

"Where are we going?"

"Put on your Teva sandals, please."

"Not until you explain . . ." I said, refusing to put them on.

"Put your shoes on," he said. "And I promise we'll talk on the way, OK?"

"I give you something, you give me something. Isn't that how it works?"

"Do you want to get the money and free your friend from jail and pay off his expensive lawyer or not? More importantly, do you want this evil thing in the right hands and out of your life—out of the baby's life—or not?" A cold chill went down my spine. He wasn't bullshitting. Not that he ever did—except maybe always, such as when he pretended to be dead.

I said nothing. "The sooner we do this thing, the sooner you get back to our"—he hesitated—"your son." As much as I tried to stay stoic, my heart melted a bit. Pantera always knew how to touch me in a way no one else could. I always just knew that Pantera was Terry's father—and now here he was. I had decided when he was born that I would never have a DNA test to definitively determine whether Pantera or Donald—the only two men I'd ever loved and both of whom I now knew would remain in my life forever—was Terry's biological father. Pantera suddenly showing up, though, gave me cause to doubt. The cold, hard fact was that Donald never disappeared. He'd always stayed close by. And I thought Donald was the biggest bad boy I'd ever known. Ha!

OK, enough! Snap out of it. You are his mother and that's all that counts. You've got something in your possession that can cause terrible harm to everyone who comes into contact with it and maybe the whole world. Your friend is in prison, possibly for life, for crimes he certainly didn't commit. Focus.

So, grabbing my sturdy sandals out of my bag and slipping them on, I said, "You're sure about all this?" I meant the pages, not the biology of my son.

"I am."

"Are you doing this for the benefit of the buyer, the Vatican, or who exactly?" I asked.

"For you," was his answer. This man who was by design virtually indistinguishable in a crowd was in reality the most distinguishably unique and complex man I'd ever known—and as a reporter I've known more than my fair share of complex, famous, infamous, off-the-wall, let alone off-the-beaten-track humans, and even nonhumans. I guess that's why after hating the guy, I ended up falling hard for him back then.

"It's complicated. And illegal."

"Who are you also doing this for then?" I demanded. "I won't be duped again by you. Who is it for?"

"I need to make sure the thing can never harm you or the baby," he said. "And yes, your friend will profit handsomely."

"And you? You won't?" I asked sternly.

"I'm not the issue here," he answered, heading toward the door. "Roy will get his money. And more. Trust me."

I just shot him a look that said: "Seriously?"

Pantera asked me to wait—and not run off—and twenty minutes later he was back, knocking like a human being this time. He walked in wearing a yarmulke, an official Israeli guide badge with the name Avi Schulman on his jacket pocket, sunglasses, and his eye patch. "You look very Moshe Dayan." I chuckled.

He must have been told that many times but all he said was, "Ready?" I nodded. "OK, you need to put your passport in the wall safe," he said, handing me a false one, which ID'd me, complete with photo, as Maryellen O'Connor.

"For security."

"Nobody can get away with these things nowadays," I said, shaking my head. Again he just looked blank. "Anyway, what's the problem? You think we'll be robbed by Hasidic gypsies looking to steal my identity?"

I saw he was carrying a gun in a shoulder holster under his jacket.

"Anything's possible," he said, one-up snarking me in that superior way only he could.

He handed me a plastic bag. "You need to put these on."

I looked inside. It was a Yankees baseball hat, terrible sunglasses, and a pin-on ponytail.

"Hello?"

"I want you to look like a clueless tourist, not like a hot reporter with a stolen relic."

Don't even think about what he just said. Who cares if he thinks you're hotter than Emily Ratajkowski? Well, he never said that.

"Oy vey," I said instead, and he smiled at me like he meant it. I wasn't in any mood to smile back. "A fake ponytail? Seriously?"

"You have a relic worth ten million dollars. Someone's already been murdered and another is sitting in jail. Just put the wig on, *please.*"

"Then put the freaking gun away, *please,*" I mocked him as I pulled my hair back and pinned the ponytail on, slipping it through the back of the cap. "The last thing Avi Schulman and I need is to end up in jail on a weapons charge."

He opened the door. It was useless to argue.

"Wait. Let me try my parents one more time before we leave."

"Use this," he said, handing me his satellite phone.

"Why?" I asked. "I bought a package."

"It's safer. You need to keep yours off. Period."

Dad picked up after a few rings "Dad, it's me."

"Ali! Hi, honey! Didn't know it was you. Came up as 'unknown caller.' Anyway, we're just coming out of the Midtown Tunnel. Should be at your place in ten minutes tops. Can't wait to see the little fella. How are things there?"

"Complicated, Dad, complicated. I just wanted to make sure everything was on track. My keys are with security and I've left a page of instructions for Terry on the table."

"Ali, I think Mom knows how to take care of a baby." We both laughed.

"Daddy? Just call me when Terry comes back. He's off with my neighbors at a brunch. OK?"

"Sure bet." We hung up. I would feel a thousand times better once Terry was back in the arms of the Russos. I would tell them to get rid of that terrible Voynich Manuscript, too. Perhaps Mr. Engles had been right to warn me to burn the damned thing. I didn't want any of that ugly, filthy, evil stuff around Terry ever again.

Pantera was waiting impatiently. "I asked you to put the gun away," I said, fighting again for the upper hand. Of course, he completely ignored me. Where was he supposed to put it? In the plastic bag? Instead he opened the door and stood there until I followed him out.

Here we go again!

22

We walked through a lower-level exit, bypassing the front desk, thank God. Who knows what the hell they must have thought, what with security having been sent up, then as quickly sent away from my room not five minutes after I had checked in.

We began to walk. I was once again reminded of how Jerusalem is like no other city in the world: ancient, modern, the sacred site of three different religions, home of endless warring and countless deaths because of those three different religions.

Pantera knew his way around—*what a shock*—as he did every-where it seemed. We passed the entrance to something called the LOWER COURT OF ISRAEL with its massive security, and then another called UNDERGROUND PRISONS, which weirdly enough was a new building. We turned and found ourselves on a huge shopping street. Old buildings, new merchandise, and then a modern street, no cars but with a sleek twenty-first-century rail train running down the middle. Jewelry stores, outdoor cafés. My stomach was beginning to growl—out loud—so when we turned onto Heleni HaMalka, Pantera plopped me down on a chair, walked into The Coffee Bean (yes, they have one there, too), and brought me out a double espresso with plenty of sugar and two croissants. I guess he remembered how I could chow down.

"Just wait here a second," he said and walked down a few doors to a bar called the Voice of Free Jerusalem, of all things, and came back out and walked into a tailor shop you'd never notice if you didn't know the city. Thank God he didn't go into the tattoo and piercing joint as well.

The Coffee Bean was full of Hasidim, hipsters, and fashionistas in equal number. I felt like I was in Williamsburg, Brooklyn.

He came back as I finished off the second croissant, not even embarrassed that I could eat like I had two stomachs. Was it the fact that I was back together with Terry's presumed dad or was it just that I was nearing starvation—as usual?

I got up and we started walking on Heleni HaMalka once more, this time on a narrow sidewalk until we came to the Russian Compound. Again, he stopped and he spoke to someone who must have been waiting for him because he handed him a slip of paper. We proceeded on, passing the huge Russian Orthodox church. Everything religious was bigger here.

"Why are we walking instead of driving or taking a cab?"

"You really need to stop questioning every single thing."

"No. I'm a reporter."

We walked on, and he stopped to point out the Mount of Olives in the distance.

"Who cares?" I said. "This is not a real guided tour."

"For the purposes of those who are most probably watching us, it is."

"Right. OK, then," I said, going along with it. "So that's where Judas did—or did not—betray Jesus. The Garden of Gethsemane," I said, pronouncing it "Geth-sem-a-nee." He started to smirk.

"What?"

"Gest-ta-meen, is how you say it," he said, putting in all the Hebrew guttural sounds. Or at least that's what it sounded like.

"Sorry. I don't speak Hebrew," I said sarcastically. Then, "Let me guess, you do."

"Not well."

"Pantera? Shut up in every language. Anyway, now that I've read the published version of what's left of *The Gospel of Judas,* I'm not so sure which version of the betrayal is even true. Nor do I care. What I care about is that selling the missing pages can get Roy sprung, and it will get the thing out of my life."

"I can foresee a battle ahead," he said. "The pages rightfully belong to Egypt—although Israel will lay claim to them and so will the Vatican. It's kind of like trying to sell a stolen masterpiece from the Louvre. Make no mistake, though, the bastards who killed Paulo are only interested in the information on those pages, not just the dollar value of them alone." Then he stopped dead. "Alessandra . . ."

I stopped him. "I know what you're about to say. Those pages may contain the most important, most dangerous information imaginable. It's vital that it's put into the right hands."

He looked out at the view, not at me. "Correct. But unless they are destroyed and unless you are no longer associated, then you and the baby are not safe."

"But how do we do that? Where the hell is that other key?"

He started pointing out monuments as though he was a real

guide. "Neither of you can be exposed to it any longer. The temperature changes you experienced are usually followed by—well, some people start speaking in tongues. Some we believe have had visions. Some see the past, some the future."

I asked, "We? Who is 'we'?" He, of course, didn't answer.

"All right then," I said, also pointing to things like a tourist. "But clearly a baby can't even speak, let alone speak in tongues, but Terry had started speaking—at a crazy pace—as soon as I came into possession of that goddamned tube. And there was an inexplicable cold that would fill my apartment . . ."

Panic rising, I tried to say as calmly as possible, "But he's safe now that it's out of there?"

"He—baby Pantera—is safer spiritually, at least, with the pages out of there than he was with them in your home."

"Terry! His name is Terry. So don't ever call him Pantera again."

"Jesus, sorry, he was named after me."

"Not as sorry as I am."

He started walking, as though he hadn't just taken a shot to the gut.

I decided I had to bring the temperature back down a few hundred degrees. Only this man could make me behave this irrationally.

"So," I started, "you don't have to be brought up to speed on the Gospel? Or why or how in hell it ended up in a bank vault in my old hometown of Hicksville, Long Island?"

"It's a well-known story," he answered vaguely. I decided to believe him because, well, it had been written about—including the bank, and Morris Golden's name was easy enough to trace back.

Anyway, whatever transpired in the Garden of Gest-ta-meen," I said, making fun of his pronunciation, "is key, I think. Which reminds me . . ." I reached into my bag and hauled out the ancient key with the modern glitter glued to it.

"What the hell is that?" he asked.

"It's a key on a chain . . ."

"I know that."

"I don't know what it's for, but I had to decorate it," I answered, brushing loose glitter off my hands. We were passing behind the Jerusalem police headquarters with its high barbed wire, unmarked white cars, and guard booth. I was surprised he didn't stop to pick up something from an Israeli secret agent or someone here, too.

"You should be imprisoned for that alone," he said, looking at the key. I let it pass. He obviously did need to be brought up to speed on some things.

We kept rushing along and he said, "You have no idea what it is, but you felt the need nonetheless to decorate it with *briller*?"

"Does that mean 'glitter'?"

"I guess."

"Jesus. You are such a pretentious ass."

"No, I just don't do arts and crafts in my spare time. I haven't done any gluing since *cours élémentaire* in France."

"Like I said, such a pretentious ass." Despite the horror of what we were living through, without any preamble—Paulo's and possibly Mr. Engles' murders, the knock-down, drag-out, call-the-cops hotel room battle—we had fallen into the same smart-ass repartee as we had before we fell into each other's arms last year. Was it *only* last year that we had made wild, unbridled, insanely passionate love in Carcassonne? After I lost him I couldn't imagine feeling like I wanted anyone to touch me ever again. Now that included him. Mostly him.

"Enough sweet talk," he said, managing to be sarcastic without any nastiness to his tone. Damned French. Or whatever the hell he was. "Where did you get this key and why did you bring it with you? I won't even ask you why you saw the necessity to decorate it, if that's what you insist on calling the disgraceful mess you've performed on this antique."

"We're passing another prison," I said. "Watch your ass. Maybe it fits the keyhole to a cell. This country has more prisons than people."

"It's actually called the Russian women's hostel," he said, "so you should be the one watching your ass. I speak Russian." We dropped all conversation about the key, and for spite I made a big gesture of putting the chain with the key around my neck. When he didn't react, I hung it inside my shirt. No sense attracting attention by looking like a *brillered* horse's ass.

"Oh, Jesus. Let's just stop talking, sweet and otherwise." We turned left and passed a huge number of gray stone government buildings and apartments. Hard to imagine that these currently peaceful streets so often erupted in such tremendous violence. Yet amid the stone edifices there were lovely personal gardens and flowers. We passed the *mikvah* for handicapped women, an anonymous-looking building amid the ancient ones, and some other modern buildings with solar boilers and panels on top. I couldn't help but notice how many buildings had plaques dedicated to people killed in terrorist attacks.

He paused and rubbed his chin, and said, "OK, there are two options to approach the Damascus Gate. My instinct says to go right into the new gate—opened after the war to allow Christians to enter."

So we did, passing first the Notre Dame of Jerusalem with huge figures of Mary and the baby Jesus atop. We waited for the Jerusalem

Light Rail train to pass, crossed the street, and entered the gate he suggested into the Christian Quarter. Immediately, the hipsters and the Hasidim disappeared and Franciscans miraculously took their place. O! Jerusalem!

"Are they following us?" I asked, looking around.

"Perhaps . . . and don't do that! Look around like that."

It was a noisy, ugly area with a high school and a lot of parked cars on impossibly narrow, cobbled streets. We passed an old mission building; a million cheesy dying-Jesus-on-the-cross souvenir shops; cafés without the requisite charm; priests of all stripes on cell phones; graffiti on walls; small alleys with too many, too-loud Motorinos speeding past; tobacco shops; and yes, more crucified-Jesus souvenir shops. We climbed down a lot of stairs and through open tunnels that led back onto more tiny, covered streets, which got darker the farther in we went. I was glad that he hadn't listened to me about carrying his pistol. I'd been in one gunfight with this guy and I was glad he was on my side—as much as I hated him.

We walked into archway number nine, written, he told me, in Aramaic and Greek. It was a deserted, stone-covered arched alley, narrow and dark. An old, banged-up homeless man, covered in a woven, tattered blanket sat on the ground, his head down, his hand out. I was thinking it was such an odd place for someone to try to collect money, seeing how it was so dark and not heavily trafficked, when at that same second, Pantera grabbed my hand and shoved me roughly behind him. In that same split second the old man jumped up quick as an Olympian with knife drawn.

A fast look at his face told me he was not old, and not banged up. He was not as tall as Pantera, maybe five nine, but every bit as wiry. *"Den chreiázetai kan na to skeftó, Sas kátharma!"* Pantera snapped.

The man stepped back, put the knife down, and broke into a grin.

"*Gios tou vrómiko skylí!*"

"*Éna lyssalées vrómiko skylí ennoeíte!*" Pantera replied. *Dear Jesus.* What the hell was going on?

"*Pírate to mínyma mou í den tha ton gýro sto drómo sas gios enós vrómiko skylí?*"

"*Nai, vévaia, allá den boreíte na eíste pára polý prosektikoí.*"

He turned to me. "The man's an idiot. I tell, you a real idiot," and then back to the man, "*Poú boró na vro ta Korsikís?*"

"Good! But first we drink, my friend," the man said, inexplicably breaking into perfectly good English.

"*Tin epómeni forá, pal,*" Pantera answered.

Then he turned to me and said, not in a stage whisper, but out loud, "That's all he can say in English. The sonofabitch can probably say 'first we drink' in sixteen languages, but can't say 'it's on me,' in even one."

The man threw off his dirty shawl to reveal his outfit-of-contradictions underneath: a cheap, short, gray suit; pricey linen shirt; and very expensive shoes. Vuittons were my guess. He needed a shave but had a very good haircut. My reporter's curiosity was on fire. *What the hell and who the hell?*

The man reached into his lapel pocket and took out a slip of paper. Pantera went to take it. The man pulled it back.

"*Prota na kouvediasoume to kerma!*"

"*Iisoús Christós. O gios tis leípei, ase me mai afta ta skata!*" Then to me—I was tugging on his sleeve to find out what they were saying—"Baksheesh. We're arguing about baksheesh," he said disgustedly. "I saved his sorry ass once, and I'm not talking about when Greece went broke, either, but he doesn't give a crap." Pantera reached into a pocket and pulled out a gold coin. The man grinned. "Yeah, I'm glad you're happy, you thieving bastard," Pantera spat out.

The man handed him the paper. "Now we drink, my friend!"

"Go fuck yourself, my friend," he answered back, shaking his hand nonetheless. As we walked back out of the alley, he repeated, "Bastard . . ."

"But my friend . . ." the beggar in the Vuitton shoes called after him.

"What was that about?" I implored, grabbing onto his sleeve.

"Nothing."

"Something."

"Jesus, Russo," he answered. "I asked him a couple of things, he told me a couple of things. I gave him what he wanted and he told me what I wanted to know."

"What did you want to know and what did he want for whatever he gave you?" Now I wanted to know, too.

"He wanted a gold coin. I wanted information."

"What gold coin? What information?"

"He has been trying for years to get his hands on a Roman Emperor Maxentius gold medallion. OK? Does that mean anything to you? No? Shocker." We kept walking.

"Such a shit. Yes, I know who Maxentius was," I lied. "Why the beggar getup?"

"He's eccentric," he lied.

I let it drop, knowing I'd get nowhere fast. Instead I asked, "So . . . what's it worth, that coin?"

"One eight, maybe two."

"Two—what? You mean two hundred *thousand*? That's not baksheesh, that's a fortune!" I continued without waiting for an answer. "You just gave a slob in a bad suit lying in an alley a medallion worth two hundred K that we could have used as bail?"

"No."

"What do you mean, 'no'?"

"No, I gave him a coin worth two million."

23

I stopped short. "You just gave up something worth two million for . . . for . . . information?" I sputtered.

"I said, maybe two million. Maybe one eight."

"What. Is. Wrong. With. You?"

"Wrong with me? Hmm. Nothing that I know of. OK, my eye is not what it used to be and these scars make me not quite as attractive as I once was, I realize, but all in all, I'm in good shape. I have a resting heart rate of forty-five . . ."

"Is this a joke to you?"

He didn't like that. "Listen, Russo," he said sharply, almost raising his voice, but not quite. "Nothing about this is a joke. But I know what I am doing. It's not my first time at the rodeo, as you Americans like to say."

"No, we Americans do not like to say that."

He cut the banter off and gripped my arm until it smarted, although to an observer it would look like he was just a guide steering a tourist in the right direction, again pointing out nothing.

"I don't see anybody looking at us. I'm a reporter, remember?"

"You never let me forget it, remember? And they are watching us. Especially after that transaction."

"Jesus. You are not easy. Why the hell I ever got involved . . ."

"I do. Remember why, I mean." He shrugged and laughed. Then, "OK, first we go to this address," he said as though he hadn't just had a laugh, all business again. "The thing I thought was code? They're coordinates." Then, tapping his pocket, where he'd put the piece of paper for which he'd exchanged the two-million-dollar coin. So far we'd accomplished nothing. I had to stifle my frustration because frankly there was nobody to guide me *but* this man—who was pretending to be a guide.

The Christian Quarter, when it's not full of rapturous tourists, is a nasty-looking place, all ancient narrow stone streets and dark alleys. You won't find the kind of lively exchanges here—not on weekdays and out of season, or we didn't, anyway—that you find in the Jewish and Muslim Quarters. Its stone walls are drab, with mold, some littered with graffiti. The other quarters, even though dark, crowded, loud, and scary as they could be to a foreigner, had somehow, I remembered, always felt nicer than these somewhat-deserted alleyways. But the circumstances were much different now, of course.

We walked down a few steps and everything lightened up. We were entering the fancier Christian tourist attraction area, the Via Dolorosa, where Jesus had carried the cross. Apparently Jesus wasn't the only one to carry crosses around here, because out of nowhere, to the right, a youngish, bearded man dressed as Jesus was also carrying a full-sized one. Not exactly Jesus of Nazareth, more like

Jesus of Newark. From the opposite direction, a group of German tourists heading our way were doing the same. However, unlike Jesus of Newark, these German tourists and their escorts—two monks—were dressed in ridiculous shorts, complete with cameras around their necks and rosary beads around their waists. Worse, they were chanting "Hosanna" while carrying their giant cross though the streets. I briefly wondered if these crosses were rented out by the hour and returned to docking stations. The Citi Bikes of religion. So bizarre.

Since we had come from the direction we had (which didn't house any rent-a-cross shops), we arrived first at Station Eight, the Eighth Station of the Cross. Pantera touched the wall. "These are the actual marks that used to be outside the gate," he said. He ran his fingers around the stone cross carved out of the wall and said what sounded like, "Icy, ecky, nikita," then, "Nike—victory."

"Like the shoes?"

"Nike, the goddess of victory."

I always vaguely assumed somewhere in my brain that "Nike" was a Japanese word, like *konnichiwa* or Yamaha, or something.

He continued, "When Nike began infiltrating the Muslim market here they stupidly put the name 'Allah' on their shoes. Can you imagine? It would be like trainers for Jesus," he said, using the British term for sneakers.

"Right," I said.

"Anyway," he continued, "when we enter the Arab Quarter don't go trying to buy a pair of Nike knockoffs."

"You're showing off."

"Correct."

"Enough with the show-off talk. You need to come clean with me."

"About?"

I stopped walking. "About your real involvement in this whole thing. I know Paulo brought you out of hiding or whatever you call it, but now Paulo's dead. I don't trust that you had nothing to do with that, but I've no choice right now. I don't think you'd cheat me out of a dime. I think I know that about you, at least. I even get the part about you saying it was because the baby and I were in danger. But are you ultimately here because of that mysterious 'Headquarters' agency or whatever it is that you belong to? Are you on assignment?"

He hadn't stopped walking, so I had to catch up to him, the bastard. "The key to unlocking these pages from the Gospel of Judas is here. But it's held by very dangerous people. People who killed Paulo. As for your friend being charged with multiple murders?"

"Paulo?"

"Don't know."

"They need the keys *and* the pages?"

He didn't reply.

"What's your involvement—*really*?" I asked.

We were facing each other with swirls of bustling locals and tourists passing all around us, but suddenly it was as if we were alone.

"Are you asking me if I'm here because I'm part of the scheme? Or blindly following orders on an assignment?"

"I am."

"You're missing a third element," he said, turning away from me. "That I've willingly been lured out of hiding."

"Or were you part of *my* being lured here?"

"No."

"Just no?"

"Just no."

"You are really maddening."

"It's one way to make a living . . ." he joked, clearly trying to get me off the subject.

Since I knew he wouldn't go any deeper into any of it, I changed the subject and started walking again.

"I don't know if you know this," I said, "since I didn't tell you, but I have a small ruby earring. It opens one lock on the tube."

"Yes, I know." Paulo must have told him. *Paulo had clearly trusted him, but then again Paulo was now dead.*

I pushed. "And maybe my glitter key has something to do with it?"

"Don't know. But I do know that Morris Golden came to Jerusalem for an extended stay in 1982. Stayed for a month. His wife came two weeks into his visit. Stayed at the King David in a big suite. Not the kind of trip your average suburban bank manager gets to take very often."

The area we turned into was immediately livelier, the shops more crowded. "And you know this—how?"

"There's such a thing as the Internet these days. Ever heard of it?"

"That's not where you got your info. And by the way? Where the hell are we going?" I demanded.

He didn't react, only nodded, and kept on walking as though I hadn't asked. I had no choice but to catch up to him as he passed stall after outdoor stall filled with colorful jeweled scarves, electronic gizmos, small household goods, and antiques. Finally he stopped and I was so busy looking around that I crashed right into him.

I realized then where it was we had stopped and why it was we had stopped: we had come to the place along the Via Dolorosa that had changed both of our lives forever just last year: the Sixth Station of the Cross.

Carved into the stone wall were the words: 6 ST/PIA VERONICA FACIEM CHRISTI LINTEO DETERCI. My Latin wasn't great, even back in high school when it was supposed to be, but I could interpret that it meant: "Sixth Station, where Veronica rubbed the face of Christ on linen." It probably was more profound in Latin. What it meant to him and to me in any language, though, was profound beyond words. It was my turn to touch the words, the carved cross, the wall.

We didn't have to say anything. After all, without the Veil of Veronica—that piece of ancient linen cloth celebrated on this wall—Demiel ben Yusef, the second coming of Jesus Himself, could never have happened. If that hadn't happened, I would never have met Yusef Pantera and Terry would never have been conceived.

"Ready to move?" he asked, pulling back to look at me.

"Yes, I'm ready." I touched the wall again, and did something that no agnostic in my family had ever done: I made the sign of the cross.

24

We passed a restaurant with the ungodly name of Holy Rock Cafe. "You should eat," he said.

"I don't need to eat, don't want to eat, and I'd rather eat my own shoes than eat somewhere called the Holy Rock Cafe. Whadda they have? Cheeses of Nazareth Burgers?"

"Yes. And Salome on rye," he snapped back. OK, I'll grant you, he could be quick. I still hated him. "But I wouldn't eat there, either. But here's the place," he said. "Hummus Lina, best hummus in Jerusalem."

"Is this necessary? I mean, why are we stopping?"

"Because you need to eat. I can't have a partner who faints!"

"I'm not your partner and I won't faint for Christ's sake! I ate two croissants, remember?"

He shook his head and forced me inside and onto a chrome chair at a small table. Immediately a man came from behind the counter, wiping his hands on his apron. He had a big grin on his face and hugged Pantera.

"My friend!"

Another friend. How many "my friends" does this guy have?

"What can I get for you and your pretty lady?" he said, sounding more Greek than Israeli. Another bullshitter, I thought. I was anything but pretty at this point. I was sure the fake ponytail must have been hanging off the hat by now.

Pantera got up and walked to the counter and was back in a flash with a large bottle of chilled water and a big plate of spreads. There was hummus—the center scooped out and filled with olive oil— taramasalata, red pepper salad, Israeli salad, falafel, and hot crusty sesame-seeded bread.

"Dig in."

"Well, maybe just the tiniest of bites." I didn't want to, but once I started, I couldn't stop, lapping up the spreads with the bread and not coming up for air. I realized Pantera was laughing at me.

"What?"

"Nothing. I'm glad you're eating."

"No one has ever uttered those words to me before in my life. Even when I was a kid and didn't want to eat my vegetables—and my mother's a pediatrician!"

"My friend" brought out something made with cheese, semolina, pistachio, and honey. Even though I couldn't, I did.

We got up and started walking again, although I now felt like I was seventeen months pregnant. The area abruptly changed. We had entered the Muslim section.

Immediately there were butcher shops with whole carcasses hanging up, fresh-caught fish, and thousands upon thousands of stalls with every kind of garment imaginable from burqas to yoga pants.

The women were either in burqas or modest clothing with head scarves, while most of the men were in regular western garb. Arabic music was pumping out of various stalls and everyone seemed to be hawking everything at once. Normally, I love walking the souks of the world finding crazy, exotic things that too often turn out to be stupid knockoffs. But now, the sights, the din, the insanity of women with nothing but eye slits sitting on the ground selling vegetables was sensory overload.

We stopped and he told me to stand aside while he spoke to someone at a stall. We continued on and reached an arched stairway with several dozen steps that led to another street, at the front of which was a small house covered in colorful paintings.

"It means the occupant is a Muslim who completed the hajj."

"Meaning they've been to Mecca?" I asked.

"Actually, it means they walked around the Kaaba in Mecca. A Muslim must circumambulate the Kaaba, the most sacred site in Islam, seven times, in a counterclockwise direction."

Like I cared at that point if the person had walked around the moon, but my reporter self couldn't help but ask, "Why seven?"

"Muslims believe—like all other religions—in the metaphysical world. They believe it is made up of seven layers, or spheres. The universe we live in is the first . . . all sacred numbers. But then again, this also relates to what Jesus related to Judas. Sacred numbers are the secret codes in all religions."

"I'm sorry I asked. Enough comparative religion for one day," I sniped without understanding how important sacred numbers were about to become to us. "It's a meteorite inside, that much I know." Pantera shrugged.

Then he knocked on the door, which opened a crack. A few words were exchanged in Arabic and we continued on our way—to where, I couldn't imagine.

"What was that about?" I asked.

"It was nothing."

"It was something."

"No. Listen, the less I discuss with you about what I do, the less information they can nail you on," he said, taking my arm.

"*Sí*, Don Pantera."

He grinned and kept walking, turning around to say, "You are such a wiseass."

"Yes. Granted," I wise-assed back, aping him with, "it's not as exciting as being an international man of mystery, I know, but it's a living."

We approached something called the Prison of Christ, and he stopped. It was in an old, kind of banged-up Greek building. Very unprepossessing.

"The coordinates 31.780231° N, 35.233991° E? Right here."

"Here?" I wondered.

"There has to be something here. What it is, I don't know."

"I can't even imagine, but I'm pretty fair at puzzles . . ."

"Well, the sooner we figure this out, the sooner you'll be back with your boy." Since he did nothing without first having thought it through, I noted how he was sticking strictly to the more civilized "your" now.

"Ready?"

"Sure," I said and I followed him down the old flight of stairs. The stairwell was narrow, dark, and nasty. The sides were sooty, the spaces between the ancient blocks of stone crudely filled in with black paint. One of the stones had rough, hand-painted lettering in both Greek (he said) and English, reading, PRISON OF CHRIST. Above the entrance to the stairwell was just a single painted icon of Jesus.

"Can you imagine a place of such significance being so open?"

"Not if the Vatican controlled it, that's for sure," he said.

This was the prison where the Greeks believe Jesus had been held prior to the crucifixion, although it had never been proven. St. Peter's Basilica, on the other hand, merely held the tomb of St. Peter and it was worth billions and guarded as closely as the White House. This was probably because this prison was Greek Orthodox territory. If it wasn't Greek, the Catholic Church would have gilded it in gold and turned it into a giant basilica/cash cow a long, long time ago.

The prison's stark, unremarkable, unmolested, uncommercialized appearance reminded me of the House of the Virgin Mary near Ephesus, Turkey. These were two of the most important sacred sites in all of Christendom, yet each remained untouched and unclaimed by the Church.

A single bulb illuminated the cave-like hole of a prison hewn out of the rock. We were completely alone. It was a tiny space, the ceiling barely taller than a man's head. Pantera took a flashlight out of his jacket and shone it into the darkest areas. "The lucky few got to sleep in those," he said, shining the light onto a few rectangular, trunk-sized holes cut into the rock.

There were also, every few feet along the rough cave walls, "handles" carved out of the stone, but they seemed to be handles that held nothing. "What are they?" I asked. I wished I hadn't asked.

"That's where the others, who weren't so lucky, got to live—attached to the wall. The prisoners were lashed to the walls on those with their arms up."

"How long did they stay like that?" I asked, alarmed.

"Until they were tried, found guilty, and crucified . . . or died from starvation, thirst, dysentery, and don't ask."

I imagined what this place had been like two thousand years earlier. Dank, dark, covered in feces, blood, vomit, and urine. The stuff of life, the end products of death. *Why do these handle things remind me of something? What?*

He shone his flashlight around the walls and you could practically hear the screams. I was getting light-headed from the lack of air and the tightness of the area. The spirits of the tortured dead haunted this place; you could feel it on your skin, banging in your brain, pounding inside your heart.

To think that this was where Jesus might have spent his last night on Earth was almost as incomprehensible as the crucifixion itself. How many thousands of people had ended their lives in this terrible dungeon below the earth, chained to the walls, beaten, screaming, dying?

I didn't imagine it could still happen. I was wrong.

I had a little penlight attached to my key ring that I always kept as part of my life as a diligent New Yorker. I shone it up to the ceiling and was shocked by what I saw. "What the hell is that? Idiots have graffiti'd the ceiling! Look," I added, moving the light around. "That part looks like ancient graffiti, though . . ." I pointed to carved ancient lettering on the ceiling. "Is that possible?"

"It certainly does," he said. "Aramaic, by the looks of it."

"The chains of our Lord did not bind Him!" I said excitedly. "The secret is above where He hung below! Could that be what Roy's father's note meant?"

He didn't answer and ran his fingers on the scribbles carved out.

"I assumed it meant the crucifixion," I added, pointing, "but damn! Can it mean that He was one of the ones who was chained right here and that the secret is up there?"

Pantera knitted his brow, still without saying anything.

"No? Yes? Hello? Is that why the coordinates led here?"

He began mouthing some words—he seemed to be interpreting the words or whatever they were—and then without preamble (as in no warning, zero, zilch), he grabbed me and kissed me hard on the mouth.

25

I would have told him to back the hell off, but, well, I didn't. It wasn't because I would ever want him to kiss me like that ever again, absolutely positively most definitely not. For sure. Really. No, *non, nyet*. I didn't tell him to back off because, well, this guy gave out compliments approximately once every lifetime, and I'd just been the recipient of his entire lifetime's quota. That's the only reason I didn't shove him away. And of course, we were in a sacred place. And I really believed that was why. At the time, anyway.

Pantera let me go. He whistled and let out a quiet, "Holy shit!"

Well, maybe not so sacred. "What?"

"This graffiti?" he said. "It's Aramaic all right, but a very ancient, rare form of Aramaic."

"Yes, and . . . ?"

He took out his bizarre-looking smart phone and started photographing the ceiling.

"Isn't it too dark in here to get a clear shot?" I asked.

He showed me one photo. It was as clear as if *National Geographic* had sent one of their top shooters to capture the images.

"Remember I told you about sacred numbers?" he said, looking from the photos to the ceiling.

"Yes."

"There," he said pointing, "is the number thirteen, and right next to it, there? That says, 'Judas'!"

"What? Are you kidding me?"

"Clear as day, 'Judas'!"

"Was Judas here?"

"No. Maybe it's the writing of Jesus Himself, or one of His followers who may also have been held here. Look at this," he said, flashing his light on the ceiling.

"Those scratchings?"

"This says, 'Fear not losing what you find.'" Then, "Here, look, seven spices and this looks like a bird of some kind."

"And what is that one next to it?"

"It's hardly visible. Something about the word of 'Tetragrammaton' being rotted, or rot, or rotten."

"Who?"

"Tetragrammaton," he answered. "Transliteration of Hebrew name of God or Yahweh. But I'm not really sure about the 'rot' part since it's scratched over and worn."

"An early atheist or disbeliever? Sounds like Judas himself. Couldn't have been the scrawling of Jesus, then."

"Not necessarily. Remember, Jesus was a very angry man. He wasn't the lamb-petting, New Agey, love-is-all-you-need being he's been mythologized into."

"What about turn the other cheek?" I challenged like any good reporter.

"Remember, please," he lectured as though five seconds ago he hadn't kissed me passionately, "the stories in the Bible, like other histories of the time, were not actual history for the most part."

"You sure know how to seduce a girl." I laughed.

"Is that what I was doing?" he said, the haughty French bastard.

"You bet. Or you're trying your best, at least," I, the haughtier American, snarked back.

He continued, unfazed. "You're probably right." He laughed. Then, "In those days, history merely meant storytelling mixed with the truth. History is 'his story.'"

"Similar to news nowadays," I answered.

"You said it, not me." He grinned. "But at least everyone back then knew these were stories, not truth—stories that have gotten twisted with time. For instance, many believe Jesus was referring to only other Jews when He said to turn the other cheek. In fact, He says in Matthew, 'Do not think that I have come to bring peace on Earth. I have not come to bring peace, but the sword.' And in Luke: 'And if you don't have a sword, sell your cloak and buy one!' Does that sound like a pacifist to you?"

"No, it sounds like you!" I sure couldn't argue Gospel with the man who'd been part of the team that had actually once cloned Jesus from the cloth that bears His image: il Volto Santo.

"But this," he said, shining the light on the spices and something next to them, "these are Egyptian hieroglyphs. Very curious. Very, very curious."

As we were studying them my cell rang, and I nearly tore my bag apart trying to get to it. Finally, word from home.

"I told you to keep your damned phone off," Pantera seethed. "For Christ's sake!" I ignored him completely.

"Hi, honey." Mom.

"Mom! Hi. Everything OK?"

"I can hardly hear you," she yelled.

"I'm in ah, a prison. Let me go back outside." I could hear her demanding to know why I was in prison and thinking I might have scared the bejesus out of her. So to speak.

Pantera followed, but I signaled him that it was my parents. I didn't want him to hear my conversation and said, "Hey, go grab us a falafel or something."

He laughed and shook his head at me. "I'll grab us a water," he said and pointed to a coffee shop.

"Can the water, grab me a double espresso."

"Right. Be careful, I'll just be a minute," he said as I nodded off-handedly, gesturing that I'd meet him right at the top of the stairs.

I found a spot where I could hear Mom clearly. She had put her phone on speaker. I could hear my dad moving things around in the background.

"What are you doing in prison?" she asked, not as panicked as I feared, since I'd interviewed everyone from Mafia dons to pacifist nuns in jails around the world.

"*I'm* not in prison," I assured her. "Visiting an ancient one is all."

"You're sightseeing?" she asked, surprised.

"No, part of the trail. More importantly, how's Terry?"

"Everything's fine, dear. I mean, I assume it is. We're in your apartment, but Terry and your neighbors aren't back yet. Which apartment did you say they live in?"

"They're in F right down the hall."

"Oh, that's what I told Dad and he went down the hall and knocked on their door but they're not there, either."

"I thought I told you they were taking Terry to some Norwegian thing at the U.N. or something. Should have been back by now for sure, though," I said, a slight panic beginning to bubble up inside. "I left Dane's cell phone number—he's the husband—on the pad on the kitchen counter. Not that he knows how to use his phone."

"They took a baby to the United Nations?"

People walking by the crowded ancient street took no notice of me because they were all on their own phones or staring into them or staring down at rosary beads. Even so, I was watching for anyone/anything that even hinted of suspicion.

"They want to show him off to their fancy friends, I guess," I explained to Mom.

"I guess," she repeated rather suspiciously.

"Please call me the minute they're back."

"Will do. We're dying to see Terry. By the way, are you alone in Israel?"

"Not exactly. I met an acquaintance who's helping me with the story."

"That sounds mysterious. A man?" she asked hopefully, wanting me to get back to real life and stop pining over "that goddamned, irresponsible adventurer," as she'd called Pantera even though she'd never even met him.

"Yes, a *man*," I joked, exaggerating the "man" part.

"A man-man or a work man?"

"Both."

"Oh boy."

I've always had a hard time lying to my mother. For one thing she has supersonic mom telepathy and could always tell when I was lying.

I figured I'd just get it over with. "See, the thing is, Mom? That man—the one I told you about who I thought was dead?"

"Not that goddamned, irresponsible adventurer?" She yelled so loudly half of Jerusalem could hear her through my phone. "The one you insist is *my* grandson's father?"

"Yes, that one. The goddamned, irresponsible adventurer–slash–your grandson's alleged father. He's not as dead as I thought."

I could hear the disgust before the explosion. "Run like your ass is on fire, Alessandra," she exclaimed. I could feel her blood pressure rising on the other side of the world. "He's trouble! Big, big . . ."

"Don't I know it."

"Well." She sniffed. "Then why are you thousands of miles away with him?" She didn't wait for an answer. "I suppose you know what the hell you're doing—*not*. You always pick the bad boys. You know if the creep has shown up now, when you're onto something huge, that he's only after the reward money for that relic."

"I've got my suspicions, yes."

"Don't sleep with him!"

"Jesus, Mom, can't you put a lid on it?"

"Of course not," she answered. "Wait. Dad wants to talk to you."

Dad was used to Mom's outbursts and ignored it, just saying, "Hi, Ali. So, I think I'll walk over to the Norwegian embassy and pick Terry up instead of waiting around."

"OK, Dad, but you don't have to . . ." I knew they'd had a long flight and he must be exhausted, especially since he'd had that bout of *tourista,* but I was also glad he'd offered. The sooner Terry was with Mr. & Dr. Grandparents, the better I'd feel.

"I insist. He *is* my grandson," he tried to joke. "I don't want any damned old fools teaching him otherwise." It came out more like a concern than a joke.

Mom got back on. "Men," she said, as though that explained away all the problems in the world.

We hung up with her assuring me that she'd call the second Terry was home.

Even though I had no reason to be concerned—not really— something was nagging at me. I tried to shake it off. Perhaps my father's unease had made *me* unnecessarily uneasy, too.

As I turned, I spotted a Greek Orthodox monk in a brown robe heading toward the prison. *Damn. Closing time. We need a few more minutes down there,* I thought. *I shouldn't have asked for a coffee.*

I went to check the hours-of-operation sign at the top of the stairs, but as I read: 5:00 P.M. DAILY, I felt a gun shoved into the back of my neck. "Move," the monk said, and forced me back down the dark stairs, locking the gate behind him.

26

The monk shoved me hard and I fell on the stone steps, nearly tumbling down the whole flight. He yanked me to my feet by my jacket, and with the gun now against my temple, locked the door behind us.

He shoved me against the wall and ordered in broken English, "Put your hands up, bitch!" I did so, trying to figure out my options, if any.

With his free hand, he shackled me onto the carved-out stone handles that had shackled thousands of prisoners in the time of Christ. He turned over my bag and rifled through it, then dumped everything out onto the floor. Nothing of interest.

"Where are the pages?" he demanded.

"I don't have them. Not with me."

"Here's the deal then, lady," he said in an accent that I couldn't recognize, but that sounded vaguely Spanish. "Two men have already died. Hand over the pages or the killings continue."

"I don't have the pages," I insisted, struggling against the shackles.

"We begin with your son."

"What do you know of my son?" I cried out, panic growing.

"I know you want him alive more than you want to hold on to the resurrection pages," he said, waving the gun around.

"How can I get the pages to you if you kill me?"

"You tell me where they are, and if they are where you say they are, we won't kill your son, and you might get to live, too. If you don't or if you lie . . ."

"How do I know you won't kill me as soon as I tell you where the pages are?"

He pointed the gun at me and shot. I could feel the bullet whiz by my head.

The prison was sealed, so you could probably set off a bomb in there and it wouldn't have been heard from the outside. "I can get closer, Ms. Russo. It's up to you. One bit of you at a time . . ." I instinctively turned my head toward the wall as another shot rang out. Again, I felt it whiz by but didn't feel it hit me. Then another, which shot out the lightbulb, and then another. I felt blood splatter all over my face. *Was this what it felt like to die? No pain?*

I heard a thump and then a cry of pain. *Had it come from me? How could it? I'm handcuffed to the wall.*

I felt myself being unshackled and lifted up and over a man's shoulder.

"It's me. It's OK," he said.

"Pantera?" I asked, the pitch black obscuring everything.

He placed me gently on the steps. I could hear him hoisting the shooter and I heard groans and cries and the sound of metal scraping the wall.

He came back, and I heard him say, "Are you all right? Have you been shot?"

"I don't know. I don't think so . . ."

He lifted me again and carried me up the stairs and unlocked the door, and then locked it again behind us. As soon as we emerged into the fading sunlight, religious people hurrying by, he felt my body up and down for wounds.

He put his fingers to the side of my head. "Your hair will grow back, and you've got a nasty black eye looming," Pantera said as I touched my head where I'd felt the bullet whiz by. "But you'll be OK."

"What?"

"We need to get the fuck out of here. Now."

"He said he'd kill my son . . ." I cried out, grabbing his shirt.

"Now he can't."

"How did you get in there? It was locked!"

"You didn't think I paid two eight just for information, did you?" he asked, not expecting an answer, shoving the key back into an inside jacket pocket.

"But when they . . . whoever . . . don't hear from him . . ."

He just grabbed my hand and hurried me out of there. We ran into a tailor shop that somehow had a hidden stairway inside that led us to the other side of the Old City and through the gate.

"I need to call home," I insisted.

"Use this," he said, handing me his satellite phone. "I took the chip out of your phone. You can't be trusted," he said. "That's how we were tracked here."

"It wasn't my fault!" I argued against reason.

Using his phone, I called my dad's cell and he picked up. "Dad, it's me!"

"Almost at the Norwegian embassy now, Ali."

"Dad, listen to me carefully. There's a chance that some very bad people are after Roy's relic. And Daddy? Those bad people are on to my whereabouts—and I'm panicked that they know Terry's as well."

He started to ask a million questions, and I asked him to just listen, as time was precious. "Go get Terry. Tell the Judsons not to walk home with you, as the thieves may in fact have a bead on the Judsons as well. Don't panic when the cops show up. I'm calling now."

"Dear God, Ali . . ."

I cut him off. "Dad, please hurry. You can't call me back. I'll call you. Please hurry."

Next call was to Donald. I gave him a quick rundown and he said he'd have his cop friends on it immediately.

"They'll surround the fucking embassy if they have to. Don't worry, Larry used to work security over there."

"Now I'm really worried. How could any country trust that fool?" I said. "And Donald? Any word on Roy?"

"Yeah, and it ain't good. Don't ask."

"What?" Of course I asked.

"I said, don't ask. You can't do anything from Israel, and he's got Mad Dog on the case."

"OK, but call Bob Brandt. Let him know I've got this situation and have him call the damned police commissioner if he has to."

"On it."

I next tried the Judsons, even though I knew Dane wouldn't ever answer a phone. No answer.

I turned to Pantera. "I'll feel better in a half hour from now when the baby's home with my parents, and Donald's got the cops on it."

"Yes, you will," he lied, and then before asking me for the fake passport, he sent out a text, which he also wouldn't discuss. He then stopped next to a motorcycle, which had been parked on that other side of the gate, and hopped on. It had a plaque written in both Hebrew and English reading: ALL-ISRAEL TOURING COMPANY ל ישרא כל נסיעות תברח

He handed me a helmet with ל ישרא כל נסיעות תברח emblazoned on it, as well as a Star of David for good measure.

"Get on."

"The last thing I want to do is weave in and out on the back of this thing with Snake Plissken," I said, referring to Kurt Russell's character in *Escape from New York.*

"It's temporary," he said, pointing to the patch. "Or so the doctors say."

"I'm happy for you," I retaliated, meaning no such thing, hands on my hips, feet planted firmly on terra firma. "You're like a circus danger act, riding a bike in traffic with one eye!"

"Jesus Christ," he said, really pissed off now. "Get on the goddamned bike, Alessandra," he yelled above the roar, "so you can get home to our son."

I reluctantly climbed on, grabbed him around the waist, and screamed just as loudly over the din, "My son. He's *my* son!"

We sped out, me holding on for dear life, so I could get home to *my* son whose life I held so dear. The local streets, as expected, were very slow and packed with traffic at this hour. It was a Friday as well, and people were rushing to get home before sundown. The fact that everything would be closed for the Sabbath very shortly made it all the worse. The last thing we needed was to deal with a mostly shuttered city when time was of the essence, I told him.

He said it would work to our advantage. *Right.*

We were able to skirt around on the bike, cutting in and out illegally. When we made it onto route 424, the traffic was much better—mostly because we were heading into the desert and you could count the settlements and houses on one hand.

"Where are we going?" I screamed as we sped along.

"Like you'd know? We're headed to Karmei Yosef. It's near the Tel Gezer." He was right; I had no idea what he was talking about.

After an hour of endless nothing, punctuated by the occasional something, we entered an area with a sign reading TEL GEZER, which led into some kind of an upscale development in the desert. I'm referring to it as a development, but it's a development in the desert in the same way that say, Palm Springs, is a development in the desert. Most of us can't even begin to think about affording to live in such a desert.

We drove around the back where the houses were concentrated, across the dry, sandy, rocky soil that was freckled with wild cacti and sprinkled with lazy, feral cats.

Beautiful, tasteful houses—in the middle of some kind an archeological dig!

He steered the motorcyle down into a valley. It was completely dark now, and the dig, closed off to prying eyes, spies, and thieves, was shuttered for the day, or actually, shuttered until sundown on Saturday.

We pulled up behind one of the digs, Pantera turned off the bike, and we dismounted. There was just one guard posted in a uniform that looked vaguely military outside a tiny guard shack. He immediately started approaching.

"Walk with me," Pantera instructed as he took off his helmet, revealing his yarmulke. He opened his jacket and I saw he even had tzitzit hanging down (the white tassels worn by Orthodox Jewish men, which remind them to obey the commandments).

"Like hell I will," I answered. "That guy's carrying a machine gun!"

He just looked at me in that exasperated way he had down to a science, grabbed my hand, pulled me toward the guard, and spoke to him in Hebrew. The guard kept shaking his head and saying what in any language sounded like, "Get your asses out of here or I'll kill you with my large gun."

I tugged on Pantera's sleeve and he brushed me away. "Do you speak English?" I begged.

"Your client, she wants me to speak in English? Yes?" The guard mocked me in his heavy Israeli accent. "Yes, I can speak English and this is what I say: lady, you hired here a guide who doesn't know the rules, and he's wearing a yarmulke but wants to enter a site after sundown."

Pantera started to protest, but the guard cut him off. "And this part of the dig is not open to tourists in any case. The whole area is closed for thirty minutes already."

"But my friend," Pantera continued like a cheeseball in English with an astoundingly good, thick Israeli accent, "this lady came all the way from the United States. Here, let me show you." He reached into his pocket and pulled out my fake passport. "Look, look for yourself," he said, handing it to him. I gasped. It had a couple hundred shekels lying inside it.

The guard, taken off guard, literally, was aghast. "Is this a bribe?" he said, straightening up with indignation.

"No, no bribe, my friend," Pantera said, meaning, "Yes, yes bribe, my friend."

Pantera then reached into his inside jacket pocket like he was reaching for a gun, causing the guard to turn his gun on us. Pantera, in a move so quick and so smooth, neither of us saw it coming, kicked the guard in the throat. The poor schmuck fell, out cold on the hot, desert sand.

"They should have posted two guards," he said casually to me, reaching into his pocket once again, and this time pulling out a hypodermic needle, which he stuck into the unconscious man's thigh.

"Oh my God! Oh dear God! Did you just kill him, too? A man in the army, yet? What have you done?"

"No, I didn't kill him. He will wake up—tomorrow—with a helluva headache."

"He's in the Israeli army, for God's sake!"

"No, this one's not army, just a rent-a-guard. Grab his weapon, will you?"

"No, I will not steal a gun. And excuse me, but how stupid was that move—knocking the guy out? When he doesn't check in on schedule—just like that other one in the prison—they'll come looking!"

"No, it's Shabbat so they won't be calling him tonight. It's not like this is a military installation. It's just another one of fifty million digs going on in Israel all the time."

"And the other?"

"Who knows? My guess is the real monk in charge will figure that another monk locked up before him. Now, please, grab his damned weapon."

"No, I won't. What did you do to him?" I demanded.

"Brazilian jujitsu. Unexpected, no matter how well trained," he said, reaching for the weapon himself. "Not that this guy is trained well. He's not even Israeli-born. Or Jewish."

"And you know that—how?"

"Too dumb to be Israeli-trained. And real Jews don't work on Shabbat for nonessential, nondefense jobs."

"Maybe his shift was just ending!" I was looking every which way for cops to come barreling our way to kill us on the spot.

Pantera just pointed to his own watch. "Jee*sus,* Russo!"

"I want to call home. See if Terry's home with my folks yet."

"No can do. Even though this is an untraceable satellite phone, they managed to find us before. So it's off and staying that way."

"They . . ."

"They. The guys who killed Paulo, the guys who know about Terry, the ones who tracked us to prison. This will serve you better," he said. He handed me the guard's machine gun, grabbed a hard hat with a light on it that was sitting inside the small guard shack, and we walked right into the dig site.

The site was deserted, but there had clearly been plenty of activity earlier, which was centered about five hundred yards away. We walked over the dusty desert grounds and reached the area where the equipment had been left for safekeeping until work resumed after the Sabbath. There wasn't anything above ground, just the mouth to a hole in the ground with a wooden platform.

Pantera put the hard hat on, took the machine gun from me and strapped it on his back, stuffed his pistol into my backpack, and shone the hat's light down into the hole.

I could see the cave was more like a stone tunnel—something dug out by human hands—with uneven, primitive steps carved into it. Pantera descended, advising me to keep a lookout.

"Don't do anything foolish," he warned, looking back up at me as he started down.

Now it was my turn to look exasperated. He was the one going into a black hole after knocking out a guard, and he was telling me not to do anything foolish?

"I think you've taken care of that for both of us," I said as he reached the bottom step. I could see his shadow from the light as he looked around and then walked out of my line of vision.

Where did he go? What if the guard stirs? What if he wakes and calls the authorities? What if . . . ?

I was alternately looking back for the guard and looking down into the hole. I didn't know which was more anxiety-producing— expecting the guard or not seeing Pantera reemerging. I was perspiring so heavily that the sweat was rolling down into my eyes. I grabbed an old bandana out of my bag and tied it around my forehead. It also seemed to be getting hotter instead of the other way around as day progressed into evening.

After five minutes, I gave up waiting and tried calling in the softest voice possible, "Pantera! You there? Yusef, where are you?"

Nothing.

Should I climb down? Should I run away? Did he get hurt? Oh shit. Time is running out. This is the last thing I need!

"Pantera!" I called out again, this time somewhat more stridently. Nothing.

I began pacing and then covering up my tracks for no reason whatsoever. Why weren't any emergency lights or the dig's nighttime lights on? Suddenly I found myself standing in the blackness of the desert under the same stars where the ancients had stood contemplating heaven. Me? I was contemplating hell. Alone. And so I began a panicky personal argument with myself. Anything to keep from going mad.

Should I climb into the hole? Are you insane? Go down into a dig, a black hole, with the penlight attached to your key ring for light? No!

Yes. It's the only choice. He might be hurt. What do you care—you hate him—remember? Yes, but you're in the middle of the desert with a knocked-out guard.

There wasn't a choice. I switched on the penlight, should have grabbed a hard hat, but didn't. Immediately spotlights came on in the distance, around the guard shack. I switched the penlight off, realizing that it might have been too late and I might have alerted the authorities, so I began to climb down backward into the hole, step by slippery, uneven makeshift step.

The crunching under my feet belied the fact that the steps were incredibly slimy. What the hell? I slipped down two of the steps and barely caught myself. It wasn't like the archeological site exactly had a railing.

"Pantera! Where the hell are you?"

27

The hand-dug tunnel wasn't high enough to stand in, so I got down on all fours with the penlight in my mouth. I could see another light coming toward me, also at the same height.

I took the light out of my mouth. "Yusef!" I called out.

"Shh," came the reply. Has to be him! Only an arrogant ass like him would say that at a time like this.

As the crawling figure with a shining light approached, I could see it was. "Quickly! Follow me," he said.

"I may have alerted the authorities to our location when I turned on my penlight."

"Just follow me."

"I thought no one would check up on the guard on Shabbat."

"The lights come on automatically at a set time, I would think. So I wouldn't worry about them coming down here."

"No?"

"No."

I began to follow him, the walls of the tunnel closing in on me like a tomb. Then I understood why they really might not want to come searching in this tunnel. The sound began as flapping wings, followed by a high-pitched chirping like injured birds—or God, even mice—screaming in the tunnel.

The flapping, light at first, kept increasing in intensity until it became the deafening flailing of a million wings. The horrible chirping, too, magnified until it sounded like a giant ship being scraped against a metal pier. Neither sound was the kind I had heard when flocks of birds were flying overhead.

"There are birds in here? In a tunnel?" I whispered, trying to overcome a sudden feeling of revulsion.

"No." Then, "*Duck!*"

"Ducks?"

Out of the blackness, the flapping of wings and chirping engulfed us in sound, and then enveloped us in a horrifying, suffocating animal stench. Something brushed my face and I jumped, trying not to scream. It happened again, then again and again. My face, arms, legs, and torso were being slammed by wings and my ears by high-pitched squeals, while from above a bombardment of sticky globs hit my head, my face, my everywhere.

These aren't birds! I'm being hit with leather wings!

"What are they?" I screamed.

"Bat swarm! Duck down! Cover your face!"

I realized there were now hundreds of flying, screeching, swooping, swarming rodents, seeking to get out of the cave and into the night—all at once.

"What is dropping down on us?" I cried, trying frantically to get the horrible sticky stuff out of my eyes and nostrils.

"Guano! Stop talking, and keep your mouth closed," he warned. "Get down."

"Bat shit? Oh shit!"

I threw my body down flat right on top of the slippery, disgusting, guano-covered stone ground, and stuffed my hand in my mouth to keep from screaming.

Pantera crawled over and climbed on top of me, his entire body covering mine. He put his hands over my head as a shield. "Just bats. Just bats. Shhh. Just bats, let them pass . . ."

"Oh God! Oh God!"

"Bats . . . that's all. Israel is full of them. Nothing to be frightened of . . ." Maybe nothing for him, but I was terrified.

Even with Pantera on top of me, I began to heave, the bile splashing on the tunnel floor. How much worse could this get? Answer: Much. Perhaps it was better that I didn't know the horror yet to come.

I tried to catch my breath but as soon as I did, I gagged again.

"OK, OK, it's OK," he tried to soothe.

No, it was definitely *not* OK.

With the bats still swarming, brushing and splashing us, Pantera said, "I'm going to slide off of you now. Stay down. But we need to start moving forward when you can. I'll be right here. Just let me know when you can move."

"I can move. I *want* to move on . . . to wherever."

He crouched beside me. "You need answers. I know you need answers. All I can tell you is that . . . well, that information I was given by the ah, gold coin man, along with the key led us first to the Prison of Christ and consequently, here."

"What is this place?"

"A burial cave."

"What?"

"A mile-long burial tunnel. It leads to tombs."

"Tombs," I said, more of a statement than a question.

"Tombs from the time of Jesus."

He shone the light and I could see shelves cut into the rock. "In ancient Israel, tombs and catacombs were like homes for the dead," he said as I crawled on my belly. He was clearly trying to refocus this city girl. "Homes for the dead," he repeated, "as opposed to burial chambers. These areas held the body until it decomposed, and then the bones were stored in an ossuary—a bone box."

"Right, I've heard of that."

"The tombs were cut into the rock, like here," he said, shining his light onto what might have been a shelf cut into the rough rock wall. "They laid the bodies on these shelves until they decomposed."

I heaved again. And again. "Pretty."

When I got my rhythm back, I managed to sit up a bit and croak out, "Did that gold-coin guy tell you the other key was down *here*?"

"No, well, not exactly. What we have to do is crawl to the end."

"Then?"

"Then. Well, then we'll see. Can you crawl now?" he asked, handing me a flask from his backpack and offering me some water. "Here, clean your mouth out. Then sip. Not too much or too quickly. You're probably beginning to get dehydrated."

I rinsed, spat, and then took a sip of the cool, clean water. I've never even had a martini taste that wonderful. "Whew. Thanks. Yes, I think I'm good to go now."

He shone the light on my face. "Really, I'm OK." He wiped my face with his fingers, and then rubbed his hands on his pants.

I could see bat guano. I heaved again. He tried to take it out of my hair, but it was stuck and I yelped.

"Just leave it, just leave it!"

"Bats may be the least of it, unfortunately," he said. "There are reptiles and all kinds of things living down here."

"Oy. Let's go, please. Get this over with."

I got back up on all fours and began to crawl. A snake—or what seemed like a snake in the dark—passed over my hand and I jumped up so fast I hit my head. I touched my head, and yes, it was bleeding. "Shit! I'm an idiot!" I seethed under my breath.

We kept crawling. Rodents, maybe smelling the blood, came around and we batted them away although three were attached to my back. Bugs, spiders, and all manner of underground life *came* to life to feast upon us as we steadily crawled forward, the light on Pantera's hard hat guiding the way. Sort of.

After an hour, we came to the end of the tunnel. I was bitten, scratched, bleeding, and covered in bat shit. But there was the metaphoric light at the end of the tunnel: a door.

"What the hell?"

Pantera shone the light and illuminated an ancient wooden door with a huge handle. He tried it.

"Locked. I don't want to create any noise, but I have to open it." He reached for his gun.

"Wait!"

He looked at me curiously, and I reached inside my T-shirt and pulled out the giant glittered key on the key chain, and pointed it toward the keyhole.

"Maybe nuts, but try this before you go shooting your way in. And by the way, you are not *just* bat shit, but you're covered in it *too*."

He grinned. "You should see what you look like. A bat shit facial."

"You're a regular laugh riot." I slipped the chain off my neck, and with shaking hands, attempted to put the glittered key into the keyhole, but I couldn't get it in. I pulled it back and rubbed the glops of excess glue and glitter off and onto my jacket and tried again. Nothing. Then it hit me. I rubbed the key on my guano-covered pants and then smeared it all around the key and into the keyhole with my bare fingers—without retching this time.

The old key was so slippery I could hardly hold onto it, but it went into the lock more easily. I could hardly contain my excitement and joy—yes, joy—when I felt the equally old bolt budge a tiny bit inside the mechanism. "Aggh," I strained, "I think it's beginning to move."

Pantera reached to take over.

"Don't even think about it, bub. This one's all mine," I gritted, rubbing guano into the lock itself.

He stepped back and I kept straining until it began to turn micrometer by micrometer, finally clanging into place and disengaging the bolt. I pulled back, looked at my handiwork, and did a happy dance like a kid, guano falling out of my hair.

He just shook his head and grinned again, the space between his teeth showing even in the darkness.

"Never doubt the power of *briller* and guano!"

"*Briller* and guano." He laughed back, practically admitting defeat. "It could replace WD-40."

I tried, but couldn't help suppress a grin, too. He reached over and wiped more guano from the corner of my eye.

The small triumph of conquering the cave crawl, the bats, the vermin, and having the key open the door made us giddy. For a moment. And for a moment—just a moment—despite being in a tomb, covered in bat droppings, with a gash on my head and a patch of my hair singed off, I felt like I was deep into some great news story instead of being smack in the middle of a nightmare.

"Are you ready?"

"I'm ready," I answered. "I can't wait to get someplace where I can call home to make sure everything's OK."

He didn't look at me. Not good. Even so, I let him be the one to press down on the door handle's old metal lever, which he finally got to budge after being rusted shut for God knows how long. He pushed the door with his shoulder, but it wouldn't budge so he leaned his shoulder into it.

"Pardon me," he said, and reached into my hair and took out a glop of guano. "And wipe the smug look off your face," he said, pretending to threaten me with a handful of bat droppings.

"It's too dark to see if I have a smug look on my face."

"I can smell the smug," he joked.

"That's bat shit you smell. And by the way? You've got a frigging hard hat on, so your hair is probably clean."

"Jesus, no wonder your ex-husband wanted to leave you in war-torn Iraq."

"As a matter of fact, I'm the one who carried him home from there. On a stretcher in a cargo transport plane."

He pushed again. "Once more with feeling . . . move, dammit!"

"How about pulling it instead of pushing?" I said.

He glared at me and shoved hard. Nothing.

Reluctantly he pulled it inward, and I could hear the squeak, and the ancient, stuck-with-time door budged open a crack! *Ha!* A tiny shaft of light appeared on the side of the cave wall. As he was applying more guano to the hinges, without acknowledging my suggestion, I peered into the crack.

I turned to face him, astounded, then turned back and peered back in, to make sure of what I'd seen in the dim light. Astounding.

"What is it?" he asked. "What do you see in there?"

"Either a stairway to heaven, or Liberace lived here. I'm looking, I swear, at a glass staircase!"

28

———

Without uttering a word, Pantera came up behind me, his body almost touching mine, and I still felt an old stirring, dammit. He peered over my head into the crack in the doorway. I remembered then that he was more than a head taller than me.

"Perfect," he finally whispered almost in my ear.

"What?"

"Perfect." He took both of my hands and put them on the lower part of the massive door handle, which I gripped as he placed his own above mine. "Pull!"

We pulled and pulled again, as he popped on more guano to keep the creaking to a minimum. Finally the heavy door began to open millimeter by millimeter until there was just enough room for us to fit through. The shaft of light—dim as it was—illuminated the glass stairs and its elaborately braided banisters.

"Let's go. Hold on to my jacket and stay right behind me . . ."

I grabbed the back of his jacket while he grabbed onto a banister.

"Unbelievable. This thing's made of crystal, not ordinary glass." Then reaching down, he said "And so are the steps."

"Glass steps into a tomb? What the . . . ?"

"Or out of a tomb . . ."

"You don't think it leads to another tomb, one level higher? Maybe above for the nobility, servants below . . ."

"I sure as hell paid a king's ransom to get the location." Then to himself, "This better be right or that miserable bastard is counting down his last minutes on Earth."

Unlike almost everyone else on Earth that says things like that without meaning it, when Pantera said such a thing, he meant it. Literally. It *would,* I figured, actually *be* "my friend's" last days on Earth. I couldn't help but to compare them: Donald took shots with a camera, but this one preferred taking shots with a Glock.

We climbed the fifteen or so stairs, and saw that at the top there was a gold door built into the rough tunnel walls. "Shit. Not again!"

"Yes, again."

"How do we get in, and if we do, where in the hell does it lead to?"

Shining a light on the door, then around it, Pantera touched it and whispered, "Twenty-four karat—the entire thing." We could see that it was also engraved with images and hieroglyphs, so he took out a pen with a miniature camera and photographed the door from top to bottom.

"What's with the 1960s spy equipment?"

"Jesus Christ almighty, can you just stop being a reporter for a minute?"

"No. What's it say? What does it mean?"

"Not now."

"Yes, now. What's it say?"

"I disabled the alarm. OK?"

"How?"

"Didn't I just ask you to stop asking questions every second?"

"And didn't I just tell you I wouldn't?"

He pointed to a hieroglyph. "The same glyphs as in the prison. Seven spices and the bird."

He pushed his shoulder against the shimmering door, but it was locked solid.

"I thought you could figure codes out with that *Get Smart* spy pen." He ignored me.

There was no handle visible and no keyhole that I could see, so clearly my giant glitter key wasn't going to be much use opening this door.

"Think, think," he said to himself aloud, and I swear he actually was beginning to break a sweat.

"Were there any other numbers on that piece of paper the man sold you?" I asked, trying for any clue possible. "Maybe there's a code key built in somewhere."

"No, I felt all around for any kind of keypad. Nothing." He looked again at the paper. "Let me think. What am I missing?"

I interjected, "What about those coordinates? Could they be the combination here as well?"

"Could be . . ."

"Maybe like in the old movies, you have to say it aloud." He just looked at me like I was nuts. Ignoring him, I picked the note out of my bag, and looked at the coordinates: 31.780231° N, 35.233991° E. I whispered them.

The door did not swing open magically. In fact, it didn't even budge.

Pantera looked up at the ceiling one foot above our heads, exasperated. "There's got to be a way to open this door from this side. Has to be a way . . ."

"Maybe there's a remote somewhere . . ."

"Unlikely that they would keep such a thing around for any random person to pick up and use," he said, feeling all around the outer edges of the door.

"Like random people would crawl several miles through a bat swarm to look for a remote?"

"Depends what's on the other side. This staircase did lead here directly from a working archeological site. Remember?" Without waiting for an answer, he said, "Read me those numbers again—the coordinates—would you?"

I read him off the sequence.

He shone the light on his hard hat onto the door, and said, "Now one at time."

"Thirty-one."

"No, let me try three and one."

"Try what?"

"The symbols and numbers on these wheels—right here—are Egyptian."

"And by the way, what the hell is a gold Egyptian door doing in Israel?"

"Same as why in hell is there a crystal staircase here? Stolen artifacts."

"The stairwell looks a lot more Vegas than Sumerian to me."

He felt around and then touched two places on the door. We went through the entire sequence, him touching each symbol that corresponded, finally coming to the end of the numbers. Nothing.

"Oh wait," I said, "There's an *E* at the end. An *E*."

He found what must have been the equivalent or something and touched it. Nothing.

He shone the light over the entire door again. "It tells the story, oddly, of the Dog Star and the Dog-faced God."

"Well, that's hardly got anything to do with Judas," I said.

"Maybe," he said, feeling around the door. "The Egyptian calendar system was based on the rising of Sirius, the Dog Star, the brightest star in the sky, which happened each year just before the annual summer flooding of the Nile. That's where the expression 'the dog days of summer' comes from."

"And this is important right now—how?"

"The Greater Dog, Canis Major, was important to civilizations all over the globe, unbeknownst to one another. Ancient Greeks, Sumerians, Babylonians, and even a tribe, the Dogon, from what is now Mali, revered it. I believe it was even hinted at in the Judas Gospel."

"Really? And?"

"Here, look." He pointed to an inscribed drawing of a man with a dog's head. "It's the dog-faced god, Anubis, a jackal. Anubis was the Egyptian protector god of the dead. And he was connected to the star Sirius. Some believe that the gods came from Sirius.

"This star was also associated with the Egyptian god Osiris, whose parts were scattered, and his wife, Isis, resurrected him. Also a god of the dead and resurrection."

"This is what you paid for? A history lesson on a door?" I asked. Now it was my turn to be exasperated.

"This may be a door from the tomb of a nobleman or even a pharaoh honoring the star, Sirius."

"Right. You once told me you went to MIT and studied astrophysics. Think, for God's sake—what are we missing here?"

"I'm trying to figure it out, as you may have guessed," he said, annoyed and putting me behind him as he put his ear to the door.

"What the . . . ?"

"What is it?"

"Listen," he said as I, too, put my ear to the door to hear what the hell was going on on the other side. There was the sound of strange exotic music—live music, by the sound of it—and drumming, followed by high-pitched chanting, a flute, and the sound of rhythmically pounding feet.

"What the hell?"

"Hell is probably right," Pantera said, shaking his head at the sounds behind the door.

29

He took some kind of micro listening device from his bag and put his ear to it, exclaiming, "Excuse my French, but *c'est quoi ce bordel!*"

"You are the only man pretentious enough to say, 'Excuse my French' and then say something in French!"

He listened for a few more seconds, not giving me much.

"What?"

"Dogon."

"I beg your pardon? You mean, 'doggone'—as in, say, 'doggone right'?"

"I mean, didn't I just tell you about the civilizations that worshipped the star Sirius and the dog-faced god, Anubis?"

I nodded.

"Well, there is a tribe in Mali, curiously enough named Dogon—as in 'dog,' as I said."

"Or 'no god' if you spell it backward," I threw in.

"True," he said. "That's even more curious, actually. Because the Dogon did then and still do worship the star Sirius. They believe that about thirty-two hundred years ago a group of fishlike beings—Nommo—from Sirius visited them. These beings told them about the dwarf star orbiting Sirius, called Sirius B, which was invisible to the naked eye and wasn't even photographed until 1970!"

"Geez. That's too weird for words."

"It gets weirder. It's smaller than the planet Earth, yet one teaspoon of Sirius B is so dense that it weighs five tons."

"Remind me not to visit. I'd weigh five million tons there. And no pun intended, but seriously? What does that have to do with getting this door opened?"

I could see his exasperation with me even in the dim light. "It's a connection! The Dogon probably originated in Egypt. They knew things at the time of the Egyptians that weren't proven true until the 1970s, as I said. Even now it's impossible to explain how they knew some of these things without going into alien theories."

I broke in, "So it was discovered right around the time that the Gospel of Judas was discovered. And Judas hinted at another galaxy in his Gospel. But again . . . what does this have to do with the door . . . ?"

"The drums, the chanting," he answered without removing his listening device. "For sure the people on the other side of this door aren't celebrating Shabbat! It's Dogon."

"I won't ask how you know, but how in hell do you know . . ."

"I spent a year with the tribe . . . well, it doesn't matter."

"Of course you did and of course it doesn't. Whether they're praying to a cat-faced dog or a raccoon-legged fish—it won't matter if we can't open the door."

"I've got an idea," he said, reaching for his satellite phone in his backpack and punching something in. Yes, somehow his phone worked even down there.

"Here! Look at this," he said, holding out the phone.

I grabbed it from him. "I thought you shut it off. Liar! I'm calling home. I need to find out if my parents picked up Terry."

He grabbed it back. "I told you it's not safe."

I grabbed it back. "You're lying. Why don't you want me to call home?"

Trust no one. I started dialing.

He grabbed it back again. "It's offline. You can't dial out. You've got to trust me on this right now."

"But it's safe to surf the Web?"

"That's not what I'm doing. I swear on Terry's life."

"You don't care about Terry's life!" I shot back.

"I do," was his answer. Then, shoving the phone at me, he said, "Read these to me very slowly." It was an entry from some astronomy book.

"Oookay . . ."

He shone the light on the gold door again and I read, "It says, 'The position of Sirius is . . .'"

"Slowly now, one at a time."

"RA."

"Ra! That's the sun god, right here," he whispered excitedly, touching a symbol RA on the door, "exactly as in the prison!"

When I read, "Oh six H," he looked around and pointed as he touched six separate etchings. "Horus" (the eagle-headed god). I then read, "Forty-five M, oh eight point nine," and in turn he found and touched each of the matching symbols. Finally I read, "Dec: sixteen, forty-two," and then "fifty-eight." He touched what he called a "civil calendar"—a round disc, and touched each in turn, one month and three days: sixteen, forty-two, and fifty-eight days of the year. Nothing.

Then something.

A small creaking sound, then another. The mechanism on the dead bolt was slowly sliding back! "Whoever stole this door configured this touch-locking system. The calculations match the hieroglyphs in the prison!"

"Damn! We're good!" I said, almost jumping up and down on the glass stairs.

He pushed on the heavy, large, gold door and it opened a bit. We peeked into a candlelit, ultramodern, white, high-ceilinged room, the walls covered with modern artwork, and shelves with ancient artifacts. There was no furniture to speak of, but kneeling on the floor were a group of people, some robed, some—both men and women—topless (thirteen of them to be precise), their heads to the floor, chanting. A few others circled the people on the floor, playing on African drums and clay pipes. At the center, there was a perfectly round fire pit that was lit, the incense-infused logs burning brightly.

Behind them all, sitting in an elaborate chair, was another robed figure—this robe embroidered in gold—calmly petting a beautiful, medium-sized brown dog—a Pharaoh Hound to be precise.

The figure on the chair, a man with a full, long black beard and a shaved head, then rose and walked over to the fire pit, still holding and stroking his dog. As we watched, Pantera covered my mouth to keep me from screaming as the man held the dog aloft. The poor thing sensed what was happening and began struggling to break free, howling pitifully. The man pulled a knife from the pocket of his robe, and in a split second, slit the dog's throat. After a few more seconds the little guy just stopped moving. Then, holding the dead beast's body over the pit, he let its blood drain into the fire, the blood spitting and sizzling as the crowd ooh'd and aah'd. When the little dog's blood was drained completely, the head man or whatever he was, tossed the dog's body into the fire pit, sparks flying as the stench of burning hair and flesh nauseatingly filled the beautiful space. They all knelt and began applauding, then broke into chanting and dancing, their faces glowing in the firelight as the dog's body shriveled and burned until it was charred.

When the dog's body had been totally consumed by the flames, they all came 'round to kiss the mad monk.

"Jesus H. Christ. What savages!" I whispered to Pantera when he finally took his hand off my mouth. "What? What? Just say it!"

"This guy—the chief muck-a-muck there?—his name's Jean-Carlos Acevedo, aka the Prophet Jeremiah. He's got the missing earring. I knew that 'monk' looked familiar. Must be his brother."

"The son of a bitch who just cooked a dog? What?"

"International drug dealer out of Andalusia. Two-bit street hustler, made himself a small fortune as a professional gambler. He managed to triple that in the black market antiquities game. He is the reason Morris came here in 1982."

Then I remembered what I'd forgotten about Morris that I'd been trying desperately to remember a few days earlier.

"Geez," I whispered, smacking my head with my hand. "I remember when I was a kid, Mr. Golden," I said, reverting back to what I called him then, "took to wearing a small red stone on his lapel, I just assumed it was a 'manager of the year' lapel pin or something. It was the other earring. Damn!" Then, "How would he know this guy, though?"

"After the so-called prophet conveniently found God, he must have also found Morris. And lo and behold! God turned out to be none other than Jean-Carlos himself. Now he's into all kinds of black magic. Even formed his own religion. As L. Ron Hubbard once said, 'If you want to get rich, you start a religion.'"

"Jesus, Mary, and Joseph!"

"Well, I don't think they went into it for the money . . ." he quipped.

"Your humor escapes me at the moment."

"Rule one: if you lose your sense of humor, you lose."

"I wasn't aware you had a sense of humor."

"No? Stick around."

"I'm not the one who had the problem sticking around—remember?"

"I remember very clearly. Anyway, I believe that your mood dictates success or failure."

I pretended to ignore him because, well, because he was right. Plus he was a pain in the ass.

I hate him. No, seriously, I really hate him.

"His followers," Pantera continued, "show up to perform his rituals, which they think God gave him in visions."

"How very Prophet Muhammad of him," I said.

"The Prophet Muhammad worked for millions of Muslims, he must figure, so why not for the Prophet Jeremiah?"

"Insane."

"No, smart. In fact, Acevedo's feeding them a hodgepodge of all kinds of ceremonies he's cobbled together from many ancient rituals. Like now, his followers are chanting a Dogon rite. Since Dogon's got the world 'dog' in it and the Dogon worshiped the Dog Star, Acevedo—excuse me, the Prophet Jeremiah—must have figured that sacrificing a dog would be very on-point high drama."

"On point? Disgusting and tragic is more like it," I added, still whispering. "But what's in it for him?"

"Same as any good televangelist. Money. He's got followers all over the world. They pay him the long green to pray for them. And he's got the whole God complex thing going on, too. The guy grew up in a Spanish orphanage. His mother, when she came around, was a prostitute."

"Oh crap. The murdered prostitutes out in Gilgo?"

"Doubtful, but maybe Acevedo's twisted game became Morris's real-life obsession. Ritual murder of the girls."

"And—what?—Jean-Carlos told him to murder girls?"

"Maybe Morris bought into Acevedo's whole mash-up."

"And oh, by the way? You know all this about Acevedo—why?"

"I've run into him along the way."

"I'll bet you have. So apparently did Morris and look how he ended up. It seems Morris signed on with every religious scam artist of every stripe he could find."

"But Morris had the pages and Acevedo paid for access. He kept the other earring. Acevedo was probably promised it, along with the missing pages, when Morris dropped."

"Goddamn! Morris promised more people a piece of the action than Max Bialystock!"

"Who?" he asked. Finally something he didn't know.

"The producer in *The Producers,*" I said. "Or is Mel Brooks too lowbrow for you?"

"Such a wiseass," he said.

"You bet."

We watched as Acevedo's followers filed out and drove away in several cars and one large van. Then the big man himself opened the windows, looked out, and went into another room. He came back wearing a tight T-shirt and silk pajama-type pants. He looked like an athlete in his prime, even though he was probably in his early fifties. When I looked down, I saw he was barefoot, carrying a bottle of wine and a glass in one hand, and an AK-47 in the other.

He laid them all on the floor next to the chair, sat down, and put his feet up on the fire pit where the little dog's bones were still smoldering, the rancid odor filling the air.

Acevedo poured himself a glass of wine and lit a joint. He took a remote control from his pants pocket and pointed it. Immediately an ear-splitting scream of "Mother!" came roaring out of the hidden speakers. It made me jump a foot high on the stairs, and I was lucky to catch hold of the slippery glass banister to keep from tumbling down and making a racket.

The very heavy-metal riff of guitars pounding over and over into the quiet, starry desert night followed "Mother!" It was an old recording of Jim Morrison's. Acevedo picked up the AK-47 and stroked it like he still had the dog in his lap. He smiled and took a long hit off the joint and let out a laugh. Or it looked like he did, because the music overwhelmed any other sounds.

Ah, the good life.

"Now what?"

"Now we go and get what we came for. Are you ready for this?"

"Ready." *Sort of.*

30

We shut off our flashlights and closed the door, leaving just enough room for us to shimmy through as we flattened ourselves against the wall and crept into the adjacent room, a big kitchen. The lights were on—not good—and Pantera did a quick sweep.

"Let's move."

Following as closely behind as I could, we inched our way back into the room where Jean-Carlos was still sipping and toking, the music still blasting.

The staircase up was to the left, and somehow we managed to make it to the stairwell without him hearing. We climbed each step as quietly as possible, hugging the wall for fear of casting shadows.

The upstairs portion of the house was as sleek, expensive, and modern as the downstairs had been. There were several rooms, one with a double door, which we figured to be the bedroom.

We walked into a library room, which was very elegantly appointed—filled with ancient books and artifacts.

"What are we looking for?"

"The other earring. The missing other key."

A sound behind us! Shit.

I spun around. In the doorway stood a gorgeous woman, clad only in a G-string, vast ringlets of hair cascading all the way down to her waist.

"What?" she called out and started to run.

In a flash, Pantera had her by the wrists, forcing her to the ground, gun to her head. "Not a sound—understand?" he said without much effect, as though he were asking for directions.

She whispered back in Hebrew. It seemed like "what" was the only word she knew in English.

He knew better and asked, in English, "Do you know of the Judas papers?"

Lady Godiva shook her head. He pressed the gun farther into her temple. She shook her head again, twisting to get free.

Good luck with that, sister.

"Well, fuck me," I heard a man say behind us with a heavy accent. I turned. Acevedo was standing in the doorway with the AK-47 pointed right at me.

"You got a woman, I got a woman," he said to Pantera. Then he burst into song, screaming the lyrics of a 1960s Jr. Walker rock song: "'I said shotgun! Shoot 'em 'fore he runs now!'"

I was paralyzed. Pantera didn't budge. There were no tells, no change of expression, no pulling the gun from the woman's temple.

"I'll just take what I came for, and your woman won't die, Juan-Carlos."

Acevedo broke into a laugh. "My woman? Jesus, Pantera. *¿Esta pedazo de basura?* I don't even remember her name! Kill her if you like. It'll save me from having to do it myself."

The woman started to sob harder.

"Now, as for you?" Acevedo continued. "I don't think you can say the same about this fine, if filthy, piece of ass you've got," he said, glancing with disgust at my guano-covered hair. "See, I remember what you like. You like them whole. I know you wouldn't want her once I rip a side of her face off. Aggh, messy!"

Pantera answered just as coolly, like these two were having a nice conversation, "You could do that, but then I'd have to do the same . . ."

"I told you, be my guest. I don't even know the *puta*'s name."

"It's Noelia."

Acevedo was taken off guard, looked surprised.

"Noelia Acevedo. Your half-sister."

Oh, Jesus. This was more disgustingly twisted than I wanted to even think about.

"No, she is not . . ."

"She is," Pantera mocked. "I have a copy of your sex tape. And better still, I have you both on video shooting smack, snorting coke, you name it."

"My followers know I used to live a sinful life—before I found God."

"Would that be very recently then? Because I just acquired the links and they were shot a month ago—one in the Old City, one right here in your humble abode. Dated."

"You're a liar."

"Yes, that's true," Pantera answered. "Still, if my associates don't hear from me in a few minutes, the link gets activated and sent to every news outlet and every worshipper on your mailing lists—of which there are hundreds of thousands."

Acevedo, enraged, made a lunge for him, but Pantera sidestepped, grabbing Noelia by the hair and dragging her with him, never taking the gun from her temple.

In the split second that Acevedo lost his cool and let anger overtake him, I jumped out of the way and started to make a run for it out the door. Acevedo, as fast and nimble as Pantera, grabbed me by the neck and forced me to the ground on my knees.

"I will kill this bitch," he screamed.

"No, you won't," Pantera answered without changing expression. He looked at his watch, tugging at the woman's hair in the process. "In five minutes the video goes out. There is even expert testimony identifying the Prophet Jeremiah's sex-slave, former-stripper, half-sister. And, two minutes after that? Another file, with all of your personal information, goes to the syndicate."

"Syndicate," Acevedo replied, without affect.

"As in the Orthodox Jewish Russian Mob–slash–syndicate. Your enemies from the bad old days. Nasty boys but very pious."

Acevedo was beginning to break a sweat.

"Somehow those guys, smart as they are, never figured out the whole Juan-Carlos turned Prophet Jeremiah scam. They know you're in Israel, but they're looking for the old you—the one who didn't have surgery. The one who didn't grow a full beard, shave his head, and find God."

Acevedo started sweating for real now. With the machine gun inches from my head, Acevedo demanded, "What the fuck do you want, Pantera? I thought we were good. That thing was all settled . . ."

"Well, *that* thing was settled, sure, but this thing?" he said, nodding his head in my direction. "This is a whole *new* thing. Maybe some of your followers will forgive you. You can always take that chance."

"What the hell do you want?"

"I want the key to the Judas pages."

"No. I can't do that. And you know why I can't do that."

"I want the key to the Judas pages."

"Why? You can't sell the pages. They're too hot."

"I'm not here to negotiate."

"It's not here."

"Bullshit." Pantera pulled at the woman's hair so hard she cried out. "The clock's ticking."

"Go ahead and kill her, I don't care."

"But you do care if you lose your followers, your fortune, and this scam. Not to mention your life."

Was this really happening? Was Pantera really so cool under pressure, or more likely, was he that stone cold?

"Did Golden tell you the pages held the secret to eternal life?" Pantera continued, yanking the woman across several more feet by her hair.

The woman begged her brother for her life. *"¡Pedazo de mierda! ¡Por el amor de Dios!"*

Pantera looked at his watch. "Two minutes."

"Wait, stop. Jesus wanted to create a movement. He had the code. Those pages—those fucking pages have the code. We can share the secret . . ."

"Yusef, please, we can go in on this together, we can have all the power in the world!"

Pantera just laughed. "Tell that to your brother who you sent to ambush us at the Prison of Christ. If he's still alive, that is. Now give me the fucking key, Acevedo. And take the gun off the woman." That would be me.

Acevedo answered, still not moving the gun from my head. "I swear I'll find you and get it back and when I do, you're a dead man, Yusef."

"I don't doubt that. Unless I have the secret to resurrection, in which case, good luck killing me off. The key, please." Pantera looked crisp and cool, while I was sweating like a pregnant nun.

Does Pantera want the pages for himself? *Was that what this was really all about? Have I been had? Am I a dead woman? What about Terry? Roy?*

Shit. No scenario was a good scenario.

Acevedo pulled me up and, still holding the gun, began to move toward the double doors of the bedroom as Pantera, still holding onto the naked half-sister, gun to her head, followed closely behind. Acevedo led us into the bedroom, which looked shockingly small. Everything was white, starched, pristine. That all changed when he pushed a button on a white nightstand next to the bed. The wall on one side slid open, leading into a huge and very Victorian room. The walls were painted bronze and were hung with all kinds of bondage equipment.

There were whips and chains hung as neatly as a gardener's tools, a bench with straps, a small cage, a morgue table, a suspension-looking frame, and yes, what looked like a torture rack from the Spanish Inquisition. Hell, there was even a dentist's chair, of all things.

"Nice place you nice young couple have put together here," Pantera quipped, pressing the gun so hard into the sister's head that she again cried out.

"Please! Don't shoot me!"

"Then please don't annoy me," he answered. Turning to Acevedo, he said, "The key?"

Acevedo pulled me over to a large inverted cross and moved it aside. A keypad was revealed, and I could now see that the cross was hanging on a nearly seamless door. He punched in some numbers and it opened. He took a box carefully out and laid it down on the bench.

"Open it," Pantera said. "And take the gun off my friend there. Drop the weapon and, for Christ's sake, enough with your bullshit. Let her go," he ordered, pointing the gun briefly away from the sister and toward Acevedo.

Acevedo reluctantly did as he was told and as soon as I was released, I picked up his assault rifle.

"Open it."

He unlocked the box to reveal a tiny, very thin, gold cross. Pantera picked it up and turned it around in his hands, feeling it with his fingers. "Ah," he said. "Very clever. But where is the ritual? You know you have it."

"I don't! I swear I don't. The old bastard, Golden, he has it."

"What do you mean he has it? He's dead."

"Yes, but . . . the son . . ."

"What about him?" Pantera said and stuck the gun in Noelia's mouth.

"He's got the book. It's in that book. It's mine. Morris left it to me. It's all useless without it."

"What fucking book? I'm getting tired of your bullshit."

"I don't know; he wouldn't tell me. He brought it here, but wouldn't tell me what it was! Some ancient thing. Big, with pictures."

"Not good enough!"

The Voynich Manuscript! The only way we could get the key was to let Pantera know I had the book. But I'd deal with him later.

"The Voynich Manuscript?" I cried.

Acevedo nodded.

"I know where it is," I whispered to Pantera.

Pantera looked satisfied, and so without moving the gun, he ordered Acevedo onto his knees and shoved Noelia down onto hers.

"Do me a favor, would you?" he said to me. "Get me that cat-o'-nine-tails." Then, "Oh wait," he said casually, "I better call off Headquarters. We're almost out of time here. And if one of us gets killed? Oh Jesus, you don't want to know!"

The guy's good, I'll give him that. Was he faking the whole Headquarters involvement in this thing? I mean, wasn't this a personal job, after all? Yes. But was it for Terry—or for himself? But then again, with him, you never knew who he was doing anything for at any given time.

Pantera forced Noelia into the dentist's chair as Acevedo looked on helplessly. "Keep your gun on the holy man, will you?" he asked me.

He gagged Noelia, placing the handle of the whip over a gag at her mouth. He then tied the straps of the whip together behind her back. He asked me for other leather straps and tied her to the chair, her hands across her chest, as she wept and tried to break free.

Even in my terror, I couldn't help but to think how weird it was that she was crying about being tied up in her own bondage room, yet.

What kind of world did these people live in? I again felt sick. Pantera noticed, out of the corner of his eye, and said, "Come on now, steady with that gun . . ."

"Right." As I kept the AK-47 trained on Acevedo, Pantera knocked him out with one punch, then carried him to the medieval rack and put one of the hideous black face masks studded with nails that were hanging nearby, nail side down, on his face. He then tied him up with his arms and legs stretched out in an X shape. Pantera turned the rack a few times, enough to wake Acevedo, who began screaming, trapped inside the mask. I winced and turned away from the scene in this modern dungeon. I couldn't help but think back to the dungeon of Christ where people had suffered and died and how these two sickos had built a private dungeon for their incestuous pleasure.

"Good? Good," Pantera said. "Please pick up the box, will you?" I picked it up as he said to the half-siblings, "Don't worry, pal. You won't die. The housekeeper gets here at—what?—nine?"

The helpless, perverted drug lord turned phony prophet moaned and struggled to free himself, but he had been trapped inside his own perversion. Literally. Pantera took the little cross out of the box and stuck it in his jacket pocket and snapped it shut.

As we calmly (well, one of us was calm, anyway) walked down and out into the night, Pantera breathed in the fresh air. Tapping his pocket, he said, "What makes the desert beautiful is that somewhere it hides a well."

"Did you make that up?"

"Hardly. Antoine de Saint-Exupéry."

"You are one crazy bastard, Pantera."

He laughed—a big, hearty laugh—breaking the silence of the night, and threw his arm around my shoulder. "Yeah."

But how crazy was he? I still had no idea. I shrugged his arm off my shoulder.

Pantera, too, was back to all business in an Israeli minute, commanding, "Keep up with me," as he put the hard hat back on his head and turned on the light. He grabbed my hand and we began to run, or rather he ran, dragging me behind. The night was pitch black and I was hitting the wall for real this time.

When we got back to his motorcycle, the guard was still passed out. He knelt down and checked him for vitals. "All good."

"Not if you're him it's not." I gasped, out of breath.

"He'll be OK. It'll *all* be OK. Trust me, it'll be OK."

I had no choice but to at least let him think that I trusted him. *Trust no one.*

We hopped aboard and drove back onto the now-deserted highway. I demanded that he stop at a local rest stop and give me his phone.

"Please. I have to check on my son."

"But keep it very, very short," he said, handing me the phone. My father picked up before it had even finished ringing once.

"Hey, Dad. How's everything? Terry back?" He hesitated. "Dad?"

"Ali, I don't understand, but the Norwegian embassy said there was no function there today. They don't know who the Judsons even are!"

"What? There's some mistake. Did you call their cell phone?"

"Of course. Several times. So I came home, knocked on their door, and even asked the doorman. I don't want you to get panicked, but he said he wasn't on duty when they left, and he came on at six this morning."

"And?" I was panicking now. "And the police?"

"They're on their way . . . Oh wait. There's the intercom." The intercom was attached to the doorman station in the lobby.

I heard my mother pick it up and then scream.

"Oh my God. Oh my God."

"Dad!" I demanded, "What is it? What's going on there?"

"Honey, wait, I'm getting it from Mom."

"No. Put her on the phone! Now!"

"Ali, oh Ali," my mother cried. "The overnight doorman told Anthony that they left sometime in the middle of the night. They had a lot of baggage with them."

"Was Terry with them? Did they take him? Is he—God forbid—in their apartment alone?"

Pantera was by my side in a flash. I was shaking so hard, I put my cell on speaker so he could hear.

"Dad's calling nine-one-one right now. The maintenance men are coming up to unlock their door." Hysteria gripped me. I heard a low animal sound in the distance but didn't realize it was coming from me.

The cell went dead in my hands. I demanded that Pantera put

the chip back into mine. "They need to contact me, goddamn it! We've lost precious time!"

He did so and handed me back the phone. It immediately began to ding. It was a text without identification.

The message on the screen was as simple as it was horrific:

Baby Terry is a very bad boy.

I immediately texted back:

Where is my baby? Show me my son!

Good luck with that one. Since those on the other end of the text had probably an even more secure line than Pantera's satellite phone, my text came back as "not delivered."

Then another text:

Calling the authorities in will only make it worse.

In the meantime, Pantera was busy on his own phone. I fell to my knees, pounding the ground, and Pantera bent down and scooped me up into his arms.

"I . . . I . . . don't know what they want!" I screamed. "They must want Terry to replace their own dead son."

"No. They want the pages."

"What? Are you serious? They've got my son!"

I jumped up when my phone dinged again: "Unknown caller." It was just a link.

I hit the link with my finger shaking and the screen filled with the image of a crib with a baby inside. His face was turned away from the screen, but I saw that the baby was swaddled in a black, rough-looking blanket, screaming.

Next, Raylene leaned into the crib as the camera zoomed in and panned around to show the baby's face. It *was* my Terry with tears streaked all down his face as he struggled to break free of the coarse swaddle.

Is that a bruise on his little cheek? Oh dear God!

I couldn't tell, because the camera then turned to focus back on Raylene. She had a black scarf covering part of her face. It wasn't a disguise. It was a costume.

"Alessandra," she began, her Caribbean accent surfacing for the first time since I'd known her. "Bring us what we need or the baby dies," she said. "Tell anyone about this video and the baby dies. Fail us and the baby dies." Pantera, with his own phone, had been recording it.

The camera then panned back down to the crib. There was a gun resting at Terry's swaddled feet. As his screams increased, the camera cut to Dane, who was dressed not unlike the followers of Acevedo. "We want the pages. We want the keys to the kingdom." The screen went dark. I stared down at it and mumbled, "They're hurting Terry! I'll give them whatever they want! Roy will understand."

I went to read the original text again but it was no longer available.

Pantera said nothing, just stood up and punched something into his phone.

I attacked. "You? Is this your doing? Do you want to live forever? Is that it? Did you set me up? Did you arrange for those people to move into my building? Or are you in this for your own good?"

He grabbed me. "No! I want what you want. Safety for Terry and the goddamned destruction of these pages that have the power to destroy all that is good left on Earth."

"They have Terry," I screamed. "I'll give them everything I have! The pages, the keys, the fucking Voynich Manuscript!"

"I believe the Judsons are still in New York," he said.

"Bullshit. How do you know?"

He didn't answer me but only said, "We'll be back in New York in a few hours."

"How? I can't imagine there's even a flight until tomorrow!"

"Let's go."

"How can you be so freaking calm? Our son"—there, I'd said it. If he was out for the pages, maybe I could touch a part of whatever soul he might have left. "Our son," I repeated, "has been kidnapped!"

I called my parents back. "We're in the Judsons' apartment," Dad said. "The police had the building manager open it . . . Terry's not here."

"Daddy! They stole him! The Judsons kidnapped Terry!"

He gasped. "But honey, you don't know that. Not for sure."

"Dad! Listen to me. They called. They sent a video. They've got him!"

Just then I heard a cop in the background say, "What the hell?"

Dad handed the phone to my mother and apparently went to where the officers were. I heard screams, and men yelling.

"Holy shit!"

"What the eff is that thing?"

"Get out, get out!"

"*¡Es el Diablo!*"

"What?" I screamed. "What is it?"

Someone grabbed the phone from my father. "This is Detective Barracato," a man said.

"They stole my baby! They stole my baby!"

"Please, Mrs. Russo. Give me as much information as you can."

"What did they find? Is it my son?" I screamed. I couldn't stop screaming despite the detective urging me to calm down.

"No, no, Mrs. Russo. There was a false wall. Jesus Christ, but there's a life-sized wax figure of a teenage boy in there! Fully clothed from the 1960s or something. There's a transistor radio in there and a box full of stuff . . ."

Her son! She'd had Makenson recreated in wax. I felt like I was going to faint. She'd had a full-sized voodoo doll made of the boy. Pantera took the phone from me. He calmly gave them information I didn't know he had about Terry and me. I looked at him. *Why does he know all this? He's in on the whole thing.*

Instead of explaining how he knew what he knew, he got back on the motorcycle and indicated for me to do the same.

"We need to go to the hotel right now and get the pages."

"I want to go home!"

"We're almost there. Almost there."

He dialed up someone and I heard him say a bunch of numbers, then another bunch but with dots and slashes thrown in.

"Good, good, thanks." Then, as calmly as if he were giving me the weather forecast for the weekend, he said, "We've got a flight."

"There's no flight out tonight anymore! Where the hell are you trying to take me?"

"Home. I know a guy."

"You know a lotta guys. Which guy?" I said, refusing to get back on the back of the bike.

"A guy. I know you don't trust me, but I'm all you've got now.

I've come through before—we've come through for each other. You have to trust me."

And my choices were . . . ? Exactly. I got on the bike and we drove back to the hotel. A man—a Pantera kind of man—was waiting outside and handed me a leather bag with the contents from my safe and we got into his car and he sped us to Ben Gurion Airport. We bypassed the commercial areas and went directly to Laufer Aviation, which services private jets.

A VIP check through customs and we were aboard a plane, no name on the outside, the likes of which I'd never seen. The plane was outfitted with tables, chairs, computer terminals, and plush cream-colored leather seats that we strapped into for takeoff.

Once airborne, I was shaking and crying. Excoriating myself for leaving Terry with my "beloved" neighbors. The flight attendant came by and offered food and drinks, of which I was having none. "Sleep is what you need," Pantera said.

I put my head in my hands and began to moan. "I should have known there was something wrong with them. Why didn't I guess it when Dane got freaked out at the rare book shop? I just thought . . ."

"How could you know?"

I turned on Pantera in a flash. "Don't frigging placate me. Don't! I don't even know what you're in this for. I don't trust you, and I shouldn't have trusted them."

"I wasn't placating you. I was merely telling you that—"

"You know nothing about me or Terry, so you can't tell me anything."

"I know more than, well, than you think. You think I haven't kept an eye on you and Terry?"

"I don't care. I just don't want any harm to come to Terry."

"One step at a time. These things are never easy."

"These things? Is kidnapping part of your everyday *things*?"

"Whoa, I'm not the bad guy here."

I looked at him. I didn't need to spell it out. My disgust spoke for me.

He put his hand on top of mine, and I pulled it away. So he gripped both of my hands in his and said, "I know you don't understand why I didn't come to you, why I let you think I was dead."

"Are you serious right now?"

"I do understand. But you don't."

"No? How's this? You let me think you were dead. You understand that? You understand there was—I meant, God forbid, *is*—a baby boy named Terry? Please give me a break. You don't understand shit. I also understand that you want to get your hands on the ten-million-dollar pages. For yourself or this Headquarters place you work for."

"Not true," he shot back, standing up.

"Siddown, mister! Here's what else I understand: You spent God knows how many years raising Demiel ben Yusef, because it was all part of the quote 'great experiment' unquote, but you never came when you had your own boy? That's what I understand. Do you?"

I didn't give him a second to answer, rushing right on. "And now I don't even *have* my son. You understand, you say? Maybe all of this is somehow connected to you."

He simply got up and looked out the window. Then he looked at the monitor on the wall that tracked every second of our flight.

"I killed Maureen in Manoppello to save your life, and then you played dead, you bastard!"

He turned back toward me. "Goddammit, Russo, we saved each other's lives! Listen, I don't know if I could have prevented the kidnapping from happening, so I won't play 'what if?' with you again.

Won't happen. But what I do know is that since I first laid eyes on you outside the U.N.—when you and Dona charmed your way into Demiel's trial after the doors were shut . . ." He trailed off.

I didn't ask him to continue. I didn't want to hear it.

After a breath, he went on, nonetheless. "All I wanted to do was . . ." He walked back and stood one millimeter from me—most of him almost touching most of me.

He grabbed my face in his hands, forced me to look into his eyes, and whispered, "All I *ever* wanted to do from the first second I laid eyes on you, was to grab you and never let you go. Maybe that's just another thing you'll never understand."

Don't let him get to you . . . don't!

"Just accept this fact," he went on as I fought back tears—I so needed somebody, anybody to lean on right then—but I remained stoic against his words. "I can never and will never tell you why I couldn't come to you. I need you to believe that it wasn't because I didn't want you, didn't ache for you with every single cell in my body, didn't—don't—long to see my son, hold my own flesh and blood."

I pulled away. "You need? *You* need?" I said, trying to convince myself that what was coming out of my mouth was genuine, after what we had shared together, and what we had done together.

"What are you? A desperado, attached to some bullshit thing called 'Headquarters' or whatever you call that espionage–slash–terrorist group these days?"

"Clearly you don't know," he snapped back, "what I am or what we do, so don't go off half-cocked about things you know nothing about, Alessandra."

Using his first name back at him, I seethed, "*Yusef.* I know you've done things I never want to know about, and I mean that, but what

I do know is *this*—this thing that's happened with my boy? That's my life, that's Terry's life." I was running out of breath, I was so angry. "He's my little baby, my tiny, helpless boy! My child is the one you rejected, you son of a bitch!" I stood and turned my back to him.

He grabbed me and spun me around, and instead of the fury I expected, he threw his arms around me and tried to rock me back and forth, tried to wipe away the tears of anger and fear running down my face. I struggled against his strong grip, but he had the strength of a twenty-year-old boxer.

He leaned in and kissed me hard, whispering through his open mouth. "Don't do this now. We . . ."

I violently turned my face away from him, and slapped him hard. "Stop it. Just stop it!"

He turned and walked down the aisle, and opened a door. I saw a small bed made up and beyond that another door. "The bathroom's in there," he said, as though nothing had happened. "You can clean up and then rest. You need to rest."

"You need to stop telling me what you think I need to do," I said, walking past him and slamming the door.

32

_____

Too exhausted to even think about showering—despite the guano—I stripped off my filthy clothes, washed my face, and brushed my teeth with the amenities provided. I slipped on an Egyptian cotton robe hanging on the door, which I figured probably belonged to some mogul's mistress. I flopped onto the bed looking more like that mogul's hard-living drunken mother than anybody's pampered mistress. Pantera was nowhere to be seen, and I tossed and turned, occasionally dropping off for a second, only to jump back awake, my heart pounding.

Then I saw the photo attached to the bedside table: Mossad and Gisele! The two impossibly good-looking people on the flight into Israel. Pantera had been guiding this expedition since before I'd left New York!

After many more restless hours, Pantera came in and stood by the bed. "We're landing in less than forty-five minutes," he said. "Maybe you want to get a shower and something to eat."

I pointed to the photo. "Friends of yours?"

"For your safety."

"A supermodel and a rich guy who looks like an Israeli secret agent?"

"Hardly. Just friends. It's their plane."

"Right. Kind of them to fly commercial on the way in."

"You need to eat," he simply said.

"A shower, yes, but no, I can't eat."

"Yes to both," he said, leaving me in bed and closing the door behind him.

A quick look at the clock told me it was 12:45 A.M.

That would mean we'd land around 1:30 A.M. in New York.

I climbed into the small shower and turned the hot water on and tried to let the scalding water soak the pain out of me. It didn't work. I washed all of the bat shit out of my hair. I felt cleaner, but not better. I climbed out and put on the robe and wrapped a towel around my head and sat back down on the bed.

We were almost home. Would I be able to trade what I had—the tube, both keys, the pages, and that old book—for Terry? Was it too late? In the whole mess I'd actually completely forgotten about Roy. If it hadn't been for his father, Morris, both his son—and mine—would be safe right now. I hoped Morris Golden was rotting in some awful hell even Dante couldn't have conjured up.

And what if those pages really did contain Jesus' secret teachings about resurrection, as they surely seemed to?

What if, in exchange for the life of my little boy, I was giving these monsters all the power in the world, and worse, the power to kill every little boy, girl, adult, and elder who didn't bow to their rule? The power to destroy, ironically enough, Christianity itself?

My mind was spinning so violently that I felt dizzy. I tried to clear my brain to think it through.

Why would only these pages be stolen if they weren't the ones that contained Jesus' ultimate secrets? Didn't Acevedo go from guttersnipe son-of-a-whore to a religious cult leader living like an Egyptian pharaoh complete with ancient Egyptian-style sister-wife once he met Morris Golden? Isn't he now a self-appointed god, worshipped by people worldwide? And this with just a glimpse into the pages of Judas and the very words of Jesus. How could he have done that alone—without at least part of some secret knowledge?

What if we really are in fact about to hand over to the worst sub-humans on earth the secrets of life and death as imparted by the most evolved being ever to walk the earth? Those secrets at the disposal of terrorists could start the beginning of the end of life on earth as we know it . . . Armageddon.

On the other hand, if I *didn't* hand over the pages, my Terry, my miracle baby, would be the one destroyed. He'd be tortured and killed because his mother was worried she might give away hypothetical secrets to people with whom she'd been so stupid as to entrust his well-being in the first place. I began to picture his little body being brutalized, burned, punched, battered, and maybe even ritually sacrificed. I couldn't get the picture of Acevedo's little dog out of my mind.

And what if the choice comes down to every child on Earth or mine?

What if?

I got up and opened the door. "Pantera!"

"Yes?" he said, knowing I was about to demand something big. Answers.

"I don't know what your involvement is in this thing—really— but if you have anything to do with Terry's kidnapping? I don't care if you are the biggest secret agent in the universe, I will—"

He grabbed my shoulders and shook me gently. "Stop it! Terry is my son, too, whether you admit to it or not. I would never, *never* harm him!" Then gently, "Or you."

"No, but maybe you'd try to steal him so that you could train him up like your father trained you up. Bring him into this black ops world of yours with the secret to resurrection. An army of men who would never die!" I was screaming and out of breath. He reached for me.

"Don't touch me! Just don't touch me!"

"I would give up my life gladly for him," he said. "And you know I would for you."

"Yes, and with Jesus' secret to resurrection, you'd never have to. But oh right, I remember how you gladly died for me already. Oops. But here you are!"

"Stop! We don't have the energy to waste fighting with each other."

"OK, since you won't come clean with me . . ."

"How do I prove I'm not lying?" he said, sounding defeated, which I knew he wasn't.

"OK, you can tell me what I believe you already know."

"And what do you believe I already know?"

"Whether it's true that these pages contain the most dangerous secret in the world."

"I made a solemn vow when . . . it's not something . . ."

"Yes. It. Is. *Something.* Tell me what it is!"

He sat on the bed and put his clasped hands between his knees, his head down.

I hovered over him. "Tell me, goddammit! Tell me! My son's life is at stake."

He sighed. "Once you know this you cannot unknow it. Do you understand this?"

"Just tell me!"

"The pages, as Acevedo confirmed, *do* contain the secret to resurrection. Jesus' resurrection, and the code to resurrect any other person who would put these together with another formula. We always suspected that . . ."

I turned to face him, my mouth open. "You mean . . . ?"

"Yes. Without this book, the Voynich Manuscript, the pages are useless. Just as without Judas there could be no Jesus story. No betrayal, no so-called resurrection, no grand and glorious story upon which the richest religion in the world could be built."

"Why would Judas take on that role—to be the most hated man in history?"

"He was fated to it. Look at the other Gospels—the accepted Gospels—Judas was the only apostle taught the esoteric knowledge by his master. The rest were just retellings of what they supposedly saw and heard as a group. Judas was given the secrets of life and resurrection. Therefore he *had* to be part of the grand scheme because he was the most trusted of them all. He was behind the resurrection and those pages contain most of the secret."

I sat there, open-mouthed. "What? Are you saying it was all a scam—Jesus' death and resurrection?"

"No, I'm saying that he knew the secret and gave it to Judas, so that he could complete the process after Jesus died!"

"But why Judas?"

"Like I said, I believe he was Jesus' most beloved, trusted disciple outside of Mary Magdalene. But Mary was of this Earth. Jesus was not, and perhaps neither was Judas."

"Why do you say that, Pantera? I thought you were a great believer!"

"I am. But remember, it's clear in what was saved of the Gospel of Judas when Judas said, 'the realm of Barbelo.'"

"Is that an acronym for heaven? Or is he talking about another galaxy?"

He didn't answer, of course. So I said, "Is this proof that Jesus is not the son of God as the Church would have us believe, but a being from another realm, whatever the hell that means?"

"Yes."

"And the Immaculate Conception?"

"An angel came down to a young girl and impregnated her? An angel? They had no word for what came to Mary back in those days," he said. "Beings that flew perhaps in a craft of some sort, or could levitate, could pass through dimensions of time and space? A being, who left Mary's child with the knowledge imprinted on his brain to resurrect. He could not be left here to die."

"Ah," I said. "We could be hung out to dry for trying to push that one."

"You bet. But the truth is still out there . . ." he said.

I jumped in. "Jesus Himself brought the dead back to life—we know He did. So you're saying He gave Judas the knowledge, too? So that he could bring Jesus back after the crucifixion?"

"Yes, that's exactly what I'm saying."

"My God," I said, my mind thinking back. "Raylene was raised as a young girl in the Caribbean, and she said her grandmother was a voodoo priestess of some kind. She was deported from Haiti because of something she did. Like what? Failing to raise the dead?"

"The voodoo rites are totally different. They most probably stun the victims and then when they seem as though they're dead, they miraculously bring them back to life. Or so it seems. That's why they're zombies—their brains have been so damaged by whatever they gave the victims in the first place that they seem to be walking dead people."

"The wax figure in the Judsons' wall was probably supposed to represent her dead son. They were after the secret to resurrection!"

"That's what too many people are after and that's the reason no one should ever have it. Can you imagine the ability to resurrect the dead in the hands of ISIS or Kim Jong-un—the ability to raise an army that could never die—as you had suggested?"

"And you've known about these pages for—how long?"

"I've known about them since they went missing on the black market. But we—"

I cut him off: "We?"

"Headquarters, the organization I'm associated with."

I shot him a look. "And *they* want the pages, I assume? That's who you wanted to sell them to?"

"Yes. They will destroy them, or perhaps consecrate them. Whichever they would see best to do with them."

"And—what?—they get to decide?"

"They get to decide many things."

"Like?"

"Like many things you think happen naturally."

I thought about what I was doing to Roy. "This was all supposed to be for Roy. Now he'll rot in jail because of me. But it's not a choice."

"No. It's not a choice," he repeated.

"You know, Raylene, the wife. She and her husband, Dane,

claimed to have been manufacturers of organic medicines. Probably voodoo and black-magic potions. Who knows? But I'll bet when the boy died, she tried to raise him from the dead with her grandmother's help or maybe her grandmother's spells or whatever, and failed. Maybe she never forgave herself. Dedicated herself to finding the cure—for death."

"That sounds right."

"I don't even think Dane was the boy's father, so I don't know what skin he has in this game."

"Alessandra," Pantera said, looking away. "Don't you get it? Whoever has all the marbles wins. All the power and money in the world. The owner becomes the new Jesus—for good *or* evil. That person would have the power over life and death. Can you imagine? They could keep dictators alive forever. Every lunatic with their fingers on the bomb; every cult leader, terrorist, you name it— whoever was in their fold. But they'd present themselves as spiritual beings to the public—never admit that there were still pages that could be stolen by others. They'd always be safe—because *they'd* always be alive. And Terry will be safe as long as we can hand them what they want."

"The choice, then, is between my son and all the children on Earth." There—I'd said it out loud. He just looked down. "And then they'd come for us anyway."

"Yes."

I felt like J. Robert Oppenheimer, father of the atomic bomb: "Now I am become Death, the destroyer of worlds."

"Yusef, if I do this, I am not just becoming Death, the destroyer of worlds. I become the modern-day Judas."

Then I heaved up everything in my stomach.

33

I scraped the guano off my dirty clothes as best as I could and strapped myself in for landing. The second we were on the ground, I immediately turned my cell phone back on to see if my parents or Detective Barracato had called. They had. Several messages in fact—all from earlier today. Well, technically, yesterday—it was after two A.M. All said the same thing: following up all leads, call the minute you land, blah, blah.

"They haven't found him!" I cried. Pantera didn't look surprised.

As we were deplaning I got a text:

You have returned from Israel. Were you successful in obtaining the necessary items?

I showed Pantera the text as we walk-ran toward customs and immigration.

"The kidnappers tracked you," he said, nearly at a full gallop, "but they don't know you are with someone. They don't know you are with me."

"Is that good—or not?"

"I think so," he said in his usual "this could mean this and that could mean that" undercover-speak.

"Stop the cloak-and-dagger. Should we let them know I'm not alone in this or not? I don't even know if it's good that I'm with you . . ." Was Pantera in it for himself and his mysterious group, or was he in it for his son and me?

"If you can text them back," he said, "say 'Leaving airport, will text from cab.'"

This time the text went through. They had opened the lines of communication.

We bypassed the snaking taxi line and jumped into a black car. The driver had been holding a sign saying MR. & MRS. LAPOINTE.

"Don't ask," Pantera said. I did. "I have no idea who Mr. and Mrs. LaPointe are," he whispered, settling into the backseat.

"Oh geez . . ."

He took his phone out, punched something in, and told the driver, "Ninety-Sixth Street and Second Avenue."

"What the hell? Ninety-Sixth?"

"The text was *generated* from Ninety-Sixth and Second Avenue."

A silence descended between us as we sped along, finally entering the Midtown Tunnel—where we came to a complete standstill.

The driver turned around, "Sorry, Mr. LaPointe, tunnel maintenance."

Pantera then texted back the kidnappers on my phone:

Show me proof that my baby is alive and well, and I will hand over the pages.

He hit "send" but the phone beeped. The signal had been lost. So we waited and waited. After twenty or so minutes, we finally exited at Thirty-Seventh Street, and the text was sent.

Within seconds, as we moved up Third Avenue, a text came back:

Display the pages & see the child.

He texted back:

I can show you the tube and the keys. I haven't opened the tube.
Not good enough.

I was frightened that they'd know the cops were involved after being told, warned, and threatened not to involve them.

I had once trusted Pantera, more than I trusted the authorities. I was a rogue myself—never played by the rules. Until recently.

And look what had happened. When I *had* played it strictly by the rules—being a good mommy, never giving Terry anything that wasn't organic, and not even leaving him before this with anyone who wasn't family or his beloved sitter, Anna—well, technically, Donald wasn't family any longer, but he had been more of a father to Terry than Pantera ever was, and would have, like Pantera claimed, killed for Terry.

I'm a reporter; my instincts about people are usually spot-on, but yes, the Judsons had fooled me. Just because they looked my parents' age didn't mean they were my parents. Trust no one.

Pantera broke my train of thought—he was always good at that. "How old were you when you and Roy became friends in Hicksville? Were you there when the old man went from mild-mannered bank manager to a nightmare father and husband?"

"What?"

"I'm trying to track this thing in my mind."

I grabbed his jacket lapels and tugged like a madwoman. "How did you even know that I *knew* Roy as a kid, let alone that there was any connection to his father? That we grew up in Hicksville, Long Island?"

"You told me once. Where you grew up." He'd answered too quickly.

"When? When first we met so romantically last year," I answered, sarcasm dripping, "did I tell you that tidbit when we were running from the French police? Or was it when Interpol was chasing us? Between shooting those men atop Montségur at the castle and killing Maureen? When did I stop to tell you the story of my frigging life, Pantera—when?"

I knew for sure I had never discussed my growing-up years with him. He had known about Roy when we first discussed it in Israel, yes, but not where I'd grown up. Had he slipped?

Pantera tried to mollify me, saying, "You told me that night in, well, in Carcassonne."

Yes, I'd definitely had too much *vin de pays* that night, that's a fact, and we had ended up in bed, which is also a fact, but still . . .

He interrupted my train of thought with, "It's my *business* to find things out before I go off blind into a situation. You forgot."

"I didn't forget what you do for a living, because I don't actually know what you do for a living. Spy? Professional assassin? International man of mystery? Asshole?"

"All of the above," he said.

"Jesus." I wasn't convinced that I hadn't caught him in a lie, but right at this moment, he was the only shot I had of getting Terry back. I'd deal with the consequences later, kill him if I had to, to get my son home.

Maybe he set up the Judsons for some bizarre scheme of his own. What? Plus he already had the pages in hand. Who in hell could I trust? Right. No one.

Then in—what?—an attempt to mollify me, he added, "The truth? We were provided everything about you the minute Demiel chose you from the crowd."

"Shut up, please."

The driver's phone rang and I could hear a furious voice coming through. Ugh. The dispatcher. The poor driver turned around, frantic. "Aren't you Mr. and Mrs. LaPointe?"

Pantera handed him two hundred dollars over the seat. "Yes, we are," he said, and the driver went back to the phone and shut the plastic safety panel between us.

Pantera wasted not a second more—we had a signal again—and sent off the two high-res photos. An immediate text came back.

We need to see the pages.

I grabbed the phone and texted back,

I need to see my boy.

Nothing. As we pulled up to Ninety-Sixth Street and got out of the car, I mumbled a brief "Sorry, but it was life or death" apology to the driver, and re-texted the kidnappers again.

I need to see live feed of my baby.

A patrol car slowed down to have a look at us, and parked across the street. Maybe it was because there was so little action on the block at this time of day and the Second Avenue Subway tunnel was still under construction and therefore vulnerable to terrorists or something, or maybe Detective Barracota had a tail on me.

"Not good," I said.

"Not good," Pantera repeated back to me. He took my arm and walked over to the Merrion Square sports bar, which was still open, and sat down at the bar where we could still see the patrol car.

He ordered us a couple of beers and waited. A half hour later, my phone rang, breaking the quiet of the bar at this hour. I answered it and a live feed popped up. It was a baby all right, but he/she was facing away from the camera and screaming.

The screaming baby was placed in an old-fashioned black pram with black drapery over it in what looked like a wet, dark, and terrible tunnel. "Oh my God!" I cried out, my hands to my mouth, causing the bartender to come rushing over.

"Everything all right, lady?"

Pantera waved him away, laughing. "Real Madrid is down," he said, which the bartender inexplicably accepted as a normal reaction to a soccer loss.

"Where is he?" I said into the phone. "Where is he?"

The answer came back—a man's voice this time. Or so I thought it could be. *Dane?* They were using an electronic voice modulator this time. He/It said, in that horrible, horror-movie voice, "The boy is right underneath you. In the tunnel." Then came a horrible screech of metal. The kind of screech the subway makes as it's roaring into the station, metal against metal.

34

The screeching of metal abruptly stopped, but in the immediate quiet that followed, so did the screeching of the baby.

"Let me see my baby!" I cried. Pantera looked at the bartender, and I looked at Pantera, then back at the bartender. *Shit*. I thought a look of recognition came over the barkeep's face. Had I been made? I hadn't even thought that the story of the baby's kidnapping might have made it to the news. How? That meant Terry might already be . . .

Pantera went over to deal with the bartender. Would the man behind the bar on this slow night be able to keep quiet—knowing what was at stake? Would he call the tabloids for cash—or the cops, even? Maybe surreptitiously start taking his own video, which would go viral in seconds, making him the most famous bartender in the world and destroying any chance we had of getting Terry back?

In the meantime, the person on the other end wouldn't let me see Terry—or whichever baby was in that carriage—and turned the camera instead to what looked like a man in a hoodie—it must have been the person from whom the voice had come. The face was hidden in the darkness of the tunnel's dim light.

"We'll be waiting," Hoodie said as the filthy water dripped all around and dangerously close to the pram. "The pages must be intact, and they must be authentic. If the police show up or are aware of this in any way, the boy dies. If you try to play fast and loose, the boy dies. If you attempt to do anything other than what you are instructed to do, we tip over the carriage," he said, and someone else's hand reached out to grab the handle. The hand on the pram—an older woman's hand—began to rock it, first gently, then harder and harder. Raylene!

I clenched my fists in terror as we watched the pram, perched on the edge of the unfinished subway platform, freezing, dirty water dripping down onto it. The hooded figure shone a light on a fat rat as it scurried by, followed by others.

"Any deviation from the instructions and the boy dies. We will see you inside the tunnel. We'll give you five minutes to get down." The phone went dead.

"There's that construction elevator that takes workers down into the tunnel over there. I did a story on the Second Avenue Subway construction," I told Pantera. "But the cops are parked across the street. And it's gotta be locked up."

"There's a guard in a booth there," he added. "Must be armed."

"Well, guards never seem to be a problem for you. The NYPD is another story altogether . . ." I said, biting my nails, which were already so bitten down they were bleeding. I could see that the bartender was trying to pretend he wasn't listening to our heated conversation in the nearly empty joint.

I whispered to Pantera, "Do you think he's filming us on a phone or something?" *Are you my enemy or my friend? Do you want to save your son or become the most powerful man in the universe?*

"No," Pantera said. "I took care of the barkeep, but he doesn't have the ability to turn off the security cams. It's a problem . . . I don't know who he'll alert the second we're outta here."

"I can't worry about that now," I said, worried to death that the cops would show up in force and destroy everything. "Terry's down there. He's on the subway tracks! What do we do? What do we do?" I suppressed the urge to vomit onto the bar.

Cool and unshaken, Pantera reached into his shirt pocket and pulled out a pack of Gauloises—which I thought didn't exist any longer. He put one between his lips but didn't light it. "Old habits die hard," he said, as though we were having a romantic drink in Marseille or something. I couldn't believe it! Then, "As for Terry, the subway is still under construction. Any trains they have down there would be just to test the tracks . . . there's no actual service yet."

"How do you know that? You're not even an American, let alone a New Yorker! You're saying crap to calm me down."

"No. I'm not." Period, the end, nothing else.

"The cops don't even know you're back in the country—let alone sitting in a bar! You give them too much credit."

"And you don't give them enough."

He said nothing more—well, not to me anyway—and instead picked up his phone and dialed it. Then: "Yes, correct. Right now."

Within a few seconds, the cherry atop the parked cop car started swirling and the cruiser took off at top speed with the siren blaring.

I just looked at him, and he shrugged. "I know a guy."

This guy had a guy for every occasion.

"Let me have the tube and the keys," he said. "It's safer in my bag than yours." *Then you'll have nothing to barter.*

"They can grab you and take your bag. They can't take it from me," he said. Again, I was putting my trust in a man who had proved he wasn't worth my trust.

I reluctantly handed him the tube and the keys. My choice was—what?

He paid the bill, left a tip, and we walked out as casually as possible. It was still dark at this hour, but the sun would be coming up soon. "Now what?"

"We go down there," he said, pointing to the immense aboveground housing of the Second Avenue Subway's construction elevator.

As we crossed the street I could see a guard was in a booth next to the elevator's metal frame with his headset on, apparently listening to music—or so I thought. Lax for such an important guard station. Maybe that was good? I didn't ask.

Before we got to the booth, I stopped and turned to Pantera, choking back tears that were desperate to pop out from a combination of nerves, fear, and in no small part, terror.

Pantera took both of my shoulders in his hands and squared them up. "I know this is the worst thing in the world for you. But it's about to get worse. You need to be laser focused."

Who could I trust? No one, that's who. What if . . . ?

This time it was his sat phone that rang just as we approached the guard booth. He let me listen as a modulated voice instructed, "Tell the guard you are here about rail AD three five four. That's rail AD three five four." Click.

We walked up to the booth. The guard was saying something into the wire of his headset. Apparently he hadn't been listening to music. I jumped ahead and said into the booth's speaker, "We're here about rail AD three four five." As soon as it was out of my mouth I realized it might be a setup.

The guard stood up. "What did you say?"

"We're here about rail AD three five four," Pantera answered, as though I hadn't made a mistake, my heart pumping out of my chest.

"Roger that," the guard answered like he was a real cop. He looked like a retired cop, actually. Within a minute or so, the construction elevator ascended and a burly guy in a hard hat inside the cage said, "Get in." We slowly descended sixty feet down through a hole cut into the bedrock of Manhattan that had been reinforced on the sides with steel rods.

We got out and stepped into the partially finished Second Avenue Subway tunnel—a Gothic cathedral of the modern age—a round, arched concrete ceiling that looked to be as high as that of any great cathedral but which was dripping water. Bare bulbs strewn along the sides lit the unfinished tunnel. It was more of the same as far as the eye could see in this dim light. A rat scurried by our feet, already making a home in the tunnel. It attacked a wet sandwich that had fallen into a puddle, which a construction worker must have left.

We came to an area that was even more of a futuristic nightmare than the rest of the tunnel—hundreds upon hundreds of round steel poles that were supporting a wooden open floor above. It was like walking through a steel version of a forest out of *Grimm's Fairy Tales*. The floor was thick and muddy, the mud soaking through my sneakers. It was also dank and damp and very cold and if I could have reached out and killed every one of the kidnappers for taking my Terry down into this hellhole I would have.

Pantera grabbed my hand in the dim light and squeezed it, saying nothing. At one point, we passed an area where the stone from the original rock was exposed and a line of curved iron spikes that had been hammered in were protruding out menacingly. Familiar. Familiar—why? Then it hit me. The whole underground hole in the ground was so similar—again—to the Prison of Christ, where we'd been just hours before; where the clues led us all the way back here to the prison of my son.

As my eyes adjusted to the light, I squinted but all I could see ahead were thousands more feet of arched tunnel that looked like a nightmare mirror that endlessly reflects back upon itself. We must have sloshed ten blocks thru this hellhole before I heard it. It was a mere echo of a sound at first that grew a bit louder with each hundred or so feet. It was the unmistakable cry of a baby!

I started to run on the wet floor, when the man in the hard hat grabbed my arm to stop me. I slipped and fell onto the wet ground. Pantera lifted me up.

The man growled, and then said in what sounded like a Russian accent, "No more of that or you die right here!"

"Understood." The crying grew more intense. Was it Terry's voice? His cry? It was impossible to know what was the real cry and what was the echo as the sound became like a solid thing—constant and constantly repeating in this echoing hall of mirrors sixty feet below the street.

We waded through an area that was at least four inches deep with cold, black water before we came to the area where the tracks had been laid down thus far.

There was even the beginning of a crude platform. And there they were—standing in the grim light on that half-completed platform—five people and a baby carriage with a screaming baby inside. They say a mother always knows her own child's cry even in a roomful of screaming babies, but this baby's cry was so throaty and raspy I wasn't sure. Accompanying the crying was a horrible croupy-type of cough.

It didn't sound like Terry, but Terry had never been as sick as this baby sounded, either. No matter whose baby it was, the little thing was very sick and had gone hoarse from coughing and crying. The sound nearly killed me on the spot.

"What have you done to the baby?" I cried out.

There was no reply, nor did any of them move to comfort the infant, to pick him up, to soothe him.

"He sounds very sick! Please. Give him back to me!"

"When the exchange is completed to our satisfaction," a woman said. It was Raylene, no mistaking it.

I could make them out a little clearer now. They were dressed for winter, each wearing a head covering. Was the baby dressed as warmly? Raylene wore a long women's coat with a triangular scarf tied under her chin. Another person—must have been "Hoodie" himself—wore a ski jacket over a hooded sweatshirt. A third person was in a long black coat with the collar pulled up—Dane? A fourth man wore a flat-brimmed woolen cap pulled down low. He was holding an assault rifle by his side. The fifth one wore a trench coat, a woolen scarf over his nose and mouth, and a fedora on his head. All were wearing knee-high waders on their feet.

I moved forward. I was so close . . .

"Stop! Stay right there," the Russian warned.

"You take one more step and we kill the kid," Hoodie added. That voice, unmodulated now, was so familiar. At that, the suited man with the assault rifle moved to the carriage.

Then the man in the fedora very calmly spoke, his voice muffled by the scarf. "Give the tube and the keys to the man who brought you down, please."

Pantera answered, "Let me see the baby before we hand anything over," even as the baby continued to scream and cough. My fury boiled up at him for negotiating at this point, but things were about to take an unexpected turn. Fedora said, "Ever the negotiator, Mr. Pantera? Even with your son's life?" Pantera squinted to try to make out who was speaking but it was impossible.

My God. They knew Pantera? The Judsons knew Pantera? So he supposedly wasn't in on it, but the kidnappers knew him? And he had the ransom in his bag. Was this Pantera's own scheme gone terribly awry?

My confusion, fear, and frustration were mounting at these stupid cat-and-mouse games with my son's life. I cried out, "Enough!" and tried to grab Pantera's bag away from him but he threw his arm out to hold me back.

I screamed into the tunnel, "Give me the baby! Please. We'll give you what you want."

I knew I had subconsciously stopped referring to the infant in the carriage as "Terry." Perhaps I was too terrified to think it wasn't him, maybe I was too terrified to think it was and he was as sick as this baby sounded.

"The baby. We must see the baby," Pantera countered.

"You can hear the baby, you don't need to see him," Fedora said as the suited figure with the cap and the assault rifle rocked the old-fashioned black pram back and forth over the edge of the rough subway platform, the front two wheels going over and then back again onto the platform.

I threw my hand up to my mouth as someone started singing, "Hush, little baby, don't say a word, Mama's gonna buy you . . ." and then, "What *are* you going to buy him, Mama—a brutal death on a subway track?"

Raylene spoke then: "Quickly now. The sun will be coming up. The workers will be coming down any minute. They can either find a dead baby on the tracks or they can find it's just another day in paradise down here. Up to you," she mocked as the pram was rocked farther and farther over the edge of the platform.

I reasoned with Pantera, "Even if it's not my Terry, this baby needs to be in a hospital." He shook his head, squeezed my hand, and then carefully took the tube and keys from his bag.

The Russian in the hard hat moved to grab the pages just as Fedora called out, "Hold on. C! Our associate will come to get them and we need to examine them to make sure they are authentic."

That would be the man in the hoodie, who immediately began to walk the seventy-five feet that separated us as the baby continued to scream and cough.

This guy has a very weird, loping gait. Where? Where have I seen that before?

It was so cold down there, and now the baby was coughing so hard that he couldn't catch his breath. It sounded like pneumonia. "Please! Please, the pages are real—let me have my baby! He's cold and frightened and sick. He's so scared!" I pleaded, my heart breaking. I was so close to getting him back—if this baby even *was* Terry.

Instead the approaching man in the hoodie—which was zipped up over his mouth and secured tightly enough so that just his eyes were showing—said in a gruff, clearly disguised voice, "Shut the hell up. This kid is fearless."

The kid is fearless? That's what Donald had said when he left my apartment after babysitting. That's what Donald said, goddammit! Could it be him*? The only man besides my father that I really trusted in the world?*

I let out a cry, and Pantera looked at me and held my arm. "Steady now. Steady."

"I . . . I . . ." I tried to say but couldn't get the words out.

The hooded figure came nearer and held his gloved hand out. Pantera handed over the tube and the keys, and Hoodie turned to walk back to the others. I had to stuff my hand in my mouth to keep from saying, "Donald? Is that you, Donald?"

As he loped away—*it has to be a fake gait*—I could see the pram was still being rocked back and forth precariously over the edge of the platform.

He handed her the tube, someone took out a light, and Raylene quickly inserted the keys, inspected the pages without removing them completely, quickly locked the tube back up, and handed it to Fedora.

After a minute or two—each one ticking by to the sound of the baby struggling now to breathe—one of them announced, "We will make the exchange."

I broke from Pantera and began cautiously making my way down the platform toward the baby. "Stop!" Pantera yelled as the man in the suit dropped the carriage with the coughing baby onto the tracks. They never had any intention of letting Terry live!

The Russian got off a round and grazed me in the arm.

I dropped and began crawling toward the baby on the tracks as all hell broke out. Pantera took out the Russian first, shooting him at close range—just as the elevator banged down. I could hear the voices of the sandhogs coming down into the tunnel to work. They must have heard the shot, because sirens went off. I heard an engine start up and a headlight turned on at the other end of the track. The test train!

Pantera and Hoodie began firing at each other as Raylene took aim at the baby carriage, which was upside down on the track—the baby underneath it. I leaped toward her and knocked her back onto the tracks, where she landed facedown, inside the wet filthy track, unable to move for fear of being electrocuted, as what seemed like hundreds of rounds were exchanged. I saw the man in the suit with the assault rifle fall, then saw Hoodie fall, perhaps wounded, perhaps dead.

I kicked Raylene out of my way, and she inched almost on top of the now-active third rail. The man in the overcoat screamed, "Raylene!" and jumped into the tracks to save her, grabbing onto her arm. An old carton of orange juice, which had been discarded by someone, was laying nearby and I grabbed it and threw it on top of them, remembering from chemistry class that acid was a good conductor of electricity. I heard a scream, then immediately smelled burning flesh as pungent as when I'd imagined it in Montségur.

I tiptoed carefully, trying to avoid the same fate. My arm was gushing blood. I pulled the pram up and off the now-silent baby. I handed the lifeless little being up to Pantera on the platform just as the test train approached. Pantera pulled me up with one strong arm as he held the baby in the other. I heard the terrible crunch of the woman and the pram being crushed.

There was carnage all around, blood mixing with the unfinished wet floor.

"Is he alive?" I cried, taking him gently from Pantera.

Pantera just looked at me. "Please God," I whispered, "please." No atheists— or agnostics— in fox holes. Yes, while it *was* my own sweet Terry, he was now hardly breathing—or maybe not at all. I laid him down on the platform, and could see he was battered, cut up everywhere, and very, very sick. He was barely alive, and he was dying.

Frantically, using the techniques I'd learned in my well-baby classes, I tilted his head back and sealed my mouth over his tiny lips, pinched his nose, and blew in his mouth five times. I gave him thirty chest compressions—how hard could I press without doing further damage?—two more rescue breaths, and then suddenly, someone was pulling me off Terry as I struggled to hold on. The tunnel was filling up with SWAT cops. Then when they gave the all clear, down rushed firefighters and EMS. I remember screaming as they pulled me away from my baby amid the dead and dying all around us.

I heard a voice—it sounded somewhat familiar, and it was coming from someone trying to hold me. "Ms. Russo, Ms. Russo? You're wounded. You need to go to the hospital. It's Detective Barracota—I'm here. We spoke on the phone from Israel?"

I broke from him and ran to the EMS workers who were working on Terry.

"He's breathing, he's breathing . . ." a female EMS worker told me. "He's breathing, honey, he's breathing." They had put an oxygen mask on him.

"Is his spine broken?" I screamed. "They threw him on the tracks." He was covered in blood.

Pantera's arms surrounded me. The woman said, "I'm sorry, ma'am, but we don't know anything yet," as she and a man lifted his little broken body onto a tiny baby board and covered him with blankets. "We need to be in the ambulance!" I cried, grabbing onto her arm.

"I'm sorry," she responded as kindly as she could while trying to get the baby out of there. "Just one of you can ride. Which one is the parent?"

"We both are," I said. "We both are."

35

At New York's Metropolitan Hospital, Terry was rushed into the ER, and they let me stay by his side as they patched my arm up. I just had a flesh wound, but the baby? That was another story.

Terry was placed in a little metal crib as the blood seemed to gush from wounds everywhere. I leaned in to him and sang in his ear once again my own words to Brahms' Lullaby: "Terry boy, Mommy's boy, Mommy loves you so much, 'cause you're handsome and you're nice, and you're Mommy's best boy. Terry boy, Mommy's boy, Mommy loves you so much, Terry boy, Mommy's boy, Mommy loves you so much," over and over as they tried to get him to breathe normally.

The monitors were blazing and suddenly, somehow, there were my parents and Dona and my brother, Arlo, in from California, by my side. And about a million cops until the doctors shooed everyone away. My mother, fiercely determined not to be turned away, showed the ER nurses her credentials and even they were cowed by her and permitted her to stay with me.

A dome-shaped oxygen tent was placed over Terry's crib, and we held on to each other staring down at my infant boy as the doctors tried to staunch the bleeding.

Worse than they actually were—thank God—and that only a few required stitches. The others could be closed with surgical strips. At least there was that.

We watched, helpless, as my suffering baby struggled for every breath—even my mother was helpless in a situation like this. Yes, she was a pediatrician, but it wasn't her hospital and she wasn't an ER doc. She checked that his legs and arms were moving.

Terry looked so tiny in there, fighting for his life. I knew that Mom knew he had a slim chance of making it.

I leaned close to the tent and began the lullaby again. My mother, her arm around me, said, "When he's strong enough, they will have to take him for an MRI, you know. You understand that?"

We both understood what she meant: They needed to assess possible spinal damage.

It was a very, very long night of touch and go. Several times, the team came running back in when Terry stopped breathing. My mother and I just plopped down on the floor whenever they asked us to move.

By noon, the doctors felt that Terry was strong enough to be brought down to the basement for an MRI, which was vital. They sedated him and Terry was moved with a board on his back. I cried as the horrible noise began, knowing my little boy was again in a black tunnel with no one to hold him. It must have been at least twenty agonizing minutes.

Back in the ER in his little crib with the oxygen tent over it, the orthopedist gave us the news. And it was good. So good, in fact, that I began to actually breathe for the first time in I don't know how long. The little guy had no spinal cord damage. That being said, however, he was far from out of the woods. It was still minute-to-minute, but Terry was finally sleeping in fits and starts with the help of the oxygen and being hydrated and medicated via IV.

Mom begged me to take a break, to go get a cup of coffee for five minutes, but I wouldn't leave. They let Dad come in, who took over the plea patrol: "We're here. Please get some coffee and a donut for yourself. Just right outside in the hallway there's a nice coffee cart."

No.

Dad left and came back in with the heavy artillery: Gramma. My beloved grandmother must have rushed out so quickly that she was still in pajamas, robe, and fuzzy bedroom slippers. "Go get a donut and coffee. You're going to give me a heart attack and I'll die on the spot if you don't do what I'm telling you," she threatened, rubbing her chest.

Nobody refused Gramma—especially Gramma in pajamas, who I knew from experience pretended to have a heart attack if we didn't do what she asked—so I went to get a coffee. "I'll be right here, honey," Gramma said, shuffling me out as she plopped down on the floor next to my mother.

Dad and I found Dona standing with Pantera right outside the door. How long had he been here?

The hallway, too, was full of cops. I could see Dona had been crying, and when I came out, she grabbed me and hugged me like she'd never let me go. Then, Pantera took one hand and she took the other and walked me down the hall.

Barracota was standing near the coffee cart with a bunch of suits.

"Give us a moment alone," Pantera asked—well, he actually *told* Detective Barracota.

The detective just nodded and said, "I'm here when you're ready to speak to us."

"My baby's fighting for his life. He's only a little tiny thing," I cried, completely breaking down again. "I can't. I can't do anything right now but concentrate on him. I know you need to do whatever. Are they all dead—the kidnappers?"

"We don't know, Ms. Russo," Barracota said.

Pantera walked away with the detective, saying, "I can sort out some of what you need."

Dona and I sat down in the seating area near the coffee cart—which was, for such a sad place, incongruously decorated with happy decorations and stickers of smiley faces drinking coffee, suggesting, HOT! HOT! HOT! CHOCOLATE! and HAVE A SUPER DELISH DONUT! *Jesus.*

Dona tried to bring me back to life. "Do you want a super delish donut? Never mind, I'm getting you one. You need the sugar."

She brought the coffee and half a dozen donuts over. Yes to the joe, no to the donuts. I took a sip. She had poured in what tasted like six sugars. She shrugged, sitting down next to me. "I figured you wouldn't eat a donut."

After no more than two or three minutes, I got up, intending to go back into the ER. Pantera came over and indicated for me to sit back down and then he sat next to me on the other side. "I need to show you something," he said, opening his phone.

"What?"

"It's the cop video."

"That's the last thing I need to see now!" I snapped.

"Seriously, what the *hell* is wrong with you?" Dona stood up and glared at him like she would have killed him if there weren't so many cops around. "*Geezits,* Mr. Pantera," she seethed. Dona is very Christian and, unlike most reporters I know, she doesn't take the name of Jesus in vain. "You are one insensitive son of a bitch." She could, however, curse like a sailor, using every other word in her arsenal. She then attempted to snatch the phone away. It didn't work. He was much nicer with my friends than he was with, well, anybody else.

"Please just look at it," he insisted, ignoring her demands and gently turning my face to the phone. "It's important." Dona let out a huff when I opened my eyes to watch, even as she stood—all six feet of her—hovering over us like a giant protective mama bird.

The cops, I could see in the video, had brought huge spotlights down, so the tunnel was completely illuminated and filled with NYPD uniforms, SWAT team members, detectives, and forensics people.

"How did you get this video?" I foolishly asked, turning away from the horror.

He shrugged.

"Please just watch," he urged again. I saw detectives and what must have been the medical examiner—all in protective gear—turning over the body of the man in the suit.

Dona leaned down to put her arms around me, and Pantera said, "Looks like they had Terry down in the tunnel for about twenty-four hours. It was a holiday yesterday so the sandhogs were off.

"Thus, the desperation to get you down there immediately," he said. "They didn't think Terry would make it."

"Of course with the secret to . . ." I stopped. "This innocent baby lying in there had nothing to do with anything!"

Dona, tears forming, deliberately looked at me only. "But Terry's made of your incredible stock. He'll make it. He'll make it."

The next video showed the cops pulling up the mangled, blood-soaked, electrocuted body of the woman in the black coat and the man who'd tried to save her. Dona and I both reflexively turned away. "You don't need to look," he said. "You know who they are."

I wanted to make sure, however. The cops were just zipping the yellow body bag over the woman's charred face in a two-second shot. All that remained intact was one thing: an oversized, ornate cross hanging around her neck. Next came the body of Dane.

"Jesus Christ, why?" I cried to the now-dead sons of bitches.

They'd already hauled off the dead Russian, but I still am not sure I was ready for what came next. The next person was still re-markably alive. The video showed him, blood soaking thru the blankets, being lifted onto a gurney and rushed onto the elevator.

"The kid's fearless!" kept running through my head. At first I couldn't tell, even with the hoodie pulled back, if it was indeed Donald, because they'd placed an oxygen mask over his face. *Donald, is that you? Please don't let it be you. But it has to be you.*

I heard Pantera's voice call out in the video, "Hey, scumbag! We gave you a fake tube," he said, which caused Hoodie to turn his face toward the camera. Greed wins out over logic every time. *No. It couldn't be* him!

"Jesus H. Christ," I yelled out. "Larry. It's fucking Larry! Bas-tard! I can't believe that he was smart enough to pull this off," I screamed, shaking my head and jumping up in disbelief. "He was only in my apartment that one time, when Donald babysat for me."

Pantera answered, "Well, I don't know that *he* pulled it off. More likely they recruited him to get to you through Donald." Then, almost rhetorically, he added, "Must have stolen an extra key when he was in your apartment alone with your ex-husband or handed it off to your neighbors to make a copy before you noticed it missing."

"I can't imagine. You're not saying Donald was in on it?" *Well, not unless he was the one in the trench coat and fedora, but—no, it couldn't be,* I thought to myself. *Donald would never let any harm come to Terry. Or maybe he would. Was he that angry that Terry is Pantera's child?*

"No, not Donald," I continued. "I don't think he knew any of the players except for Larry as far as I can figure. He loves Terry."

"I believe that," Pantera said without malice.

Realizing, finally, that not all of the kidnappers had been accounted for yet, I asked, "But what about the last man—the one in the trench coat and fedora? If Dane was the mastermind . . ."

Pantera looked down. "I'm not sure and there's no more video. There *was* one more person and he got away." He paused and looked down. "With the tube and the keys."

"So you *don't* have . . . ? You said it was a fake tube."

"It wasn't," Pantera answered.

We were all the new Judases, then. I'd traded my son for the knowledge in those pages, and the Judsons had traded their lives for the shot at resurrection, yes, but the man in the fedora? Who the hell was he and what was he trading for eternal life?

"I wonder why Raylene so wanted the secret to resurrection when her son was so long dead? So past bringing back to life? Just crazy, I guess." I put my head in my hands. "And I trusted her with my precious little son!"

Pantera put his hand on my shoulder. "Yes. But whoever they were dealing with wanted the pages more."

"I bet the Voynich Manuscript is no longer in my apartment, either. The man who got away is the one with all the marbles now," I lamented, disgusted that I'd started this filthy business.

"My God." I let it soak in and sat there for a few minutes in stunned silence. We all did, although Dona didn't understand the import of what it all actually meant. As the horror of what we'd done to save my boy filled me, my mother came rushing down the hall, breathless. "You need to go back in . . . Please hurry! Terry's . . ."

Without giving her a chance to finish, my heart in my throat, I bolted up and ran down the hall, slamming through the swinging doors of the ER, my mother shouting something behind me, trying to catch up. I paid zero attention to her, no idea what she was shouting.

I made it to Terry's crib literally in seconds. "Is he breathing?" I cried, shoving the nurses out of my way. Tears pouring down my face, I reached under the tent and experienced the second miracle of my baby's life—the first one was his even being born after they told me I could never have a child. Terry's eyes were open. He turned his sweet baby face toward my voice, his body full of tubes, his breathing steadier. Then? Sick as he was, he managed a tiny giggle. Once more, I experienced that thrill of hearing my baby's laugh—the purest, most gorgeous sound in the universe. Never more so than it was right at that second.

Then he coughed that terrible croupy sound again.

All I wanted to do was grab him out of the oxygen tent and kiss him and hug him and kiss him some more. But I couldn't. So I squeezed his little hand, trying not to disturb the tubes, and cried, "I am so sorry I let them take you. I will never let you out of my sight ever again. Mommy is so sorry. I love you so much and I am so sorry . . ."

The big arms of Pantera were suddenly around me, pulling me away, up to his chest. "Shh. It was not your fault."

I just let the tears flow into and all over him. "It *was* and I won't ever even try to forgive myself."

"It wasn't and you have nothing to forgive yourself for."

Maybe. But still.

The ER doors opened and they must have given the OK because my family came rushing through. Crying. We're Italian, after all. Even my brother, Arlo, the corporate lawyer, who I always suspected was a WASP and had been switched at birth was drying his eyes on his expensive shirtsleeve.

It was a great moment.

Except for one thing.

To save our own flesh and blood, we had given—to the Devil himself, a man who had nearly killed our son—all the power on Earth. And by my reckoning, powers well beyond this Earth as well.

What *had* we done? And then there was Roy. In the horror, I'd nearly forgotten about my dear friend. He was rotting in a cell, and might remain in jail for the rest of his life. My beloved hero firefighter. My true brother.

36

For four agonizing days Terry remained in the pediatric step-down unit—one unit up from the ER, which meant he was not as critical as when he'd been brought in, but he was not out of the woods by a long shot. He had pneumonia, as I'd feared. Watching my baby and hearing him struggling for breath will forever remain the most terrifying sound in my life. It was almost worse than all that had come before.

There was a bed for me next to Terry's crib, and two big sleeping recliners for family. Pantera catnapped in one, often with my mom or dad catching some sleep in the other.

It was the only funny scenario in the midst of all that sadness. Yusef Pantera's life had been spent making things happen behind the scenes: he was complex, unknown, unattached, untraceable, unknowable, and yet here he was around the clock with my insanely knit-together family, punctuated by pop-ins from Dona and yes, Donald.

Pantera is as opaque as steel and the Russos are as transparent as glass. Dad helps low-income families get what they need, Mom helps sick and impoverished kids get healthy, and Arlo, well, he helps white-collar one percenters stay out of jail. Then there's Gramma. Gramma makes lasagna, which helps everyone feel better about everything.

Even though I make a living by covering events like coups, terror attacks, assassinations, tsunamis, hurricanes, death and disease, and war and the horrors of it—all without ever missing a deadline—this time I wrote nothing, and even left the press briefings to Terry's doctors, my parents, my brother, and Mad Dog, who loves a camera like, well, like a mad dog loves a postman's leg.

Of course Pantera was never out front, either—because as the rumor mills had it, he was—what?—Terry's baby daddy/an international man of mystery hired by Mad Dog to rout out the kidnappers/a professional assassin/an archeologist with ties to the (!) Russian/Chinese/you-name-it Mob. Rumors were flying. Some were closer to the truth than not, I suspected.

While sitting in the hospital, I once asked Pantera, between bouts of hysteria, how someone like him who probably didn't even exist on paper, felt with the ever-present press desperate to get a glance of me and "my" mystery man.

In his usual articulate way, he shrugged. "It's fine." I knew it wasn't.

Then there was the Donald problem. I felt that if it weren't for Donald, there would have been no Larry, and if there had been no Larry, there would have been no kidnapping. My resentment was out of control and Donald's regret knew no bounds. Larry was either a moron pawn in a high-stakes international scam, or a con man of the first order. Since Donald himself was a savvy, award-winning photojournalist who'd seen even more than I had of every disaster and war zone of the past decade, and had hung out in every sleazy back-alley bar in every dangerous city in every marginal country on the planet, I knew he'd have been able to spot a con. What was Larry's story?

I imagined Larry, if he were still alive, was now shackled to a bed in Bellevue with all the other sick and wounded convicts. "I hope they put that son of a bitch in the infectious disease unit, and the bastard comes down with Ebola!" I screamed at Donald, who shook his head in rage and said, "That fuckin' piece of shit better hope he never gets out." I knew he meant it. Donald had many friends in many low places.

In the meantime, the press was continually surrounding the building, desperate to "make" my "unknown accomplice" who had killed all those people and helped me rescue my baby in the tunnel. The headline in *The Standard* read: TERMINATOR TO K'NAPPERS: DROP DEAD, while other tabloids ran with: CLARK KENT UNMASKED! They had nothing. And: DIRTY HARRY CLEANS UP SUBWAY. That was true.

So far, I didn't think many people bought into the rumor that the mystery man was also the mystery father of my baby. Most people thought Donald was the actual dad and since I had always felt it was not most people's business, we just left it at that.

Pantera would usually leave at night and return the next morning without managing to get caught on camera by even one of the paps on stakeout (the supermarket tabloids were offering big money for a clear shot—double if they got us coming and going together). They couldn't get one of me, because I never left the hospital, but him? How did they miss catching even one shot? Oh right. He's never been seen unless he wanted to be seen.

During that first week, a few journos occasionally managed to sneak inside the hospital, but the cops made swift work of them.

While chasing my colleagues out did make me feel guilty, seeing as how I am a member of the working press myself, it also made me feel enormously relieved to be left alone as a desperate mother in pain.

I had no desire to report on or to explain to my colleagues what I/we had been through. Usually people like me resented people like me. People like me prevented people like me from doing my job: i.e., reporting the news, getting the "get."

My big "gets" went to Dona, the only person I'd talk to. She was freelancing video feeds to *The Standard,* which went up on the Web instantly. Even though our outlets were rivals, the only way they could get Dona, contractually, would be to share the feed with Fox.

My boss, Bob, didn't pressure me, and he and his wife, Carrie— who were on the approved list of visitors—came by the hospital to sit with us. They are staunch Catholics, so they'd stop by St. Pat's every day and light candles for Terry, while my Jewish friends prayed, my Hindu friends made offerings to Ganesh and Kali, my Muslim friends prayed to Allah, and my Protestant friends, well, they drank to Terry's health. In other words we pretty well had it covered for every god anybody could think of.

On the fourth day, as Pantera and I sat beside Terry's crib, he checking his phone, I finally brought up the unspeakable "what if?" elephant in the room.

"Yusef, I need to talk about something." He looked at me like I was going to ask him to move in with my parents.

When I found it harder to actually ask than I thought it would be, he said, "Whatever it is, it can't be as bad as what you've been through." It was nice that he never put himself in my equation, re-spectfully understanding that genetics aside, I was the one who had given birth to and single-parented Terry.

So I tried to include him by making a joke, but it was slimmer than a new iPhone. "Yes, we have been through hell and back. And—hey!—we have to be the only two people who've been through this much and have only had sex once!" What a knee slapper that wasn't.

"There's Roy. We lost the tube, which means I lost his get-out-of-jail-free card. I not only gave up the secret of resurrection to the worst human on the planet, I gave up Roy's life as well."

"Roy's good," Pantera said.

"What? You went to see him?"

"No."

"So how do you know?"

"His bail is paid. He gets out today. By tomorrow things should begin to be cleared up."

"What are you talking about?"

"His bail is paid," he repeated. "Within probably a week or so evidence will be found that will exonerate him and reveal the real serial murderer. DNA for each of the dead prostitutes." I just stared at him. He'd done this somehow.

"You're paying the bail?"

"No."

"Who, then?"

Instead of answering, he said, "He will be released, that's what's important."

"But that doesn't mean they won't still accuse him of killing his dad, right?"

"It's all fine," he answered.

I stared at him, sick. "You didn't plant . . ."

"No, I didn't."

I didn't believe him. "But he's not cleared?"

"Not yet. But the evidence will be so compelling that they'll drop the charges. Unless . . ."

"Unless?"

"Unless something else happens."

"Well, clearly nothing else will happen because Roy had nothing to do with murdering anybody."

"Perhaps," Pantera said in his offhand, maddening way.

I was grateful that Roy was going to be freed, but I needed to know: "Who the hell is going to pay the bail?"

"His lawyer can't give up that information."

"Hold on a minute, bub," I seethed. "You are talking to *my* friend—Mad Dog—who *I* got to take Roy's case? And neither of you thought to talk to me first?" I was furious.

Pantera placated me. "We both thought you had more important issues to deal with, and we wanted to come to you with good news for a change." OK, placated, but not fully on board with the story. "A confidential bail angel? Right."

"So, baby," Pantera countered, calling me a name that had only come out of his mouth once before—that night we made love in Carcassonne—and clearly aimed at getting me off the subject, "I wanted to discuss something else with you."

"Isn't one bombshell per day enough? And by the way? I want to discuss something with you, too."

"Shoot," he said.

"Not a great choice of words, by the way," I said, giving him a sideways wise-guy glance. "So, the Judsons. I mean, how in hell did they end up on the same floor as me? I mean, was it planned from day one, do you think?"

"It's a stretch to think they would know about Roy one day inheriting the pages, but . . . who knows what and who they knew?"

"But they apparently did. The bastards. In fact, they were just lying in wait for the old man to kick off. Now that I think about it, and I've been thinking about it a lot, you know Roy was up at my apartment a thousand times—I even introduced him to the Judsons several times casually in the elevator or whatever."

"Nothing they did was casual."

"Ain't that the truth? I've kicked myself a million times over it. How did I not see that at the time?"

"You weren't looking for it. They gave you no reason to even look."

"Good con artists never do," I spat out.

He smiled. "No, they never do. That's why they're good."

He grabbed my hand and said, "On another note entirely? I've been looking over what we've got. The missing pages aren't the only pages that contain, or once contained, secret esoteric information. It's just that the others are rotted out. But—and here's what has never been known—Judas says he did not hang himself as it says in Matthew, nor did he fall down and explode as it says in Acts. The thirty pieces of silver? Never used for his grave in Potter's Field."

"My God. Are you saying Judas was resurrected as well?"

"I'm saying perhaps he just went to the 'realm of Barbelo.'"

Was that a joke? Hilarious.

He ignored me and continued, "I don't think that the man who is now in possession of the pages will necessarily be able to interpret them or carry out the resurrection ritual alone. That's why there was a whole cabal of them plotting this together."

"But fedora man can sell those pages or collaborate with someone."

"They are so hot now, he may die well before even a low-life black market antiquities dealer would touch them. And personally? I don't believe he has much longer to live."

"I doubt if he'll just keel over and die."

"I wasn't suggesting that he would."

"Neither was I."

"Anyway, back to the topic at hand," he said, maddeningly. "I believe Judas was speaking about other realms, other dimensions, other solar systems."

"Coming from the mouth of a physicist, or so you claim."

"Yes, I do and so I am," he answered. With that one you could never tell if he was being sarcastic or just speaking the truth. Then, "But I often take breaks from stargazing to spy, kill, and do other soldier-of-fortune errands as I may have mentioned to you." That was definitely sarcasm, and even I reluctantly smiled. Sometimes I hated him for making me feel the opposite of what I absolutely knew I shouldn't feel, which is how I ended up in that horrible spot to begin with. He was just so freaking smart. And tough. So of course, I was beginning to hate him all over again. Or so I told myself.

On a roll, he continued, "It's interesting, in light of all this, that history has turned the men who were with Jesus at Gethsemane into martyrs, but in fact, they weren't heroes. They scattered at His arrest. According to the accepted Gospels, none of the male disciples were mentioned as witnessing the crucifixion. Apparently they didn't have the balls to stand by their Lord. The Gospel of John says there was one unnamed 'beloved disciple' present. Why is this disciple unnamed when Mary Magdalene, and Mary, mother of Jesus, and several other women are clearly mentioned?"

"Wait. So you think . . ."

"Yes, I think the unnamed beloved disciple was Judas. I am convinced of it, in fact."

"I'm not sure . . ."

"The early Church fathers who, by the way, even pushed out Jesus' own family to gain control—especially when Paul came along—rewrote history. It's almost one hundred percent certain that Paul never even met Jesus—he lived in Turkey—although he supposedly resided in Jerusalem as a child. Yes, the disciples had horrible deaths but they weren't brave martyrs. They are considered martyrs because they died for Christ, but they didn't live for Him, despite becoming the Church's embodiment of Him."

Terry awoke just then, and began to cry. I stroked him, still not able to hold him for all the IVs in his little body. "The only secret I need to know right now," I said, "is how to get Terry out of the hospital and back home. And I think that's strictly medical."

"Ah, ye of little faith."

"Actually, faith in the medical profession is all I've got. Remember we're agnostics and my mother's a doctor."

"So am I," he answered. "Of the scientific kind, but also an agnostic, meaning one who questions everything. I believe nothing. And everything."

37

I thought about what he'd said. "What I believe now is in my love for her little boy. I sit here willing Terry to get better, and, yes, I'm sending up prayers to whatever god I hope is listening to me. But I also know I made a pact with the devil. My son for everyone else."

He looked down. "Do you trust me?"

Did I? Yes. I actually did, so I nodded my head.

"Then I have to ask you to trust me one more time," he said. "This will be made right."

An awkward silence followed, so I really didn't expect what happened next. Pantera leaned into me, tilted my head back, and kissed me, his tongue just slightly exploring my mouth. I let him engulf me, let his arms surround me. I wanted to stop him, I really did, but instead I pulled him in even tighter and kissed him like I'd never kissed a man before. He kissed me with all the power and passion of a man who'd kissed too many women before, but somehow had never kissed anyone he loved before. Was I fooling myself?

I kissed him with the kind of abandon I hadn't known in a very long time because for the first time in what seemed like a lifetime, our precious son, our Terry, was getting stronger, right next to us—even if he was in a little hospital crib.

Even though life in the cocoon of that pediatric hospital room was still moment-to-moment for us, and the unknown was too frightening for me to contemplate, that one moment, at least, was a good moment. A very good moment.

As week one entered into week two, the crowds of reporters outside the hospital thinned, and the flood of paparazzi that'd been trying to sneak in slowed to a trickle. The media was on to the next story, the next Hollywood scandal, the next tragedy that wouldn't, with any luck, touch them personally.

Pantera showed up early to the hospital on day nine, just as Terry had gone down for a nap. He hadn't asked and I hadn't offered my apartment, and I had no idea where he went after he left the hospital each day. I just didn't want him or anyone in our home until Terry was back home with me. At any rate, Pantera showed up that morning with warm croissants, espresso, and some fresh-cut fruit.

"I really need to teach you the concept of the New York bagel with a schmear," I said. "And I don't mean pineapple bagels or some other abomination of nature." Then I told him why no bagels in the world tasted like New York bagels: it's our water, stupid!

"Then, why," he asked sarcastically, "do New Yorkers pay three bucks for a pollution-causing, plastic bottle filled with French water?"

"Because they are misguided fools who've never met *you,* so they buy all that French hype," I teased. "I, however, know the truth!" I was definitely feeling lighter. I was actually sort of back to my old self. "I will never give Terry anything but New York tap," I finished, somewhat triumphantly.

"Before we get any deeper into the merits of fake mineral water versus tap water," he said, bringing my dissertation to an unceremonious halt, "I want to go over something with you."

"This sounds serious. Leave it to you to bring a grenade to the party."

He shook his head and grinned. "You are such a pain in the ass. Maybe Peter was right about women."

"Peter who? Some spy friend of yours?"

"No, actually in the Gospel of Thomas, Peter says to Jesus, 'Tell Mary'—that would be Magdalene—'to leave us, for women are not worthy of life.' He must have meant spiritual life," he joked. Sort of.

"So I heard. You know, that's what's so great about you—you sure know how to tell a joke!"

"Anyway, moving on," he continued in that way he had of cutting you off while still not making you feel cut off. "Forget Thomas's Gospel. I have again been studying the pages of the Gospel of Judas."

My heart leapt. "You got them back?" I asked, so excited I almost did the happy dance right there and then.

"Oh God, no. Sorry. I have been studying the old pages. And I think I came across something that the scholars missed. Or just overlooked. They weren't looking for a code, they were too busy trying desperately to interpret what was not rotted away."

"Well, of course . . ." I said, as he pulled his laptop and a hardcover copy of *The Gospel of Judas* out of his bag. "Please get out your iPad," he said.

I unplugged my iPad. He pulled his chair next to mine. "Here, look where Judas tells Jesus, 'I know who you are and which place you came from. You came from the realm of the immortal Barbelo.'"

I pulled the quote up on my Kindle version. "Got it. Yes, I'd read that portion before."

"Well, I have been looking for a code, something that was missing: a reason that the disciples who were the possible real betrayers of Jesus didn't want this Gospel to ever be spread." He showed me his screen. There was an equation of some kind. "Look at this. I believe the letters in the word 'Barbelo,' B-A-R-B-E-L-O, are encoded. Each letter stands for another letter."

"Well, in theory that's great, but that's English—and Jesus and Judas spoke Aramaic."

"If the Gospel had been found back then, nobody would be able to understand it. Perhaps that was the whole point."

"I for one don't understand it two thousand years later! Sorry, but it sounds like a stretch."

"Not really."

He continued, unfazed as usual. "Anyway, if you believe in the very concept of life—that we're here right now, that we and everything around us exists as a reality, well then, imagining that an evolved being such as Jesus would be able to map a code in a language not spoken during his manifestation on Earth? Light stuff—the time/space continuum."

"OK, so just say I do buy this code business. Have you figured out these so-called encoded words?"

He showed me the equation on paper. It read: $B=S$, $A=I$, $R=R$, $E=I$, $L=U$, $O=S$.

"I'm sorry I don't understand," I said.

"Decoded, 'Barbelo' stands for 'Sirius.' Aside from that, the suffix of 'Barbelo' is 'E.L.O.,' as in 'elohim,' which is found over two thousand times in the Old Testament. It means 'gods.' Plural. In Genesis, for example, when God says, 'Let us make man in *our* image.' Not *my* image, but 'our image.'"

"I'm getting this . . ."

"The suffix for 'Sirius' is 'U.S.,' as in 'we.' In short, 'God is us.' As Jesus said in Luke: 'The kingdom of God is in the midst of you.'"

"Interesting . . ."

"Yes, and it gets more so. Take the roots of the words. The root word of 'Sirius' is 'Siri,' which means 'secret' in Swahili. God's secret? Jesus spoke in parables to the others, but I believe he spoke in code to Judas."

"Code? Like, 'Hey, buddy, you're going to take the hit for this whole crucifixion thing'?"

Pantera pointed to a page in the Judas Gospel. "See? Look here: 'And the Aeon then appeared with his generation, in whom the cloud of knowledge and the angel is called El . . .'"

Clearly the O had rotted away to complete the word "Elo."

"So you believe that this 'realm Barbelo'—where Judas says Jesus comes from—is actually the star, 'Sirius'?"

"It certainly appears that way."

"So, we're back to the Dog Star, the one that was the key to unlocking the tomb door that led into Acevedo's house!" I said, knocking my hand against my head in a "duh" gesture.

"Right you are," he said. "Sirius A, the Dog Star, the brightest star in our night sky. Remember the Dogon tribe that I told you about, who knew about the stars of Sirius, which were not visible to the naked eye?"

I nodded, remembering.

He opened a screen and pointed to an image of their rotation, saying, "That pattern of rotation that they described? Well, the rotation of one around the other forms an almost perfect double helix—the human DNA pattern!"

"Are you telling me that Jesus and Judas were somehow identifying Sirius as the star where human creation began?"

"I am. Have you ever heard of 'panspermia'?"

"Pan-sperm-ia? If I have, it certainly had nothing to do with the universe and more to do with wannabe lover boys!"

He shook his head and grinned that gap-tooth grin that always made me go weak. "It's the theory that if life exists throughout the universe, it can be distributed by asteroids, comets, and meteoroids when they enter Earth's atmosphere. It's even speculated that spacecraft can leave contamination in the form of microorganisms."

"So even our spacecraft could have done that elsewhere?"

"American and Russian spacecraft or probes have landed on the moon, Jupiter, Venus, Mars, and Mercury, and even on asteroids."

"So you're saying perhaps an asteroid crashed into the Earth zillions of years ago that was carrying some microscopic form of life that eventually evolved into human life?"

"Yes, that's exactly what I'm saying."

"I'm freaking out right now. How do you prove this?"

"We don't."

"True. I can imagine the reaction when I tell my boss one day that I want to go with the story—at least this part of the story—that the remnants of a disputed, mostly destroyed Gospel, which has been examined by scholars with a fine-tooth comb, contains coded information that they all missed—such as how we came from Sirius. Such as how our DNA duplicates the rotation pattern of the star system Sirius, and that Judas believed that Jesus came from there. Or perhaps it's just that the God particle—whatever it may be—came to Earth from there. He'll say no one will believe it."

"But how would you rationalize that theory in the face of the accepted fact that Jesus was born of a mortal woman," he challenged.

"Correct," I answered. "An angel came down and impregnated

a young teenage girl. But that's what some folks today would now call alien abduction, or alien visitation!"

"Maybe no one will. Maybe no one even should."

"Meaning?"

"There was a reason that Jesus gave the information only to Judas. There was a divine reason the Gospel rotted away soon after it was found. And now? The less focus on what's out there and still intact, the better. For the world's sake."

I was shocked "What? Are you a physicist or a spiritualist, *Dr.* Pantera?"

"I am a realist, *Ms.* Russo. You want to pick which parts you want to reveal. I choose to reveal none of it."

38

Early the next morning, my cell phone rang. Roy! We'd been speaking when we could, and I hadn't wanted to discuss it on the phone, but had been assured by Mad Dog that he knew he'd be getting out any day now.

His bail had been posted and even *he* didn't know by whom. Mad Dog said it was between him and "the, ah, benefactor."

"Who is it—Miss Havisham?"

Roy corrected me. "Magwitch, actually." Ten million big ones. Had to be Pantera. I had no idea he was even rich. Rich is one thing, parting with ten million for someone you didn't know? Clearly somebody—Pantera, probably—knew more than he was saying.

I came clean to him finally about what had happened, about Terry and how the tube had been stolen. Up until then he'd assumed the "benefactor" was the one negotiating to buy the pages.

Since there is no proper way to react to finding out that your best friend almost lost her baby to help you out, but that she lost your ten million in the process, sweet Roy just said, "But Terry's going to be OK?"

"Terry is very banged up for an infant, but we believe he'll be OK, yes. Your prayers will help . . ."

"I don't know if anybody's listening to me anymore, but I will." Then, "Or maybe somebody is. If you lost the tube with the pages, how is it possible that my bail got paid? Ten million. How?"

"I know a guy, who knows a guy," I said, imitating Pantera.

"Wow. But I'll pay whoever it is back. Somehow. The old man's house has gotta be worth something, for starters."

"I hope so," I answered.

Roy wanted to come visit the baby and me, but I told him I didn't want any more media circuses than we'd already had. The truth is, I just wasn't ready to introduce them. Pantera had met enough of my real and extended family, and I wasn't ready to deal with anything more right then.

The next days consisted, thankfully, of feeding Terry when he woke, and researching possible answers that might have been hidden in the available text every minute that he slept. It gave my mind the rest that it so desperately needed.

Terry still wasn't ready to come home, but in a way I felt we were safer in this hospital. Cops were posted 24/7 near the hospital door, so between me, Pantera, the armed cop, the hovering nurses, and the equally concerned doctors, the baby was as safe as he could be under the circumstances.

It didn't take a scholar (although none had discovered it) to figure out that the Judas Gospel was written in code—which was in contradiction to many of the scholars and clerics who'd put the

words down to the rantings of a madman. I also began to really believe that these were the words Jesus had spoken to Judas, which
had been passed down in secret for hundreds of years until they
were lost, almost forever. And the more I read, the more I suspected
that what Pantera had suggested—about what was written of the
origins of our species, the codes, etc.—were closer to the real truth
than not.

The Judas Gospel sounded like crazy talk—until you broke it
down into sacred geometry, a concept I had not known about
before this.

What I learned, which the physicist part of Pantera explained,
is that sacred geometry means that God, the Supreme Being, call it
what you will, created the universe according to a geometric plan—
and that all life and all creation are in line with this geometric
language.

Simply put, pi—as well as the square roots of 2, 3, 4, and 5—are
the essences of sacred geometry. Even the word "geometry" comes
from Greek: "geos" (Earth) and "metron" (to measure). These patterns are repeated over and over throughout the universe in all
life—are all part of the universal pattern.

Ancient and sacred man-made sites from the Mayan, Inca, Hindu,
and Sumerian temples to Stonehenge and the Great Pyramid all
used this geometry. Even the so-called Cydonian monuments on
Mars adhered to it.

The Earth and Moon have the same proportions as the dimensions of the Great Pyramid, which can be *directly* obtained using
the Pythagorean triangle.

Therefore when Judas speaks of twelve and six angels, three hundred and sixty luminaries as well as twelve rulers, he's speaking in
the language of sacred geometry.

Also on Friday the thirteenth of October 1307, scores of Templar knights—"

"Your ancestors, if I remember what little history you almost told me about yourself once," I interrupted.

He continued without addressing what I'd said. "Right. As I was trying to say, on Friday the thirteenth of October 1307, scores of Templars were arrested and charged with everything from homosexuality to bank fraud and heresy. The indictment called it, *'Dieu n'est pas content.'*"

"God is not pleased?"

"Yes, correct. Thus the unlucky number 'thirteen' is the antithesis of a sacred number. But on the other hand, at one point in the Gospel, Jesus calls Judas 'the thirteenth.' Wouldn't that mean it's a lucky number?"

"Your logic escapes me."

"Well, Jesus excoriates the other disciples, but never Judas. Even in the accepted King James Version. He loves the guy. Also, Judas is suggesting here that Jesus had a foreknowledge of what was to come—therefore Jesus *had* to be in on the whole thing. If not, he wouldn't have been the all-knowing Savior. Jesus even points Judas out at the Last Supper but doesn't attempt to stop him. *Somebody* had to do it in order for the prophesy to be fulfilled and Judas may have loved his Lord so much that he was willing to become the most hated man in history."

"Ah, but Jesus calls him the 'thirteenth daimon'—which is 'devil.'"

"Interestingly enough, many ancient, magical texts use that term to mean 'spirit' or 'god.' In fact, it's even been interpreted to mean beings that are between human and divine."

He immediately pointed to something from the old book in his hands. "Here, look. It says that there are actually thirteen—not

How would a condemned, crazy, desert dweller—or an equally nutty scribe hundreds of years later, repeating the story—know about geometry two thousand years ago?

We began looking carefully at the specific numbers: six, for example, is said to harness the power of spirit and bring that spirit into matter. Twelve, the symbolic number of the universe, is mentioned a hundred and eighty-seven places in the Bible (twenty-two times in Revelations alone). There are twelve apostles, twelve people on a jury, twelve days of Christmas, twelve tribes of Israel, twelve Jyotirlingas in Hindu Shaivism, twelve Olympian gods, twelve Imams in Shi'a Islam, twelve signs of the zodiac corresponding to twelve months in a year, twelve petals in the heart chakra, twelve hours of day, and twelve hours of night.

My head was about to explode. I yelled out to Pantera, "Not to mention that twelve is Joe Namath's sacred Jets number!"

"Irreverent wiseass!"

Back to business.

One night as we shared some of Gramma's homemade meat-loaf in Terry's hospital room, Pantera picked his head up from his laptop screen to say out of nowhere, "Thing of it is, when Judas supposedly betrayed Jesus, there were only eleven apostles left—correct?"

"Why, you sweet-talkin' thing!" I kidded him. Then, "So you're saying twelve *wasn't* a sacred disciple number?"

"Ah, but it was!" he answered. "It was so sacred, in fact, that the apostles replaced Judas with Matthias, giving Matthias the honor, after a coin toss, of becoming the twelfth apostle. Judas then became the thirteenth apostle—the bad-luck number.

"There were thirteen present at the Last Supper, which led to His betrayal or His alleged betrayal, and then to His crucifixion.

twelve—dimensions, and that thirteen is last dimension, the dimension of divine communion and is actually a void. Judas was the thirteenth disciple, hence he was the chosen one to complete the task of Jesus—He who contains all the possibilities!"

Whatever was real and whatever was false in what we were deducing, and whether Judas was a demon or a godlike compatriot of Jesus, the book's original scribe certainly knew and understood the concepts of love, loyalty in a crazy way, and sacred geometry in a secret, coded way. Did the missing pages contain, whether in code or not, the formula for resurrection and life everlasting? I believe they did.

As we toiled away over the next several days in that hospital room, trying to figure out the whole code that might have been hidden within the text, I remembered something else—something we had completely overlooked or hadn't thought significant at the time. "Remember in the Prison of Christ—there was something scrawled about God's word being rotten, or rot—something like that?"

"Yes . . . ," he said, looking up over the ancient book he was holding.

"Well, maybe, just maybe, secrets lie also not only in what's left but what's rotted away! Maybe it was all part of some divine plan."

"Why, Ms. Russo, you sound almost like a believer. For a dyed-in-the-wool agnostic, I mean. I'm impressed."

"Oh, go shoot somebody or whatever you do on your days off," I said. "I really don't care if you think I'm barking up the wrong tree, but I'm going to give up trying to find the secrets in what's left and look instead at what's rotted away. I'm a reporter and what I do is figure out whodunit and who done what." He wasn't buying it, but I hadn't been buying what he'd been selling at first, either.

After staying up most of one night—Terry had been very cranky and had tried to pull out the tubes—I was drifting off to sleep when something jumped out at me.

And so it began—as clearly as if the words had never been disguised. What I discovered were messages from Jesus to the people of the future, the people of the future whose civilization was being held hostage to worldwide terrorist attacks, global warming, tsunamis, devastating earthquakes, hurricanes, nuclear plant disasters, rampant "religious" beheadings, and rapes, not to mention the unthinkable beginnings of a Christian holocaust in the Middle East. Never again? Until the next time.

We were now living in a time that in many ways was every bit as primitive and barbaric as the time of Jesus—but now the primitives had sophisticated bombs that could in fact end civilization. Just as we were facing the end of civilization in the cradle of civilization in the very area of the world where Jesus had lived, what was perhaps a new message from Jesus had come. Had He known that this Gospel's hidden code would be discovered when it was most needed?

I couldn't believe what had been right before my eyes. Or more precisely what hadn't been before my eyes: many of the rotted parts of the words in the Judas Gospel were affirmations of human life: spirituality, creation, God, life, mother, even almost a signature of the Savior.

When Pantera arrived the next morning with the croissants, fruit, and coffee—he never did capitulate to my lecture on bagels—I said, "Sit down and take a deep breath. Have I got something for *you*!"

I had broken what I believe is the code in the rotted-away parts of words. I placed my yellow legal pad on the hospital tray table and said, "These are all the parts of the words that were rotted away. Look!

"Ra, the Egyptian sun god; Thor, the god of lightning; and *negli*? It's 'from the gods' in Hebrew, and it's also Sanskrit for 'finding unity in diversity.' Look here: 'genes—DNA and the Sirius rotation pattern.'

"Ur, the Scandinavian ruler of the beginning; An, the prefix for the solar deities of Egypt; Se, the divine tree of life; Pli, for Pleiades; Thi, the Sirius Big Dog; and Ove, for egg. Ca, as in Kaaba—from the asteroid matter, the material inside the cuboid building at the center of Islam's most sacred mosque.

"It's Jesus talking to us," I said when I'd finished. "He's telling us where we came from, and that we must prevail and give thanks and be in the light no matter how dark the days are ahead. Which is exactly what I needed to remember during this whole, horrible ordeal."

"You never fail to surprise me," he said. Then he surprised *me*. Laughing out loud, he grabbed me and kissed me.

I pulled back and stared at him. "And you never fail to surprise me!"

We both laughed as I sort of shoved him away, despite wanting nothing more than to have him kiss me again and again, and more to the point to be in a big bed with him for endless days exploring not some ancient manuscript, but every single bit of him. This was hardly the time or the place.

But the feel, the smell, and the maleness of him made me stupid for him, crazy to have him climbing all over me and me all over him, until we were both exhausted, only to do it all over again. And again. I wanted that. I wanted to feel him inside of me, filling me up like no man ever could again. I knew he wanted me at least as much as I wanted him. More.

But what the hell would happen when we actually *could*? Should I even put myself in that position? I was still reeling from our first encounter. When we made love again, I knew it would be even more intense, passionate, and all-consuming than it had been the first time.

Then what? I couldn't picture him giving up his secret life, his off-the-grid life, doing whatever black ops thing he did for God and country—albeit which God and whose country still remained unclear. Nor did I want him to—no more than I'd want to give up my own life as a reporter. I couldn't breathe if I couldn't write, and I just didn't know if he would be able to breathe if he was tied down to even a semi-normal life. Pantera didn't live his life like anyone else. And that was another reason I couldn't get enough of him.

But the fact remained, however, that as real as our *baby* was, his father, Yusef Pantera, was the opposite of real. He was a desperado fantasy man, a mystery man with brains. What could come of it all?

All I knew for sure was that when we finally got our hands on each other, it would be unforgettable. But could it possibly be sustainable? That was something else altogether.

39

Three weeks and four days after the horror began, the heads of pediatrics, Dr. Rodriguez and Dr. Singn, came into Terry's room. Instead of their usual grim-but-trying-to-appear-optimistic looks, they were actually smiling. Smiling!

"Well, Alessandra, I've got a bit of news for you!" Rodriguez said, trying to contain his giddiness. They asked me to step out into the corridor and to take Terry with me. I gently grabbed my baby boy up in my arms—he was finally free of the horrible tubes—and followed the docs out.

The corridor was filled with people—doctors, nurses, aides, orderlies, administrators, my family, the cops on the case—everyone was there. They burst into applause and broke out singing my special Terry lullaby, "Terry boy! Mommy's boy! Mommy loves you so much, 'cause you're handsome and you're nice, and you're Mommy's best boy!" Pantera—not one for public parties—wasn't around. I didn't care. This was for my boy and me.

Holding Terry close in his little hospital gown, I burst into tears and so did every other person in the hall. Big tough guys, stoic doctors, the cops, seen-the-worst-things-in-the-world pediatric nurses, and even the electrician, were all shamelessly crying. Mad Dog—whom I'd discovered was a huge crybaby but only when happy—was mopping his tears with a wad of Kleenex.

The hospital staff presented Terry with his very own official TOUGH GUY onesie, followed by a giant cake.

Dr. Singn said, "I speak for everyone here when I tell you that we can't remember a day as happy as today." I looked puzzled.

He continued, "Why? Because today is the day that we kick Terry Russo and his entire family outta here!"

I was speechless. Somehow the day I'd prayed for, longed for, and dreamed of was here. I was so overwhelmed that I couldn't think of anything to say other than to go around and kiss every single person. That's when I finally missed Pantera. Where was he anyway?

To get ready to go home, Mom and I dressed Terry in one of the fifty-six thousand outfits she'd bought him—a little baseball cap, shoes, and socks. I'm not prejudiced at all, and I mean that, but he *is* the cutest baby ever born in the history of the entire human race.

As Mom was packing up all the stuff I'd managed to accumulate—my toiletries, pajamas, and clothes, none of which I ever wanted to see again—the door opened and I heard, "Ready to take your son home?"

I turned around. It was Pantera. I grinned at him. "Yes, I'm *so* ready to take our son home." He put his arm around me and for a moment we looked like your average, normal family: mom, dad, baby, and grandma.

For a long moment I stood there soaking up the miracles in my life: my Terry, who was never supposed to have been possible in the first place—a miracle baby who became again, at only six months old, a miracle survivor; my mother, who was impossibly loyal and competent no matter what kind of insanity she faced and no matter what I had put her through; Yusef Pantera, the man I loved more than I thought it was possible—but whom I'd also sometimes hated in equal measure—a man I *know* I'd seen die fifteen months earlier in a building collapse.

A few minutes later Dad came into the room with Terry's stroller/car seat, and we strapped Terry in. My big Italian family had a procession of cars waiting: my father and brother in one; Mad Dog and Dona in the next; and a black All City SUV with a driver, waiting for my mother, Terry, Pantera, and me. Donald didn't show up because, well, he finally must have gotten it through his head that Terry really wasn't his son.

There also were three cop cars and an unmarked vehicle with a few plainclothes cops riding shotgun, probably *with* shotguns following. What a way to stay anonymous!

Loath as I was to do it, before I got into the car, I posed for a few news photographers outside the hospital—somebody had leaked our exit. But these were my colleagues, and I was, after all was said and done, one of them.

Somehow Pantera was never in any photo that ran anywhere. Never even got caught in one lousy "get" on any site anywhere. Not on Instagram, Facebook, nor Twitter. No-*where*! The man was good. At what, I still wasn't sure, but he was good at it anyway.

The whole entourage—minus the cops who were stationed outside—barreled into my apartment, never thinking for a moment that my little *nuclear* family might want to be alone at home for the first time. We'd been through hell, but we were on our way back.

The Judsons were dead, Father Paulo and Mr. Engles were dead, the fedora man was missing, and so were the missing pages of Judas. At least we were alive, and Terry was home safe—I hoped, at least—forever.

But no one made mention of any of this, nor did they mention the fact that the apartment down the hall was very conspicuously sealed off with yellow crime scene tape. Gramma, who'd been mysteriously missing from the hospital that morning, was already in my apartment and had prepared a huge feast for upward of one thousand guests: veal cutlet parmigiana, eggplant parmigiana, lasagna, meatballs, and just in case there wasn't enough, sausage and peppers.

Terry was already used to a million people around so he took the whole raucous fiesta in stride and fell into a deep sleep in my arms at the table. Gratefully, I put him down in his own little crib—which I'd dreamed about.

It got better. Roy showed up mid-meal and we drank to everyone's health and well-being.

After the meal and before the cannolis, I threw them out. I sent Mad Dog home with a goody bag the size of a pro baller's locker. I handed Dad the still-tied-with-string box of cannolis from Caffe Palermo, aka the "Cannoli King of Little Italy," joking, "Leave the gun, take the cannoli."

I closed the door behind them and leaned back against it with a giant sigh. "Good to be home!" I said.

"Good to be home," Pantera repeated, taking me into his arms. I looked up at him and smiled.

He took my face in his hands and kissed me, his mouth open, his tongue exploring the inside of my mouth. I responded as hungrily as a woman who hadn't been fed in years. He pushed me against the door and began slowly unbuttoning my shirt, kissing every inch that was exposed with each button. It was excitingly, excruciatingly slow. He tore off my old white broadcloth shirt and moved the straps of my bra down onto my shoulders and down my arms with the tips of his fingers, unhooking the back and tossing it onto the floor.

Then thrusting himself against me and kissing me hard, he began unbuttoning my jeans just enough so that he could put his fingers inside. I was nearly exploding—and I was still half dressed—and he was still fully dressed!

I began to pull off my own jeans when he stopped me. "No," he said. He continued exploring me until I screamed with pleasure—unable to be quiet, and afraid the cops outside would start banging on the door!

He finally removed my jeans and slowly slid off my panties.

He stepped a micromillimeter away from me and pulled off his own shirt and pants. For the first time—and only the second time in our lives—we were naked together. I slipped off his eye patch, and was surprised to see that he really wasn't missing an eye. It was just stitched up and healing. From what? Who knows?

With his mouth on mine he whispered, "I love you, I love you, I love you, Russo."

"And I love you, Pantera."

I wrapped my legs around him, and we made crazy, passionate love against the door, on the couch, on the sink, and finally again in bed. As we were making love, I climbed on top and said, "I wish you were me." He looked at me quizzically.

"Why?"

"Because I want you to know what you feel like," I said.

He rolled me over and said, while moving very slowly, "You mean like this?" Oh yeah.

Life was good. Life was very good. I wrote my story—leaving out the secret that was in the lost pages. I did say that the only disciple that Jesus loved and trusted—besides His wife, Mary Magdalene—was Judas. That the only being that He trusted with the esoteric knowledge of the universe was Judas. I didn't say that Jesus told him—in code—that all life sprung from the star system Sirius. That Jesus planned His own end on Earth. That Jesus charged Judas, His most beloved, with the ultimate secret, the ultimate task: with His own resurrection.

That somewhere, somehow, right now, someone was figuring out the secret to resurrection because I'd given it to him.

My story on *The Standard*'s Web site went viral—and there wasn't a country that didn't pick it up and herald it front page and home page. I turned down interview requests from *60 Minutes, The New York Times,* BuzzFeed, *The Washington Post,* The Huffington Post, VICE, Newser, *The New York Times International Edition,* CNN, NBC, MSNBC, NPR, *Today, CBS This Morning, Good Morning America,* you name it—for the time being. I told them all—and after I filed my story, I told Bob, too, that I wanted to spend time alone with my family. I didn't know if I meant the three of us or just Terry and me.

The next few days were spent in a complete dream state. When Terry napped we made love. We ordered in, we cooked, we watched movies, and sometimes we'd talk around how one day he'd have to take care of the "situation," i.e., the man in the fedora. We never talked about *how* he'd take care of the man-in-the-fedora situation, however.

On the third night Pantera made French onion soup and a rustic cassoulet. "So wait," I said, eating so fast it was like I'd never tasted food before, "you can make a girl scream like you do, have the body of Death, the brain of Carl Sagan, and you cook? What next? Do you sing opera, too?"

"Only on special occasions. But you're not so bad yourself. You can do that thing that you do, that I can't do, that drives me insane."

"Really! And what's that?"

I was expecting him to praise some sex trick I thought I'd mastered. He said instead, "You can write." I hit him playfully over the head with my napkin and he ducked.

"Did I ever tell you I hate the French?" I teased. We laughed until we squirted Bordeaux out of our noses.

The dream couldn't last—could it?—but we enjoyed it like it would be forever.

Then my doorbell rang. I opened it and one of the building's security guards was standing there. Beyond him, I could see a tremendous commotion in the hall.

"Ms. Russo! Ms. Russo! You gotta see this."

I grabbed Terry and Pantera and I ran down the hall. What I saw will live with me forever. The maintenance men were cleaning out the Judsons' storage closet, which they'd rented on our hall. Apparently no one had thought to tell the police and the police hadn't thought to ask whether the couple had any other units of any kind in the building.

Inside the storage room, which is ceiling height and probably six-by-six-feet wide, was a standing refrigerated unit. I assumed, knowing the Judsons, that they'd put in a large wine refrigerator. But when a security guard opened the door, I screamed and turned Terry toward my chest.

It was the perfectly preserved body of a teenaged boy! He was dressed exactly as the wax boy had been—in bell-bottoms, a printed shirt, a Nehru jacket, and boots. His hair was shoulder length and he was wearing aviator sunglasses and holding a transistor radio. This was no wax boy, though. It was the preserved corpse of Makenson! Raylene's dead son. They had not just made and stored the full-sized voodoo wax figure of him, but had mummified the real boy as well.

"Oh my God," I cried out, clutching Terry. "That's why they were so desperate for the . . ." I caught myself before I said "resurrection" out loud. Raylene had wanted to bring her boy back to life—and was willing to sacrifice mine to do it. Her voodoo grandmother's secrets for raising the dead didn't do it, so she met a rich man and together they devoted their lives to giving her the one thing all his money actually *could* buy: resurrection.

The hall once again started filling with cops.

I could see Detective Barracota barreling out of the elevator first, shooing all the neighbors away. "Nothing to see here, folks." That had to be the biggest lie ever to come out of the mouth of, well, anyone. Ever.

"Jesus God Almighty on the Cross," Barracota exclaimed when he got to the storage unit. "Now I've seen it all."

I explained everything I knew about Raylene's dead son. But I left something out. I didn't tell him that the man in the fedora now had in his hands the secret to resurrect anyone at any time.

"I think you deserve some good news for a change, Ms. Russo. And I've got some."

"OK, anything's good news after that, Detective."

"Suffolk P.D. believes they got the Gilgo Beach Killer. Some old sicko doctor who lives out there."

Relief washed over me even as I had an uncomfortable feeling that perhaps somehow Pantera was behind this. For me. But would he nail an innocent man?

"Congratulations on Roy being exonerated," Pantera said calmly once we went back to the apartment.

"Yes. Great news," I said suspiciously. Then, "But you know . . . even that good news doesn't undo the other. The lost pages, the manuscript in the hands of a maniac. I know what I've done can't be undone. I foolishly just wanted a few days to pretend that it could."

"It's not what you've done, baby, it's what I need to do."

Trying to reassure myself, I said, "But we have time, right? It will take years to interpret, let alone to create the formula—even if the man in the fedora does now have the Voynich Manuscript as well. He can't have those resources."

"But he'll make a deal with people who do. Terrorists or God knows who."

"They'd have to know how to interpret the formula, too."

His look said it better than words: terrorists have all the money in the world to find whatever they need.

Acevedo paid plenty for just a chance at the prize. But since those days the stakes had changed. It wasn't even the same game any longer.

And so, my idyll stopped abruptly. Back to reality.

I had to live with the reality of what I'd done to save my son.

But could I?

40

Because it had been planned well in advance, and because I didn't want to upset my parents before I actually needed to upset my parents, we proceeded with the plans we'd made for our first night out as though nothing had changed.

My parents, as arranged, came over to babysit. It was to be my first time away from Terry for more than a few minutes since the day he was rescued.

It was too late to cancel the evening out, and I felt I owed my parents one good night with the baby. And frankly, I just couldn't deal with the conversation about what I'd done—not yet.

I had gotten us a table at Rao's—a big score. On any other night, I would have been proud to show off my own "juice" in my town to my man.

Pantera had taken me to his joints in Montségur and Carcassonne in France last year, and I had wanted to take him to my New York hangouts now that he was here.

But real life has a way of happening, as they say, while we're busy making plans.

My friend Frankie Pellegrino (aka "Frankie No" because he said "no" to everyone who tried get a reservation at the legendary Rao's), called me with an impossible table opening. Rao's is a tiny restaurant in East Harlem on 114th Street and Pleasant Avenue. It's old-time Italian, and it's such an impossible reservation to get that occasionally one is auctioned off for charity. I once saw a Rao's reservation-only (food not included) go for fifty thousand dollars at a charity auction.

Pantera and I got there at eight and our table was waiting. Frankie broke into tears and kissed me over and over. "My darling baby . . . and how is baby Terry? And how are you?"

We kissed and hugged and cried. Finally, Frankie said, "And who is this handsome gentleman?" eyeing Pantera suspiciously.

I introduced them, knowing full well that telling Frankie the name of my mystery man—that man whose identity everyone wanted to know—would never be spoken outside of this place ever. We were there, the reservation had been made, and my parents had come to babysit, so for a few hours I decided to try to forget what I'd traded for the life of my son—and worse, what the devastating consequences could be.

I would deal with it the next day and the day after that and probably every day that I lived after that, in fact.

We settled into our booth and ordered like we were just a regular, happy couple.

We had the seafood salad, lemon chicken, and pasta with red sauce and meatballs. At one point I said to Pantera, "Hey, buddy, gimme five bucks."

He grinned and handed it over. Five bucks gave me ten songs

on Rao's jukebox with songs that hadn't changed in twenty-five years. At least. I first hit, "My Girl" knowing for sure that Frankie would sing it. He didn't disappoint, and in fact came right up to our table.

"Excuse me, sir," he said to Pantera, and took my hand and gestured for me to stand so we could sing together, "I've got sunshine on a cloudy day. When it's cold outside, I've got the month of May. Well, I guess, you'll say, what can make me feel this way? My girl. Talkin' 'bout my girl . . ."

By the second chorus the whole place had joined in, and I caught Pantera grinning out of the corner of my eye, with that stupid gap between his teeth. How I loved him at that second.

I plopped back down on the bench of the booth and we ate and drank too much, pretending things were the same as they were when we'd gotten up that morning. But they weren't and so the conversation eventually had to—and did—take a turn for the serious.

As espresso was served, Pantera said to me, "You know . . . I can't let this matter go unsettled." I bit the side of my lip, trying not to cry.

"Yes, I realize that, and I love you for it. I also hate you for it."

"I can't leave the pages loose to wander the world."

"But whoever the Judsons were in league with—the man in the fedora—has *already* got his hands on those secrets! It's already too . . ." I was grasping at straws. "You said it would be all right. Did you lie to me just to give me a few days of peace?"

"I've never lied to you. And I *will* never lie to you."

"But you *have* lied to me before. You let me think you were dead."

"You assumed that I was dead and I let you assume that because you—you and Terry—are everything. But because of who I am, you would never be safe. So let's not have that conversation. I can't do it again. I can't and I won't."

"That's not enough—saying it isn't enough anymore! I need to know what happens now. What are you planning to do? What happens to *us*?"

He didn't answer, so I asked again, just as just the tenth song that I'd queued up on the jukebox came on. It was a real oldie—1962— Barbara Lynn's "You'll Lose a Good Thing."

Pantera took his finger and wiped away a tear just forming in my eye, and grabbed my hand and brought me to my feet. "Not now." We stood close to each other, and I reluctantly put my arms around his neck. He gently took my right hand in his and brought our hands close in.

"Old school, remember?"

"Old school. I didn't forget."

The words to Barbara Lynn's song this time were as ironically apt as the words had been back in Carcassonne when we'd danced to the song of his choice.

"If you should lose me, oh yeah, you'll lose a good thing . . ."

I melted into him and we danced slow and easy while the tears rolled down my cheeks. "I love you, Russo," he whispered, his hands in my hair, his breath on my cheek. This time I didn't say anything back. I couldn't. I wiped my tears on his chest. I didn't want anyone to know.

When the song finished, people in the restaurant began whistling and hooting. "Hot!" one guy yelled. No one had any clue about what was going on between us. They just saw two people mad for each other dancing the way they all wished they would one day with someone they were that crazy about.

No matter that all hell was about to break loose in the world, when we were pressed against each other, swaying to the old R & B tune, it was still magical. How could everything be so wrong with two people so wild for each other?

We got back to the table and finished our espressos in silence, just staring at each other. He took my hand and squeezed it.

"I will fix this. I will make it right. You know that."

I looked at him, pressed my lips together, and nodded my head. I finally said, "I know that. And I know I can't talk you out of doing it your way."

"No, you can't. It won't be right while that son of a bitch is walking this Earth."

"I know that, too."

We just sat there for a few more minutes in silence until Pantera finally said, "Let me go settle up with Frankie in the back."

"How did you know that's what you do at Rao's?" I laughed miserably at him. "And besides, it's my treat tonight."

"It's never your treat. Old school, remember?" He kissed me lightly on the forehead and got up from the booth. I watched his lean and gorgeous frame saunter into the back room to settle the bill.

I stood up, grabbed my coat, and started walking—I passed the jukebox, the bar, the kitchen, and finally made it to the front door. It had started to rain so I put my collar up and my head down, opened the door, and climbed the few steps up and out to the sidewalk.

My cell phone rang. I thought it was him, but when I looked at the screen it read: "Councilman Alonzo Curry." I let it go to voice mail.

I stood in the rain for a moment on the sidewalk, just thinking. Then I turned on my heel and began walking up Pleasant Avenue past the school.

I raised my hand. "Taxi!"

41

Bin Jawwād, Libya

The man in the fedora made his way along the broken city street. The city, which lay on the former front line between Libya's two rival governments, didn't look like the bustling area he remembered from days past. Many of the villagers, fishermen, oil workers, shepherds, clerics, and shopkeepers had fled—some to encampments in the desert, some to join ISIS, others had died in the fighting, and still others had simply disappeared.

The man, however, was unafraid as he stood in the broken archway of partially destroyed building, his suit and fedora covered in dust. He knew he was being watched, but he wasn't afraid because he had a big connection there—the biggest.

The sun blazing down, he pulled out his handkerchief to wipe his forehead and looked around. He was surprised that his friend Sheik Abu Ali al-Turkmani hadn't sent an armed escort to greet him. *What nerve!* The two men *had* agreed that he'd be at this secret location at this precise time.

Feral dogs roamed freely looking for food and the man was beginning to get nervous. *Nothing to worry about,* he told himself. After all, he had all the power in the world, and he was about to have all the riches, too, once he shared the secret he had inside his briefcase with al-Turkmani.

Minutes ticked by slowly and it seemed to be getting hotter. About forty-five minutes after he'd arrived, however, he finally heard the sound of motors. He could see a huge amount of dust billowing in the distance. Ah! Armoured vehicles were heading his way. The escorts!

The man patted his battered briefcase the way people do when they pat their pockets to make sure they still have their wallets. He'd traveled across continents with his treasure and wasn't about to lose it now. Some—well, the two people who knew what he carried at any rate—would call him a thief. Say it wasn't his by right; that he'd stolen it.

But they were lowlifes who didn't deserve to have it, never did, and couldn't even comprehend that it rightly belonged in the possession of a man who truly understood the power and beauty of it.

Not that he wasn't willing to share that which he'd nearly died to protect—he was a man of principles and great understanding, after all. But this secret, he knew, was almost too great for one man alone. So he had decided to share it—for the right price, that is. He was a generous man, a holy man, but he wasn't a foolish man, as he liked to say. He'd never made money in his lifetime, but it never mattered—until now.

The right price he had in mind had so many zeroes he could hardly count them. But he and his old friend Sheik al-Turkmani would work it out.

More importantly, the other thing that the oil-rich sheik could provide aside from cold, hard cash for him personally—was the ability and the funds to actually extract the precise formula he knew was coded in there somewhere.

And they say ISIS can't be trusted, he thought to himself even as he shooed away ragged children who popped up out of nowhere begging for money or a piece of bread.

Some might question why he'd share this secret with the likes of al-Turkmani—a known terrorist. But "some" would be unsophisticated peasants who didn't understand the ways of the world.

He and al-Turkmani had been friends for decades. They both believed in God, albeit different concepts of God. But when allied together? They could bring world peace—by threatening Armageddon. Armies of men who could never die led by two men with eternal life!

As he saw it, one man in the East and one in the West could control the world.

As he was musing and thinking about zeroes, two armored vehicles and a jeep finally made their way to where he stood—a stretch of what was once a nice street.

The bearded man being driven in the jeep was wearing a checked keffiyeh wrapped turban-style, sunglasses, fatigues, and was armed with two Uzis and an AK-47.

"Get in. We take you to al-Turkmani," he barked in broken English.

"But sirs! How do I know you are who you say you are?" the dour man inquired.

"Get in," the bearded man snapped in response.

When he didn't budge, two men from the armored vehicle got out and grabbed him and physically threw him into the jeep—and got in with him, rifles at the ready.

"Well, I never," he protested. "Wait until Sheik al-Turkmani hears of your rough treatment!"

"Shut up," the driver said.

"Are you really taking me to the sheik?" the now terrified man screamed.

No one answered as they kept driving deep into the desolate desert for nearly an hour, finally arriving in front of what looked to be the only intact house in the area.

There! Relief settled over him as he spotted his old friend on the broken concrete porch. The man in the fedora stood up, waved, and shouted, *"Tahiat ya sdyqy! Allah yakun maeakum!"* He hoped he'd gotten it right as what he'd meant to say was, "Greetings my friend! God be with you!"

Al-Turkmani waved back and then waved toward the men in the vehicles.

Before he realized what was happening, two of the men grabbed him and dragged him out of the jeep. All the while he held on to his bag for dear life. The men knocked the bag out of his hands and onto the ground, bound his hands and feet in zip ties, and threw him down on his knees in the dust, the rosary that was still around his waist dragging on the ground.

Al-Turkmani approached him, and much to his shame, the man in the fedora soiled himself, crying, "Why have you done this to me, my friend?"

The sheik, a tall, handsome man in his seventies, stood in front of him. He had a long beard, his white *thobe* (robe) impeccably tailored, his white keffiyeh worn loose and secured with a black cord.

"You not a friend, but a traitor to Allah!"

"No! No! I want to share with you a great treasure!"

"I paid you ten million American dollars," the sheik shouted.

The man was confused. "No, we never even discussed price. I know not of what you speak!"

"Liar! I wired ten million dollars to the bank account of your Jew lawyer, Rosenberg, and it was received and withdrawn. Now my informant tells me that in exchange you have brought *Iblīs* to me—not the secret to eternal life! You bring *Iblīs*!" The sheik was referring to the Muslim word for "devil."

"I bless?" the man repeated incorrectly, then thinking he was on the right track, added, "Yes, yes, that's right: I bless you!" misunderstanding the word entirely.

Even the sheik was taken aback at the lack of respect.

"You filth! You are the great liar. You bring *Iblīs* disguised as the secret power of the Son of the Holy Mother Mary, a woman beloved and respected by the Prophet Muhammad, himself!"

"Yes, Christ was born from the Holy Mother Mary," the confused man answered. *What is he talking about?* he thought to himself. "I bring you the secret of the Son. The secret to resurrection! Life everlasting!"

"Liar! You wage war against Allah," the sheik raged. "My sources confirmed that you have betrayed me—who you called 'friend.' You are the handmaiden of the Americans—trying to bring this filth into our land. Allah will never fail in his promise to the righteous, and you have betrayed the righteous!"

The sheik's men first took the Voynich Manuscript from the bag, then the tube, and finally the small bag containing the "keys." The sheik carefully inserted the little cross into one minuscule hole in the cap of the tube, which was clearly visible in the bright sun, and then screwed the post of the ruby earring into the other hole. As soon as he heard the tiny sound of the locks unlocking, he unscrewed the brass cap on the end and tossed it to the ground.

The terrified, hog-tied man pleaded, "My friend, we made a pact—remember? *Inna Al Alam Yamloukohou Al Montasar*—the world belongs to the victor! You are the victor. I am the victor."

The sheik spat on him and then took a long, curved knife out from under his *thobe*. "You are a thief and the prophet of a false god." *Bn el Metanaka!*"

Al-Turkmani sat on the back of the hogged-tied man as if he were a donkey, grabbed his head, and put the knife to his throat, causing the fedora to fall to the ground. When al-Turkmani yanked his head back with great force, the now-hatless prisoner started to weep again. The sheik leaned down and whispered in his ear, "*Inna Al Alam Yamloukohou Al Montasar,* my friend."

Was this a test of his loyalty, the man wondered? He said, "Yes, yes, I am your loyal friend. Together we have the secret of resurrection!" The sheik moved his mouth away from the man's ear, and the man visibly relaxed.

The sheik then bent the man's head back as far as it would go and began methodically sawing his head off like a butcher would a lamb's. The blood spurted with the force of water from a split hose. It splayed out over the sand and splattered the man's body and clothes, his hat, as he struggled to breathe against the pain and the inevitable. With what he had left, he gurgled, "Jesus save my soul" as his head came off.

As the headless body of the man who'd called himself Father Arturo Elias slumped forward, al-Turkmani reached down, picked up the head, and held the trophy proudly to the wild cheering of his men.

Al-Turkmani plopped Elias's head face forward on the corpse's raised buttocks. Rifles raised, the men shouted, "*Allahu akbar!*"

The sheik ordered the men to hand him the open brass tube. "*Iblīs!*" he spat, dropping the ancient pages out like they were feces in the sand. His crazed men stomped on the pile before al-Turkmani himself lit a match and threw it onto the crumpled papyri that were the missing pages of the Gospel of Judas—the pages that contained the greatest power in the universe: Jesus' secret teachings for resurrection and eternal life.

He then took what may have been the last remaining authentic copy of the Voynich Manuscript and lit it, too, on fire. It caught very quickly in the arid climate. Despite the magnitude of the words each had contained, the book and the ancient papyri made for a surprisingly small pyre.

The wind, as though the breath of God himself, suddenly blew strong, causing the ashes to fly up and scatter wildly across the desert sands.

On a nearby rooftop, a sandy-haired man with three days' growth of beard—was he American, English, French, what?—remained flattened, observing the spectacle through his S1240 D/N Stabiscope binoculars. He'd wait until dark to make his way back to Tripoli, where there was a big money backgammon game waiting for him in a backstreet café favored by gunrunners and mercenaries.

He smiled to himself. It had worked as smoothly as a clean shot between the eyes—without his having to raise his own rifle once. His woman would have been pleased. Not that she'd ever know that a terrorist had unknowingly paid her friend's bail, or that both the pages and the cursed book were forever destroyed.

It had been a good day. It had been a *very* good day.

❖

Five Months Later
New York City

Alessandra Russo put Terry (who was back to being a regular, age-appropriate baby boy) down for the night, and picked up her phone to check for messages. It had rung earlier, but she'd been knee-deep in kids and family—at Terry's first birthday party!

One voice mail.

"Hey, it's your favorite councilman. Shamelessly I'm leaving you message one hundred forty-eight or maybe it's message one hundred forty-nine by now. I hoped I might help you to exorcise the ghosts of last year past. What I mean is, would you like to be my date, yes as in a real date, to the governor's New Year's Eve party? It's the inaugural for the Second Avenue Subway opening, at, I'm going to say it now, the Ninety-Sixth Street Station. Come on, Ali, take that first ride with me. Kick the crap out of those damned ghosts."

She shook her head and laughed.

Gee-zis! The guy really is shameless. Flattering—but shameless.

And then for reasons she refused to acknowledge, Alessandra Russo didn't do what she'd done one hundred and forty-eight or maybe one hundred and forty-nine times before: she didn't hit "delete."